ABSALOM, ABSALOM!

Books by William Faulkner
available from Vintage

Absalom, Absalom!
As I Lay Dying
Collected Stories
A Fable
Flags in the Dust
Go Down, Moses
The Hamlet
Intruder in the Dust
Knight's Gambit
Light in August
The Mansion
Pylon
The Reivers
Requiem for a Nun
Sanctuary
Selected Letters of William Faulkner
The Sound and the Fury
Three Famous Short Novels:
Spotted Horses, Old Man, The Bear
The Town
The Uncollected Stories of William Faulkner
The Unvanquished
The Wild Palms

WILLIAM FAULKNER

ABSALOM, ABSALOM!

THE CORRECTED TEXT

VINTAGE BOOKS

A DIVISION OF RANDOM HOUSE
New York

Vintage Books Edition, February 1987

Copyright © 1986 by Jill Faulkner Summers

All rights reserved under International and Pan-American Copyright Conventions. Published in the United States by Random House, Inc., New York, and simultaneously in Canada by Random House of Canada Limited, Toronto. Originally published in hardcover by Random House, Inc., in 1936. Copyright 1936 by William Faulkner. Copyright renewed 1964 by Estelle Faulkner and Jill Faulkner Summers. This new and corrected edition was originally published, in hardcover, by Random House, Inc., in 1986.

Library of Congress Cataloging in Publication Data
Faulkner, William, 1897–1962.
　Absalom, Absalom!
　I. Polk, Noel. II. Title.
PS3511.A86A65　1987　　　813'.52　　　86-40168
ISBN 0-394-74775-5 (pbk.)

Designed by Robert Bull

Manufactured in the United States of America

10　9　8　7　6　5　4　3

PUBLISHER'S NOTE

This new edition of *Absalom, Absalom!* is the first corrected version of the novel to appear in paperback
since the book was originally published in 1936. The
text is based on a comparison—under the direction of
Noel Polk—of the first edition, Faulkner's holograph
manuscript, the typed setting copy, and the working
galley proofs. An editor's note on the corrections fol-
lows the text.

ABSALOM, ABSALOM!

I

From a little after two oclock until almost sundown of the long still hot weary dead September afternoon they sat in what Miss Coldfield still called the office because her father had called it that—a dim hot airless room with the blinds all closed and fastened for forty-three summers because when she was a girl someone had believed that light and moving air carried heat and that dark was always cooler, and which (as the sun shone fuller and fuller on that side of the house) became latticed with yellow slashes full of dust motes which Quentin thought of as being flecks of the dead old dried paint itself blown inward from the scaling blinds as wind might have blown them. There was a wistaria vine blooming for the second time that summer on a wooden trellis before one window, into which sparrows came now and then in random gusts, making a dry vivid dusty sound before going away: and opposite Quentin, Miss Coldfield in the eternal black which she had worn for forty-three years now, whether for sister, father, or nothusband none knew, sitting so bolt upright in the straight hard chair that was so tall for her that her legs hung straight and rigid as if she

3

had iron shinbones and ankles, clear of the floor
with that air of impotent and static rage like children's feet, and talking in that grim haggard amazed
voice until at last listening would renege and hearing-sense self-confound and the long-dead object of
her impotent yet indomitable frustration would appear, as though by outraged recapitulation evoked,
quiet inattentive and harmless, out of the biding and
dreamy and victorious dust.

Her voice would not cease, it would just vanish.
There would be the dim coffin-smelling gloom
sweet and oversweet with the twice-bloomed wistaria against the outer wall by the savage quiet September sun impacted distilled and hyperdistilled,
into which came now and then the loud cloudy
flutter of the sparrows like a flat limber stick
whipped by an idle boy, and the rank smell of female
old flesh long embattled in virginity while the wan
haggard face watched him above the faint triangle of
lace at wrists and throat from the too tall chair in
which she resembled a crucified child; and the voice
not ceasing but vanishing into and then out of the
long intervals like a stream, a trickle running from
patch to patch of dried sand, and the ghost mused
with shadowy docility as if it were the voice which
he haunted where a more fortunate one would have
had a house. Out of quiet thunderclap he would
abrupt (man-horse-demon) upon a scene peaceful
and decorous as a schoolprize water color, faint
sulphur-reek still in hair clothes and beard, with
grouped behind him his band of wild niggers like

beasts half tamed to walk upright like men, in attitudes wild and reposed, and manacled among them
the French architect with his air grim, haggard, and
tatter-ran. Immobile, bearded and hand palm-lifted
the horseman sat; behind him the wild blacks and
the captive architect huddled quietly, carrying in
bloodless paradox the shovels and picks and axes of
peaceful conquest. Then in the long unamaze
Quentin seemed to watch them overrun suddenly
the hundred square miles of tranquil and astonished
earth and drag house and formal gardens violently
out of the soundless Nothing and clap them down
like cards upon a table beneath the up-palm immobile and pontific, creating the Sutpen's Hundred,
the *Be Sutpen's Hundred* like the oldentime *Be Light.*
Then hearing would reconcile and he would seem
to listen to two separate Quentins now—the Quentin Compson preparing for Harvard in the South,
the deep South dead since 1865 and peopled with
garrulous outraged baffled ghosts, listening, having
to listen, to one of the ghosts which had refused to
lie still even longer than most had, telling him about
old ghost-times; and the Quentin Compson who
was still too young to deserve yet to be a ghost but
nevertheless having to be one for all that, since he
was born and bred in the deep South the same as she
was—the two separate Quentins now talking to one
another in the long silence of notpeople in not-
language, like this: *It seems that this demon—his name
was Sutpen—(Colonel Sutpen)—Colonel Sutpen. Who
came out of nowhere and without warning upon the*

*land with a band of strange niggers and built a planta-
tion—(Tore violently a plantation, Miss Rosa Coldfield says)—tore violently. And married her sister Ellen
and begot a son and a daughter which—(Without gentleness begot, Miss Rosa Coldfield says)—without gentleness. Which should have been the jewels of his pride
and the shield and comfort of his old age, only—(Only
they destroyed him or something or he destroyed them or
something. And died)—and died. Without regret, Miss
Rosa Coldfield says—(Save by her) Yes, save by her.
(And by Quentin Compson) Yes. And by Quentin
Compson.*

"Because you are going away to attend the college at Harvard they tell me," she said. "So I dont
imagine you will ever come back here and settle
down as a country lawyer in a little town like Jefferson since Northern people have already seen to it
that there is little left in the South for a young man.
So maybe you will enter the literary profession as so
many Southern gentlemen and gentlewomen too
are doing now and maybe some day you will remember this and write about it. You will be married
then I expect and perhaps your wife will want a new
gown or a new chair for the house and you can write
this and submit it to the magazines. Perhaps you will
even remember kindly then the old woman who
made you spend a whole afternoon sitting indoors
and listening while she talked about people and
events you were fortunate enough to escape yourself when you wanted to be out among young
friends of your own age."

"Yessum," Quentin said. *Only she dont mean that* he thought. *It's because she wants it told.* It was still early then. He had yet in his pocket the note which he had received by the hand of a small negro boy just before noon, asking him to call and see her—the quaint, stiffly formal request which was actually a summons, out of another world almost—the queer archaic sheet of ancient good notepaper written over with the neat faded cramped script which, due to his astonishment at the request from a woman three times his age and whom he had known all his life without having exchanged a hundred words with her or perhaps to the fact that he was only twenty years old, he did not recognise as revealing a character cold, implacable, and even ruthless. He obeyed it immediately after the noon meal, walking the half mile between his home and hers through the dry dusty heat of early September and so into the house (it too somehow smaller than its actual size— it was of two storeys—unpainted and a little shabby, yet with an air, a quality of grim endurance as though like her it had been created to fit into and complement a world in all ways a little smaller than the one in which it found itself) where in the gloom of the shuttered hallway whose air was even hotter than outside, as if there were prisoned in it like in a tomb all the suspiration of slow heat-laden time which had recurred during the forty-three years, the small figure in black which did not even rustle, the wan triangle of lace at wrists and throat, the dim face looking at him with an expression speculative, urgent, and intent, waited to invite him in.

It's because she wants it told he thought *so that people whom she will never see and whose names she will never hear and who have never heard her name nor seen her face will read it and know at last why God let us lose the War: that only through the blood of our men and the tears of our women could He stay this demon and efface his name and lineage from the earth.* Then almost immediately he decided that neither was this the reason why she had sent the note, and sending it, why to him, since if she had merely wanted it told, written and even printed, she would not have needed to call in anybody—a woman who even in his (Quentin's) father's youth had already established (even if not affirmed) herself as the town's and the county's poetess laureate by issuing to the stern and meagre subscription list of the county newspaper poems, ode eulogy and epitaph, out of some bitter and implacable reserve of undefeat; and these from a woman whose family's martial background as both town and county knew consisted of the father who, a conscientious objector on religious grounds, had starved to death in the attic of his own house, hidden (some said, walled up) there from Confederate provost marshals' men and fed secretly at night by this same daughter who at the very time was accumulating her first folio in which the lost cause's unregenerate vanquished were name by name embalmed; and the nephew who served for four years in the same company with his sister's fiancé and then shot the fiancé to death before the gates to the house where the sister waited in her wedding gown on the eve of the wedding and then fled, vanished, none knew where.

It would be three hours yet before he would learn why she had sent for him because this part of it, this first part of it, Quentin already knew. It was a part of his twenty years' heritage of breathing the same air and hearing his father talk about the man; a part of the town's—Jefferson's—eighty years' heritage of the same air which the man himself had breathed between this September afternoon in 1909 and that Sunday morning in June in 1833 when he first rode into town out of no discernible past and acquired his land no one knew how and built his house, his mansion, apparently out of nothing and married Ellen Coldfield and begot his two children—the son who widowed the daughter who had not yet been a bride —and so accomplished his allotted course to its violent (Miss Coldfield at least would have said, just) end. Quentin had grown up with that; the mere names were interchangeable and almost myriad. His childhood was full of them; his very body was an empty hall echoing with sonorous defeated names; he was not a being, an entity, he was a commonwealth. He was a barracks filled with stubborn backlooking ghosts still recovering, even forty-three years afterward, from the fever which had cured the disease, waking from the fever without even knowing that it had been the fever itself which they had fought against and not the sickness, looking with stubborn recalcitrance backward beyond the fever and into the disease with actual regret, weak from the fever yet free of the disease and not even aware that the freedom was that of impotence.

("But why tell me about it?" he said to his father that evening, when he returned home, after she had dismissed him at last with his promise to return for her in the buggy; "why tell me about it? What is it to me that the land or the earth or whatever it was got tired of him at last and turned and destroyed him? What if it did destroy her family too? It's going to turn and destroy us all someday, whether our name happens to be Sutpen or Coldfield or not."

"Ah," Mr Compson said. "Years ago we in the South made our women into ladies. Then the War came and made the ladies into ghosts. So what else can we do, being gentlemen, but listen to them being ghosts?" Then he said, "Do you want to know the real reason why she chose you?" They were sitting on the gallery after supper, waiting for the time Miss Coldfield had set for Quentin to call for her. "It's because she will need someone to go with her—a man, a gentleman, yet one still young enough to do what she wants, do it the way she wants it done. And she chose you because your grandfather was the nearest thing to a friend which Sutpen ever had in this county, and she probably believes that Sutpen may have told your grandfather something about himself and her, about that engagement which did not engage, that troth which failed to plight. Might even have told your grandfather the reason why at the last she refused to marry him. And that your grandfather might have told me and I might have told you. And so, in a sense, the affair, no matter what happens out there tonight, will still be in the family; the skeleton (if it be a skeleton) still in the closet. She may believe that if it hadn't been for your grandfather's friendship, Sutpen could never have got a foothold here, and that if he had not got that foothold, he could not have married Ellen. So maybe she considers you partly responsible through heredity for what happened to her and her family through him.")

Whatever her reason for choosing him, whether it was that or not, the getting to it, Quentin thought, was taking a long time. Meanwhile, as though in inverse ratio to the vanishing voice, the invoked ghost of the man whom she could neither forgive nor revenge herself upon began to assume a quality almost of solidity, permanence. Itself circumambient and enclosed by its effluvium of hell, its aura of unregeneration, it mused (mused, thought, seemed to possess sentience, as if, though dispossessed of the peace—who was impervious anyhow to fatigue—which she declined to give it, it was still irrevocably outside the scope of her hurt or harm) with that quality peaceful and now harmless and not even very attentive—the ogre-shape which, as Miss Coldfield's voice went on, resolved out of itself before Quentin's eyes the two half-ogre children, the three of them forming a shadowy background for the fourth one. This was the mother, the dead sister

Ellen: this Niobe without tears who had conceived to the demon in a kind of nightmare, who even while alive had moved but without life and grieved but without weeping, who now had an air of tranquil and unwitting desolation, not as if she had either outlived the others or had died first, but as if she had never lived at all. Quentin seemed to see them, the four of them arranged into the conventional family group of the period, with formal and lifeless decorum, and seen now as the fading and ancient photograph itself would have been seen enlarged and hung on the wall behind and above the voice and of whose presence there the voice's owner was not even aware, as if she (Miss Coldfield) had never seen this room before—a picture, a group which even to Quentin had a quality strange, contradictory and bizarre; not quite comprehensible, not (even to twenty) quite right—a group the last member of which had been dead twenty-five years and the first, fifty, evoked now out of the airless gloom of a dead house between an old woman's grim and implacable unforgiving and the passive chafing of a youth of twenty telling himself even amid the voice *Maybe you have to know anybody awful well to love them but when you have hated somebody for forty-three years you will know them awful well so maybe it's better then maybe it's fine then because after forty-three years they cant any longer surprise you or make you either very contented or very mad.* And maybe it (the voice, the talking, the incredulous and unbearable amazement) had even been a cry aloud once, Quentin thought, long ago when she was a girl—of young and indomitable unregret, of indictment of blind circumstance and savage event; but not now: now only the lonely thwarted old female flesh embattled for forty-three years in the old insult, the old unforgiving outraged and betrayed by the final and complete affront which was Sutpen's death:

"He wasn't a gentleman. He wasn't even a gentleman. He came here with a horse and two pistols and a name which nobody ever heard before, knew for certain was his own anymore than the horse was his own or even the pistols, seeking some place to hide himself, and Yoknapatawpha County supplied him with it. He sought the guarantee of reputable·men to barricade him from the other and later strangers who might come seeking him in turn, and Jefferson gave him that. Then he needed respectability, the shield of a virtuous woman, to make his position impregnable even against the men who had given him protection on that inevitable day and hour when even they must rise against him in scorn and horror and outrage; and it was mine and Ellen's father who gave him that. Oh, I hold no brief for Ellen: blind romantic fool who had only youth and inexperience to excuse her even if that; blind romantic fool, then later blind woman mother fool when she no longer had either youth or inexperience to excuse her, when she lay dying in that house for which she had exchanged pride and peace both and nobody there but the daughter who was already the same as a widow without ever having been a bride and was, three years later, to be a widow sure enough without having been anything at all, and the son who had repudiated the very roof under which he had been born and to which he would return but once more before disappearing for good, and that as a murderer and almost a fratricide; and he, fiend blackguard and devil, in Virginia fighting, where the chances of the earth's being rid of him were the best anywhere under the sun, yet Ellen and I both knowing that he would return, that every man in our armies would have to fall before bullet or ball found him; and only I, a child, a child, mind you, four years younger than the very niece I was asked to save, for Ellen to turn to and say, 'Protect her. Protect Judith at least.' Yes, blind romantic fool, who did not even have that hundred miles of plantation which apparently moved our father nor that big house and the notion of slaves underfoot day and night which reconciled, I wont say moved, her aunt. No: just the face of a man who contrived somehow to swagger even on a horse—a man who so far as anyone (including the father who was to give him a daughter in marriage) knew either had no past at all or did not dare reveal it—a man who rode into town out of nowhere with a horse and two pistols and a herd of wild beasts that he had hunted down singlehanded because he was stronger in fear than even they were in whatever heathen place he had fled from, and that French architect who looked like he had been hunted down and caught in turn by the negroes—a man who fled here and hid, concealed himself behind respectability, behind that hundred miles of land which he took from a tribe of ignorant Indians, nobody knows how, and a house the size of a courthouse where he lived for three years without a window or door or bedstead in it and still called it Sutpen's Hundred as if it had been a King's grant in unbroken perpetuity from his great grandfather —a home, position: a wife and family which, being necessary to concealment, he accepted along with the rest of respectability as he would have accepted the necessary discomfort and even pain of the briers and thorns in a thicket if the thicket could have given him the protection he sought.

"No: not even a gentleman. Marrying Ellen or marrying ten thousand Ellens could not have made him one. Not that he wanted to be one, or even be taken for one. No. That was not necessary since all he would need would be Ellen's and our father's names on a wedding license (or on any other patent of respectability) that people could look at and read just as he would have wanted our father's (or any other reputable man's) signature on a note of hand because our father knew who his father was in Tennessee and who his grandfather had been in Virginia and our neighbors and the people we lived among knew that we knew and we knew they knew we knew and we knew that they would have believed us about who and where we came from even if we had lied, just as anyone could have looked at him once and known that he would be lying about who and where and why he came from by the very fact that apparently he had to refuse to say at all. And the very fact that he had had to choose respectability to hide behind was proof enough (if anyone needed further proof) that what he fled from must have been some opposite of respectability too dark to talk about. Because he was too young. He was just twenty-five and a man of twenty-five does not voluntarily undertake the hardship and privation of clearing virgin land and establishing a plantation in a new country just for money; not a young man without any past that he apparently cared to discuss, in Mississippi in 1833, with a river full of steamboats loaded with drunken fools covered with diamonds and bent on throwing away their cotton and slaves before the boat reached New Orleans;—not with this just one night's hard ride away and the only handicap or obstacle being the other blackguards or the risk of being put ashore on a sandbar and at the remotest, a hemp rope. And he was no younger son sent out from some old quiet country like Virginia or Carolina with the surplus negroes to take up new land, because anyone could look at those negroes of his and tell that they may have come (and probably did) from a much older country than Virginia or Carolina but it wasn't a quiet one. And anyone could have looked once at his face and known that he would have chosen the River and even the certainty of the hemp rope, to undertaking what he undertook even if he had known that he would find gold buried and waiting for him in the very land which he had bought.

"No. I hold no more brief for Ellen than I do for myself. I hold even less for myself, because I had had twenty years in which to watch him, where Ellen had had but five. And not even those five to see him but only to hear at second hand what he was doing, and not even to hear more than half of that since apparently half of what he actually did during those five years nobody at all knew about, and half of the remainder no man would have repeated to a wife, let alone a young girl; he came here and set up a raree show which lasted five years and Jefferson paid him for the entertainment by at least shielding him to the extent of not telling their womenfolks what he was doing. But I had had all my life to watch him in, since apparently and for what reason Heaven has not seen fit to divulge, my life was destined to end on an afternoon in April forty-three years ago, since anyone who even had as little to call living as I had had up to that time would not call what I have had since, living. I saw what had happened to Ellen, my sister. I saw her almost a recluse, watching those two doomed children growing up whom she was helpless to save. I saw the price which she had paid for that house and that pride; I saw the notes of hand on pride and contentment and peace and all to which she had put her signature when she walked into the church that night, begin to fall due in succession. I saw Judith's marriage forbidden without rhyme or reason or shadow of excuse; I saw Ellen die with only me, a child, to turn to and ask to protect her remaining child; I saw Henry repudiate his home and birthright and then return and practically fling the bloody corpse of his sister's sweetheart at the hem of her wedding gown; I saw that man return—the evil's source and head which had outlasted all its victims—who had created two children not only to destroy one another and his own line, but my line as well, yet I agreed to marry him.

"No. I hold no brief for myself. I dont plead youth, since what creature in the South since 1861, man woman nigger or mule, had had time or opportunity not only to have been young but to have heard what being young was like from those who had. I dont plead propinquity: the fact that I, a woman young and at the age for marrying and in a time when most of the young men whom I would have known ordinarily were dead on lost battlefields, that I lived for two years under the same roof with him. I dont plead material necessity: the fact that, an orphan a woman and a pauper, I turned naturally not for protection but for actual food to my only kin: my dead sister's family: though I defy anyone to blame me, an orphan of twenty, a young woman without resources, who should desire not only to justify her situation but to vindicate the honor of a family the good name of whose women has never been impugned, by accepting the honorable proffer of marriage from the man whose food she was forced to subsist on. And most of all, I do not plead myself: a young woman emerging from a holocaust which had taken parents security and all from her, who had seen all that living meant to her fall into ruins about the feet of a few figures with the shapes of men but with the names and statures of heroes;—a young woman I say thrown into daily and hourly contact with one of these men who, despite what he might have been at one time and despite what she might have believed or even known about him, had fought for four honorable years for the soil and traditions of the land where she had been born (and the man who had done that, villain dyed though he be, would have possessed in her eyes, even if only from association with them, the stature and shape of a hero too) and now he also emerging from the same holocaust in which she had suffered, with nothing to face what the future held for the South but his bare hands and the sword which he at least had never surrendered and the citation for valor from his defeated Commander-in-Chief. Oh he was brave. I have never gainsaid that. But that our cause, our very life and future hopes and past pride, should have been thrown into the balance with men like that to buttress it—men with valor and strength but without pity or honor. Is it any wonder that Heaven saw fit to let us lose?"

"Nome," Quentin said.

"But that it should have been our father, mine and Ellen's father of all of them that he knew, out of all the ones who used to go out there and drink and gamble with him and watch him fight those wild negroes, whose daughters he might even have won at cards. That it should have been our father. How he could have approached papa, on what grounds;

what there could have been beside the common civility of two men meeting on the street, between a man who came from nowhere or dared not tell where and our father; what there could have been between a man like that and papa—a Methodist steward, a merchant who was not rich and who not only could have done nothing under the sun to advance his fortunes or prospects but could by no stretch of the imagination even have owned anything that he would have wanted, even picked up in the road—a man who owned neither land nor slaves except two house servants whom he had freed as soon as he got them, bought them, who neither drank nor hunted nor gambled;—what there could have been between a man who to my certain knowledge was never in a Jefferson church but three times in his life—the once when he first saw Ellen, the once when they rehearsed the wedding, the once when they performed it;—a man that anyone could look at and see that, even if he apparently had none now, he was accustomed to having money and intended to have it again and would have no scruples about how he got it—that man to discover Ellen inside a church. In church, mind you, as though there were a fatality and curse on our family and God Himself were seeing to it that it was performed and discharged to the last drop and dreg. Yes, fatality and curse on the South and on our family as though because some ancestor of ours had elected to establish his descent in a land primed for fatality and already cursed with it, even if it had not rather been

our family, our father's progenitors, who had incurred the curse long years before and had been
coerced by Heaven into establishing itself in the
land and the time already cursed. So that even I, a
child still too young to know more than that,
though Ellen was my own sister and Henry and
Judith my own nephew and niece, I was not even
to go out there save when papa or my aunt was with
me and that I was not to play with Henry and Judith
at all except in the house (and not because I was four
years younger than Judith and six years younger
than Henry: wasn't it to me that Ellen turned before
she died and said 'Protect them'?)—even I used to
wonder what our father or his father could have
done before he married our mother that Ellen and
I would have to expiate and neither of us alone be
sufficient; what crime committed that would leave
our family cursed to be instruments not only for that
man's destruction but for our own."

"Yessum," Quentin said.

"Yes," the grim quiet voice said from beyond the
unmoving triangle of dim lace; and now, among the
musing and decorous wraiths Quentin seemed to
watch resolving the figure of a little girl, in the prim
skirts and pantalettes, the smooth prim decorous
braids, of the dead time. She seemed to stand, to
lurk, behind the neat picket fence of a small, grimly
middleclass yard or lawn, looking out upon the
whatever ogreworld of that quiet village street with
that air of children born too late into their parents'
lives and doomed to contemplate all human behav-

ior through the complex and needless follies of
adults—an air Cassandralike and humorless and profoundly and sternly prophetic out of all proportion
to the actual years even of a child who had never
been young. "Because I was born too late. I was
born twenty-two years too late—a child to whom
out of the overheard talk of adults my own sister's
and my sister's children's faces had come to be like
the faces in an ogre-tale between supper and bed
long before I was old enough or big enough to be
permitted to play with them, yet to whom that sister
must have to turn at the last when she lay dying,
with one of the children vanished and doomed to be
a murderer and the other doomed to be a widow
before she had even been a bride, and say, 'Protect
her, at least. At least save Judith.' A child, yet whose
child's vouchsafed instinct could make that reply
which the mature wisdom of her elders apparently
could not make: 'Protect her? From whom and from
what? He has already given them life: he does not
need to harm them further. It is from themselves
that they need protection.' "

It should have been later than it was; it should
have been late, yet the yellow slashes of mote-palpi-
tant sunlight were latticed no higher up the impalpable wall of gloom which separated them; the sun
seemed hardly to have moved. It (the talking, the
telling) seemed (to him, to Quentin) to partake of
that logic- and reason-flouting quality of a dream
which the sleeper knows must have occurred, still-
born and complete, in a second, yet the very quality

upon which it must depend to move the dreamer (verisimilitude) to credulity—horror or pleasure or amazement—depends as completely upon a formal recognition of and acceptance of elapsed and yet-elapsing time as music or a printed tale. "Yes. I was born too late. I was a child who was to remember those three faces (and his, too) as seen for the first time in the carriage on that first Sunday morning when this town finally realised that he had turned that road from Sutpen's Hundred in to the church into a race track. I was three then, and doubtless I had seen them before; I must have. But I do not remember it. I do not even remember ever having seen Ellen before that Sunday. It was as though the sister whom I had never laid eyes on, who before I was born had vanished into the stronghold of an ogre or a djinn, was now to return through a dispensation of one day only, to the world which she had quitted, and I a child of three, waked early for the occasion, dressed and curled as if for Christmas, for an occasion more serious than Christmas even, since now and at last this ogre or djinn had agreed for the sake of the wife and the children to come to church, to permit them at least to approach the vicinity of salvation, to at least give Ellen one chance to struggle with him for those children's souls on a battle-ground where she could be supported not only by Heaven but by her own family and people of her own kind; yes, even for the moment submitting himself to redemption, or lacking that, at least chiv-alrous for the instant even though still unregenerate.

That is what I expected. This is what I saw as I stood there before the church between papa and our aunt and waited for the carriage to arrive from the twelve mile drive. And though I must have seen Ellen and the children before this, this is the vision of my first sight of them which I shall carry to my grave: a glimpse like the forefront of a tornado, of the carriage and Ellen's high white face within it and the two replicas of his face in miniature flanking her, and on the front seat the face and teeth of the wild negro who was driving, and he, his face exactly like the negro's save for the teeth (this because of his beard, doubtless)—all in a thunder and a fury of wildeyed horses and of galloping and of dust.

"Oh, there were plenty of them to abet him, assist him, make a race of it; ten oclock on Sunday morning, the carriage racing on two wheels up to the very door to the church with that wild negro in his christian clothes looking exactly like a performing tiger in a linen duster and a top hat, and Ellen with no drop of blood in her face, holding those two children who were not crying and who did not need to be held, who sat on either side of her perfectly still too, with in their faces that infantile enormity which we did not then quite comprehend. Oh yes, there were plenty to aid and abet him; even he could not have held a horse race without someone to race against. Because it was not even public opinion that stopped him, not even the men who might have had wives and children in carriages to be ridden down and into ditches: it was the minister himself, speaking in the name of the women of Jefferson and Yoknapatawpha County. So he quit coming to church himself; now it would be just Ellen and the children in the carriage on Sunday morning, so we knew now that at least there would be no betting now, since no one could say if it was an actual race or not, since now, with his face absent, it was only the wild negro's perfectly inscrutable one with the teeth glinting a little, so that now we could never know if it were a race or a runaway, and if there was triumph, it was on the face twelve miles back there at Sutpen's Hundred, which did not even require to see or be present. It was the negro now, who in the act of passing another carriage spoke to that team too as well as to his own—something without words, not needing words probably, in that tongue in which they slept in the mud of that swamp and brought here out of whatever dark swamp he had found them in and brought them here:—the dust, the thunder, the carriage whirling up to the church door while women and children scattered and screamed before it and men caught at the bridles of the other team. And the negro would let Ellen and the children out at the door and take the carriage on around to the hitching grove and beat the horses for running away; there was even a fool who tried to interfere once, whereupon the negro turned upon him with the stick lifted and his teeth showing a little and said, 'Marster say; I do. You tell Marster.'

"Yes. From them; from themselves. And this time it was not even the minister. It was Ellen. Our aunt

and papa were talking and I came in and my aunt
said 'Go out and play' though even if I could not
have heard through the door at all, I could have
repeated the conversation for them: 'Your daughter,
your own daughter' my aunt said; and papa: 'Yes.
She is my daughter. When she wants me to interfere
she will tell me so herself'. Because this Sunday
when Ellen and the children came out of the front
door, it was not the carriage waiting, it was Ellen's
phaeton with the old gentle mare which she drove
and the stableboy that he had bought instead of the
wild negro. And Judith looked once at the phaeton
and realised what it meant and began to scream,
screaming and kicking while they carried her back
into the house and put her to bed. No, he was not
present. Nor do I claim a lurking triumphant face
behind a window curtain. Probably he would have
been as amazed as we were since we would all realise
now that we were faced by more than a child's
tantrum or even hysteria: that his face had been in
that carriage all the time; that it had been Judith, a
girl of six, who had instigated and authorised that
negro to make the team run away. Not Henry,
mind; not the boy, which would have been outrageous enough; but Judith, the girl. As soon as papa
and I entered those gates that afternoon and began
to go up the drive toward the house, I could feel it.
It was as though somewhere in that Sunday afternoon's quiet and peace the screams of that child still
existed, lingered, not as sound now but as something for the skin to hear, the hair on the head to

hear. But I did not ask at once. I was just four then; I sat in the buggy beside papa as I had stood between him and our aunt before the church on that first Sunday when I had been dressed to come and see my sister and my nephew and niece for the first time, looking at the house (I had been inside it before too, of course, but even when I saw it for the first time that I could remember I seemed already to know how it was going to look just as I seemed to know how Ellen and Judith and Henry would look before I saw them for the time which I always remember as being the first). No, not asking even then, but just looking at that huge quiet house, saying 'What room is Judith sick in, papa?' with that quiet aptitude of a child for accepting the inexplicable, though I now know that even then I was wondering what Judith saw when she came out the door and found the phaeton instead of the carriage, the tame stableboy instead of the wild man; what she had seen in that phaeton which looked so innocent to the rest of us—or worse, what she had missed when she saw the phaeton and began to scream. Yes, a still hot quiet Sunday afternoon like this afternoon; I remember yet the utter quiet of that house when we went in and from which I knew at once that he was absent without knowing that he would now be in the scuppernong arbor drinking with Wash Jones. I only knew, as soon as papa and I crossed the threshold, that he was not there: as though with some almost omniscient conviction (that same instinctive knowledge which enabled me to tell Ellen that it was not from him that Judith would need protection) knowing that he did not need to stay and observe his triumph—and that, in comparison with what was to be, this one was a mere trivial business even beneath our notice too. Yes, that quiet darkened room with the blinds closed and a negro woman sitting beside the bed with a fan and Judith's white face on the pillow beneath a camphor cloth, asleep as I supposed then: possibly it was sleep, or would be called sleep: and Ellen's face white and calm and papa said 'Go out and find Henry and ask him to play with you, Rosa' and so I stood just outside that quiet door in that quiet upper hall because I was afraid to go away even from it because I could hear the sabbath afternoon quiet of that house louder than thunder, louder than laughing even with triumph.

" 'Think of the children,' papa said.

" 'Think?' Ellen said. 'What else do I do? What else do I lie awake at night and do but think of them?' Neither papa nor Ellen said Come back home. No: This occurred before it became fashionable to repair your mistakes by turning your back on them and running. It was just the two quiet voices beyond that blank door which might have been discussing something printed in a magazine; and I, a child standing close beside that door because I was afraid to be there but more afraid to leave it, standing motionless beside that door as though trying to make myself blend with the dark wood and become invisible, like a chameleon, listening to the living spirit, presence, of that house, since some of Ellen's life and breath had now gone into it as well as his, breathing away in a long neutral sound of victory and despair, of triumph and terror too.

" 'Do you love this——' papa said.

" 'Papa,' Ellen said. That was all. But I could see her face then as clearly as papa could have, with that same expression which it had worn in the carriage on that first Sunday and the others. Then a servant came and said our buggy was ready.

"Yes. From themselves. Not from him, not from anybody, just as nobody could have saved them, even himself. Because he now showed us why that triumph had been beneath his notice. He showed Ellen, that is: not I. I was not there; it was six years now, during which I had scarcely seen him. Our aunt was gone now and I was keeping house for papa. Perhaps once a year papa and I would go out there and have dinner, and maybe four times a year Ellen and the children would come in and spend the day with us. Not he; that I know of, he never entered this house again after he and Ellen married. I was young then; I was even young enough to believe that this was due to some stubborn coal of conscience, if not remorse, even in him. But I know better now. I know now that it was simply because since papa had given him respectability through a wife there was nothing else he could want from papa and so not even sheer gratitude, let alone appearances, could force him to forego his own pleasure to the extent of taking a family meal with his wife's people. So I saw little of them. I did not have time now to play, even if I had ever had any inclination. I had never learned how and I saw no reason to try to learn now even if I had had the time.

"So it was six years now, though it was actually no secret to Ellen since it had apparently been going on ever since he drove the last nail in the house, the only difference between now and the time of his bachelorhood being that now they would hitch the teams and saddle horses and mules in the grove beyond the stable and so come up across the pasture unseen from the house. Because there were plenty of them still; it was as if God or the devil had taken advantage of his very vices in order to supply witnesses to the discharge of our curse not only from among gentlefolks, our own kind, but from the very scum and riffraff who could not have approached the house itself under any other circumstances, not even from the rear. Yes, Ellen and those two children alone in that house twelve miles from town, and down there in the stable a hollow square of faces in the lantern light, the white faces on three sides, the black ones on the fourth, and in the center two of his wild negroes fighting, naked, fighting not like white men fight, with rules and weapons, but like negroes fight to hurt one another quick and bad. Ellen knew that, or thought she did; that was not it. She accepted that—not reconciled: accepted—as though there is a breathing-point in outrage where you can accept it almost with gratitude since you can say to yourself, *Thank God this is all; at least I*

now know all of it—thinking that, clinging still to
that when she ran into the stable that night while the
very men who had stolen into it from the rear fell
back away from her with at least some grain of
decency, and Ellen seeing not the two black beasts
she had expected to see but instead a white one and
a black one, both naked to the waist and gouging at
one another's eyes as if their skins should not only
have been the same color but should have been covered with fur too. Yes. It seems that on certain occasions, perhaps at the end of the evening, the
spectacle, as a grand finale or perhaps as a matter of
sheer deadly forethought toward the retention of
supremacy, domination, he would enter the ring
with one of the negroes himself. Yes. That is what
Ellen saw: her husband and the father of her children standing there naked and panting and bloody
to the waist and the negro just fallen evidently, lying
at his feet and bloody too save that on the negro it
merely looked like grease or sweat—Ellen running
down the hill from the house, bareheaded, in time
to hear the sound, the screaming, hearing it while
she still ran in the darkness and before the spectators
knew that she was there, hearing it even before it
occurred to one spectator to say, 'It's a horse' then
'It's a woman' then 'My God, it's a child'—ran in,
and the spectators falling back to permit her to see
Henry plunge out from among the negroes who had
been holding him, screaming and vomiting—not
pausing, not even looking at the faces which shrank
back away from her as she knelt in the stable filth

to raise Henry and not looking at Henry either but up at *him* as he stood there with even his teeth showing beneath his beard now and another negro wiping the blood from his body with a towsack. 'I know you will excuse us, gentlemen,' Ellen said. But they were already departing, nigger and white, slinking out again as they had slunk in, and Ellen not watching them now either but kneeling in the dirt while Henry clung to her, crying, and *he* standing there yet while a third nigger prodded his shirt or coat at him as though the coat were a stick and he a caged snake. 'Where is Judith, Thomas?' Ellen said.

" 'Judith?' he said. Oh, he was not lying; his own triumph had outrun him; he had builded even better in evil than even he could have hoped. 'Judith? Isn't she in bed?'

" 'Dont lie to me, Thomas,' Ellen said. 'I can understand your bringing Henry here to see this, wanting Henry to see this; I will try to understand it; yes, I will make myself try to understand it. But not Judith, Thomas. Not my baby girl, Thomas.'

" 'I dont expect you to understand it,' he said. 'Because you are a woman. But I didn't bring Judith down here. I would not bring her down here. I dont expect you to believe that. But I swear to it.'

" 'I wish I could believe you,' Ellen said. 'I want to believe you.' Then she began to call. 'Judith!' she called in a voice calm and sweet and filled with despair: 'Judith honey! Time to come to bed.'

"But I was not there. I was not there to see the two Sutpen faces this time—once on Judith and once on the negro girl beside her—looking down through the square entrance to the loft."

II

It was a summer of wistaria. The twilight was full of it and of the smell of his father's cigar as they sat on the front gallery after supper until it would be time for Quentin to start, while in the deep shaggy lawn below the veranda the fireflies blew and drifted in soft random—the odor, the scent, which five months later Mr Compson's letter would carry up from Mississippi and over the long iron New England snow and into Quentin's sitting-room at Harvard. It was a day of listening too—the listening, the hearing in 1909 even yet mostly that which he already knew since he had been born in and still breathed the same air in which the church bells had rung on that Sunday morning in 1833 (and, on Sundays, heard even one of the original three bells in the same steeple where descendants of the same pigeons strutted and crooned or wheeled in short courses resembling soft fluid paint-smears on the soft summer sky);—a Sunday morning in June with the bells ringing peaceful and peremptory and a little cacophonous—the denominations in concord though not in tune—and the ladies and children, and house negroes to carry the parasols and flywhisks, and

34

even a few men (the ladies moving in hoops among
the miniature broadcloth of little boys and the pantalettes of little girls, in the skirts of the time when
ladies did not walk but floated) when the other men
sitting with their feet on the railing of the Holston
House gallery looked up, and there the stranger
was. He was already halfway across the square when
they saw him, on a big hard-ridden roan horse, man
and beast looking as though they had been created
out of thin air and set down in the bright summer
sabbath sunshine in the middle of a tired foxtrot—
face and horse that none of them had ever seen
before, name that none of them had ever heard, and
origin and purpose which some of them were never
to learn. So that in the next four weeks (Jefferson
was a village then: the Holston House, the courthouse, six stores, a blacksmith and livery stable, a
saloon frequented by drovers and peddlers, three
churches and perhaps thirty residences) the stranger's name went back and forth among the places of
business and of idleness and among the residences in
steady strophe and antistrophe: *Sutpen. Sutpen.
Sutpen. Sutpen.*

That was all that the town was to know about him
for almost a month. He had apparently come into
town from the south—a man of about twenty-five as
the town learned later, because at the time his age
could not have been guessed because at that time he
looked like a man who had been sick. Not like a man
who had been peacefully ill in bed and had recovered to move with a sort of diffident and tentative

amazement in a world which he had believed himself on the point of surrendering, but like a man who
had been through some solitary furnace experience
which was more than just fever, like an explorer say,
who not only had to face the normal hardship of the
pursuit which he chose but was overtaken by the
added and unforeseen handicap of the fever also and
fought through it at enormous cost not so much
physical as mental, alone and unaided and not
through blind instinctive will to endure and survive
but to gain and keep to enjoy it the material prize
for which he accepted the original gambit. A man
with a big frame but gaunt now almost to emacia-
tion, with a short reddish beard which resembled a
disguise and above which his pale eyes had a quality
at once visionary and alert, ruthless and reposed in
a face whose flesh had the appearance of pottery, of
having been colored by that oven's fever either of
soul or environment, deeper than sun alone beneath
a dead impervious surface as of glazed clay. That
was what they saw, though it was years before the
town learned that that was all which he possessed at
the time—the strong spent horse and the clothes on
his back and a small saddlebag scarcely large enough
to contain the spare linen and the razors, and the
two pistols of which Miss Coldfield told Quentin,
with the butts worn smooth as pickhandles and
which he used with the precision of knitting needles; later Quentin's grandfather saw him ride at a
canter around a sapling at twenty feet and put both
bullets into a playing card fastened to the tree. He

had a room in the Holston House but he carried the key with him and each morning he fed and saddled the horse and rode away before daylight, where to the town likewise failed to learn, probably due to the fact that he gave the pistol demonstration on the third day after his arrival. So they had to depend on inquiry to find out what they could about him, which would of necessity be at night, at the supper table in the Holston House dining room or in the lounge which he would have to cross to gain his room and lock the door again, which he would do as soon as he finished eating. The bar opened into the lounge too, and that would or should have been the place to accost him and even inquire, except for the fact that he did not use the bar. He did not drink at all, he told them. He did not say that he used to drink and had quit, nor that he had never used alcohol. He just said that he would not care for a drink; it was years later before even Quentin's grandfather (he was a young man too then; it would be years yet before he would become General Compson) learned that the reason Sutpen did not drink was that he did not have the money with which to pay his share or return the courtesy; it was General Compson who first realised that at this time Sutpen lacked not only the money to spend for drink and conviviality, but the time and inclination as well: that he was at this time completely the slave of his secret and furious impatience, his conviction gained from whatever that recent experience had been—that fever mental or physical—of a need for haste, of time fleeing

beneath him, which was to drive him for the next
five years—as General Compson computed it,
roughly until about nine months before his son was
born.

So they would catch him, run him to earth, in the
lounge between the supper table and his locked door
to give him the opportunity to tell them who he was
and where he came from and what he was up to,
whereupon he would move gradually and steadily
until his back came in contact with something—a
post or a wall—and then stand there and tell them
nothing whatever as pleasantly and courteously as a
hotel clerk. It was the Chickasaw Indian agent with
or through whom he dealt and so it was not until he
waked the County Recorder that Saturday night
with the deed, patent, to the land and the gold Spanish coin, that the town learned that he now owned
a hundred square miles of some of the best virgin
bottom land in the country, though even that
knowledge came too late because Sutpen himself
was gone, where to again they did not know. But he
owned land among them now and some of them
began to suspect what General Compson apparently
knew: that the Spanish coin with which he had paid
to have his patent recorded was the last one of any
kind which he possessed. So they were certain now
that he had departed to get more; there were several
who even anticipated in believing (and even in saying aloud, now that he was not present) what
Sutpen's future and then unborn sister-in-law was
to tell Quentin almost eighty years later: that he had

found some unique and practical way of hiding loot and that he had returned to the cache to replenish his pockets, even if he had not actually ridden with the two pistols back to the River and the steamboats full of gamblers and cotton- and slavedealers to replenish the cache. At least some of them were telling one another that when two months later he returned, again without warning and accompanied this time by the covered wagon with a negro driving it and on the seat with the negro a small, alertly resigned man with a grim, harried Latin face, in a frock coat and a flowered waistcoat and a hat which would have created no furore on a Paris boulevard, all of which he was to wear constantly for the next two years—the sombrely theatric clothing and the expression of fatalistic and amazed determination—while his white client and the negro crew which he was to advise though not direct went stark naked save for a coating of dried mud. This was the French architect. Years later the town learned that he had come all the way from Martinique on Sutpen's bare promise and lived for two years on venison cooked over a camp fire, in an unfloored tent made of the wagon hood, before he so much as saw any color or shape of pay. And until he passed through town on his way back to New Orleans two years later, he was not even to see Jefferson again; he would not come, or Sutpen would not bring him, to town even on the few occasions when Sutpen would be seen there, and he did not have much chance to look at Jefferson on that first day because the wagon did not stop.

Apparently it was only by sheer geographical hap that Sutpen passed through town at all, pausing only long enough for someone (not General Compson) to look beneath the wagon hood and into a black tunnel filled with still eyeballs and smelling like a wolfden.

But the legend of Sutpen's wild negroes was not to begin at once, because the wagon went on as though even the wood and iron which composed it, as well as the mules which drew it, had become imbued by sheer association with him with that quality of gaunt and tireless driving, that conviction for haste and of fleeing time; later Sutpen told Quentin's grandfather that on that afternoon when the wagon passed through Jefferson they had been without food since the previous night and that he was trying to reach Sutpen's Hundred and the river bottom to try to kill a deer before dark, so he and the architect and the negroes would not have to spend another night without food. So the legend of the wild men came gradually back to town, brought by the men who would ride out to watch what was going on, who began to tell how Sutpen would take stand beside a game trail with the pistols and send the negroes in to drive the swamp like a pack of hounds; it was they who told how during that first summer and fall the negroes did not even have (or did not use) blankets to sleep in, even before the coon-hunter Akers claimed to have walked one of them out of the absolute mud like a sleeping alligator and screamed just in time. The negroes could speak no English yet and doubtless there were more than Akers who did not know that the language in which they and Sutpen communicated was a sort of French and not some dark and fatal tongue of their own.

There were many more than Akers, though the others were responsible citizens and landowners and so did not have to lurk about the camp at night. In fact, as Miss Coldfield told Quentin, they would make up parties to meet at the Holston House and go out horseback, often carrying lunch. Sutpen had built a brick kiln and he had set up the saw and planer which he had brought in the wagon—a capstan with a long sapling walking-beam, with the wagon team and the negroes in shifts and himself too when necessary, when the machinery slowed, hitched to it—as if the negroes actually were wild men; as General Compson told his son, Quentin's father, while the negroes were working Sutpen never raised his voice at them, that instead he led them, caught them at the psychological instant by example, by some ascendancy of forbearance rather than by brute fear. Without dismounting (usually Sutpen did not even greet them with as much as a nod, apparently as unaware of their presence as if they had been idle shades) they would sit in a curious quiet clump as though for mutual protection and watch his mansion rise, carried plank by plank and brick by brick out of the swamp where the clay and timber waited—the bearded white man and the twenty black ones and all stark naked beneath the croaching and pervading mud. Being men, these spectators did not realise that the garments which Sutpen had worn when he first rode into Jefferson were the only ones in which they had ever seen him, and few of the women in the county had seen him at all yet. Otherwise, some of them would have anticipated Miss Coldfield in this too: in divining that he was saving his clothes, since decorum even if not elegance of appearance would be the only weapon (or rather, ladder) with which he could conduct the last assault upon what Miss Coldfield and perhaps others believed to be respectability— that respectability which, according to General Compson, consisted in Sutpen's secret mind of a great deal more than the mere acquisition of a chatelaine for his house. So he and the twenty negroes worked together, plastered over with mud against the mosquitoes and, as Miss Coldfield told Quentin, distinguishable one from another by his beard and eyes alone and only the architect resembling a human creature because of the French clothes which he wore constantly with a sort of invincible fatality until the day after the house was completed save for the windowglass and the ironware which they could not make by hand and the architect departed—working in the sun and heat of summer and the mud and ice of winter, with quiet and unflagging fury.

It took him two years, he and his crew of imported slaves which his adopted fellow citizens still looked on as being a good deal more deadly than any beast he could have started and slain in that country. They worked from sunup to sundown while parties of horsemen rode up and sat their horses quietly and watched, and the architect in his formal coat and his Paris hat and his expression of grim and embittered amazement lurked about the environs of the scene with his air something between a casual and bitterly disinterested spectator and a condemned and conscientious ghost—amazement, General Compson said, not at the others and what they were doing so much as at himself, at the inexplicable and incredible fact of his own presence. But he was a good architect; Quentin knew the house, twelve miles from Jefferson, in its grove of cedar and oak, seventy-five years after it was finished. And not only an architect, as General Compson said, but an artist since only an artist could have borne those two years in order to build a house which he doubtless not only expected but firmly intended never to see again. Not, General Compson said, the hardship to sense and the outrage to sensibility of the two years' sojourn, but Sutpen: that only an artist could have borne Sutpen's ruthlessness and hurry and still manage to curb the dream of grim and castlelike magnificence at which Sutpen obviously aimed, since the place as Sutpen planned it would have been almost as large as Jefferson itself at the time; that the little grim harried foreigner had singlehanded given battle to and vanquished Sutpen's fierce and overweening vanity or desire for magnificence or for vindication or whatever it was (even General

Compson did not know yet) and so created of
Sutpen's very defeat the victory which, in conquering, Sutpen himself would have failed to gain.

So it was finished then, down to the last plank and
brick and wooden pin which they could make themselves. Unpainted and unfurnished, without a pane
of glass or a doorknob or hinge in it, twelve miles
from town and almost that far from any neighbor,
it stood for three years more surrounded by its formal gardens and promenades, its slave quarters and
stables and smokehouses; wild turkey ranged within
a mile of the house and deer came light and colored
like smoke and left delicate prints in the formal beds
where there would be no flowers for four years yet.
Now there began a period, a phase, during which
the town and the county watched him with more
puzzlement yet. Perhaps it was because the next step
toward that secret end which General Compson
claimed to have known but which the town and the
county comprehended but dimly or not at all, now
required patience or passive time instead of that
driving fury to which he had accustomed them; now
it was the women who first suspected what he
wanted, what the next step would be. None of the
men, certainly not those who knew him well
enough to call him by name, suspected that he
wanted a wife. Doubtless there were some of them,
husbands and bachelors both, who not only would
have refused to entertain the idea but would even
have protested against it, because for the next three
years he led what must have been to them a perfect

existence. He lived out there, eight miles from any neighbor, in masculine solitude in what might be called the halfacre gunroom of a baronial splendor. He lived in the spartan shell of the largest edifice in the county, not excepting the courthouse itself, whose threshold no woman had so much as seen, without any feminised softness of window pane or door or mattress; where there was not only no woman to object if he should elect to have his dogs in to sleep on the pallet bed with him, he did not even need dogs to kill the game which left footprints within sight of the kitchen door but hunted it instead with human beings who belonged to him body and soul and of whom it was believed (or said) that they could creep up to a bedded buck and cut its throat before it could move.

It was at this time that he began to invite the parties of men of which Miss Coldfield told Quentin, out to Sutpen's Hundred to camp in blankets in the naked rooms of his embryonic formal opulence; they hunted, and at night played cards and drank, and on occasion he doubtless pitted his negroes against one another and perhaps even at this time participated now and then himself—that spectacle which, according to Miss Coldfield, his son was unable to bear the sight of while his daughter looked on unmoved. Sutpen drank himself now, though there were probably others beside Quentin's grandfather who remarked that he drank very sparingly save when he himself had managed to supply some of the liquor. His guests would bring whiskey out with them but he drank of this with a sort of sparing calculation as though keeping mentally, General Compson said, a sort of balance of spiritual solvency between the amount of whiskey he accepted and the amount of running meat which he supplied to the guns.

He lived like that for three years. He now had a plantation; inside of two years he had dragged house and gardens out of virgin swamp, and plowed and planted his land with seed cotton which General Compson loaned him. Then he seemed to quit. He seemed to just sit down in the middle of what he had almost finished, and to remain so for three years during which he did not even appear to intend or want anything more. Perhaps it is not to be wondered at that the men in the county came to believe that the life he now led had been his aim all the time; it was General Compson, who seemed to have known him well enough to offer to lend him seed cotton for his start, who knew any better, to whom Sutpen ever told anything about his past. It was General Compson who knew first about the Spanish coin being his last one, as it was Compson (so the town learned later) who offered to lend Sutpen the money to finish and furnish his house, and was refused. So doubtless General Compson was the first man in the county to tell himself that Sutpen did not need to borrow money with which to complete the house, supply what it yet lacked, because he intended to marry it. Not the first person: the first man, since, according to what Miss Coldfield told Quentin seventy-five years later, the women in the county had been telling one another and their husbands as well that Sutpen did not intend to quit there, that he had already gone to too much trouble, gone through too much privation and hardship, to settle down and live exactly as he had lived while the house was being built save that now he had a roof to sleep under in place of an unfloored wagon hood. Probably the women had already cast about among the families of the men who might now be called his friends, for that prospective bride whose dowry might complete the shape and substance of that respectability Miss Coldfield anyway believed to be his aim. So when, at the expiration of this second phase, three years after the house was finished and the architect departed, and again on Sunday morning and again without warning, the town saw him cross the square, on foot now but in the same garments in which he had ridden into town five years ago and which no one had seen since (he or one of the negroes had ironed the coat with heated bricks, General Compson told Quentin's father) and enter the Methodist church, only some of the men were surprised. The women merely said that he had exhausted the possibilities of the families of the men with whom he had hunted and gambled and that he had now come to town to find a wife exactly as he would have gone to the Memphis market to buy livestock or slaves. But when they comprehended whom it was that he had apparently come to town and into church to invest with his choice, the assurance of the women became one with the men's surprise, and then even more than that: amazement.

Because the town now believed that it knew him. For two years it had watched him as with that grim and unflagging fury he had erected that shell of a house and laid out his fields, then for three years he had remained completely static, as if he were run by electricity and someone had come along and removed, dismantled the wiring or the dynamo, while the women of the county gradually convinced it that he was merely waiting to find a wife with a dowry to finish it with. So that when he entered the Methodist church that Sunday morning in his ironed coat, there were men as well as women who believed that they had only to look around the congregation in order to anticipate the direction his feet would take him, until they became aware that he had apparently marked down Miss Coldfield's father with the same cold and ruthless deliberation with which he had probably marked down the French architect. They watched in shocked amazement while he laid deliberate siege to the one man in the town with whom he could have had nothing in common, least of all, money—a man who obviously could do nothing under the sun for him save give him credit at a little cross-roads store or cast a vote in his favor if he should ever seek ordination as a Methodist minister—a Methodist steward, a merchant not only of modest position and circumstances but who already had a wife and family of his own, let alone a dependent mother and sister, to support out of the proceeds of a business which he had brought to Jefferson ten years ago in a single wagon—a man with a name for absolute and undeviating and even puritan uprightness in a country and time of lawless opportunity, who neither drank nor gambled nor even hunted. In their surprise they forgot that Mr Coldfield had a marriageable daughter. They did not consider the daughter at all. They did not think of love in connection with Sutpen. They thought of ruthlessness rather than justice and of fear rather than respect, but not of pity or love: besides being too lost in amazed speculation as to just how Sutpen intended or could contrive to use Mr Coldfield to further whatever secret ends he still had. They were never to know: even Miss Rosa Coldfield did not. Because from that day there were no more hunting parties out at Sutpen's Hundred, and when they saw him now it would be in town. But not loafing, idling. The men who had slept and matched glasses with him under his roof (some of them had even come to call him Sutpen without the formal Mister) watched him pass along the street before the Holston House with a single formal gesture to his hat and go on and enter Mr Coldfield's store, and that was all.

"Then one day he quitted Jefferson for the second time," Mr Compson told Quentin. "The town should have been accustomed to that by now. Nevertheless, his position had subtly changed, as you will see by the town's reaction to this second return. Because when he came back this time, he was in a sense a public enemy. Perhaps this was because of what he brought back with him this time: the material he brought back this time, as compared to the simple wagon load of wild niggers which he had brought back before. But I dont think so. That is, I think it was a little more involved than the sheer value of his chandeliers and mahogany and rugs. I think that the affront was born of the town's realization that he was getting it involved with himself; that whatever the felony which produced the mahogany and crystal, he was forcing the town to compound it. Heretofore, until that Sunday when he came to church, if he had misused or injured anybody, it was only old Ikkemotubbe, from whom he got his land—a matter between his conscience and Uncle Sam and God. But now his position had changed, because when, about three months after he departed, four wagons left Jefferson to go to the River and meet him, it was known that Mr Coldfield was the man who hired and dispatched them. They were big wagons, drawn by oxen, and when they returned the town looked at them and knew, no matter what they might have contained, that Mr Coldfield could not have mortgaged everything that he owned for enough to fill them; doubtless this time there were more men than women even who pictured him during this absence with a handkerchief over his face and the two pistol barrels glinting beneath the candelabra of a steamboat's saloon, even if no worse: if not something performed in the lurking dark of a muddy landing and with a knife from behind. They saw him pass, on the roan horse beside his four wagons; it seems that even the ones who had eaten his food and shot his game and even called him 'Sutpen' without the 'Mister', didn't accost him now. They just waited while reports and rumors came back to town of how he and his now somewhat tamed negroes had installed the windows and doors and the spits and pots in the kitchen and the crystal chandeliers in the parlors and the furniture and the curtains and the rugs; it was that same Akers who had blundered onto the mudcouched negro five years ago who came, a little wild-eyed and considerably slack-mouthed, into the Holston House bar one evening and said, 'Boys, this time he stole the whole durn steamboat!'

"So at last civic virtue came to a boil. One day and with the sheriff of the county among them, a party of eight or ten took the road out to Sutpen's Hundred. They did not go all the way because about six miles from town they met Sutpen himself. He was riding the roan horse, in the frock coat and the beaver hat which they knew and with his legs wrapped in a piece of tarpaulin; he had a portmanteau on his pommel and he was carrying a small woven basket on his arm. He stopped the roan (it was April then, and the road was still a quagmire) and sat there in his splashed tarpaulin and looked from one face to the next; your grandfather said that his eyes looked like pieces of a broken plate and that his beard was strong as a curry-comb. That was how he put it: strong as a curry-comb. 'Good morning, gentlemen,' he said. 'Were you looking for me?'

"Doubtless something more than this transpired at the time, though none of the vigilance committee ever told it that I know of. All I ever heard is how the town, the men on the gallery of the Holston House saw Sutpen and the committee ride onto the square together, Sutpen a little in front and the others bunched behind him—Sutpen with his legs and feet wrapped neatly in his tarpaulin and his shoulders squared inside the worn broadcloth coat and that worn brushed beaver cocked a little, talking to them over his shoulder and those eyes hard and pale and reckless and probably quizzical and maybe contemptuous even then. He pulled up at the door and the negro hostler ducked out and took the roan's head and Sutpen got down, with his portmanteau and the basket and mounted the steps, and I heard how he turned there and looked at them again where they huddled on their horses, not knowing what to do exactly. And it might have been a good thing that he had that beard and they could not see his mouth. Then he turned, and he looked at the other men sitting with their feet on the railing and watching him too, men who used to come out to his place and sleep on the floor and hunt with him, and he saluted them with that florid, swaggering gesture to the hat (yes, he was underbred. It showed like this always, your grandfather said, in all his formal contacts with people. He was like John L. Sullivan having taught himself painfully and tediously to do the schottische, having drilled himself and drilled himself in secret until he now believed it no longer necessary to count the music's beat, say. He may have believed that your grandfather or Judge Benbow might have done it a little more effortlessly than he, but he would not have believed that anyone could have beat him in knowing when to do it and how. And besides, it was in his face; that was where his power lay, your grandfather said: that anyone could look at him and say, *Given the occasion and the need, this man can and will do anything*) and went on into the house and commanded a chamber.

"So they sat on their horses and waited for him. I suppose they knew that he would have to come out sometime: I suppose they sat there and thought about those two pistols. Because there was still no warrant for him, you see: it was just public opinion in an acute state of indigestion; and now other horsemen rode into the square and became aware of the situation, so that there was quite a posse waiting when he walked out onto the gallery. He wore a new hat now, and a new broadcloth coat, so they knew what the portmanteau had contained. They even knew now what the basket had contained because he did not have that with him now either, though doubtless at the time it merely puzzled them more than ever. Because, you see, they had been too busy speculating on just how he was planning to use Mr Coldfield and, since his return, too completely outraged by the belief that they now saw the results even if the means were still an enigma, to remember about Miss Ellen at all.

"So he stopped again doubtless and looked from face to face again, doubtless memorising the new faces, without any haste, with still the beard to hide whatever his mouth might have shown. But he seems to have said nothing at all this time. He just descended the steps and walked on across the square, the committee (your grandfather said it had grown to almost fifty by now) moving too, following him across the square. They say he did not even look back. He just walked on, erect, with the new hat cocked and carrying in his hand now that which must have seemed to them the final gratuitous bafflement and even insult, with the committee riding along in the street beside him and not quite parallel, and others who did not happen to have horses at the moment joining in and following the committee in the road, and ladies and children and women slaves coming to the doors and windows of the homes as they passed to watch as they went on in grim tableau, and Sutpen, still without once looking back, entered Mr Coldfield's gate and strode on up the brick walk to the door, carrying his newspaper cornucopia of flowers.

"They waited for him again. The crowd was growing fast now—other men and a few boys and even some negroes from the adjacent houses, clotting behind the eight original members of the committee who sat watching Mr Coldfield's door until he emerged. It was a good while and he no longer carried the flowers, and when he returned to the gate, he was engaged to be married. But they did not know this, because as soon as he reached the gate, they arrested him. They took him back to town, with the ladies and children and house niggers watching from behind curtains and behind the shrubbery in the yards and the corners of the houses, the kitchens where doubtless food was already beginning to scorch, and so back to the square where the rest of the able-bodied men left their offices and stores to follow, so that when he reached the courthouse, Sutpen had a larger following than if he actually had been the runaway slave. They arraigned him before a justice, but by that time your grandfather and Mr Coldfield had got there. They signed his bond and late that afternoon he returned home with Mr Coldfield, walking along the same street as of the forenoon, with doubtless the same faces watching him from behind the window curtains, to the betrothal supper with no wine at table and no whiskey before or after. I have heard how during none of his three passages that day through that street did his bearing alter—the same unhurried stride to which that new frock coat swung, the same angle to the new hat above the eyes and the beard. Your grandfather said that some of the faience appearance which the flesh of his face had had when he came to town five years ago was gone now and that his face had an honest sunburn. And he was not fleshier either; your grandfather said that was not it: it was just that the flesh on his bones had become quieter, as though passive after some actual breast-ing of atmosphere like in running, so that he actu-ally filled his clothes now, with that quality still swaggering but without braggadocio or belliger-ence, though according to your grandfather the quality had never been belligerence, only watchful-ness. And now that was gone, as though after the three years he could trust his eyes alone to do the watching, without the flesh on his bones standing sentry also. Two months later, he and Miss Ellen were married.

"It was in June of 1838, almost five years to the day from that Sunday morning when he rode into town on the roan horse. It (the wedding) was in the same Methodist church where he saw Ellen for the first time, according to Miss Rosa. The aunt had even forced or nagged (not cajoled: that would not have done it) Mr Coldfield into allowing Ellen to wear powder on her face for the occasion. The powder was to hide the marks of tears. But before the wed-ding was over the powder was streaked again, caked and channelled. Ellen seems to have entered the church that night out of weeping as though out of rain, gone through the ceremony and then walked back out of the church and into the weeping again, the tears again, the same tears even, the same rain. She got into the carriage and departed in it (the rain) for Sutpen's Hundred.

"It was the wedding which caused the tears: not marrying Sutpen. Whatever tears there were for that, granted there were tears, came later. It was not

intended to be a big wedding. That is, Mr Coldfield
seems not to have intended it to be. Of the two men
(I dont speak of Ellen, of course: in fact, you will
notice that most divorces occur with women who
were married by tobacco-chewing j.p.'s in country
courthouses or by ministers waked after midnight,
with their suspenders showing beneath their coat-
tails and no collar on and a wife or spinster sister in
curl papers for witness. So is it too much to believe
that these women come to long for divorce from a
sense not of incompleteness but of actual frustration
and betrayal? that regardless of the breathing evidence of children and all else, they still have in their
minds even yet the image of themselves walking to
music and turning heads, in all the symbolical trap-
pings and circumstances of ceremonial surrender of
that which they no longer possess? and why not,
since to them the actual and authentic surrender can
only be (and have been) a ceremony like the breaking of a banknote to buy a ticket for the train)—of
the two men, it was Sutpen who desired (or hoped:
I have this from something your grandfather let
drop one day and which he doubtless had from
Sutpen himself in the same accidental fashion, since
Sutpen never even told Ellen that he wanted it,
which—the fact that at the last minute he refused to
support her in her desire and insistence upon it—
accounts partly for the tears) the big wedding, the
full church and all the ritual. Mr Coldfield apparently intended merely to employ, use, the church,
apart from its spiritual significance, exactly as he

might or would have used any other object, concrete or abstract, to which he had given a certain amount of his time. He seems to have intended to use the church into which he had invested a certain amount of sacrifice and doubtless self-denial and certainly actual labor and money for the sake of what might be called a demand balance of spiritual solvency, exactly as he would have used a cotton gin in which he considered himself to have incurred either interest or responsibility, for the ginning of any cotton which he or any member of his family, by blood or by marriage, had raised—that, and no more. Perhaps this was due to the same tedious and unremitting husbandry which had enabled him to support mother and sister and marry and raise a family on the proceeds of that store which ten years ago had fitted into a single wagon; or perhaps it was some innate sense of delicacy and fitness (which his sister and daughter did not seem to possess, by the way) regarding the prospective son-in-law whom just two months ago he had been instrumental in getting out of jail. But not from any lack of courage regarding the son-in-law's still anomalous position in the town. Regardless of what their relations before that had been and of what their future relations might be, if Mr Coldfield had believed Sutpen guilty at the time of any crime, he would not have raised a finger to take Sutpen out. He might not have gone out of his way to keep Sutpen in jail, but doubtless the best possible moral fumigation which Sutpen could have received at the time in the eyes of his fellow citizens was the fact that Mr Coldfield signed his bond— something he would not have done to save his own good name even though the arrest had been a direct result of the business between himself and Sutpen— that affair which, when it reached a point where his conscience refused to sanction it, he had withdrawn from and let Sutpen take all the profit, refusing even to allow Sutpen to reimburse him for the loss which, in withdrawing, he had suffered, though he did permit his daughter to marry this man of whose actions his conscience did not approve. This was the second time he did something like that.

"When they were married, there were just ten people in the church, including the wedding party, of the hundred who had been invited; though when they emerged from the church (it was at night: Sutpen had brought in a half dozen of his wild negroes to wait at the door with burning pine knots) the rest of the hundred were there in the persons of boys and youths and men from the drovers' tavern on the edge of town—stock traders and hostlers and such who had not been invited. That was the other half of the reason for Ellen's tears. It was the aunt who persuaded or cajoled Mr Coldfield into the big wedding. Sutpen had not expressed himself. But he wanted it. In fact, Miss Rosa was righter than she knew: he did want, not the anonymous wife and the anonymous children, but the two names, the stainless wife and the unimpeachable father-in-law, on the license, the patent. Yes, patent, with a gold seal and red ribbons too if that had been practicable. But

not for himself. She (Miss Rosa) would have called
the gold seal and the ribbons vanity. But then, so
had vanity conceived that house and, in a strange
place and with little else but his bare hands and
further handicapped by the chance and probability
of meddling interference arising out of the disapprobation of all communities of men toward any situation which they do not understand, built it. And
pride: she admitted to you that he was brave; perhaps she will even allow him pride: the same pride
which wanted such a house, which would accept
nothing less, and drove through to get it at whatever
cost and then lived in it, alone, on a pallet on the
floor for three years until he could furnish it as it
should be furnished—not the least of which furniture was that wedding license. She was quite right.
It was not just shelter, just anonymous wife and
children that he wanted, just as he did not want just
wedding. But he never told Ellen, nor anyone; in
fact, when the female crisis came, when Ellen and
the aunt tried to enlist him on their side to persuade
Mr Coldfield to the big wedding, he refused to support them. He doubtless remembered even better
than Mr Coldfield that two months ago he had been
in jail; that public opinion which at some moment
during the five preceding years had swallowed him
even though he never had quite ever lain quiet on
its stomach, had performed one of mankind's natural and violent and inexplicable volte faces and
regurgitated him. And it did not help him any that
at least two of the citizens who should have made

two of the teeth in the outraged jaw served instead as props to hold the jaw open and impotent while he walked out of it unharmed.

"Ellen and the aunt remembered this too. The aunt did. Being a woman, she was doubtless one of that league of Jefferson women who on the second day after the town saw him five years ago, had agreed never to forgive him for not having any past, and who had remained consistent. Since the marriage was now a closed incident, she probably looked upon it as the one chance to thrust him back into the gullet of public opinion which had tried at last to refuse him, not only to secure her niece's future as his wife but to justify the action of her brother in getting him out of jail and her own position as having apparently sanctioned and permitted the wedding which in reality she could not have prevented—this, as Miss Rosa told you, for the sake of that big house and the position and state which the women realised long before the men did that he not only aimed at but was going to attain. Or maybe women are even less complex than that and to them any wedding is better than no wedding and a big wedding with a villain preferable to a small one with a saint.

"So the aunt even used Ellen's tears; and Sutpen, who probably knew about what was going to happen, becoming as the time drew near graver and graver. Not concerned: just watchful, like he must have been from the day when he turned his back upon all that he knew—the faces and the customs—

and (he was just fourteen then, he told your grand-father. Just the same age that Henry was that night in the stable which Miss Rosa told you about, which Henry could not quite stand up to) set out into a world which even in theory, the average geographical schooling of the normal boy of fourteen, he knew nothing about, and with a fixed goal in his mind which most men do not set up until the blood begins to slow at thirty or more and then only because the image represents peace and indolence or at least a crowning of vanity, not the vindication of a past affront in the person of a son whose seed is not yet, and would not be for years yet, planted. That same alertness which he had to wear day and night without changing or laying aside, like the clothing which without doubt and for a time at least he had to sleep in as well as live in, and in a country and among a people whose very language he had to learn and where because of this he was to make that mistake which if he had acquiesced to it would not even have been an error and which, since he refused to accept it or be stopped by it, became his doom; —that unsleeping care which must have known that it could permit itself but one mistake; that alertness for measuring and weighing event against eventual-ity, circumstance against human nature, his own fallible judgment and mortal clay against not only human but natural forces, choosing and discarding, compromising with his dream and his ambition like you must with the horse which you take across country, over timber, which you control only through your ability to keep the animal from realising that actually you cannot, that actually it is the stronger.

"His was the curious position now. He was the solitary one. Not Ellen. She not only had the aunt to support her, but the fact that women never plead nor claim loneliness until impenetrable and insurmountable circumstance forces them to give up all hope of attaining the particular bauble which at the moment they happen to want. And not Mr Coldfield. He had not only public opinion but his own disinclination for the big wedding to support it without incongruity or paradox, as Ellen had her aunt as well as her own desire for the big wedding to support it without incongruity or paradox. While Sutpen wanted the big wedding more than Ellen did, or for a deeper reason than she did, yet his judgment forewarned him how the town would take it even more than Mr Coldfield's did. So while Ellen was using her tears not only to coerce her father but to persuade Sutpen to put his weight into the balance on her side, he had but one enemy—Mr Coldfield. But when he refused her, when he remained neutral, he had three, counting the aunt. Then (the tears won; Ellen and the aunt wrote out a hundred invitations—Sutpen brought in one of the wild negroes who carried them from door to door by hand—and even sent out a dozen more personal ones for the dress rehearsal) when they reached the church for the rehearsal on the night before the wedding and found the church itself

empty and a handful of men from the town's purlieus (including two of old Ikkemotubbe's Chick-
asaws) standing in the shadows outside the door, the
tears came down again. Ellen went through the rehearsal, but afterward the aunt took her home in a
state very near hysteria, though by the next day it
had become just quiet intermittent weeping again.
There was some talk even of putting the wedding
off. I dont know who it came from, perhaps from
Sutpen. But I know who vetoed it. It was as though
the aunt were now bent, no longer on merely
thrusting Sutpen down the town's throat, but
thrusting the wedding itself. She spent all the next
day going from house to house, the invitation list in
her hand, in a house dress and a shawl and one of
the Coldfield negroes (they were both women) following her, perhaps for protection, perhaps just
sucked along like a leaf in the wake of that grim
virago fury of female affront; yes, she came to our
house, though your grandfather had never intended
anything else but to attend the wedding: the aunt
must have had no doubts about Father since Father
had helped take Sutpen out of jail, though she was
probably past all ratiocination by then; she came to
our house too. Father and your grandmother were
just married then and Mother was a stranger in
Jefferson and I dont know what she thought except
that she would never talk about what happened:
about the mad woman whom she had never seen
before, who came bursting into the house, not to
invite her to a wedding but to dare her not to come,

and then rushed out again. Mother could not even tell what wedding she meant at first, and when Father came home he found Mother in hysterics too, and even twenty years later Mother could not tell what actually happened. There was nothing comic in it to her. Father used to tease her about it, but even twenty years after that day, when he would tease her I have seen her begin to raise her hand (perhaps with the thimble on one finger) as though to protect herself and the same look come into her face that must have been there when Ellen's aunt departed.

"She covered the town that morning. It did not take her long and it was complete; by nightfall the circumstances of the situation had spread not only beyond the town but beneath it, penetrating the livery stable and the drovers' tavern which was to supply the guests who did attend it, not only as notice but as a blanket threat and dare. Ellen of course was not aware of this, anymore than the aunt herself was, or would have believed what was going to happen even if she had been clairvoyant, could actually have seen the rehearsal of events before time produced them. Not that the aunt would have considered herself insulated against being thus affronted, she simply could not have believed that her intentions and actions of the day could have any result other than the one for which she had surrendered for the time not only all Coldfield dignity but all female modesty as well. Sutpen I suppose could have told her, but doubtless he knew that the aunt

would not have believed him. Probably he did not
even try: he just did the only thing he could do,
which was to send out to Sutpen's Hundred and
bring in six or seven more of his negroes, men on
whom he could depend, the only men on whom he
could depend, and arm them with the lighted pine
knots which they were holding at the door when the
carriage came up and the wedding party got out.
And this is where the tears stopped, because now the
street before the church was lined with carriages
and buggies, though only Sutpen and possibly Mr
Coldfield remarked that instead of being drawn up
before the door and empty, they were halted across
the street and still occupied, and that now the ban-
quette before the church door was a sort of arena
lighted by the smoking torches which the negroes
held above their heads, the light of which wavered
and gleamed upon the two lines of faces between
which the party would have to pass to enter the
church. There were no catcalls yet, no jeering; evidently neither Ellen nor the aunt suspected that
anything was wrong.

"Because for the time Ellen even walked out of
the weeping, the tears, and so into the church. It was
empty yet save for your grandfather and grandmother and perhaps a half dozen more who might
have come out of loyalty to the Coldfields or perhaps to be close and so miss nothing of that which
the town, as represented by the waiting carriages,
seemed to have anticipated as well as Sutpen did. It
was still empty even after the ceremony started and

concluded. Because Ellen had something of pride too, or at least that vanity which at times can assume the office of pride and fortitude; besides, nothing had happened yet. The crowd outside was quiet yet, perhaps out of respect for the church, out of that aptitude and eagerness of the Anglo-Saxon for complete mystical acceptance of immolated sticks and stones. She seems to have walked out of the church and so into it without any warning whatever. Perhaps she was still moving beneath that pride which would not allow the people inside the church to see her weep. She just walked into it, probably hurrying toward the seclusion of the carriage where she could weep; perhaps her first intimation was the voice shouting, 'Look out! Dont hit her now!' and then the object—dirt, filth, whatever it was—passing her, or perhaps the changing light itself as she turned and saw one of the negroes, his torch raised and in the act of springing toward the crowd, the faces, when Sutpen spoke to him in that tongue which even now a good part of the county did not know was a civilised language. That was what she saw, what the others saw from the halted carriages across the street—the bride shrinking into the shelter of his arm as he drew her behind him and he standing there, not moving even after another object (they threw nothing which could actually injure: it was only clods of dirt and vegetable refuse) struck the hat from his head, and a third struck him full in the chest—standing there motionless, with an expression almost of smiling where his teeth showed through the beard, holding his wild negroes with that one word (there were doubtless pistols in the crowd; certainly knives: the negro would not have lived ten seconds if he had sprung) while about the wedding party the circle of faces with open mouths and torch-reflecting eyes seemed to advance and waver and shift and vanish in the smoky glare of the burning pine. He retreated to the carriage, shielding the two women with his body, ordering the negroes to follow with another word. But they threw nothing else. Apparently it was that first spontaneous outburst, though they had come armed and prepared with the ones they did throw. In fact, that seemed to have been the entire business which had come to a head when the vigilance committee followed him to Mr Coldfield's gate that day two months before. Because the men who had composed the mob, the traders and drovers and teamsters, returned, vanished back into the region from which they had emerged for this one occasion like rats; scattered, departed about the country—faces which even Ellen was not to remember, seen for the night or the meal or just the drink at other taverns twenty and fifty and a hundred miles further on along nameless roads and then gone from there too; and those who had come in the carriages and buggies to see a Roman holiday, driving out to Sutpen's Hundred to call and (the men) to hunt his game and eat his food again and on occasion gathering at night in his stable while he matched two of his wild negroes against one another as men match game cocks or perhaps even entered the ring himself. It blew away, though not out of memory. He did not forget that night, even though Ellen, I think, did, since she washed it out of her remembering with tears. Yes, she was weeping again now; it did, indeed, rain on that marriage."

III

If he threw her over, I wouldn't think she would
want to tell anybody about it *Quentin said.*

Ah *Mr Compson said again* After Mr Coldfield
died in '64, Miss Rosa moved out to Sutpen's Hundred to live with Judith. She was twenty then, four
years younger than the niece whom, in obedience to
her sister's dying request, she set out to save from
the family's doom which Sutpen seemed bent on
accomplishing, apparently by the process of marrying him. She (Miss Rosa) was born in 1845, with her
sister already seven years married and the mother of
two children and Miss Rosa born into her parents'
middleage (her mother must have been at least forty
and she died in that childbed and Miss Rosa never
forgave her father for it) and at a time when—
granted that Miss Rosa merely mirrored her parents'
attitude toward the son-in-law—the family wanted
only peace and quiet and probably did not expect
and maybe did not even want another child. But she
was born, at the price of her mother's life and never
to be permitted to forget it, and raised by the same
spinster aunt who tried to force not only the elder
sister's bridegroom but the wedding too down the

throat of a town which did not want it, growing up
in that closed masonry of females to see in the fact
of her own breathing not only the lone justification
for the sacrifice of her mother's life, not only a living
and walking reproach to her father, but a breathing
indictment ubiquitous and even transferable of the
entire male principle (that principle which had left
the aunt a virgin at thirty-five) above dust. So for the
first sixteen years of her life she lived in that grim
tight little house with the father whom she hated
without knowing it—that queer silent man whose
only companion and friend seems to have been his
conscience and the only thing he cared about his
reputation for probity among his fellow men—that
man who was later to nail himself in his attic and
starve to death rather than look upon his native land
in the throes of repelling an invading army—and
the aunt who even ten years later was still taking
revenge for the fiasco of Ellen's wedding by striking
at the town, the human race, through any and all of
its creatures—brother nieces nephew-in-law herself
and all—with the blind irrational fury of a shedding
snake; who had taught Miss Rosa to look upon her
sister as a woman who had vanished not only out of
the family and the house but out of life too, into an
edifice like Bluebeard's and there transmogrified
into a mask looking back with passive and hopeless
grief upon the irrevocable world, held there not in
durance but in a kind of jeering suspension by a man
(his face the same which Mr Coldfield now saw and
had seen since that day when, with his future son-in-

law for ostensible yokemate but actually whip, Mr
Coldfield's conscience had set the brakes and, surrendering even his share of the cargo, he and the
son-in-law had parted) who had entered hers and
her family's life before she was born with the
abruptness of a tornado, done irrevocable and incalculable damage, and gone on—a grim mausoleum
air of puritan righteousness and outraged female
vindictiveness in which Miss Rosa's childhood (that
aged and ancient and timeless absence of youth
which consisted of a Cassandra-like listening beyond closed doors, of lurking in dim halls filled with
that presbyterian effluvium of lugubrious and vindictive anticipation while she waited for the infancy
and childhood with which nature had confounded
and betrayed her to overtake the precocity of convinced disapprobation regarding any and every
thing which could penetrate the walls of that house
through the agency of any man, particularly her
father, which the aunt seems to have invested her
with at birth along with the swaddling clothes) was
passed.

Perhaps she saw in her father's death, in the resulting necessity upon her as not only an orphan but
a pauper, to turn to her next of kin for food and
shelter and protection—and this kin the niece
whom she had been asked to save—; perhaps she
saw in this fate itself supplying her with the opportunity to observe her sister's dying request. Perhaps
she even saw herself as an instrument of retribution:
if not in herself an active instrument strong enough

to cope with him, at least as a kind of passive symbol
of inescapable reminding to rise bloodless and without dimension from the sacrificial stone of the
marriage-bed. Because until he came back from Virginia in '66 and found her living there with Judith
and Clytie——(Yes, Clytie was his daughter too:
Clytemnestra. He named her himself. He named
them all himself: all his own get and all the get of
his wild niggers after the country began to assimilate them. Miss Rosa didn't tell you that two of the
niggers in the wagon that day were women?

No, sir *Quentin said.*

Yes. Two of them. And brought here neither by
chance nor oversight. He saw to that, who had
doubtless seen even further ahead than the two years
it actually took him to build his house and show his
good intentions to his neighbors until they allowed
him to mix his wild stock with their tame, since the
difference in tongue between his niggers and theirs
could have been a barrier only for a matter of weeks
or perhaps even days. He brought the two women
deliberately; he probably chose them with the same
care and shrewdness with which he chose the other
livestock—the horses and mules and cattle—which
he bought later on. And he lived out there for almost
five years before he had speaking acquaintance with
any white woman in the county, just as he had no
furniture in his house and for the same reason: he
had at the time nothing to exchange for it them or
her. Yes. He named Clytie as he named them all, the
one before Clytie and Henry and Judith even, with

that same robust and sardonic temerity, naming
with his own mouth his own ironic fecundity of
dragon's teeth which with the two exceptions were
girls. Only I have always liked to believe that he
intended to name her Cassandra, prompted by some
pure dramatic economy not only to beget but to
designate the presiding augur of his own disaster,
and that he just got the name wrong through a
mistake natural in a man who must have almost
taught himself to read)——When he returned home
in '66, she had not seen him a hundred times in her
whole life. And what she saw then was just that
ogre-face of her childhood seen once and then repeated at intervals and on occasions which she could
neither count nor recall, like the mask in Greek
tragedy interchangeable not only from scene to
scene but from actor to actor and behind which the
events and occasions took place without chronology
or sequence and leaving her actually incapable of
saying how many separate times she had seen him
for the reason that, waking or sleeping, the aunt had
taught her to see nothing else. On those guarded and
lugubrious and even formal occasions when she and
the aunt went out to Sutpen's Hundred to spend the
day and the aunt would order her to go and play
with her nephew and niece exactly as the aunt might
have ordered her to play a piece for company on the
piano, she would not see him even at the dinner
table because the aunt would have arranged the visit
to coincide with his absence; and probably Miss
Rosa would have tried to avoid meeting him even if

he had been there. And on the four or five occasions
during the year when Ellen would bring the children in to spend the day at her father's, the aunt
(that strong vindictive consistent woman who
seems to have been twice the man that Mr Coldfield
was and who in very truth was not only Miss Rosa's
mother but her father too) cast over these visits also
that same atmosphere of grim embattled conspiracy
and alliance against the two adversaries, one of
whom—Mr Coldfield—whether he could have held
his own or not, had long since drawn in his picquets
and dismantled his artillery and retired into the impregnable citadel of his passive rectitude: and the
other—Sutpen—who probably could have engaged
and even routed them but who did not even know
that he was an embattled foe. Because he would not
even come to the house to the noon meal. His reason
may have been because of some delicacy for his
father-in-law, the true reason for and beginning of
the relationship between whom and himself neither
the aunt nor Ellen nor Miss Rosa ever knew, which
Sutpen was to divulge to but one man—and that
under the pledge of confidence as long as Mr Coldfield lived—out of regard for Mr Coldfield's carefully nurtured name for immaculate morality—and
which, your grandfather said, Mr Coldfield himself
never divulged for the same reason. Or perhaps the
reason was the one which Miss Rosa told you and
which the aunt gave her: that now since he had got
out of his father-in-law all which Mr Coldfield possessed that Sutpen could have used or wanted, he

(Sutpen) had neither the courage to face his father-in-law nor the grace and decency to complete the ceremonial family group even four times a year. Or perhaps it was the reason which Sutpen gave himself and which the aunt refused to believe because of that very fact: that he did not get to town every day and when he did he preferred to spend it (he used the bar now) with the men who gathered each noon at the Holston House.

That was the face which, when she saw it at all, was across his own dining table—the face of a foe who did not even know that it was embattled. She was ten now and following the aunt's dereliction (Miss Rosa now kept her father's house as the aunt had done until the night the aunt climbed out the window and vanished) there was not only no one to make her try to play with her nephew and niece on those days formal and funereal, she did not even have to go out there and breathe the same air which he breathed and where, even though absent, he still remained, lurked, in what she called sardonic and watchful triumph. She went out to Sutpen's Hundred just once a year now when, in their Sunday clothes, she and her father drove the twelve miles in a stout battered buggy behind the stout scrubby team, to spend the day. It was now Mr Coldfield who insisted on the visits, who had never gone out with them while the aunt was there, perhaps from a sense of duty, which was the reason he gave and which in this case even the aunt would have believed, perhaps because it was not the true one, since

doubtless even Miss Rosa would not have believed
the true one: which was that Mr Coldfield wanted
to see his grandchildren regarding whom he was in
a steadily increasing unease of that day when their
father would tell the son at least of that old business
between father and grandfather which Mr Coldfield
was not sure yet that his son-in-law had never told.
Though the aunt was gone, she still managed to
bequeath and invoke upon each of these expeditions
something of the old flavor of grim sortie, more than
ever now against a foe who did not know that he
was at war. Because now that the aunt was gone,
Ellen had reneged from that triumvirate of which
Miss Rosa tried without realising it to make two.
Now she was completely alone and facing across the
dinner table and without support now even from
Ellen (at this time Ellen went through a complete
metamorphosis, emerging into her next lustrum
with the complete finality of actual re-birth);—
facing across the table the foe who was not even
aware that he sat there not as host and brother-in-
law but as the second party to an armistice. He
probably did not even look at her twice as compared
with, weighed against, his own family and children
—the small slight child whose feet, even when she
would be grown, would never quite reach the floor
even from her own chairs, the ones which she
would inherit nor the ones—the objects—which she
would accumulate as complement to and expression
of individual character, as people do, as against Ellen
who, though small-boned also, was what is known

as fullbodied (and who would have been, if her life
had not declined into a time when even men found
little enough to eat and the end of her days had been
without trouble, fullbodied indeed. Not fat: just
rounded and complete, the hair white, the eyes still
even young, even a faint bloom yet on what would
be dewlaps and not cheeks any longer, the small
plump ringed unscarified hands folded in tranquil
anticipation of the food, on the damask before the
Haviland beneath the candelabra which he had
fetched to town years and years ago in wagons, to
the astonished and affronted outrage of his fellow
citizens), and against Judith already taller than
Ellen, and Henry though not as tall for sixteen as
Judith was for fourteen, yet giving promise of someday standing eye to eye with his father;—this creature, this face which hardly ever spoke during the
meal, with eyes like (as you put it) pieces of coal
pressed into soft dough and prim hair of that peculiar mouselike shade of hair on which the sun does
not often shine, against Judith's and Henry's out-of-
doors faces: Judith with her mother's hair and her
father's eyes and Henry with his hair halfway between his father's red and Ellen's black and eyes of
a bright dark hazel;—this small body with its air of
curious and paradoxical awkwardness like a cos-
tume borrowed at the last moment and of necessity
for a masquerade which she did not want to attend:
that aura of a creature cloistered now by deliberate
choice and still in the throes of enforced apprentice-
ship to, rather than voluntary or even acquiescent

participation in, breathing—this bound maidservant
to flesh and blood waiting even now to escape it by
writing a schoolgirl's poetry about the also-dead—
the face, the smallest face in company, watching him
across the table with still and curious and profound
intensity as though she actually had some intimation
gained from that rapport with the fluid cradle of
events (time) which she had acquired or cultivated
by listening beyond closed doors not to what she
heard there but by becoming supine and receptive,
incapable of either discrimination or opinion or in-
credulity, to the prefever's temperature of disaster
which makes soothsayers and sometimes makes
them right, of the future catastrophe in which the
ogre-face of her childhood would apparently vanish
so completely that she would agree to marry the late
owner of it.

That may have been the last time she saw him.
Because they quit going out there. Mr Coldfield
quit. There had never been any day set for the visit.
One morning he would merely appear at breakfast
in the decent and heavy black coat in which he had
been married and had worn fifty-two times each
year since until Ellen married and then fifty-three
times a year after the aunt deserted them until he put
it on for good the day he climbed to the attic and
nailed the door behind him and threw the hammer
out the window and so died in it. Then Miss Rosa
would retire and reappear in the formidable black or
brown silk which the aunt had chosen for her years
ago and which she continued to wear on Sundays

and occasions even after it was worn out, until the
day when her father decided that the aunt would not
return and permitted Miss Rosa to use the clothing
which the aunt had left in the house the night of her
elopement. Then they would get into the buggy and
depart, Mr Coldfield first docking the two negroes
for the noon meal which they would not have to
prepare and (so the town believed) charging them
for the crude one of left-overs which they would
have to eat. Then one year they did not go. Doubtless Mr Coldfield failed to come to breakfast in the
black coat, and more days passed and still he did not,
and that was all. Perhaps he felt, now that the grandchildren were grown, that the draft on his conscience had been discharged what with Henry away
at the State University at Oxford and Judith gone
even further than that:—into that transition stage
between childhood and womanhood where she was
even more inaccessible to the grandfather of whom
she had seen but little during her life and probably
cared less anyway—that state where, though still
visible, young girls appear as though seen through
glass and where even the voice cannot reach them;
where they exist (this the hoyden who could—and
did—outrun and outclimb, and ride and fight both
with and beside her brother) in a pearly lambence
without shadows and themselves partaking of it; in
nebulous suspension held, strange and unpredictable, even their very shapes fluid and delicate and
without substance; not in themselves floating and
seeking but merely waiting, parasitic and potent and

serene, drawing to themselves without effort the post-genitive upon and about which to shape, flow into back, breast; bosom, flank, thigh.

Now the period began which ended in the catastrophe which caused a reversal so complete in Miss Rosa as to permit her to agree to marry the man whom she had grown up to look upon as an ogre. It was not a volte face of character: that did not change. Even her behavior did not change to any extent. Even if Charles Bon had not died, she would in all probability have gone out to Sutpen's Hundred to live after her father's death sooner or later, and once she had done so she would have probably passed the remainder of her life there, as she doubtless expected to do when she did go out. But if Bon had lived and he and Judith married and Henry had remained in the known world, she would have moved (if she had moved) out there only when she was ready to, and she would have lived (if she had lived) in her dead sister's family only as the aunt which she actually was. It was not her character: despite the probably six years since she had actually seen him and certainly the four years which she had spent feeding her father secretly at night while he hid from Confederate provost marshals in the attic and at the same time writing heroic poetry about the very men from whom her father was hiding and who would have shot him or hung him without trial if they had found him—and incidentally of whom the ogre of her childhood made one and (he brought home with him a citation for valor in Lee's own hand) a good one—the face which she carried out there to live for the rest of her life was the same face which had watched him across the dinner table and which he likewise could not have said how many times he had seen it nor when and where, not for the reason that he was unable to forget it but because he could probably not have remembered it enough to have described it ten minutes after looking away, and from behind which the same woman who had been that child now watched him with that same grim and cold intensity.

Although she was not to see Sutpen again for years, she now saw her sister and niece more often than ever. Ellen was now at the full peak of what the aunt would have called her renegadery. She seemed not only to acquiesce, to be reconciled to her life and marriage, but to be actually proud of it. She had bloomed, as if Fate were crowding the normal Indian summer which should have bloomed gradually and faded gracefully through six or eight years, into three or four, either for compensation for what was to come or to clear the books, pay the check to which his wife, Nature, had signed his name. She was in her late thirties, plump, her face unblemished still. It was as though whatever marks being in the world had left upon it up to the time the aunt vanished had been removed, eradicated at least, from between the skeleton and the skin, between the sum of experience and the envelope in which it resides, by the intervening years of annealing and untroubled flesh. Her carriage, air, now was a little regal

—she and Judith made frequent trips to town now, calling upon the same ladies, some of whom were now grandmothers, whom the aunt had tried to force to attend the wedding twenty years ago, and, to the meagre possibilities which the town offered, shopping—as though she had succeeded at last in evacuating not only the puritan heritage but reality itself; had immolated outrageous husband and incomprehensible children into shades; escaped at last into a world of pure illusion in which, safe from any harm, she moved, lived, from attitude to attitude against her background of chatelaine to the largest, wife to the wealthiest, mother of the most fortunate. When she shopped (there were twenty stores in Jefferson now) she unbent without even getting out of the carriage, gracious and assured and talking the most complete nonsense, voluble, speaking her bright set meaningless phrases out of the part which she had written for herself, of the duchess peripatetic with property soups and medicines among a soilless and uncompelled peasantry—a woman who, if she had had the fortitude to bear sorrow and trouble, might have risen to actual stardom in the role of the matriarch arbitrating from the fireside corner of a crone the pride and destiny of her family, instead of turning at the last to the youngest member of it and asking her to protect the others.

Often twice and sometimes three times a week the two of them came to town and into the house—the foolish unreal voluble preserved woman now six years absent from the world—the woman who had quitted home and kin on a flood of tears and in a shadowy miasmic region something like the bitter purlieus of Styx had produced two children and then rose like the swamp-hatched butterfly, unimpeded by weight of stomach and all the heavy organs of suffering and experience, into a perennial bright vacuum of arrested sun—and the young girl dreaming, not living, in her complete detachment and imperviousness to actuality almost like physical deafness. To them, Miss Rosa must not have been anything at all now: not the child who had been the object and victim of the vanished aunt's vindictive unflagging care and attention, and not even the woman which her office as housekeeper would indicate, and certainly not the factual aunt herself. And it would be hard to say which of the two, sister or niece, was the most unreal to Miss Rosa in turn— the adult who had escaped reality into a bland region peopled by dolls, or the young girl who slept waking in some suspension so completely physical as to resemble the state before birth and as far removed from reality's other extreme as Ellen was from hers, driving up to the house twice and three times a week, and one time, in the summer when Judith was seventeen, stopping in on their way overland to Memphis to buy Judith clothes; yes: trousseau. That was the summer following Henry's first year at the University, after he had brought Charles Bon home with him for Christmas and then again to spend a week or so of the summer vacation before Bon rode on to the River to take the steam-

boat home to New Orleans; the summer in which
Sutpen himself went away, on business, Ellen said,
told, doubtless unaware, such was her existence
then, that she did not know where her husband had
gone and not even conscious that she was not curious, and no one but your grandfather and perhaps
Clytie ever to know that Sutpen had gone to New
Orleans too. They would enter that dim grim tight
little house where even yet, after four years, the aunt
still seemed to be just beyond any door with her
hand already on the knob and which Ellen would
fill with ten or fifteen minutes of shrill uproar and
then depart, taking with her the dreamy and volitionless daughter who had not spoken one word;
and Miss Rosa who in actual fact was the girl's aunt
and who by actual years should have been her sister
and who in actual experience and hope and opportunity should have been the niece, ignoring the
mother to follow the departing and inaccessible
daughter with myopic and inarticulate yearning and
not one whit of jealousy, projecting upon Judith all
the abortive dreams and delusions of her own
doomed and frustrated youth, offering Judith the
only gift (it of necessity offered to the bride's equipment and not the bride; it was Ellen who told this,
with shrieks of amusement, more than once) in her
power: she offered to teach Judith how to keep
house and plan meals and count laundry, receiving
for the offer the blank fathomless stare, the unhear-
ing "What? What did you say?" while even now
Ellen was shrieking with astonished appreciation.

Then they were gone—carriage, bundles, Ellen's peacock amusement, the niece's impenetrable dreaming. When they came to town next and the carriage stopped before Mr Coldfield's house, one of the negresses came out and said that Miss Rosa was not at home.

That summer she saw Henry again too. She had not seen him since the summer before although he had been home Christmas with his friend from the University, and she had heard about the balls and parties at Sutpen's Hundred during the holidays but she and her father had not gone out. And when Henry stopped with Bon on the way back to school the day after New Year's to speak to his aunt, she actually was not at home. So she did not see him until the following summer, after a full year. She was downtown, shopping; she was standing on the street talking to your grandmother when he rode past. He didn't see her; he passed on a new mare which his father had given him, in the coat and hat of a man now; your grandmother said he was as tall as his father now and that he sat the mare with the same swagger although lighter in the bone than Sutpen, as if his bones were capable of bearing the swagger but were still too light and quick to support the pomposity. Because Sutpen was acting his role too. He had corrupted Ellen in more ways than one. He was the biggest single landowner and cotton-planter in the county now, which state he had attained by the same tactics with which he had built his house—the same singleminded unflagging effort and utter disregard of how his actions which the town could see might look and how the indicated ones which the town could not see must appear to it. That is, there were some among his fellow citizens who believed even yet that there was a nigger in the woodpile somewhere, ranging from the ones who believed that the plantation was just a blind to his actual dark avocation, through the ones who believed that he had found some way to juggle the cotton market itself and so get more per bale for his cotton than honest men could, to the ones who believed apparently that the wild niggers which he had brought there had the power to actually conjure more cotton per acre from the soil than any tame ones had ever done. He was not liked (which he evidently did not want, anyway) but feared, which seemed to amuse, if not actually please, him. But he was accepted; he obviously had too much money now to be rejected or even seriously annoyed any more. He accomplished this—got his plantation to running smoothly (he had an overseer now; it was the son of that same sheriff who had arrested him at his bride-to-be's gate on the day of the betrothal) within ten years of the wedding, and now he acted his role too—a role of arrogant ease and leisure which, as the leisure and ease put flesh on him, became a little pompous. Yes, he had corrupted Ellen to more than renegadery, though, like her, unaware that his flowering was a forced blooming too and that while he was still playing the scene to the audience, behind him fate, destiny, retribution,

irony—the stage manager, call him what you will—
was already striking the set and dragging on the
synthetic and spurious shadows and shapes of the
next one.—"There goes——" your grandmother
said. But Miss Rosa had already seen him, standing
there beside your grandmother, her head hardly
reaching your grandmother's shoulder, thin, in one
of the dresses which the aunt had left in the house
and which Miss Rosa had cut down to fit herself
who had never been taught to sew either, just as she
had assumed the housekeeping and offered to teach
Judith to do the same, who had never been taught
to cook nor taught to do anything save listen
through closed doors, standing there with a shawl
over her head like she might have been fifty instead
of fifteen, looking after her nephew and saying,
"Why . . . he's shaved."

Then she stopped seeing Ellen even. That is,
Ellen also stopped coming to the house, stopped
breaking the carriage's weekly ritual of store to store
where, without getting out, Ellen bade merchant
and clerk fetch out to her the cloth and the meagre
fripperies and baubles which they carried and which
they knew even better than she that she would not
buy but instead would merely finger and handle and
disarrange and then reject, all in that flow of bright
pettish volubility. Not contemptuous, not even pa-
tronising exactly, but with a bland and even childlike imposition upon the sufferance or good
manners or sheer helplessness of the men, the mer-
chants and clerks; then to come to the house and fill

it too with that meaningless uproar of vanity, of impossible and foundationless advice about Miss Rosa and her father and the house, about Miss Rosa's clothes and the arrangement of the furniture and the food and how prepared and even the hours at which eaten. Because the time now approached (it was 1860, even Mr Coldfield probably admitted that war was unavoidable) when the destiny of Sutpen's family which for twenty years now had been like a lake welling from quiet springs into a quiet valley and spreading, rising almost imperceptibly and in which the four members of it floated in sunny suspension, felt the first subterranean movement toward the outlet, the gorge which would be the land's catastrophe too, and the four peaceful swimmers turning suddenly to face one another, not yet with alarm or distrust but just alert, feeling the dark set, none of them yet at that point where man looks about at his companions in disaster and thinks *When will I stop trying to save them and save only myself?* and not even aware that that point was approaching. So Miss Rosa did not see any of them, who had never seen (and was never to see alive) Charles Bon at all; Charles Bon of New Orleans, Henry's friend who was not only some few years older than Henry but actually a little old to be still in college and certainly a little out of place in that one where he was—a small new college in the Mississippi hinterland and even wilderness, three hundred miles from that worldly and even foreign city which was his home—a young man of a worldly elegance and assurance beyond his years, handsome, apparently wealthy and with for background the shadowy figure of a legal guardian rather than any parents— a personage who in the remote Mississippi of that time must have appeared almost phoenix-like, full-sprung from no childhood, born of no woman and impervious to time and, vanished, leaving no bones nor dust anywhere—a man with an ease of manner and a swaggering gallant air in comparison with which Sutpen's pompous arrogance was clumsy bluff and Henry actually a hobble-de-hoy. Miss Rosa never saw him; this was a picture, an image. It was not what Ellen told her: Ellen at the absolute halcyon of her butterfly's summer and now with the added charm of gracious and graceful voluntary surrendering of youth to her blood's and sex's successor, that concurrent attitude and behavior with the engagement's span with which mothers who want to can almost make themselves the brides of their daughters' weddings. Listening to Ellen, a stranger would have almost believed that the marriage, which subsequent events would indicate had not even been mentioned between the young people and the parents, had been actually performed. Ellen did not once mention love between Judith and Bon. She did not hint around it. Love, with reference to them, was just a finished and perfectly dead subject like the matter of virginity would be after the birth of the first grandchild. She spoke of Bon as if he were three inanimate objects in one or perhaps one inanimate object for which she and her family

would find three concordant uses: a garment which
Judith might wear as she would a riding habit or a
ball gown, a piece of furniture which would complement and complete the furnishing of her house
and position, and a mentor and example to correct
Henry's provincial manners and speech and clothing. She seemed to have encompassed time. She
postulated the elapsed years during which no honeymoon nor any change had taken place, out of
which the (now) five faces looked with a sort of
lifeless and perennial bloom like painted portraits
hung in a vacuum, each taken at its forewarned peak
and smoothed of all thought and experience, the
originals of which had lived and died so long ago
that their joys and griefs must now be forgotten
even by the very boards on which they had strutted
and postured and laughed and wept. This, while
Miss Rosa, not listening, who had got the picture
from the first word, perhaps from the name, Charles
Bon; the spinster doomed for life at sixteen, sitting
beneath this bright glitter of delusion like it was one
of those colored electric beams in cabarets and she
there for the first time in her life and the beam filled
with a substanceless glitter of tinsel motes darting
suddenly upon her, halting for a moment then
going on. She wasn't jealous of Judith. It was not
selfpity either, sitting there in one of those botched-
over house dresses (the clothes, castoff sometimes
but usually new, which Ellen gave her from time to
time were always silk, of course) which the aunt had
abandoned when she eloped with the horse- and

mule-trader, perhaps in the hope or even the firm
intention of never wearing such again, blinking
steadily at her sister while Ellen talked. It was probably just peaceful despair and relief at final and complete abnegation, now that Judith was about to
immolate the frustration's vicarious recompense
into the living fairy tale. It sounded like a fairy tale
when Ellen told it later to your grandmother, only
it was a fairy tale written for and acted by a fashionable ladies' club. But to Miss Rosa it must have been
authentic, not only plausible but justified: hence the
remark which sent Ellen again (she told this too, for
the childish joke it was) into shrieks of amused and
fretted astonishment. "We deserve him," Miss Rosa
said. "Deserve? Him?" Ellen said, probably shrieked
too. "Of course we deserve him—if you want to put
it that way. I certainly hope and expect you to feel
that the Coldfields are qualified to reciprocate whatever particularly signal honor marriage with anyone
might confer upon them."

Naturally there is no known rejoinder to this. At
least, as far as Ellen ever told, Miss Rosa did not try
to make one. She just saw Ellen depart and then set
about to make Judith the second only gift in her
power. She possessed two now, this one likewise
bequeathed to her by the aunt who taught her both
to keep house and how to fit clothes by climbing out
a window one night, though this second gift devel-
oped late (you might say, repercussed) due to the
fact that when the aunt left, Miss Rosa was not yet
large enough to be able to use the discarded clothing

even by cutting the garments down. She set about secretly making garments for Judith's trousseau. She got the cloth from her father's store. She could not have got it anywhere else. Your grandmother told me that at that time Miss Rosa actually could not count money, change, that she knew the progression of the coins in theory but that apparently she had never had the actual cash to see, touch, experiment and prove with; that on certain days of the week she would go down town with a basket and shop at certain stores which Mr Coldfield had already designated, with no coin nor sum of money changing lip or hand, and that later in the day Mr Coldfield would trace her course by the debits scratched on paper or on walls and counters, and pay them. So she would have to get the material from him. And as he had brought his entire business to Jefferson in one wagon, and this at a time when he had mother sister wife and children to support out of it as against now when he had but one child to support out of it, and weighed along with this that profound disinterest in material accumulation which had permitted conscience to cause him to withdraw from that old affair in which his son-in-law had involved him not only at the cost of his just profits but at the sacrifice of his original investment, his stock which had begun as a collection of the crudest necessities and which apparently could not even feed himself and his daughter from its own shelves, had not increased, let alone diversified. Yet this was where she had to go to get the material to make those intimate young girl garments which were to be for her own vicarious bridal—and you can imagine too what Miss Rosa's notion of such garments would be, let alone what her notion of them would look like when she had finished them unassisted. Nobody knows how she managed to get the material from her father's store. He didn't give it to her. He would have felt it incumbent on him to supply his granddaughter with clothes if she were indecently clad or if she were ragged or cold, but not to marry in. So I believe she stole it. She must have. She must have taken it almost from under her father's nose (it was a small store and he was his own clerk and from any point in it he could see any other point) with that amoral boldness, that affinity for brigandage of women, but more likely, or so I would like to think, by some subterfuge of such bald and desperate transparence concocted by innocence that its very simplicity fooled him.

So she didn't even see Ellen anymore. Apparently Ellen had now served her purpose, completed the bright pointless noon and afternoon of the butterfly's summer and vanished, perhaps not out of Jefferson, but out of her sister's life anyway, to be seen but the one time more dying in bed in a darkened room in the house on which fateful mischance had already laid its hand to the extent of scattering the black foundation on which it had been erected and removing its two male mainstays, husband and son—the one into the risk and danger of battle, the other apparently into oblivion. Henry had just vanished. She heard of that too while she was spending her days (and nights; she would have to wait until her father was asleep) sewing tediously and without skill on the garments which she was making for her niece's trousseau and which she had to keep hidden not only from her father but from the two negresses, who might have told Mr Coldfield—whipping lace out of ravelled and hoarded string and thread and sewing it onto garments while news came of Lincoln's election and of the fall of Sumpter and she scarce listening, hearing and losing the knell and doom of her native land between two tedious and clumsy stitches on a garment which she would never wear and never remove for a man whom she was not even to see alive. Henry just vanished: she heard just what the town heard—that on this next Christmas Henry and Bon came home again to spend the holidays, the handsome and wealthy New Orleansian whose engagement to the daughter the mother had been filling the town's ears with for six months now. They came again and now the town listened for the announcement of the actual day. And then something happened. Nobody knew what: whether something between Henry and Bon on one hand and Judith on the other, or between the three young people on one hand and the parents on the other. But anyway, when Christmas day came, Henry and Bon were gone. And Ellen was not visible (she seemed to have retired to the darkened room which she was not to quit until she died two years later) and nobody could have told from either

Sutpen's or Judith's faces or actions or behavior, and so the tale came through the negroes: of how on the night before Christmas there had been a quarrel between, not Bon and Henry or Bon and Sutpen, but between the son and the father and that Henry had formally abjured his father and renounced his birthright and the roof under which he had been born and that he and Bon had ridden away in the night and that the mother was prostrate—though, the town believed, not at the upset of the marriage but at the shock of reality entering her life: this the merciful blow of the axe before the beast's throat is cut. Though Ellen of course did not know this either.

That's what Miss Rosa heard. Nobody knows what she thought. The town believed that Henry's action was just the fiery nature of youth, let alone a Sutpen, and that time would cure it. Doubtless Sutpen's and Judith's behavior toward one another and toward the town had something to do with this. They would be seen together in the carriage in town now and then as though nothing had occurred between them at least, which certainly would not have been the case if the quarrel had been between Bon and the father, and probably not the case if the trouble had been between Henry and his father because the town knew that between Henry and Judith there had been a relationship closer than the traditional loyalty of brother and sister even; a curious relationship: something of that fierce impersonal rivalry between two cadets in a crack regiment who eat from the same dish and sleep under the same blanket and chance the same destruction and who would risk death for one another not for the other's sake but for the sake of the unbroken front of the regiment itself. That's all Miss Rosa knew. She could have known no more about it than the town knew because the ones who did know (Sutpen or Judith: not Ellen, who would have been told nothing in the first place and would have forgot, failed to assimilate, it if she had been—Ellen the butterfly, from beneath whom without warning the very sun-buoyed air had been withdrawn, leaving her now with the plump hands folded on the coverlet in the darkened room and the eyes above them probably not even suffering but merely filled with baffled incomprehension) would not have told her anymore than they would have told anyone in Jefferson or anywhere else. She probably went out there, probably once and then no more, and doubtless she did not ask, not even Judith, perhaps knowing she would not be told or perhaps because she was waiting. And she must have told Mr Coldfield that there was nothing wrong and evidently she believed that herself since she continued to sew on the garments for Judith's wedding. She was still doing that when Mississippi seceded and when the first Confederate uniforms began to appear in Jefferson where Colonel Sartoris and Sutpen were raising the regiment which departed in '61, with Sutpen, second in command, riding at Colonel Sartoris' left hand, on the black stallion named out of Scott, beneath the regimental colors which he and Sartoris had designed and which Sartoris' womenfolks had sewed together out of silk dresses. He had filled out physically from what he had been not only when he first rode into Jefferson that Sunday in '33, but from what he had been when he and Ellen married. He was not portly yet, though he was now getting on toward fifty-five. The fat, the stomach, came later. It came upon him suddenly, all at once, in the year after whatever it was happened to his engagement to Miss Rosa and she quitted his roof and returned to town to live alone in her father's house and did not ever speak to him again except when she addressed him that one time when they told her that he was dead. The flesh came upon him suddenly, as though what the negroes and Wash Jones too called the fine figure of a man had reached and held its peak after the foundation had given away and something between the shape of him that people knew and the uncompromising skeleton of what he actually was had gone fluid and, earthbound, had been snubbed up and restrained, balloonlike unstable and lifeless, by the envelope which it had betrayed.

She did not see the regiment depart because her father forbade her to leave the house until it was gone, refusing to allow her to take part in or be present with the other women and girls in the ceremony of its departure, though not because his son-in-law happened to be in it. He had never been an irascible man and before war was actually declared and Mississippi seceded, his acts and speeches of protest had been not only calm but logical and quite sensible. But after the die was cast he seemed to change overnight, just as his daughter Ellen changed her nature a few years before. As soon as troops began to appear in Jefferson he closed his store and kept it closed all during the period that soldiers were being mobilised and drilled, not only then but later, after the regiment was gone, whenever casual troops would bivouac for the night in passing, refusing to sell any goods for any price not only to the military but, so it was told, to the families not only of soldiers but of men or women who had supported secession and war only in talk, opinion. Not only did he refuse to permit his sister to come back home to live while her horse-trader husband was in the army, he would not even allow Miss Rosa to look out the window at passing soldiers. He had closed his store permanently and was at home all day now. He and Miss Rosa lived in the back of the house, with the front door locked and the front shutters closed and fastened, and where, so the neighbors said, he spent the day behind one of the slightly opened blinds like a picquet on post, armed not with a musket but with the big family bible in which his and his sister's birth and his marriage and Ellen's birth and marriage and the birth of his two grandchildren and of Miss Rosa, and his wife's death (but not the marriage of the aunt; it was Miss Rosa who entered that, along with Ellen's death, on the day when she entered Mr Coldfield's own and Charles Bon's and even Sutpen's) had been duly entered in his neat clerk's hand, until a detachment of troops would pass: whereupon he would open the bible and declaim in a harsh loud voice even above the sound of the tramping feet, the passages of the old violent vindictive mysticism which he had already marked as the actual picquet would have ranged his row of cartridges along the window sill. Then one morning he learned that his store had been broken into and looted, doubtless by a company of strange troops bivouacked on the edge of town and doubtless abetted, if only vocally, by his own fellow citizens. That night he mounted to the attic with his hammer and his handfull of nails and nailed the door behind him and threw the hammer out the window. He was not a coward. He was a man of uncompromising moral strength, coming into a new country with a small stock of goods and supporting five people out of it in comfort and security at least. He did it by close trading, to be sure: he could not have done it save by close trading or dishonesty; and as your grandfather said, a man who, in a country such as Mississippi was then, would restrict dishonesty to the selling of straw hats and hame strings and salt meat would have been already locked up by his own family as a kleptomaniac. But he was not a coward, even though his conscience may have objected, as your grandfather said, not so much to the idea of pouring out human blood and life, but at the idea of waste: of wearing out and eating up and shooting away material in any cause whatever.

Now Miss Rosa's life consisted of keeping it in herself and her father. Up to the night of the looting of the store, they had lived out of it. She would go to the store after dark with a basket and fetch back enough food to last for a day or two. So the stock, not renewed for some time before that, was considerably reduced even before the looting; and soon she, who had never been taught to do anything practical because the aunt had raised her to believe that she was not only delicate but actually precious, was cooking the food which as time passed became harder and harder to come by and poorer and poorer in quality, and hauling it up to her father at night by means of a well pulley and rope attached to the attic window. She did this for three years, feeding in secret and at night and with food which in quantity was scarcely sufficient for one, the man whom she hated. And she may not have known before that she hated him and she may not have known it now even, nevertheless the first of the odes to Southern soldiers in that portfolio which when your grandfather saw it in 1885 contained a thousand or more, was dated in the first year of her father's voluntary incarceration and dated at two oclock in the morning.

Then he died. One morning the hand did not come out to draw up the basket. The old nails were still in the door and neighbors helped her break it in with axes and they found him, who had seen his sole means of support looted by the defenders of his cause, even if he had repudiated it and them, with three days' uneaten food beside his pallet bed as if he had spent the three days in a mental balancing of his terrestrial accounts, found the result and proved it and then turned upon his contemporary scene of folly and outrage and injustice the dead and consistent impassivity of a cold and inflexible disapproval. Now Miss Rosa was not only an orphan, but a pauper too. The store was now just a shell, the deserted building vacated even by rats and containing nothing, not even goodwill since he had irrevocably estranged himself from neighbors town and embattled land all three by his behavior. Even the two negresses which he had freed as soon as he came into possession of them (through a debt, by the way, not purchase), writing out their papers of freedom which they could not read and putting them on a weekly wage which he held back in full against the discharge of the current market value at which he had assumed them on the debt—and in return for which they had been among the first Jefferson negroes to desert and follow the Yankee troops— were gone now. So when he died, he had nothing, not only saved but kept. Doubtless the only pleasure which he had ever had was not in the meagre spartan hoard which he had accumulated before his path crossed that of his future son-in-law;—not in the money but in its representation of a balance in whatever spiritual counting-house he believed would some day pay his sight drafts on self-denial and fortitude. And doubtless what hurt him most in the whole business with Sutpen was not the loss of the

money but the fact that he had had to sacrifice the
hoarding, the symbol of the fortitude and abnegation, to keep intact the spiritual solvency which he
believed that he had already established and secured.
It was as if he had had to pay the same note twice
because of some trifling oversight of date or signature.

So Miss Rosa was both pauper and orphan, with
no kin above dust but Judith and the aunt who had
been last heard of two years ago while trying to pass
the Yankee lines to reach Illinois and so be near the
Rock Island prison where her husband, who had
offered his talents for horse- and mule-getting to the
Confederate cavalry remount corps and had been
caught at it, now was. Ellen was dead two years now
—the butterfly, the moth caught in a gale and blown
against a wall and clinging there beating feebly, not
with any particular stubborn clinging to life, not in
particular pain since it was too light to have struck
hard, nor even with very much rememberance of
the bright vacuum before the gale, but just in bewildered and uncomprehending amazement—the
bright trivial shell not even to any great extent
changed despite the year of bad food, since all of
Sutpen's negroes had deserted also to follow the
Yankee troops away; the wild blood which he had
brought into the country and tried to mix, blend,
with the tame which was already there, with the
same care and for the same purpose with which he
blended that of the stallion and that of his own. And
with the same success: as though his presence alone

compelled that house to accept and retain human
life; as though houses actually possess a sentience, a
personality and character acquired not from the
people who breathe or have breathed in them so
much as rather inherent in the wood and brick or
begotten upon the wood and brick by the man or
men who conceived and built them—in this one an
incontrovertible affirmation for emptiness, deser-
tion; an insurmountable resistance to occupancy
save when sanctioned and protected by the ruthless
and the strong. She had lost some flesh of course, but
it was as the butterfly itself enters dissolution by
actually dissolving: the area of wing and body decreasing a little, the pattern of the spots drawing a
little closer together, but with no wrinkle to show
—the same smooth, almost girlish face on the pillow
(though Miss Rosa now discovered that Ellen had
been dyeing her hair evidently for years), the same
almost plump soft (though now unringed) hands on
the coverlet, and only the bafflement in the dark
uncomprehending eyes to indicate anything of present life by which to postulate approaching death as
she asked the seventeen-year-old sister (Henry up to
now was just vanished, his birthright voluntarily
repudiated; he had not yet returned to play his final
part in his family's doom—and this, your grandfather said, spared Ellen too, not that it would have
been the crushing and crowning blow but that it
would have been wasted on her since the clinging
moth, even alive, would have been incapable now of
feeling anymore of wind or violence) to protect the

remaining child. So the natural thing would have been for her to go out and live with Judith, the natural thing for her or any Southern woman, gentlewoman. She would not have needed to be asked; no one would expect her to wait to be. Because that's what a Southern lady is. Not the fact that, penniless and with no prospect of ever being otherwise and knowing that all who know her know this, yet moving with a parasol and a private chamber pot and three trunks into your home and into the room where your wife uses the hand-embroidered linen and not only takes command of all the servants who likewise know that she will never tip them because they know as well as the white folks that she will never have anything to tip them with but goes into the kitchen and dispossesses the cook and seasons the very food you are going to eat to suit her own palate;—it's not this, not this that she is depending on to keep body and soul together: it is as though she were living on the actual blood itself like a vampire, not with insatiability, certainly not with voracity, but with that serene and idle splendor of flowers arrogating to herself, because it fills her veins also, nourishment from the old blood that crossed uncharted seas and continents and battled wilderness hardships and lurking circumstances and fatalities, with tranquil disregard of whatever onerous carks to leisure and even peace which the preservation of it incurs upon what might be called the contemporary transmutable fountainhead who contrives to keep the crass foodbearing corpuscles sufficiently numerous and healthy in the stream.

That's what she would have been expected to do. But she didn't. Though Judith was an orphan too, yet Judith still had those abandoned acres to draw from, let alone Clytie to help her, keep her company, and Wash Jones to feed her as Wash had fed Ellen before she died. But Miss Rosa didn't go out there at once. Perhaps she never would have gone. Although Ellen had asked her to protect Judith, possibly she felt that Judith did not need protection yet, since if even deferred love could have supplied her with the will to exist, endure for this long, then that same love, even though deferred, must and would preserve Bon until the folly of men would stalemate from sheer exhaustion and he would return from wherever he was and bring Henry with him—Henry, victim too of the same folly and mischance. She must have seen Judith now and then and Judith probably urged her to come out to Sutpen's Hundred to live, but I believe that this is the reason she did not go, even though she did not know where Bon and Henry were and Judith apparently never thought to tell her. Because Judith knew. She may have known for some time; even Ellen may have known, only probably to Ellen at that time absence was not a qualitative state, absence into ignominy or into oblivion being identical, and so it may not have occurred to Ellen either to tell her sister, that to another the uncertainty of battle and the certainty of oblivion might be two things. Or perhaps Judith never told her mother either. Perhaps Ellen did not know before she died that Henry and Bon were now privates in the company which their classmates at the University had organised. Miss Rosa did not know it at all. The first intimation she had had in four years that her nephew was still alive was the afternoon when Wash Jones, riding Sutpen's remaining mule, stopped in front of the house and began to shout her name. She had seen him before but she did not recognise him—a gaunt gangling man malaria-ridden with pale eyes and a face that might have been any age between twenty-five and sixty, sitting on the saddleless mule in the street before the gate, shouting "Hello. Hello." at intervals until she came to the door; whereupon he lowered his voice somewhat, though not much. "Air you Rosie Coldfield?" he said.

IV

It was still not dark enough for Quentin to start, not yet dark enough to suit Miss Coldfield at least, even discounting the twelve miles out there and the twelve miles back. Quentin knew that. He could almost see her, waiting in one of the dark airless rooms in the little grim house's impregnable solitude. She would have no light burning because she would be out of the house soon, and probably some mental descendant or kinsman of him or her who had told her once that light and moving air carried heat had also told her that the cost of electricity was not in the actual time the light burned but in the retroactive overcoming of primary inertia when the switch was snapped: that that was what showed on the meter. She would be wearing already the black bonnet with jet sequins; he knew that: and a shawl, sitting there in the augmenting and defunctive twilight; she would have even now in her hand or on her lap the reticule with all the keys, entrance closet and cupboard, that the house possessed which she was about to desert for perhaps six hours; and a parasol, an umbrella too, he thought, thinking how she would be impervious to weather and season since although he had not spoken a hundred words to her in his life before this afternoon, he did know that she had never before tonight quitted that house after sundown save on Sundays and Wednesdays for prayer meeting, in the entire forty-three years probably. Yes, she would have the umbrella. She would emerge with it when he called for her and carry it invincibly into the spent suspiration of an evening without even dew, where even now the only alteration toward darkness was in the soft and fuller random of the fireflies—a fuller and more profound random in the twilight following sixty days without rain and forty-two without even dew—below the gallery where he rose from his chair as Mr Compson, carrying the letter, emerged from the house, snapping on the porch light as he passed. "You will probably have to go inside to read it," Mr Compson said.

"Maybe I can read it here all right," Quentin said.

"Perhaps you are right," Mr Compson said. "Maybe even the light of day, let alone this—" he indicated the single globe stained and bug-fouled from the long summer and which even when clean gave off but little light—"which man had to invent to his need since, relieved of the onus of sweating to live, he is apparently reverting (or evolving) back into a nocturnal animal, would be too much for it, for them. Yes, for them: of that day and time, of a dead time; people too as we are and victims too as we are, but victims of a different circumstance, simpler and therefore, integer for integer, larger, more

heroic and the figures therefore more heroic too, not
dwarfed and involved but distinct, uncomplex who
had the gift of loving once or dying once instead of
being diffused and scattered creatures drawn blindly
limb from limb from a grab bag and assembled,
author and victim too of a thousand homicides and
a thousand copulations and divorcements. Perhaps
you are right. Perhaps any more light than this
would be too much for it." But he did not give
Quentin the letter at once. He sat again, Quentin
sitting again too, and took up the cigar from the
veranda rail, the coal glowing again, the wistaria
colored smoke drifting again unwinded across
Quentin's face as Mr Compson raised his feet once
more to the railing, the letter in his hand and the
hand looking almost as dark as a negro's against his
linen leg. "Because Henry loved Bon. He repudiated blood birthright and material security for his
sake, for the sake of this man who was at least an
intending bigamist even if not an out and out blackguard, and on whose dead body four years later
Judith was to find the photograph of the other
woman and the child. So much so that he (Henry)
could give his father the lie about a statement which
he must have realised that his father could not and
would not have made without foundation and
proof. Yet he did it, Henry himself striking the blow
with his own hand, even though he must have
known that what his father told him about the
woman and the child was true. He must have said
to himself, must have said when he closed the library

door for the last time behind himself that Christmas
eve and must have repeated while he and Bon rode
side by side through the iron dark of that Christmas
morning, away from the house where he had been
born and which he would see but one time more and
that with the fresh blood of the man who now rode
beside him, on his hands: *I will believe; I will. I will.
Even if it is so, even if what my father told me is true
and which, in spite of myself, I cannot keep from knowing is true, I will still believe.* Because what else could
he have hoped to find in New Orleans, if not the
truth, if not what his father had told him, what he
had denied and refused to accept even though, despite himself, he must have already believed? But
who knows why a man, though suffering, clings,
above all the other well members, to the arm or leg
which he knows must come off? Because he loved
Bon. I can imagine him and Sutpen in the library
that Christmas eve, the father and the brother, per-
cussion and repercussion like a thunderclap and its
echo and as close; the statement and the giving of
the lie, the decision instantaneous and irrevocable
between father and friend, between (so Henry must
have believed) that where honor and love lay and
this where blood and profit ran, even though at the
instant of giving the lie he knew that it was the
truth. That was why the four years, the probation.
He must have known that it would be vain, even
then, on that Christmas eve, not to speak of what he
learned, saw with his own eyes in New Orleans. He
may even have known Bon that well by then, who

had not changed until then and so would in all probability not change later; and he (Henry) who could not say to his friend, *I did that for love of you; do this for love of me.* He couldn't say that, you see —this man, this youth scarcely twenty, who had turned his back upon all that he knew, to cast his lot with the single friend whom, even as they rode away that night, he must have known, as he knew that what his father had told him was true, that he was doomed and destined to kill. He must have known that just as he knew that his hope was vain, what hope and what for he could not have said; what hope and dream of change in Bon or in the situation, what dream that he could someday wake from and find it had been a dream, as in the injured man's fever dream the dear suffering arm or leg is strong and sound and only the well ones sick.

"It was Henry's probation; Henry holding all three of them in that durance to which even Judith acquiesced up to a certain point. She did not know what happened in the library that night. I dont think she ever did, suspected, until that afternoon four years later when she saw them again, when they brought Bon's body into the house and she found in his coat the photograph which was not her face, not her child; she just waked the next morning and they were gone and only the letter, the note, remaining, the note written by Henry since doubtless he refused to allow Bon to write—this announcement of the armistice, the probation, and Judith acquiescing up to that point, who would have refused as

quickly to obey any injunction of her father as
Henry had been to defy him yet who did obey
Henry in this matter—not the male relative, the
brother, but because of that relationship between
them—that single personality with two bodies both
of which had been seduced almost simultaneously
by a man whom at the time Judith had never even
seen—she and Henry both knowing that she would
observe the probation, give him (Henry) the benefit
of that interval, only up to that mutually recognised
though unstated and undefined point and both
doubtless aware that when that point was reached
she would, and with the same calm, the same refusal
to accept or give because of any traditional weakness
of sex, recall the armistice and face him as a foe, not
requiring or even wishing that Bon be present to
support her, doubtless even refusing to allow him to
intervene if he were, fighting the matter out with
Henry like a man first before consenting to revert
to the woman, the loved, the bride. And Bon: Henry
would have no more told Bon what his father had
told him than he would have returned to his father
and told him that Bon denied it, since to do one he
would have to do the other and he knew that Bon's
denial would be a lie and though he could have
borne Bon's lie himself, he could not have borne for
either Judith or his father to hear it. Besides, Henry
would not need to tell Bon what had happened. Bon
must have learned of Sutpen's visit to New Orleans
as soon as he (Bon) reached home that first summer.
He must have known that Sutpen now knew his

secret—if Bon, until he saw Sutpen's reaction to it, ever looked upon it as a cause for secrecy, certainly not as a valid objection to marriage with a white woman—a situation in which probably all his contemporaries who could afford it were likewise involved and which it would no more have occurred to him to mention to his bride or wife or to her family than he would have told them the secrets of a fraternal organization which he had joined before he married. In fact, the manner in which his intended bride's family reacted to the discovery of it was doubtless the first and last time when the Sutpen family ever surprised him. He is the curious one to me. He came into that isolated puritan country household almost like Sutpen himself came into Jefferson: apparently complete, without background or past or childhood—a man a little older than his actual years and enclosed and surrounded by a sort of Scythian glitter, who seems to have seduced the country brother and sister without any effort or particular desire to do so, who caused all the pother and uproar yet from the moment when he realised that Sutpen was going to prevent the marriage if he could, he (Bon) seems to have withdrawn into a mere spectator, passive, a little sardonic, and completely enigmatic. He seems to hover, shadowy, almost substanceless, a little behind and above all the other straightforward and logical even though (to him) incomprehensible ultimatums and affirmations and defiances and challenges and repudiations, with an air of sardonic and indolent detachment like that of a youthful Roman consul making the Grand Tour of his day among the barbarian hordes which his grandfather conquered, benighted in a brawling and childish and quite deadly mud-castle household in a miasmic and spirit-ridden forest. It was as if he found the whole business, not inexplicable of course, just unnecessary; that he knew at once that Sutpen had found out about the mistress and child and he now found Sutpen's action and Henry's reaction a fetich-ridden moral blundering which did not deserve to be called thinking, which he contemplated with the detached attentiveness of a scientist watching the muscles in an anesthetised frog;—watching, contemplating them from behind that barrier of sophistication in comparison with which Henry and Sutpen were troglodytes. Not just the outside, the way he walked and talked and wore his clothes and handed Ellen into the dining room or into the carriage and (perhaps, probably) kissed her hand and which Ellen envied for Henry, but the man himself—that fatalistic and impenetrable imperturbability with which he watched them while he waited for them to do whatever it would be that they would do, as if he had known all the while that the occasion would arise when he would have to wait and that all he would need to do would be to wait; that he had seduced Henry and Judith both too thoroughly to have any fear that he might not marry Judith when he wished to. Not that stupid shrewdness half instinct and half belief in luck, and half muscular habit of the senses and nerves of the gambler waiting to take what he can from what he sees, but a certain reserved and inflexible pessimism stripped long generations ago of all the rubbish and claptrap of people (yes, Sutpen and Henry and the Coldfields too) who have not quite yet emerged from barbarism, who two thousand years hence will still be throwing triumphantly off the yoke of Latin culture and intelligence of which they were never in any great permanent danger to begin with.

"Because he loved Judith. He would have added doubtless 'after his fashion' since, as his intended father-in-law soon learned, this was not the first time he had played this part, pledged what he had pledged to Judith, let alone the first time he would have gone through a ceremony to commemorate it, make what distinction (he was a Catholic of sorts) he might between this one with a white woman and that other. Because you will see the letter, not the first one he ever wrote to her but at least the first, the only one she ever showed, as your grandmother knew then: and, so we believe, now that she is dead, the only one which she kept unless of course Miss Rosa or Clytie destroyed the others after she herself died: and this one here preserved not because Judith put it away to keep but because she brought it herself and gave it to your grandmother after Bon's death, possibly on the same day when she destroyed the others which he had written her (provided of course it was she herself who destroyed them) which would have been when she found in Bon's coat the picture of the octoroon mistress and the little boy. Because he was her first and last sweetheart. She must have seen him in fact with exactly the same eyes that Henry saw him with. And it would be hard to say to which of them he appeared the more splendid—to the one with hope, even though unconscious, of making the image hers through possession; to the other with the knowledge, even though subconscious to the desire, of the insurmountable barrier which the similarity of gender hopelessly intervened;—this man whom Henry first saw riding perhaps through the grove at the University on one of the two horses which he kept there or perhaps crossing the campus on foot in the slightly Frenchified cloak and hat which he wore, or perhaps (I like to think this) presented formally to the man reclining in a flowered, almost feminised gown, in a sunny window in his chambers—this man handsome elegant and even catlike and too old to be where he was, too old not in years but in experience, with some tangible effluvium of knowledge, surfeit: of actions done and satiations plumbed and pleasures exhausted and even forgotten. So that he must have appeared, not only to Henry but to the entire undergraduate body of that small new provincial college, as a source not of envy because you only envy whom you believe to be, but for accident, in no way superior to yourself: and what you believe, granted a little better luck than you have had heretofore, you will someday possess;—not of envy but of despair: that sharp shocking terrible hopeless despair of the young which sometimes takes the form of insult toward and even physical assault upon the human subject of it or, in extreme cases like Henry's, insult toward and assault upon any and all detractors of the subject, as witness Henry's violent repudiation of his father and his birthright when Sutpen forbade the marriage. Yes, he loved Bon, who seduced him as surely as he seduced Judith—the country boy born and bred who, with the five or six others of that small undergraduate body composed of other planters' sons whom Bon permitted to become intimate with him, who aped his clothing and manner and (to the extent which they were able) his very manner of living, looked upon Bon as though he were a hero out of some adolescent Arabian Nights who had stumbled upon (or rather, had thrust upon him) a talisman or touchstone not to invest him with wisdom or power or wealth, but with the ability and opportunity to pass from the scene of one scarce imaginable delight to the next one without interval or pause or satiety; and the very fact that, lounging before them in the outlandish and almost feminine garments of his sybaritic privacy, he professed satiety but increased not only the amazement but the bitter and hopeless outrage;—Henry, the provincial, the clown almost, given to instinctive and violent action rather than to thinking, ratiocination, who may have been conscious that his fierce provincial's pride in his sister's virginity was a false quantity which must incorporate in itself an inability to endure in order to be precious, to exist, and so must depend upon its loss, absence, to have existed at all. In fact, perhaps this is the pure and perfect incest: the brother realising that the sister's virginity must be destroyed in order to have existed at all, taking that virginity in the person of the brother-in-law, the man whom he would be if he could become, metamorphose into, the lover, the husband; by whom he would be despoiled, choose for despoiler, if he could become, metamorphose into the sister, the mistress, the bride. Perhaps that is what went on, not in Henry's mind but in his soul. Because he never thought. He felt, and acted immediately. He knew loyalty and acted it, he knew pride and jealousy; he loved grieved and killed, still grieving and, I believe, still loving Bon, the man to whom he gave four years of probation, four years in which to renounce and dissolve the other marriage, knowing that the four years of hoping and waiting would be in vain.

"Yes, Henry: not Bon, as witness the entire queerly placid course of Bon's and Judith's courtship—an engagement, if engagement it ever was, lasting for a whole year yet comprising two holiday visits as her brother's guest and which periods Bon seems to have spent either in riding and hunting with Henry or as acting as an elegant and indolent esoteric hothouse bloom possessing merely the name of a city for origin history and past, about which Ellen preened and fluttered out her unwitting butterfly's Indian summer; he, the living man, was usurped, you see. There was no time, no interval, no niche in the crowded days when he could have courted Judith. You can not even imagine him and Judith alone together. Try to do it and the nearest you can come is a projection of them while the two actual people were doubtless separate and elsewhere—two shades pacing, serene and untroubled by flesh, in a summer garden—the same two serene phantoms who seem to watch, hover, impartial attentive and quiet, above and behind the inexplicable thunderhead of interdictions and defiances and repudiations out of which the rocklike Sutpen and the volatile and violent Henry flashed and glared and ceased;—Henry who up to that time had never even been to Memphis, who had never been away from home before that September when he went to the University with his countrified clothes and his saddle horse and negro groom; the six or seven of them, of an age and background, only in the surface matter of food and clothing and daily occupation any different from the negro slaves who supported them—the same sweat, the only difference being that on the one hand it went for labor in fields where on the other it went as the price of the spartan and meagre pleasures which were available to them because they did not have to sweat in the fields: the hard violent hunting and riding; the same pleasures: the one, gambling for worn knives and brass jewelry and twists of tobacco and buttons and garments because they happened to be easiest and quickest to hand; on the other for the money and horses, the guns and watches, and for the same reason; the same parties: the identical music from identical instruments, crude fiddles and guitars, now in the big house with candles and silk dresses and champagne, now in dirt-floored cabins with smoking pine knots and calico and water sweetened with molasses;—it was Henry, because at that time Bon had not even seen Judith. He had probably not paid enough attention to Henry's inarticulate recounting of his brief and conventional background and history to have remembered that Henry had a sister— this indolent man too old to find even companionship among the youths, the children, with whom he now lived; this man miscast for the time and knowing it, accepting it for a reason obviously good enough to cause him to endure it and apparently too serious or at least too private to be divulged to what acquaintances he now possessed:—this man who later showed the same indolence, almost uninterest, the same detachment when the uproar about that engagement which, so far as Jefferson knew, never formally existed, which Bon himself never affirmed or denied, arose and he in the background, impartial and passive as though it were not himself involved or he acting on behalf of some absent friend, but as though the person involved and interdict were someone whom he had never heard of and cared nothing about. There does not even seem to have been any courtship. Apparently he paid Judith the dubious compliment of not even trying to ruin her, let alone insisting on the marriage either before or after Sutpen forbade it—this, mind you, in a man who had already acquired a name for prowess among women while at the University, long before Sutpen was to find actual proof. No engagement, no courtship even: he and Judith saw one another three times in two years, for a total period of twelve days, counting the time which Ellen consumed; they parted without even saying goodbye. And yet, four years later, Henry had to kill Bon to keep them from marrying. So it must have been Henry who seduced Judith, not Bon: seduced her along with himself from that distance between Oxford and Sutpen's Hundred, between herself and the man whom she had not even seen yet, as though by means of that telepathy with which as children they seemed at times to anticipate one another's actions as two birds leave a limb at the same instant; that rapport not like the conventional delusion of that between twins but rather such as might exist between two people who, regardless of sex or age or heritage of race or tongue, had been marooned at birth on a desert island: the island here Sutpen's Hundred; the solitude, the shadow of that father with whom not only the town but their mother's family as well had merely assumed armistice rather than accepting and assimilating.

"You see? there they are: this girl, this young countrybred girl who sees a man for an average of one hour a day for twelve days during his life and that over a period of a year and a half, yet is bent on marrying him to the extent of forcing her brother to the last resort of homicide, even if not murder, to prevent it and that after a period of four years during which she could not have been always certain that he was still alive; this father who should see that man one time, yet have reason to make a six hundred mile journey to investigate him and either discover what he already and apparently by clairvoyance suspected, or at least something which served just as well as reason for forbidding the marriage; this brother in whose eyes that sister's and daughter's honor and happiness, granted that curious and unusual relationship which existed between them, should have been more jealous and precious than to the father even, yet who must champion the marriage to the extent of repudiating father and blood and home to become a follower and dependent of the rejected suitor for four years before killing him apparently for the very identical reason which four years ago he quitted home to champion; and this lover who apparently without volition or desire became involved in an engagement which he seems neither to have sought nor avoided, who took his dismissal in the same passive and sardonic spirit, yet four years later was apparently so bent upon the marriage to which up to that time he had been completely indifferent as to force the brother who had championed it to kill him to prevent it. Yes, granted that, even to the unworldly Henry, let alone the more travelled father, the existence of the eighth part negro mistress and the sixteenth part negro son, granted even the morganatic ceremony—a situation which was as much a part of a wealthy young New

Orleansian's social and fashionable equipment as his dancing slippers—was reason enough, which is drawing honor a little fine even for the shadowy paragons which are our ancestors born in the South and come to man- and womanhood about eighteen sixty or sixty one. It's just incredible. It just does not explain. Or perhaps that's it: they dont explain and we are not supposed to know. We have a few old mouth-to-mouth tales; we exhume from old trunks and boxes and drawers letters without salutation or signature, in which men and women who once lived and breathed are now merely initials or nicknames out of some now incomprehensible affection which sound to us like Sanskrit or Chocktaw; we see dimly people, the people in whose living blood and seed we ourselves lay dormant and waiting, in this shadowy attenuation of time possessing now heroic proportions, performing their acts of simple passion and simple violence, impervious to time and inexplicable—Yes, Judith, Bon, Henry, Sutpen: all of them. They are there, yet something is missing; they are like a chemical formula exhumed along with the letters from that forgotten chest, carefully, the paper old and faded and falling to pieces, the writing faded, almost indecipherable, yet meaningful, familiar in shape and sense, the name and presence of volatile and sentient forces; you bring them together in the proportions called for, but nothing happens; you re-read, tedious and intent, poring, making sure that you have forgotten nothing, made no miscalculation; you bring them together again and again nothing happens: just the words, the symbols, the shapes themselves, shadowy inscrutable and serene, against that turgid background of a horrible and bloody mischancing of human affairs.

"They came from the University to spend that first Christmas. Judith and Ellen and Sutpen saw him for the first time—Judith, the man whom she was to see for an elapsed time of twelve days, yet to remember so that four years later (he never wrote her during that time. Henry would not let him; it was the probation, you see) when she received a letter from him saying *We have waited long enough*, she and Clytie should begin at once to fashion a wedding dress and veil out of rags and scraps; Ellen, the esoteric, the almost baroque, the almost epicene objet d'art which with childlike voracity she essayed to include in the furnishing and decoration of her house; Sutpen, the man whom, after seeing once and before any engagement existed anywhere save in his wife's mind, he saw as a potential threat to the (now and at last) triumphant coronation of his old hardships and ambition, of which threat he was apparently sure enough to warrant a six hundred mile journey to prove it—this in a man who might have challenged and shot someone whom he disliked or feared but who would not have made even a ten mile journey to investigate him. You see? You would almost believe that Sutpen's trip to New Orleans was just sheer chance, just a little more of the illogical machinations of a fatality which had chosen that family in preference to any other in the county or

the land exactly as a small boy chooses one ant-hill
to pour boiling water into in preference to any
other, not even himself knowing why. They stayed
two weeks and rode back to school, stopping to see
Miss Rosa but she was not at home; they passed the
long term before the summer vacation talking together and riding and reading (Bon was reading
law. He would be, would almost have to, since only
that could have made his residence bearable, regardless of what reason he may have brought with him
for remaining;—this, the perfect setting for his dila-
tory indolence: this digging into musty Blackstone
and Coke where, of an undergraduate body still
numbered in two figures, the law school probably
consisted of six others beside Henry—yes, he corrupted Henry to the law also; Henry changed in
midterm—and himself) while Henry aped his clothing and speech, caricatured rather, perhaps, and
Bon, though he had now seen Judith, very likely the
same lazy and catlike man and it Henry who foisted
upon him now the role of his sister's intended as
during the fall term Henry and his companions had
foisted upon Bon the role of Lothario; and Ellen and
Judith now shopping two and three times a week in
town and stopping once to see Miss Rosa while on
their way by carriage to Memphis, with a wagon
preceding them to fetch back the plunder and an
extra nigger on the box with the coachman to stop
every few miles and build a fire and re-heat the
bricks on which Ellen's and Judith's feet rested,
shopping, buying the trousseau for that wedding

whose formal engagement existed no where yet save in Ellen's mind; and Sutpen, who had seen Bon once and was in New Orleans investigating him when Bon next entered the house: who knows what he was thinking, what waiting for, what moment, day, to go to New Orleans and find what he seems to have known all the while that he would find? There was no one for him to tell, talk to about it, about his fear and suspicion. He trusted no man nor woman, who had no man's nor woman's love, since Ellen was incapable of love and Judith was too much like him and he must have seen at a glance that Bon, even though the daughter might still be saved from him, had already corrupted the son. He had been too successful, you see; his was that solitude of contempt and distrust which success brings to him who gained it because he was strong instead of merely lucky.

"Then June came and the end of the school year and Henry and Bon returned to Sutpen's Hundred, Bon to spend a day or two before riding on to the River to take the steamboat home, to New Orleans where Sutpen had already gone though none knew it, least of all Ellen. He stayed but two days, yet now if ever was his chance to come to an understanding with Judith, perhaps even to fall in love with her. It was his only chance, his last chance, though of course neither he nor Judith could have known it, since Sutpen, though but two weeks absent from home, had doubtless already found out about the octoroon mistress and the child. So for the first and last time Bon and Judith might have been said to have a free field—might have been, since it was really Ellen who had the free field. I can imagine her engineering that courtship, supplying Judith and Bon with opportunities for trysts and pledges with a coy and unflagging ubiquity which they must have tried in vain to evade and escape, Judith with annoyed yet still serene concern, Bon with that sardonic and surprised distaste which seems to have been the ordinary manifestation of the impenetrable and shadowy character. Yes, shadowy: a myth, a phantom: something which they engendered and created whole themselves; some effluvium of Sutpen blood and character, as though as a man he did not exist at all. Yet there was the body which Miss Rosa saw, which Judith buried in the family plot beside her mother. And this: the fact that even an undefined and never-spoken engagement survived, speaking well for the postulation that they did love one another, since during that two days mere romance would have perished, died of sheer saccharinity and opportunity. Then Bon rode on to the River and took the boat. And now this: who knows, perhaps if Henry had gone with him that summer instead of waiting until the next, Bon would not have had to die as he did; if Henry had only gone then to New Orleans and found out then about the mistress and the child; Henry who, before it was too late, might have reacted to the discovery exactly as Sutpen did, as a jealous brother might have been expected to react, since who knows but what it was not the fact of the mistress and child, the possible bigamy, to which Henry gave the lie, but to the fact that it was his father who told him, his father who anticipated him, the father who is the natural enemy of any son and son-in-law of whom the mother is the ally, just as after the wedding the father will be the ally of the actual son-in-law who has for mortal foe the mother of his wife. But Henry did not go this time. He rode to the River with Bon and then returned; after a time Sutpen returned home too, from where and for what purpose none were to know until the next Christmas, and that summer passed, the last summer, the last summer of peace and content, with Henry, doubtless without deliberate intent, pleading Bon's suit far better than Bon, than that indolent fatalist had ever bothered to plead it himself, and Judith listening with that serenity, that impenetrable tranquillity which a year or so before had been the young girl's vague and pointless and dreamy unvolition but was now already a mature woman's—a mature woman in love—repose. That's when the letters came, and Henry reading them all, without jealousy, with that complete abnegant transference, metamorphosis into the body which was to become his sister's lover. And Sutpen saying nothing yet about what he had learned in New Orleans but just waiting, unsuspected even by Henry and Judith, waiting for what nobody knows, perhaps in the hope that when Bon learned, as he would be obliged to, that Sutpen had discovered his

secret, he (Bon) would realise that the game was up
and not even return to school the next year. But Bon
did return. He and Henry met again at the University; the letters—from Henry and Bon both now—
making weekly journeys by the hand of Henry's
groom; and Sutpen still waiting, certainly no one
could say for what now, incredible that he should
wait for Christmas, for the crisis to come to him—
this man of whom it was said that he not only went
out to meet his troubles, he sometimes went out and
manufactured them. But this time he waited and it
came to him: Christmas, and Henry and Bon rode
again to Sutpen's Hundred and even the town convinced now by Ellen that the engagement existed;
that twenty-fourth of December, 1860, and the nigger children, with branches of mistletoe and holly
for excuses, already lurking about the rear of the big
house to shout 'Christmas gift' at the white people,
the rich city man come to court Judith, and Sutpen
saying nothing even yet, not suspected yet unless
possibly by Henry, possibly Henry who brought
the matter to its crisis that same night, and Ellen at
the absolute flood's peak of her unreal and weightless life which with the next dawn was to break
beneath her and wash her, spent amazed and uncomprehending, into the shuttered room where she
died two years later;—the Christmas eve, the explosion, and none to ever know just why or just what
happened between Henry and his father and only
the cabin-to-cabin whispering of negroes to spread
the news that Henry and Bon had ridden away in

the dark and that Henry had formally abjured his home and birthright.

"They went to New Orleans. They rode through the bright cold of that Christmas day, to the River and took the steamboat, it still Henry doing the leading, the bringing, as he always did until the very last, when for the first time during their entire relationship Bon led and Henry followed. He didn't have to go. He had voluntarily made himself a pauper but he could have gone to his grandfather since although he was probably better mounted than any other at the University, not excepting Bon himself, he probably had very little money beyond what he could raise hurriedly on his horse and what valuables he happened to have on his body when he and Bon rode away. No, he didn't have to go, and he doing the leading this time too, and Bon riding beside him trying to find out from him what had happened. Bon knew of course what Sutpen had discovered in New Orleans, but he would need to know just what, just how much, Sutpen had told Henry, and Henry not telling him, doubtless with the new mare which he probably knew he would have to surrender, sacrifice too, along with all the rest of his life, inheritance, going fast now and his back rigid and irrevocably turned upon the house, his birthplace and all the familiar scenes of his childhood and youth which he had repudiated for the sake of that friend with whom, despite the sacrifice which he had just made out of love and loyalty, he still could not be perfectly frank. Because he knew that what Sutpen had told him was true. He must have known that at the very instant when he gave his father the lie. So he dared not ask Bon to deny it; he dared not, you see. He could face poverty, disinheritance, but he could not have borne that lie from Bon. Yet he went to New Orleans. He went straight there, to the only place, the very place, where he could not help but prove conclusively the very statement which, coming from his father, he had called a lie. He went there for that purpose; he went there to prove it. And Bon, riding beside him, trying to find out what Sutpen had told him,—Bon who for a year and a half now had been watching Henry ape his clothing and speech, who for a year and a half now had seen himself as the object of that complete and abnegant devotion which only a youth, never a woman, gives to another youth or a man; who for exactly a year now had seen the sister succumb to that same spell which the brother had already succumbed to, and this with no volition on the seducer's part, without so much as the lifting of a finger, as though it actually were the brother who had put the spell on the sister, seduced her to his own vicarious image which walked and breathed with Bon's body. Yet here is the letter, sent four years afterward, written on a sheet of paper salvaged from a gutted house in Carolina, with stove polish found in some captured Yankee stores; four years after she had had any message from him save the messages from Henry that he (Bon) was still alive. So whether Henry now knew about the other woman or not, he would now have to know. Bon realised that. I can imagine them as they rode, Henry still in the fierce repercussive flush of vindicated loyalty, and Bon, the wiser, the shrewder even if only from wider experience and a few more years of age, learning from Henry without Henry's being aware of it, what Sutpen had told him. Because Henry would have to know now. And I dont believe it was just to preserve Henry as an ally, for the crisis of some future need. It was because Bon not only loved Judith after his fashion but he loved Henry too and I believe in a deeper sense than merely after his fashion. Perhaps in his fatalism he loved Henry the better of the two, seeing perhaps in the sister merely the shadow, the woman vessel with which to consummate the love whose actual object was the youth:—this cerebral Don Juan who, reversing the order, had learned to love what he had injured; perhaps it was even more than Judith or Henry either: perhaps the life, the existence, which they represented. Because who knows what picture of peace he might have seen in that monotonous provincial backwater; what alleviation and escape for a parched traveller who had travelled too far at too young an age, in this granite-bound and simple country spring.

"And I can imagine how Bon told Henry, broke it to him. I can imagine Henry in New Orleans, who had not yet even been to Memphis, whose entire worldly experience consisted of sojourns at other houses, plantations, almost interchangeable with his own, where he followed the same routine which he did at home—the same hunting and cockfighting, the same amateur racing of horses on crude homemade tracks, horses sound enough in blood and lineage yet not bred to race and perhaps not even thirty minutes out of the shafts of a trap or perhaps even a carriage; the same square dancing with identical and also interchangeable provincial virgins, to music exactly like that at home, the same champagne, the best doubtless yet crudely dispensed out of the burlesqued pantomime elegance of negro butlers who (and likewise the drinkers who gulped it down like neat whiskey between flowery and unsubtle toasts) would have treated lemonade the same way. I can imagine him, with his puritan heritage—that heritage peculiarly Anglo-Saxon—of fierce proud mysticism and that ability to be ashamed of ignorance and inexperience, in that city foreign and paradoxical, with its atmosphere at once fatal and languorous, at once feminine and steel-hard—this grim humorless yokel out of a granite heritage where even the houses, let alone clothing and conduct, are built in the image of a jealous and sadistic Jehovah, put suddenly down in a place whose denizens had created their All-Powerful and His supporting hierarchy-chorus of beautiful saints and handsome angels in the image of their houses and personal ornaments and voluptuous lives. Yes, I can imagine how Bon led up to it, to the shock: the skill, the calculation, preparing Henry's puritan mind as he would have prepared a cramped and rocky field and planted it and raised the crop which he wanted. It would be the fact of the ceremony, regardless of what kind, that Henry would balk at: Bon knew this. It would not be the mistress or even the child, not even the negro mistress and even less the child because of that fact, since Henry and Judith had grown up with a negro half sister of their own; not the mistress to Henry, certainly not the nigger mistress to a youth with Henry's background, a young man grown up and living in a milieu where the other sex is separated into three sharp divisions, separated (two of them) by a chasm which could be crossed but one time and in but one direction—ladies, women, females—the virgins whom gentlemen someday married, the courtesans to whom they went while on sabbaticals to the cities, the slave girls and women upon whom that first caste rested and to whom in certain cases it doubtless owed the very fact of its virginity;—not this to Henry, young, strong-blooded, victim of the hard celibacy of riding and hunting to heat and make importunate the blood of a young man, to which he and his kind were forced to pass time away, with girls of his own class interdict and inaccessible and women of the second class just as inaccessible because of money and distance, and hence only the slave girls, the housemaids neated and cleaned by white mistresses or perhaps girls with sweating bodies out of the fields themselves and the young man rides up and beckons the watching overseer and says Send me Juno or Missylena or Chlory and then rides on into the trees and dismounts and waits. No: it would be the ceremony, a ceremony entered into, to be sure, with a negro, yet still a ceremony; this is what Bon doubtless thought. So I can imagine him, the way he did it: the way in which he took the innocent and negative plate of Henry's provincial soul and intellect and exposed it by slow degrees to this esoteric milieu, building gradually toward the picture which he desired it to retain, accept. I can see him corrupting Henry gradually into the purlieus of elegance, with no foreword, no warning, the postulation to come after the fact, exposing Henry slowly to the surface aspect—the architecture a little curious, a little femininely flamboyant and therefore to Henry opulent, sensuous, sinful; the inference of great and easy wealth measured by steamboat loads in place of a tedious inching of sweating human figures across cotton fields; the flash and glitter of a myriad carriage wheels, in which women, enthroned and immobile and passing rapidly across the vision, appeared like painted portraits beside men in linen a little finer and diamonds a little brighter and in broadcloth a little trimmer and with hats raked a little more above faces a little more darkly swaggering than any Henry had ever seen before: and the mentor, the man for whose sake he had repudiated not only blood and kin but food and shelter and clothing too, whose clothing and walk and speech he had tried to ape, along with his attitude toward women and his ideas of honor and pride too, watching him with that cold and catlike inscrutable calculation, watching the picture resolve and become fixed and then telling Henry, 'But that's not it. That's just the base, the foundation. It can belong to anyone': and Henry, 'You mean, this is not it? That it is above this, higher than this, more select than this?': and Bon, 'Yes. This is only the foundation. This belongs to anybody.': a dialogue without words, speech, which would fix and then remove without obliterating one line the picture, this background, leaving the background, the plate prepared and innocent again: the plate docile, with that puritan's humility toward anything which is a matter of sense rather than logic, fact, the man, the struggling and suffocating heart behind it saying *I will believe! I will! I will! Whether it is true or not, I will believe!* waiting for the next picture which the mentor, the corruptor, intended for it: that next picture, following the fixation and acceptance of which the mentor would say again, perhaps with words now, still watching the sober and thoughtful face but still secure in his knowledge and trust in that puritan heritage which must show disapproval instead of surprise or even despair and nothing at all rather than have the disapprobation construed as surprise or despair: 'But even this is not it': and Henry, 'You mean, it is still higher than this, still above this?' Because he (Bon) would be talking now, lazily, almost cryptically, stroking onto the plate himself now the picture which he wanted there; I can imagine how he did it—the calculation, the surgeon's alertness and cold detachment, the exposures brief, so brief as to be cryptic, almost staccato, the plate unaware of what the complete picture would show, scarce-seen yet ineradicable:—a trap, a riding horse standing before a closed and curiously monastic doorway in a neighborhood a little decadent, even a little sinister, and Bon mentioning the owner's name casually—this, corruption subtly anew by putting into Henry's mind the notion of one man of the world speaking to another, that Henry knew that Bon believed that Henry would know even from a disjointed word what Bon was talking about, and Henry the puritan who must show nothing at all rather than surprise or incomprehension;—a façade shuttered and blank, drowsing in steamy morning sunlight, invested by the bland and cryptic voice with something of secret and curious and unimaginable delights. Without his knowing what he saw it was as though to Henry the blank and scaling barrier in dissolving produced and revealed not comprehension to the mind, the intellect which weighs and discards, but striking instead straight and true to some primary blind and mindless foundation of all young male living dream and hope—a row of faces like a bazaar of flowers, the supreme apotheosis of chattelry, of human flesh bred of the two races for that sale—a corridor of doomed and tragic flower faces walled between the grim duenna row of old women and the elegant shapes of young men trim predatory and (at the moment) goatlike: this seen by Henry quickly, exposed quickly and then removed, the mentor's voice

still bland, pleasant, cryptic, postulating still the fact
of one man of the world talking to another about
something they both understand, depending upon,
counting upon still, the puritan's provincial horror
of revealing surprise or ignorance, who knew
Henry so much better than Henry knew him, and
Henry not showing either, suppressing still that first
cry of terror and grief, *I will believe! I will! I will!*
Yes, that brief, before Henry had had time to know
what he had seen, but now slowing: now would
come the instant for which Bon had builded:——a
wall, unscalable, a gate ponderously locked, the
sober and thoughtful country youth just waiting,
looking, not yet asking why? or what? the gate of
solid beams in place of the lacelike iron grilling and
they passing on, Bon knocking at a small adjacent
doorway from which a swarthy man resembling a
creature out of an old woodcut of the French Revo-
lution erupts, concerned, even a little aghast, looking first at the daylight and then at Henry and
speaking to Bon in French which Henry does not
understand and Bon's teeth glinting for an instant
before he answers in French: 'With him? An Ameri-
can? He is a guest; I would have to let him choose
weapons and I decline to fight with axes. No, no;
not that. Just the key.' Just the key; and now, the
solid gates closed behind them instead of before, no
sight or evidence above the high thick walls of the
low city and scarce any sound of it, the labyrinthine
mass of oleander and jasmine, lantana and mimosa
walling yet again the strip of bare earth combed and

curried with powdered shell, raked and immaculate and only the most recent of the brown stains showing now, and the voice—the mentor, the guide standing aside now to watch the grave provincial face—casually and pleasantly anecdotal: 'The customary way is to stand back to back, the pistol in your right hand and the corner of the other cloak in your left. Then at the signal you begin to walk and when you feel the cloak tauten you turn and fire. Though there are some now and then, when the blood is especially hot or when it is still peasant blood, who prefer knives and one cloak. They face one another inside the same cloak, you see, each holding the other's wrist with the left hand. But that was never my way';—casual, chatty, you see, waiting for the countryman's slow question, who knew already now before he asked it: 'What would you—they be fighting for?'

"Yes, Henry would know now, or believe that he knew now; anymore he would probably consider anti-climax though it would not be, it would be anything but that, the final blow, stroke, touch, the keen surgeonlike compounding which the now shocked nerves of the patient would not even feel, not know that the first hard shocks were the random and crude. Because there was that ceremony. Bon knew that that would be what Henry would resist, find hard to stomach and retain. Oh he was shrewd, this man whom for weeks now Henry was realising that he knew less and less, this stranger immersed and oblivious now in the formal, almost ritual, preparations for the visit, finicking almost like a woman over the fit of the new coat which he would have ordered for Henry, forced Henry to accept for this occasion, by means of which the entire impression which Henry was to receive from the visit would be established before they even left the house, before Henry ever saw the woman: and Henry, the countryman, the bewildered, with the subtle tide already setting beneath him toward the point where he must either betray himself and his entire upbringing and thinking, or deny the friend for whom he had already repudiated home and kin and all; the bewildered, the (for that time) helpless, who wanted to believe yet did not see how he could, being carried by the friend, the mentor, through one of those inscrutable and curiously lifeless doorways like that before which he had seen the horse or the trap, and so into a place which to his puritan's provincial mind all of morality was upside down and all of honor perished—a place created for and by voluptuousness, the abashless and unabashed senses, and the country boy with his simple and erstwhile untroubled code in which females were ladies or whores or slaves looked at the apotheosis of two doomed races presided over by its own victim—a woman with a face like a tragic magnolia, the eternal female, the eternal Who-suffers; the child, the boy, sleeping in silk and lace to be sure yet complete chattel of him who, begetting him, owned him body and soul to sell (if he chose) like a calf or puppy or sheep; and the mentor watching again, perhaps even the gambler now thinking *Have I won or lost?* as they emerged and returned to Bon's rooms, for that while impotent even with talk, shrewdness, no longer counting upon that puritan character which must show neither surprise nor despair, having to count now (if on anything) on the corruption itself, the love; he could not even say, 'Well? What do you say about it?' He could only wait, and that upon the absolutely unpredictable actions of a man who lived by instinct and not reason, until Henry should speak, 'But a bought woman. A whore': and Bon, even gently now, 'Not whore. Dont say that. In fact, never refer to one of them by that name in New Orleans: otherwise you may be forced to purchase that privilege with some of your blood from proba- bly a thousand men', and perhaps still gently, per- haps now even with something of pity: that pessimistic and sardonic cerebral pity of the intelli- gent for any human injustice or folly or suffering: 'Not whores. And not whores because of us, the thousand. We—the thousand, the white men— made them, created and produced them; we even made the laws which declare that one eighth of a specified kind of blood shall outweigh seven eighths of another kind. I admit that. But that same white race would have made them slaves too, laborers, cooks, maybe even field hands, if it were not for this thousand, these few men like myself without princi- ples or honor either, perhaps you will say. We can- not, perhaps we do not even want to, save all of them; perhaps the thousand we save are not one in a thousand. But we save that one. God may mark every sparrow, but we do not pretend to be God, you see. Perhaps we do not even want to be God, since no man would want but one of these sparrows. And perhaps when God looks into one of these establishments like you saw tonight, He would not choose one of us to be God either, now that He is old. Though He must have been young once, surely He was young once, and surely someone who has existed as long as He has, who has looked at as much crude and promiscuous sinning without grace or restraint or decorum as He has had to, to contemplate at last, even though the instances are not one in a thousand thousand, the principles of honor, decorum and gentleness applied to perfectly normal human instinct which you Anglo-Saxons insist upon calling lust and in whose service you revert in sabbaticals to the primordial caverns, the fall from what you call grace fogged and clouded by Heaven-defying words of extenuation and explanation, the return to grace heralded by Heaven-placating cries of satiated abasement and flagellation, in neither of which—the defiance or the placation—can Heaven find interest or even, after the first two or three times, diversion: So perhaps, now that God is an old man, He is not interested in the way we serve what you call lust either. Perhaps He does not even require of us that we save this one sparrow, anymore than we save the one sparrow which we do save for any commendation from Him. But we do save that one, who but for us would have been sold to any brute who had the price, not sold to him for the night like a white prostitute, but body and soul for life to him who could have used her with more impunity than he would dare to use an animal, heifer or mare, and then discarded or sold or even murdered when worn out or when her keep and her price no longer balanced. Yes: a sparrow which God Himself neglected to mark. Because though men, white men, created her, God did not stop it. He planted the seed which brought her to flower—the white blood to give the shape and pigment of what the white man calls female beauty, to a female principle which existed, queenly and complete, in the hot equatorial groin of the world long before that white one of ours came down from trees and lost its hair and bleached out—a principle apt docile and instinct with strange and ancient curious pleasures of the flesh (which is all: there is nothing else) which her white sisters of a mushroom yesterday flee from in moral and outraged horror—a principle which, where her white sister must needs try to make an economic matter of it like someone who insists upon installing a counter or a scales or a safe in a store or business for a certain percentage of the profits, reigns, wise supine and all-powerful, from the sunless and silken bed which is her throne. No: not whores. Not even courtesans:—creatures taken at childhood, culled and chosen and raised more carefully than any white girl, any nun, than any blooded mare even, by a person who gives them the unsleeping care and attention which no mother ever gives.

For a price, of course, but a price offered and accepted or declined through a system more formal than any that white girls are sold under since they are more valuable as commodities than white girls, raised and trained to fulfill a woman's sole end and purpose: to love, to be beautiful, to divert; never to see a man's face hardly until brought to the ball and offered to and chosen by some man who in return, not can and not will but *must*, supply her with the surroundings proper in which to love and be beautiful and divert, and who must usually risk his life or at least his blood for that privilege. No, not whores. Sometimes I believe that they are the only true chaste women, not to say virgins, in America, and they remain true and faithful to that man not merely until he dies or frees them, but until they die. And where will you find whore or lady either whom you can count on to do that?' and Henry, 'But you married her. You married her.': and Bon—it would be a little quicker now, sharper now, though still gentle, still patient, though still the iron, the steel—the gambler not quite yet reduced to his final trump: 'Ah. That ceremony. I see. That's it, then. A formula, a shibboleth meaningless as a child's game, performed by someone created by the situation whose need it answered: a crone mumbling in a dungeon lighted by a handful of burning hair, something in a tongue which not even the girls themselves understand anymore, maybe not even the crone herself, rooted in nothing of economics for her or for any possible progeny since the very fact that we acquiesced, suffered the farce, was her proof and assurance of that which the ceremony itself could never enforce; vesting no new rights in anyone, denying to none the old—a ritual as meaningless as that of college boys in secret rooms at night, even to the same archaic and forgotten symbols?— you call that a marriage, when the night of a honeymoon and the casual business with a hired prostitute consists of the same suzerainty over a (temporarily) private room, the same order of removing the same clothes, the same conjunction in a single bed? Why not call that a marriage too?' and Henry: 'Oh I know. I know. You give me two and two and you tell me it makes five and it does make five. But there is still the marriage. Suppose I assume an obligation to a man who cannot speak my language, the obligation stated to him in his own and I agree to it: am I any the less obligated because I did not happen to know the tongue in which he accepted me in good faith? No: the more, the more.' and Bon—the trump now, the voice gentle now: 'Have you forgot that this woman, this child, are niggers? You, Henry Sutpen of Sutpen's Hundred in Mississippi? You, talking of marriage, a wedding, here?' and Henry— the despair now, the last bitter cry of irrevocable undefeat: 'Yes. I know. I know that. But it's still there. It's not right. Not even you doing it makes it right. Not even you.'

"So that was all. It should have been all; that afternoon four years later should have happened the next day, the four years, the interval, mere anti-climax: an attenuation and prolongation of a conclusion already ripe to happen, by the War, by a stupid and bloody aberration in the high (and impossible) destiny of the United States, maybe instigated by that family fatality which possessed, along with all circumstance, that curious lack of economy between cause and effect which is always a characteristic of fate when reduced to using human beings for tools, material. Anyway, Henry waited four years, holding the three of them in that abeyance, that durance, waiting, hoping, for Bon to renounce the woman and dissolve the marriage which he (Henry) admitted was no marriage, and which he must have known as soon as he saw the woman and the child that Bon would not renounce. In fact, as time passed and Henry became accustomed to the idea of that ceremony which was still no marriage, that may have been the trouble with Henry—not the two ceremonies but the two women; not the fact that Bon's intention was to commit bigamy but that it was apparently to make his (Henry's) sister a sort of junior partner in a harem. Anyway, he waited, hoped, for four years. That spring they returned north, into Mississippi. Bull Run had been fought and there was a company organising at the University, among the student body. Henry and Bon joined it. Probably Henry wrote Judith where they were and what they intended to do. They enlisted together, you see, Henry watching Bon and Bon permitting himself to be watched, the probation, the durance: the one who dared not let the other out of his sight, not from fear that Bon would marry Judith with Henry not there to stop it, but that Bon would marry Judith and then he (Henry) would have to live for the rest of his life with the knowledge that he was glad that he had been so betrayed, with the coward's joy of surrendering without having been vanquished; the other for that same reason too, who could not have wanted Judith without Henry since he must never have doubted but what he could marry Judith when he wished, in spite of brother and father both, because as I said before, it was not Judith who was the object of Bon's love or of Henry's solicitude. She was just the blank shape, the empty vessel in which each of them strove to preserve, not the illusion of himself nor his illusion of the other but what each conceived the other to believe him to be—the man and the youth, seducer and seduced, who had known one another, seduced and been seduced, victimised in turn each by the other, conquerer vanquished by his own strength, vanquished conquering by his own weakness, before Judith came into their joint lives even by so much as girlname. And who knows? there was the War now; who knows but what the fatality and the fatality's victims did not both think, hope, that the War would settle the matter, leave free one of the two irreconciliables, since it would not be the first time that youth has taken catastrophe as a direct act of Providence for the sole purpose of solving a personal problem which youth itself could not solve.

"And Judith: how else to explain her but this

way? Surely Bon could not have corrupted her to
fatalism in twelve days, who not only had not tried
to corrupt her to unchastity but not even to defy her
father. No: anything but a fatalist, who was the
Sutpen with the ruthless Sutpen code of taking
what it wanted provided it were strong enough, of
the two children as Henry was the Coldfield with
the Coldfield cluttering of morality and rules of
right and wrong; who while Henry screamed and
vomited, looked down from the loft that night on
the spectacle of Sutpen fighting halfnaked with one
of his halfnaked niggers with the same cold and
attentive interest with which Sutpen would have
watched Henry fighting with a negro boy of his
own age and weight. Because she could not have
known the reason for her father's objection to the
marriage. Henry would not have told her, and she
would not have asked her father. Because, even if
she had known it, it would have made no difference
to her. She would have acted as Sutpen would have
acted with anyone who tried to cross him: she
would have taken Bon anyway. I can imagine her if
necessary even murdering the other woman. But
she certainly would have made no investigation and
then held a moral debate between what she wanted
and what she thought was right. Yet she waited. She
waited four years, with no word from him save
through Henry that he (Bon) was alive, because
Henry would not let Bon write her. He would not
have. And Bon would not have tried to. It was the
probation, the durance; they all three accepted it; I

dont believe there was ever any promise between Henry and Bon demanded or offered. But Judith, who could not have known what happened nor why.—Have you noticed how so often when we try to reconstruct the causes which lead up to the actions of men and women, how with a sort of astonishment we find ourselves now and then reduced to the belief, the only possible belief, that they stemmed from some of the old virtues? the thief who steals not for greed but for love, the murderer who kills not out of lust but pity? Judith, giving implicit trust where she had given love, giving implicit love where she had derived breath and pride: that true pride, not that false kind which transforms what it does not at the moment understand into scorn and outrage and so vents itself in pique and lacerations, but true pride which can say to itself without abasement *I love, I will accept no substitute; something has happened between him and my father; if my father was right, I will never see him again, if wrong he will come or send for me; if happy I can be I will, if suffer I must I can.* Because she waited; she made no effort to do anything else; her relations with her father had not altered one jot; to see them together, Bon might never have even existed—the same two calm impenetrable faces seen together in the carriage in town during the next few months after Ellen took to her bed, between that Christmas day and the day when Sutpen rode away with his and Sartoris' regiment. They didn't talk, tell one another anything, you see—Sutpen, what he had learned about Bon;

Judith, that she knew where Bon and Henry now were. They did not need to talk. They were too much alike. They were as two people become now and then, who seem to know one another so well or are so much alike that the power, the need, to communicate by speech atrophies from disuse and, comprehending without need of the medium of ear or intellect, they no longer understand one another's actual words. So she did not tell him where Henry and Bon were and he did not discover it until after the University company departed, because Bon and Henry enrolled and then hid themselves somewhere. They must have; they must have paused in Oxford only long enough to enroll before riding on, because no one who knew them either in Oxford or in Jefferson knew that they were members of the company at the time, which would have been almost impossible to conceal otherwise. Because now people—fathers and mothers and sisters and kin and sweethearts of those young men—were coming to Oxford from further away than Jefferson —families with food and bedding and servants, to bivouac among the families, the houses, of Oxford itself, to watch the gallant mimic marching and countermarching of the sons and the brothers, drawn all of them, rich and poor, aristocrat and redneck, by what is probably the most moving mass-sight of all human mass-experience, far more so than the spectacle of so many virgins going to be sacrificed to some heathen Principle, some Priapus— the sight of young men, the light quick bones, the bright gallant deluded blood and flesh dressed in a martial glitter of brass and plumes, marching away to a battle. And there would be music at night— fiddle and triangle among the blazing candles, the blowing of curtains in tall windows on the April darkness, the swing of crinoline indiscriminate within the circle of plain gray cuff of the soldier or the banded gold of rank, of an army even if not a war of gentlemen, where private and colonel called each other by their given names not as one farmer to another across a halted plow in a field or across a counter in a store laden with calico and cheese and strap oil, but as one man to another above the suave powdered shoulders of women, above the two raised glasses of scuppernong claret or bought champagne;—music, the nightly repetitive last waltz as the days passed and the company waited to move, the brave trivial glitter against a black night not catastrophic but merely background, the perennial last scented spring of youth; and Judith not there and Henry the romantic not there and Bon the fatalist, hidden somewhere, the watcher and the watched: and the recurrent flower-laden dawns of that April and May and June filled with bugles, entering a hundred windows where a hundred still unbrided widows dreamed virgin unmeditant upon the locks of black or brown or yellow hair and Judith not one of these: and five of the company, mounted, with grooms and body servants in a forage wagon, in their new and unstained gray made a tour of the State with the flag, the company's colors, the segments of silk cut and fitted but not sewn, from house to house until the sweetheart of each man in the company had taken a few stitches in it, and Henry and Bon not of these either, since they did not join the company until after it departed, who must have emerged from whatever place it was that they lurked in, emerging as though unnoticed from the roadside brake or thicket, to fall in as the marching company passed; the two of them —the youth and the man, the youth deprived twice now of his birthright, who should have made one among the candles and fiddles, the kisses and the desperate tears, who should have made one of the color guard itself which toured the State with the unsewn flag; and the man who should not have been there at all, who was too old to be there at all, both in years and experience: that mental and spiritual orphan whose fate it apparently was to exist in some limbo halfway between where his corporeality was and his mentality and moral equipment desired to be —an undergraduate at the University, yet by the sheer accumulation of too full years behind him forced into the extra-academnic of a law class containing six members; in the War, by that same force removed into the isolation of commissioned rank. He received a lieutenancy before the company entered its first engagement even. I dont think he wanted it; I can even imagine him trying to avoid it, refuse it. But there it was, he was, orphaned once more by the very situation to which and by which he was doomed—the two of them officer and man now but still watcher and watched, waiting for something but not knowing what, what act of fate, destiny, what irrevocable sentence of what Judge or Arbiter between them since nothing less would do, nothing halfway or reversible would seem to suffice —the officer, the lieutenant who possessed the slight and authorised advantage of being able to say *You* go there, of at least sometimes remaining behind the platoon which he directed; the private who carried that officer, shot through the shoulder, on his back while the regiment fell back under the Yankee guns at Pittsburg Landing, carried him to safety apparently for the sole purpose of watching him for two years more, writing Judith meanwhile that they were both alive, and that was all.

"And Judith. She lived alone now. Perhaps she had lived alone ever since that Christmas day last year and then year before last and then three years and then four years ago, since though Sutpen was gone now with his and Sartoris' regiment and the negroes—the wild stock with which he had created Sutpen's Hundred—had followed the first Yankee troops to pass through Jefferson, she lived in anything but solitude, what with Ellen in bed in the shuttered room, requiring the unremitting attention of a child while she waited with that amazed and passive uncomprehension to die; and she (Judith) and Clytie making and keeping a kitchen garden of sorts to keep them alive; and Wash Jones, living in the abandoned and rotting fishing camp in the river bottom which Sutpen had built after the first

woman—Ellen—entered his house and the last deer
and bear hunter went out of it, where he now permitted Wash and his daughter and infant granddaughter to live, performing the heavy garden work
and supplying Ellen and Judith and then Judith
with fish and game now and then, even entering the
house now who until Sutpen went away had never
approached nearer than the scuppernong arbor behind the kitchen where on Sunday afternoons he
and Sutpen would drink from the demijohn and the
bucket of spring water which Wash fetched from
almost a mile away, Sutpen in the barrel stave hammock talking and Wash squatting against a post,
chortling and guffawing;—not solitude and certainly not idleness: the same impenetrable and serene face, only a little older now, a little thinner
now, which had appeared in town in the carriage
beside her father's within a week after it was learned
that her fiancé and her brother had quitted the house
in the night and vanished, none knew why or where
and none asked, just as now none asked when she
came to town now, in the made-over dress which all
Southern women now wore, in the carriage still but
drawn now by a mule, a plow mule, soon the plow
mule, and no coachman to drive it either, to put the
mule in the harness and take it out, to join the other
women where—there were wounded in Jefferson
then—in the improvised hospital where (the nurtured virgin, the supremely and traditionally idle)
they cleaned and dressed the self-fouled bodies of
strange injured and dead and made lint of the win-

dow curtains and sheets and linen of the houses in which they had been born;—none to ask her about brother and sweetheart while they talked among themselves of sons and brothers and husbands with tears and grief perhaps but at least with certainty, knowledge; she waiting too, like Henry and Bon, not knowing for what, but unlike Henry and Bon, she not even knowing for why. Then Ellen died, the butterfly of a forgotten summer two years defunctive now—the substanceless shell, the shade impervious to any alteration or dissolution because of its very weightlessness: no body to be buried: just the shape, the recollection, translated on some peaceful afternoon without bell or catafalque into that cedar grove, to lie in powder-light paradox beneath the thousand pounds of marble monument which Sutpen (Colonel Sutpen now, since Sartoris had been deposed at the annual election of regimental officers the year before) brought in the regimental forage wagon from Charleston, South Carolina and set above the faint grassy depression which Judith told him was Ellen's grave. And then her grandfather died, starved to death nailed up in his own attic, and Judith doubtless inviting Miss Rosa to come out to Sutpen's Hundred to live and Miss Rosa declining, waiting too apparently upon this letter, this first direct word from Bon in four years and which, a week after she buried him too beside her mother's tombstone, she brought to town herself, in the surrey drawn by the mule which both she and Clytie had learned to catch and harness, and

gave to your grandmother, bringing the letter voluntarily to your grandmother, who (Judith) never
called on anyone now, had no friends now, doubtless
knowing no more why she chose your grandmother
to give the letter to than your grandmother knew;
not thin now but gaunt, the Sutpen skull showing
indeed now through the worn, the Coldfield, flesh,
the face which had long since forgotten how to be
young and yet absolutely impenetrable, absolutely
serene: no mourning, not even grief, and your grandmother saying, 'Me? You want me to keep it?'

" 'Yes,' Judith said. 'Or destroy it. As you like.
Read it if you like or dont read it if you like. Because
you make so little impression, you see. You get born
and you try this and you dont know why only you
keep on trying it and you are born at the same time
with a lot of other people, all mixed up with them,
like trying to, having to, move your arms and legs
with strings only the same strings are hitched to all
the other arms and legs and the others all trying and
they dont know why either except that the strings
are all in one another's way like five or six people all
trying to make a rug on the same loom only each
one wants to weave his own pattern into the rug;
and it cant matter, you know that, or the Ones that
set up the loom would have arranged things a little
better, and yet it must matter because you keep on
trying or having to keep on trying and then all of
a sudden it's all over and all you have left is a block
of stone with scratches on it provided there was
someone to remember to have the marble scratched

and set up or had time to, and it rains on it and the sun shines on it and after a while they dont even remember the name and what the scratches were trying to tell, and it doesn't matter. And so maybe if you could go to someone, the stranger the better, and give them something—a scrap of paper—something, anything, it not to mean anything in itself and them not even to read it or keep it, not even bother to throw it away or destroy it, at least it would be something just because it would have happened, be remembered even if only from passing from one hand to another, one mind to another, and it would be at least a scratch, something, something that *was* once for the reason that it can die someday, while the block of stone cant be *is* because it never can become *was* because it cant ever die or perish . . .' and your grandmother watching her, the impenetrable, the calm, the absolutely serene face, and crying:

" 'No! No! Not that! Think of your——' and the face watching her, comprehending, still serene, not even bitter:

" 'Oh. I? No, not that. Because somebody will have to take care of Clytie, and Father too soon, who will want something to eat after he comes home because it wont last much longer since they have begun to shoot one another now. No. Not that. Women dont do that for love. I dont even believe that men do. And not now, anyway. Because there wouldn't be any room now, for them to go to, wherever it is, if it is. It would be full already. Glutted.

Like a theatre, an opera house, if what you expect
to find is forgetting, diversion, entertainment; like a
bed already too full if what you want to find is a
chance to lie still and sleep and sleep and sleep'——"
Mr Compson moved. Half rising, Quentin took the
letter from him and beneath the dim bug-fouled
globe opened it, carefully, as though the sheet, the
desiccated square, were not the paper but the intact
ash of its former shape and substance: and meanwhile Mr Compson's voice speaking on while
Quentin heard it without listening: "Now you can
see why I said that he loved her. Because there were
other letters, many of them, gallant flowery indolent
frequent and insincere, sent by hand over that forty
miles between Oxford and Jefferson after that first
Christmas—the metropolitan gallant's idle and deli-
cately flattering (and doubtless to him, meaningless)
gesture to the bucolic maiden—and that bucolic
maiden, with that profound and absolutely inexplicable tranquil patient clairvoyance of women
against which that metropolitan gallant's foppish
posturing was just the jackanape antics of a small
boy, receiving the letters without understanding
them, not even keeping them, for all their elegant
and gallant and tediously contrived turns of form
and metaphor, until the next one arrived. But keeping this one which must have reached her out of a
clear sky after an interval of four years, considering
this one worthy to give to a stranger to keep or not
to keep, even to read or not to read as the stranger
saw fit, to make that scratch, that undying mark on

the blank face of the oblivion to which we are all doomed, of which she spoke——;" Quentin hearing without having to listen as he read the faint spidery script not like something impressed upon the paper by a once-living hand but like a shadow cast upon it which had resolved on the paper the instant before he looked at it and which might fade, vanish, at any instant while he still did: the dead tongue speaking after the four years and then after almost fifty more, gentle sardonic whimsical and incurably pessimistic, without date or salutation or signature:

You will notice how I insult neither of us by claiming this to be a voice from the defeated even, let alone from the dead. In fact, if I were a philosopher I should deduce and derive a curious and apt commentary on the times and augur of the future from this letter which you now hold in your hands—a sheet of notepaper with, as you can see, the best of French watermarks dated seventy years ago, salvaged (stolen if you will) from the gutted mansion of a ruined aristocrat; and written upon in the best of stove polish manufactured not twelve months ago in a New England factory. Yes. Stove polish. We captured it: a story in itself. Imagine us, an assortment of homogeneous scarecrows, I wont say hungry because to a woman, lady or female either, below Mason's and Dixon's in this year of grace 1865, that word would be sheer redundancy, like saying that we were breathing. And I wont say ragged or even shoeless, since we have been both long enough to have grown accustomed to it, only, thank God (and this restores my

*faith not in human nature perhaps but at least in
man) that he really does not become inured to hardship and privation: it is only the mind, the gross
omnivorous carrion-heavy soul which becomes
inured; the body itself, thank God, never reconciled
from the old soft feel of soap and clean linen and
something between the sole of the foot and the earth
to distinguish it from the foot of a beast. So say we
merely needed ammunition. And imagine us, the
scarecrows with one of those concocted plans of scare-
crow desperation which not only must but do work,
for the reason that there is absolutely no room for
alternative before man or heaven, no niche on earth
or under it for failure to find space either to pause or
breathe or be graved and sepulchred; and we (the
scarecrows) bringing it off with a great deal of élan,
not to say noise; imagine, I say, the prey and prize,
the ten plump defenceless sutlers' wagons, the scarecrows tumbling out box after beautiful box after
beautiful box stencilled each with that U. and that S.
which for four years now has been to us the symbol
of the spoils which belong to the vanquished, of the
loaves and the fishes as was once the incandescent
Brow, the shining nimbus of the Thorny Crown; and
the scarecrows clawing at the boxes with stones and
bayonets and even with bare hands and opening them
at last and finding—What? Stove polish. Gallons
and gallons and gallons of the best stove polish, not
a box of it a year old yet and doubtless still trying
to overtake General Sherman with some belated
amended field order requiring him to polish the stove
before firing the house. How we laughed. Yes, we*

laughed, because I have learned this at least during these four years: that it really requires an empty stomach to laugh with, that only when you are hungry or frightened do you extract some ultimate essence out of laughing just as the empty stomach extracts the ultimate essence out of alcohol. But at least we have stove polish. We have plenty of it. We have too much, because it does not take much to say what I have to say, as you can see. And so the conclusion and augury which I draw, even though no philosopher, is this.

We have waited long enough. You will notice how I do not insult you either by saying I have waited long enough. And therefore, since I do not insult you by saying that only I have waited, I do not add, expect me. Because I cannot say when to expect me. Because what WAS is one thing, and now it is not because it is dead, it died in 1861, and therefore what IS——(There. They have started firing again. Which—to mention it—is redundancy too, like the breathing or the need of ammunition. Because sometimes I think it has never stopped. It hasn't stopped of course; I dont mean that. I mean, there has never been any more of it, that there was that one fusillade four years ago which sounded once and then was arrested, mesmerised raised muzzle by raised muzzle, in the frozen attitude of its own aghast amazement and never repeated and it now only the loud aghast echo jarred by the dropped musket of a weary sentry or by the fall of the spent body itself, out of the air which lies over the land where that fusillade first sounded and where it must remain yet because no other space under heaven will receive it. So that means that it is dawn again and that I must stop. Stop what? you will say. Why, thinking, remembering—remark that I do not say, hoping—; to become once more for a period without boundaries or location in time, mindless and irrational companion and inmate of a body which, even after four years, with a sort of dismal and incorruptible fidelity which is incredibly admirable to me, is still immersed and obliviously bemused in recollections of old peace and contentment the very names of whose scents and sounds I do not know that I remember, which ignores even the presence and threat of a torn arm or leg as though through some secretly incurred and infallible promise and conviction of immortality.——But to finish.) I cannot say when to expect me. Because what IS is something else again because it was not even alive then. And since because within this sheet of paper you now hold the best of the old South which is dead, and the words you read were written upon it with the best (each box said, the very best) of the new North which has conquered and which therefore, whether it likes it or not, will have to survive, I now believe that you and I are, strangely enough, included among those who are doomed to live.

"And that's all," Mr Compson said. "She received it and she and Clytie made the wedding gown and the veil from scraps—perhaps scraps intended for, which should have gone for, lint and did not. She didn't know when he would come because he didn't know himself: and maybe he told Henry, showed Henry the letter before he sent it, and maybe he did not; maybe still just the watching and the waiting, the one saying to Henry *I have waited long enough* and Henry saying to the other *Do you renounce then? Do you renounce?* and the other saying *I do not renounce. For four years now I have given chance the opportunity to renounce for me, but it seems that I am doomed to live, that she and I both are doomed to live;* —the defiance and the ultimatum delivered beside a bivouac fire, the ultimatum discharged before the gate to which the two of them must have ridden side by side almost: the one calm and undeviating, perhaps unresisting even, the fatalist to the last; the other remorseless with implacable and unalterable grief and despair——" (It seemed to Quentin that he could actually see them, facing one another at the gate. Inside the gate what was once a park now spread, unkempt, in shaggy desolation, with an air dreamy remote and aghast like the unshaven face of a man just waking from ether, up to a huge house where a young girl waited in a wedding dress made from stolen scraps, the house partaking too of that air of scaling desolation, not having suffered from invasion but a shell marooned and forgotten in a backwater of catastrophe—a skeleton giving of itself in slow driblets of furniture and carpet, linen and silver, to help to die torn and anguished men who knew, even while dying, that for months now the sacrifice and the anguish were in vain. They faced one another on the two gaunt horses, two men, young, not yet in the world, not yet breathed over long enough, to be old but with old eyes, with unkempt hair and faces gaunt and weathered as if cast by some spartan and even niggard hand from bronze, in worn and patched gray weathered now to the color of dead leaves, the one with the tarnished braid of an officer, the other plain of cuff, the pistol lying yet across the saddle bow unaimed, the two faces calm, the voices not even raised: *Dont you pass the shadow of this post, this branch, Charles;* and *I am going to pass it, Henry*) "——and then Wash Jones sitting that saddleless mule before Miss Rosa's gate, shouting her name into the sunny and peaceful quiet of the street, saying, 'Air you Rosie Coldfield? Then you better come on out yon. Henry has done shot that durn French feller. Kilt him dead as a beef.' "

V

So they will have told you doubtless already how I told that Jones to take that mule which was not his around to the barn and harness it to our buggy while I put on my hat and shawl and locked the house. That was all I needed to do since they will have told you doubtless that I would have had no need for either trunk or bag since what clothing I possessed, now that the garments which I had been fortunate enough to inherit from my aunt's kindness or haste or oversight were long since worn out, consisted of the ones which Ellen had remembered from time to time to give me and now Ellen these two years dead; that I had only to lock the house and take my place in the buggy and traverse those twelve miles which I had not done since Ellen died, beside that brute who until Ellen died was not even permitted to approach the house from the front—that brute progenitor of brutes whose granddaughter was to supplant me, if not in my sister's house at least in my sister's bed to which (so they will tell you) I aspired—that brute who (brute instrument of that justice which presides over human events which, incept in the individual, runs smooth, less claw than velvet: but which, by man or woman flouted, drives on like fiery steel and overrides

*both weakly just and unjust strong, both vanquisher
and innocent victimised, ruthless for appointed right
and truth) brute who was not only to preside upon the
various shapes and avatars of Thomas Sutpen's devil's
fate but was to provide at the last the female flesh in
which his name and lineage should be sepulchred—that
brute who appeared to believe that he had served and
performed his appointed end by yelling of blood and
pistols in the street before my house, who seemed to
believe that what further information he might have
given me was too scant or too bland and free of moment
to warrant the discarding of his tobacco cud, because
during the entire subsequent twelve miles he could not
even tell me what had happened.*

*And how I traversed those same twelve miles once
more after the two years since Ellen died (or was it the
four years since Henry vanished or was it the nineteen
years since I saw light and breathed?) knowing nothing,
able to learn nothing save this: a shot heard, faint and
far away and even direction and source indeterminate,
by two women, two young women alone in a rotting
house where no man's footstep had sounded in two years
—a shot, then an interval of aghast surmise above the
cloth and needles which engaged them, then feet, in the
hall and then on the stairs, running, hurrying, the feet
of a man: and Judith with just time to snatch up the
unfinished dress and hold it before her as the door burst
open upon her brother, the wild murderer whom she had
not seen in four years and whom she believed to be (if
he was, still lived and breathed at all) a thousand miles
away: and then the two of them, the two accursed chil-*

dren on whom the first blow of their devil's heritage had but that moment fallen, looking at one another across the up-raised and unfinished wedding dress. Twelve miles toward that I rode, beside an animal who could stand in the street before my house and bellow placidly to the populous and listening solitude that my nephew had just murdered his sister's fiancé, yet who could not permit himself to force the mule which drew us beyond a walk because 'hit warn't none of mine nor hisn neither and besides hit aint had a decent bait of vittles since the corn give out in February'; who, turning into the actual gate at last, must stop the mule and, pointing with the whip and spitting first, say 'Hit was right yonder.'— 'What was right there, fool?' I cried, and he: 'Hit was' until I took the whip from him into my own hand and struck the mule.

But they cannot tell you how I went on up the drive, past Ellen's ruined and weed-choked flower beds and reached the house, the shell, the (so I thought) cocoon-casket marriage-bed of youth and grief and found that I had come, not too late as I had thought, but come too soon. Rotting portico and scaling walls, it stood, not ravaged, not invaded, marked by no bullet nor soldier's iron heel but rather as though reserved for something more: some desolation more profound than ruin, as if it had stood in iron juxtaposition to iron flame, to a holocaust which had found itself less fierce and less implacable, not hurled but rather fallen back before the impervious and indomitable skeleton which the flames durst not, at the instant's final crisis, assail; there was even one step, one plank rotted free and tilting beneath

*the foot (or would have if I had not touched it light and
fast) as I ran up and into the hallway whose carpet had
long since gone with the bed- and table-linen for lint,
and saw the Sutpen face and even as I cried 'Henry!
Henry! What have you done? What has that fool been
trying to tell me?' realised that I had come, not too late
as I had thought, but come too soon. Because it was not
Henry's face. It was Sutpen face enough, but not his;
Sutpen coffee-colored face enough there in the dim light,
barring the stairs: and I running out of the bright
afternoon, into the thunderous silence of that brooding
house where I could see nothing at first: then gradually
the face, the Sutpen face not approaching, not swim-
ming up out of the gloom, but already there, rocklike
and firm and antedating time and house and doom and
all, waiting there (oh yes, he chose well; he bettered
choosing, who created in his own image the cold Cer-
berus of his private hell)—the face without sex or age
because it had never possessed either: the same sphinx
face which she had been born with, which had looked
down from the loft that night beside Judith's and which
she still wears now at seventy-four, looking at me with
no change, no alteration in it at all, as though it had
known to the second when I was to enter, had waited
there during that entire twelve miles behind that walking mule and watched me draw nearer and nearer and
enter the door at last as it had known (ay, perhaps
decreed, since there is that justice whose Moloch's palate-
paunch makes no distinction between gristle bone and
tender flesh) that I should—the face stopping me dead
(not my body: it still advanced, ran on: but I, myself,*

that deep existence which we lead, to which the movement of limbs is but a clumsy and belated accompaniment like so many unnecessary instruments played crudely and amateurishly out of time to the tune itself) in that barren hall with its naked stair (that carpet gone too) rising into the dim upper hallway where an echo spoke which was not mine but rather that of the lost irrevocable might-have-been which haunts all houses, all enclosed walls erected by human hands, not for shelter, not for warmth, but to hide from the world's curious looking and seeing the dark turnings which the ancient young delusions of pride and hope and ambition (ay, and love too) take. 'Judith!' I said. 'Judith!'

There was no answer. I had expected none; possibly even then I did not expect Judith to answer, just as a child, before the full instant of comprehended terror, calls on the parent whom it actually knows (this before the terror destroys all judgment whatever) is not even there to hear it. I was crying not to someone, something, but (trying to cry) through something, through that force, that furious yet absolutely rocklike and immobile antagonism which had stopped me—that presence, that familiar coffee-colored face, that body (the bare coffee-colored feet motionless on the bare floor, the curve of the stair rising just beyond her) no larger than my own which, without moving, with no alteration of visual displacement whatever (she did not even remove her gaze from mine for the reason that she was not looking at me but through me, apparently still musing upon the open door's serene rectangle which I had broken) seemed to elongate and project upward something—not soul,

*not spirit, but something rather of a profoundly atten-
tive and distracted listening to or for something which
I myself could not hear and was not intended to hear
—a brooding awareness and acceptance of the inexplicable unseen inherited from an older and a purer race
than mine, which created postulated and shaped in the
empty air between us that which I believed I had come
to find (nay, which I must find, else breathing and
standing there, I would have denied that I was ever
born):—that bedroom long-closed and musty, that
sheetless bed (that nuptial couch of love and grief) with
the pale and bloody corpse in its patched and weathered
gray crimsoning the bare mattress, the bowed and un-
wived widow kneeling beside it—and I (my body) not
stopping yet (yes, it needed the hand, the touch, for
that);—I, self-mesmered fool who still believed that
what must be would be, could not but be, else I must
deny sanity as well as breath, running, hurling myself
into that inscrutable coffee-colored face, that cold implacable mindless (no, not mindless: anything but
mindless: his own clairvoyant will tempered to amoral
evil's undeviating absolute by the black willing blood
with which he had crossed it) replica of his own which
he had created and decreed to preside upon his absence,
as you might watch a wild distracted nightbound bird
flutter into the brazen and fatal lamp. 'Wait,' she said.
'Dont you go up there.' Still I did not stop; it would
require the hand; and I still running on, accomplishing
those last few feet across which we seemed to glare at one
another not as two faces but as the two abstract contra-
dictions which we actually were, neither of our voices*

raised, as though we spoke to one another free of the limitations and restrictions of speech and hearing. 'What?' I said.

'Dont you go up there, Rosa.' That was how she said it: that quiet, that still, and again it was as though it had not been she who spoke but the house itself that said the words—the house which he had built, which some suppuration of himself had created about him as the sweat of his body might have created, produced some (even if invisible) cocoon-like and complementary shell in which Ellen had had to live and die a stranger, in which Henry and Judith would have to be victims and prisoners, or die. Because it was not the name, the word, the fact that she had called me Rosa. As children she had called me that, just as she had called them Henry and Judith; I knew that even now she still called Judith (and Henry too when she spoke of him) by her given name. And she might very naturally have called me Rosa still, since to everyone else whom I knew I was still a child. But it was not that. That was not what she meant at all; in fact, during that instant while we stood face to face (that instant before my still advancing body should brush past her and reach the stair) she did me more grace and respect than anyone else I knew; I knew that from the instant I had entered that door, to her of all who knew me I was no child. 'Rosa?' I cried. 'To me? To my face?' Then she touched me, and then I did stop dead. Possibly even then my body did not stop, since I seemed to be aware of it thrusting blindly still against the solid yet imponderable weight (she not owner: instrument; I still say that) of that will to bar me from the stairs;

possibly the sound of the other voice, the single word
spoken from the stair-head above us, had already broken
and parted us before it (my body) had even paused. I
do not know. I know only that my entire being seemed
to run at blind full tilt into something monstrous and
immobile, with a shocking impact too soon and too
quick to be mere amazement and outrage at that black
arresting and untimorous hand on my white woman's
flesh. Because there is something in the touch of flesh
with flesh which abrogates, cuts sharp and straight
across the devious intricate channels of decorous ordering, which enemies as well as lovers know because it
makes them both:—touch and touch of that which is the
citadel of the central I-Am's private own: not spirit,
soul; the liquorish and ungirdled mind is anyone's to
take in any darkened hallway of this earthly tenement.
But let flesh touch with flesh, and watch the fall of all
the eggshell shibboleth of caste and color too. Yes, I
stopped dead—no woman's hand, no negro's hand, but
bitted bridle-curb to check and guide the furious and
unbending will—I crying not to her, to it; speaking to
it through the negro, the woman, only because of the
shock which was not yet outrage because it would be
terror soon, expecting and receiving no answer because
we both knew it was not to her I spoke: 'Take your hand
off me, nigger!'

I got none. We just stood there—I motionless in the
attitude and action of running, she rigid in that furious
immobility, the two of us joined by that hand and arm
which held us, like a fierce rigid umbilical cord, twin
sistered to the fell darkness which had produced her. As

a child I had more than once watched her and Judith and even Henry scuffling in the rough games which they (possibly all children; I do not know) played, and (so I have heard) she and Judith even slept together, in the same room but with Judith in the bed and she on a pallet on the floor ostensibly. But I have heard how on more than one occasion Ellen has found them both on the pallet, and once in the bed together. But not I. Even as a child, I would not even play with the same objects which she and Judith played with, as though that warped and spartan solitude which I called my childhood, which had taught me (and little else) to listen before I could comprehend and to understand before I even heard, had also taught me not only to instinctively fear her and what she was, but to shun the very objects which she had touched. We stood there so. And then suddenly it was not outrage that I waited for, out of which I had instinctively cried; it was not terror: it was some cumulative over-reach of despair itself. I remember how as we stood there joined by that volitionless (yes: it too sentient victim just as she and I were) hand, I cried—perhaps not aloud, not with words (and not to Judith, mind: perhaps I knew already, on the instant I entered the house and saw that face which was at once both more and less than Sutpen, perhaps I knew even then what I could not, would not, must not believe)— I cried 'And you too? And you too, sister, sister?' What did I expect? I, self-mesmered fool, come twelve miles expecting—what? Henry perhaps, to emerge from some door which knew his touch, his hand on the knob, the weight of his foot on a sill which knew that weight: and so to find standing in the hall a small plain frightened creature whom neither man nor woman had ever looked at twice, whom he had not seen himself in four years and seldom enough before that but whom he would recognise if only because of the worn brown silk which had once become his mother and because the creature stood there calling him by his given name? Henry to emerge and say 'Why, it's Rosa, Aunt Rosa. Wake up, Aunt Rosa; wake up'?—I, the dreamer clinging yet to the dream as the patient clings to the last thin unbearable ecstatic instant of agony in order to sharpen the savor of the pain's surcease, waking into the reality, the more than reality, not to the unchanged and unaltered old time but into a time altered to fit the dream which, conjunctive with the dreamer, becomes immolated and apotheosized: 'Mother and Judith are in the nursery with the children, and Father and Charles are walking in the garden. Wake up, Aunt Rosa; wake up'? Or not expect perhaps, not even hope; not even dream since dreams dont come in pairs, and had I not come twelve miles drawn not by mortal mule but by some chimaera-foal of nightmare's very self? (Ay, wake up, Rosa; wake up—not from what was, what used to be, but from what had not, could not have ever, been; wake, Rosa—not to what should, what might have been, but to what cannot, what must not, be; wake, Rosa, from the hoping, who did believe there is a seemliness to bereavement even though grief be absent; believed there would be need for you to save not love perhaps, not happiness nor peace, but what was left behind by widowing—and found that there was nothing there to save; who hoped to save her as you

*promised Ellen (not Charles Bon, not Henry: not either
one of these from him or even from one another) and
now too late, who would have been too late if you had
come there from the womb or had been there already at
the full strong capable mortal peak when she was born;
who came twelve miles and nineteen years to save what
did not need the saving, and lost instead yourself) I do
not know, except that I did not find it. I found only that
dream-state in which you run without moving from a
terror in which you can not believe, toward a safety in
which you have no faith, held so not by the shifting and
foundationless quicksand of nightmare but by a face
which was its soul's own inquisitor, a hand which was
the agent of its own crucifixion, until the voice parted
us, broke the spell. It said one word: 'Clytie.' like that,
that cold, that still: not Judith, but the house itself
speaking again, though it was Judith's voice. Oh, I
knew it well, who had believed in grieving's seemliness;
I knew it as well as she—Clytie—knew it. She did not
move; it was only the hand, the hand gone before I
realised that it had been removed. I do not know if she
removed it or if I ran out from beneath its touch. But
it was gone; and this too they cannot tell you: How I
ran, fled, up the stairs and found no grieving widowed
bride but Judith standing before the closed door to that
chamber, in the gingham dress which she had worn each
time I had seen her since Ellen died, holding something
in one hanging hand; and if there had been grief or
anguish she had put them too away, complete or not
complete I do not know, along with that unfinished
wedding dress. 'Yes, Rosa?' she said, like that again, and*

*I stopped in running's midstride again though my body,
blind unsentient barrow of deluded clay and breath,
still advanced: And how I saw that what she held in that
lax and negligent hand was the photograph, the picture
of herself in its metal case which she had given him, held
casual and forgotten against her flank as any interrupted pastime book.*

*That's what I found. Perhaps it's what I expected,
knew (even at nineteen knew, I would say if it were not
for my nineteen, my own particular kind of nineteen
years) that I should find. Perhaps I couldn't even have
wanted more than that, couldn't have accepted less, who
even at nineteen must have known that living is one
constant and perpetual instant when the arras-veil before what-is-to-be hangs docile and even glad to the
lightest naked thrust if we had dared, were brave
enough (not wise enough: no wisdom needed here) to
make the rending gash. Or perhaps it is no lack of
courage either: not cowardice which will not face that
sickness somewhere at the prime foundation of this factual scheme from which the prisoner soul, miasmal-
distillant, wroils ever upward sunward, tugs its
tenuous prisoner arteries and veins and prisoning in its
turn that spark, that dream which, as the globy and
complete instant of its freedom mirrors and repeats
(repeats? creates, reduces to a fragile evanescent iridescent sphere) all of space and time and massy earth,
relicts the seething and anonymous miasmal mass which
in all the years of time has taught itself no boon of death
but only how to recreate, renew; and dies, is gone,
vanished: nothing—but is that true wisdom which can*

comprehend that there is a might-have-been which is more true than truth, from which the dreamer, waking, says not 'Did I but dream?' but rather says, indicts high heaven's very self with: 'Why did I wake since waking I shall never sleep again?'

Once there was—Do you mark how the wistaria, sun-impacted on this wall here, distills and penetrates this room as though (light-unimpeded) by secret and attritive progress from mote to mote of obscurity's myriad components? That is the substance of remembering—sense, sight, smell: the muscles with which we see and hear and feel—not mind, not thought: there is no such thing as memory: the brain recalls just what the muscles grope for: no more, no less: and its resultant sum is usually incorrect and false and worthy only of the name of dream.—See how the sleeping outflung hand, touching the bedside candle, remembers pain, springs back and free while mind and brain sleep on and only make of this adjacent heat some trashy myth of reality's escape: or that same sleeping hand, in sensuous marriage with some dulcet surface, is transformed by that same sleeping brain and mind into that same figment-stuff warped out of all experience. Ay, grief goes, fades; we know that—but ask the tear ducts if they have forgotten how to weep.—Once there was (they cannot have told you this either) a summer of wistaria. It was a pervading everywhere of wistaria (I was fourteen then) as though of all springs yet to capitulate condensed into one spring, one summer: the spring and summertime which is every female's who breathed above dust, beholden of all betrayed springs held over from all irrevo-

cable time, repercussed, bloomed again. It was a vintage
year of wistaria: vintage year being that sweet conjunction of root bloom and urge and hour and weather; and
I (I was fourteen)—I will not insist on bloom, at whom
no man had yet to look—nor would ever—twice, as not
as child but less than even child; as not more child than
woman but even as less than any female flesh. Nor do
I say leaf—warped bitter pale and crimped half-fledg-
ing intimidate of any claim to green which might have
drawn to it the tender mayfly childhood sweetheart
games or given pause to the male predacious wasps and
bees of later lust. But root and urge I do insist and
claim, for had I not heired too from all the unsistered
Eves since the Snake? Yes, urge I do: warped chrysalis
of what blind perfect seed: for who shall say what
gnarled forgotten root might not bloom yet with some
globed concentrate more globed and concentrate and
heady-perfect because the neglected root was planted
warped and lay not dead but merely slept forgot?

That was the miscast summer of my barren youth
which (for that short time, that short brief unreturning
springtime of the female heart) I lived out not as a
woman, a girl, but rather as the man which I perhaps
should have been. I was fourteen then, fourteen in years
if they could have been called years while in that un-
paced corridor which I called childhood, which was not
living but rather some projection of the lightless womb
itself; I gestate and complete, not aged, just overdue
because of some caesarean lack, some cold head-nuzzling
forceps of the savage time which should have torn me
free, I waited not for light but for that doom which we

*call female victory which is: endure and then endure,
without rhyme or reason or hope of reward—and then
endure; I like that blind subterranean fish, that insulated spark whose origin the fish no longer remembers,
which pulses and beats at its crepuscular and lethargic
tenement with the old unsleeping itch which has no
words to speak with other than 'This was called light',
that 'smell', that 'touch', that other something which has
bequeathed not even name for sound of bee or bird or
flower's scent or light or sun or love;—yes, not even
growing and developing, beloved by and loving light,
but equipped only with that cunning, that inverted
canker-growth of solitude which substitutes the omnivorous and unrational hearing-sense for all the others: so
that instead of accomplishing the processional and measured milestones of the normal childhood's time I lurked,
unapprehended as though, shod with the very damp and
velvet silence of the womb, I displaced no air, gave off
no betraying sound, from one closed forbidden door to
the next and so acquired all I knew of that light and
space in which people moved and breathed as I (that
same child) might have gained conception of the sun
from seeing it through a piece of smoky glass;—fourteen, four years younger than Judith, four years later
than Judith's moment which only virgins know: when
the entire delicate spirit's bent is one anonymous cli-
maxless epicene and unravished nuptial—not that widowed and nightly violation by the inescapable and
scornful dead which is the meed of twenty and thirty
and forty, but a world filled with living marriage like
the light and air which she breathes. But it was no*

summer of a virgin's itching discontent; no summer's caesarean lack which should have torn me, dead flesh or even embryo, from the living: or else, by friction's ravishing of the male-furrowed meat, also weaponed and panoplied as a man instead of hollow woman.

It was the summer after that first Christmas that Henry brought him home, the summer following the two days of that June vacation which he spent at Sutpen's Hundred before he rode on to the River to take the steamboat home, that summer after my aunt left and papa had to go away on business and I was sent out to Ellen (possibly my father chose Ellen as a refuge for me because at that time Thomas Sutpen was also absent) to stay so that she could take care of me, who had been born too late, born into some curious disjoint of my father's life and left on his (now twice) widowed hands, I competent enough to reach a kitchen shelf, count spoons and hem a sheet and measure milk into a churn yet good for nothing else, yet still too valuable to be left alone. I had never seen him (I never saw him. I never even saw him dead. I heard a name, I saw a photograph, I helped to make a grave: and that was all) though he had been in my house once, that first New Year's Day when Henry brought him from nephew duty to speak to me on their way back to school and I was not at home. Until then I had not even heard his name, did not know that he existed. Yet on the day when I went out there to stay that summer, it was as though that casual pause at my door had left some seed, some minute virulence in this cellar earth of mine quick not for love perhaps (I did not love him; how could I? I had never even heard *his voice, had only Ellen's word for it that there was such a person) and quick not for the spying which you will doubtless call it, which during the past six months between that New Year's and that June gave substance to that shadow with a name emerging from Ellen's vain and garrulous folly, that shape without even a face yet because I had not even seen the photograph then, reflected in the secret and bemused gaze of a young girl: because I who had learned nothing of love, not even parents' love—that fond dear constant violation of privacy, that stultification of the burgeoning and incorrigible I which is the meed and due of all mammalian meat, became not mistress, not beloved, but more than even love; I became all polymath love's androgynous advocate.*

There must have been some seed he left, to cause a child's vacant fairy-tale to come alive in that garden. Because I was not spying when I would follow her. I was not spying, though you will say I was. And even if it was spying, it was not jealousy, because I did not love him. (How could I have, when I had never seen him?) And even if I did, not as women love, as Judith loved him, or as we thought she did. If it was love (and I still say, How could it be?) it was the way that mothers love when, punishing the child she strikes not it but through it strikes the neighbor boy whom it has just whipped or been whipped by; caresses not the rewarded child but rather the nameless man or woman who gave the palm-sweated penny. But not as women love. Because I asked nothing of him, you see. And more than that: I gave him nothing, which is the sum of

loving. Why, I didn't even miss him. I dont know even
now if I was ever aware that I had seen nothing of his
face but that photograph, that shadow, that picture in
a young girl's bedroom: a picture casual and framed
upon a littered dressing table yet bowered and dressed
(or so I thought) with all the maiden and invisible
lily-roses, because even before I saw the photograph I
could have recognised, nay, described, the very face. But
I never saw it. I do not even know of my own knowledge that Ellen ever saw it, that Judith ever loved it,
that Henry slew it: so who will dispute me when I say,
Why did I not invent, create it?—And I know this: if
I were God I would invent out of this seething turmoil
we call progress something (a machine perhaps) which
would adorn the barren mirror altars of every plain girl
who breathes with such as this—which is so little since
we want so little—this pictured face. It would not even
need a skull behind it; almost anonymous, it would only
need vague inference of some walking flesh and blood
desired by someone else even if only in some shadow-
realm of make-believe.—A picture seen by stealth, by
creeping (my childhood taught me that instead of love
and it stood me in good stead; in fact, if it had taught
me love, love could not have stood me so) into the
deserted midday room to look at it. Not to dream, since
I dwelt in the dream, but to renew, rehearse, the part
as the faulty though eager amateur might steal wing-
ward in some interim of the visible scene to hear the
prompter's momentary voice. And if jealousy, not
man's jealousy, the jealousy of the lover; not even the
lover's self who spies from love, who spies to watch,

taste, touch that maiden revery of solitude which is the first thinning of that veil we call virginity; not to spring out, force that shame which is such a part of love's declaring, but to gloat upon the rich instantaneous bosom already rosy with the flushy sleep though shame itself does not yet need to wake. No, it was not that; I was not spying, who would walk those raked and sanded garden paths and think 'This print was his save for this obliterating rake, that even despite the rake it is still there and hers beside it in that slow and mutual rhythm wherein the heart, the mind, does not need to watch the docile (ay, the willing) feet'; would think 'What suspiration of the twinning souls have the murmurous myriad ears of this secluded vine or shrub listened to? what vow, what promise, what rapt biding fire has the lilac rain of this wistaria, this heavy rose's dissolution, crowned?' But best of all, better far than this, the actual living and the dreamy flesh itself. Oh no, I was not spying while I dreamed in the lurking harborage of my own shrub or vine as I believed she dreamed upon the nooky seat which held invisible imprint of his absent thighs just as the obliterating sand, the million finger-nerves of frond and leaf, the very sun and moony constellations which had looked down at him, the circumambient air, held somewhere yet his foot, his passing shape, his face, his speaking voice, his name: Charles Bon, Charles Good, Charles Husband-soon-to-be. No, not spying, not even hiding, who was child enough not to need to hide, whose presence would have been no violation even though he sat with her, yet woman enough to have gone to her entitled to be received (perhaps with pleasure, gratitude) into that maiden shameless confidence where young girls talk of love— Yes, child enough to go to her and say 'Let me sleep with you'; woman enough to say 'Let us lie in bed together while you tell me what love is', yet who did not do it because I should have had to say 'Dont talk to me of love but let me tell you, who know already more of love than you will ever know or need.' Then my father returned and came for me and took me home and I became again that nondescript too long a child yet too short a woman, in the fitless garments which my aunt had left behind, keeping a fitless house, who was not spying, hiding, but waiting, watching, for no reward, no thanks, who did not love him in the sense we mean it because there is no love of that sort without hope; who (if it were love) loved with that sort beyond the compass of glib books: that love which gives up what it never had—that penny's modicum which is the donor's all yet whose infinitesimal weight adds nothing to the substance of the loved—and yet I gave it. And not to him, to her; it was as though I said to her, 'Here, take this too. You cannot love him as he should be loved, and though he will no more feel this giving's weight than he would ever know its lack, yet there may come some moment in your married lives when he will find this atom's particle as you might find a cramped small pallid hidden shoot in a familiar flower bed and pause and say, "Where did this come from?"; you need only answer, "I dont know." ' And then I went back home and stayed five years, heard an echoed shot, ran up a nightmare flight of stairs, and found—

Why, a woman standing calmly in a gingham dress before a closed door which she would not allow me to enter—a woman more strange to me than to any grief for being so less its partner—a woman saying 'Yes, Rosa?' calmly into the midstride of my running which (I know it now) had begun five years ago, since he had been in my house too and had left no more trace than he had left in Ellen's, where he had been but a shape, a shadow: not of a man, a being, but of some esoteric piece of furniture—vase or chair or desk—which Ellen wanted, as though his very impression (or lack of it) on Coldfield or Sutpen walls held portentous prophecy of what was to be;—Yes, running out of that first year (that year before the War) during which Ellen talked to me of trousseau (and it my trousseau), of all the dreamy panoply of surrender which was my surrender, who had so little to surrender that it was all I had because there is that might-have-been which is the single rock we cling to above the maelstrom of unbearable reality;—the four years while I believed she waited as I waited, while the stable world we had been taught to know dissolved in fire and smoke until peace and security were gone, and pride and hope, and there was left only maimed honor's veterans, and love. Yes, there should, there must, be love and faith: these left with us by fathers, husbands, sweethearts, brothers, who carried the pride and the hope of peace in honor's vanguard as they did the flags; there must be these, else what do men fight for? what else worth dying for? Yes, dying not for honor's empty sake, nor pride nor even peace, but for that love and faith they left behind. Because he was to die; I know that, knew that, as both pride and peace were: else how to prove love's immortality? But not love, not faith itself, themselves. Love without hope perhaps, faith with little to be proud with: but love and faith at least above the murdering and the folly, to salvage at least from the humbled indicted dust something anyway of the old lost enchantment of the heart. —Yes, found her standing before that closed door which I was not to enter (and which she herself did not enter again to my knowledge until Jones and the other man carried the coffin up the stairs) with the photograph hanging at her side and her face absolutely calm, looking at me for a moment and just raising her voice enough to be heard in the hall below: 'Clytie. Miss Rosa will be here for dinner; you had better get out some more meal': then 'Shall we go down stairs? I will have to speak to Mr Jones about some planks and nails.'

That was all. Or rather, not all, since there is no all, no finish; it not the blow we suffer from but the tedious repercussive anti-climax of it, the rubbishy aftermath to clear away from off the very threshold of despair. You see, I never saw him. I never even saw him dead. I heard an echo, but not the shot; I saw a closed door but did not enter it: I remember how that afternoon when we carried the coffin from the house (Jones and another white man which he produced, exhumed, from somewhere made it of boards torn from the carriage house; I remember how while we ate the food which Judith— yes, Judith: the same face calm cold and tranquil above the stove—had cooked, ate it in the very room which he lay over, we could hear them hammering and sawing in the back yard, and how I saw Judith once, in a faded gingham sunbonnet to match the dress, giving them directions about making it; I remember how during all that slow and sunny afternoon they hammered and sawed right under the back parlor window—the slow, maddening rasp. rasp. rasp. of the saw, the flat deliberate hammer blows that seemed as though each would be the last but was not, repeated and resumed just when the dulled attenuation of the wearied nerves, stretched beyond all resiliency, relaxed to silence and then had to scream again: until at last I went out there (and saw Judith in the barnlot in a cloud of chickens, her apron cradled about the gathered eggs) and asked them why? why there? why must it be just there? and they both stopped long and more than long enough for Jones to turn and spit again and say, 'Because hit wouldn't be so fur to tote the box': and how before my very back was turned he—one of them—added further, out of some amazed and fumbling ratiocination of inertia, how 'Hit would be simpler yit to fetch him down and nail the planks around him, only maybe Missus Judy wouldn't like hit.')—I remember how as we carried him down the stairs and out to the waiting wagon I tried to take the full weight of the coffin to prove to myself that he was really in it. And I could not tell. I was one of his pall bearers, yet I could not, would not believe something which I knew could not but be so. Because I never saw him. You see? There are some things which happen to us which the intelligence and the senses refuse just as the stomach sometimes refuses what the palate has accepted but which digestion cannot compass—

occurrences which stop us dead as though by some impalpable intervention, like a sheet of glass through which we watch all subsequent events transpire as though in a soundless vacuum, and fade, vanish; are gone, leaving us immobile, impotent, helpless; fixed, until we can die. That was I. I was there; something of me walked in measured cadence with the measured tread of Jones and his companion, and Theophilus McCaslin who had heard the news somehow back in town, and Clytie as we bore the awkward and unmanageable box past the stair's close turning while Judith, following, steadied it from behind, and so down and out to the wagon; something of me helped to raise that which it could not have raised alone yet which it still could not believe, into the waiting wagon; something of me stood beside the gashy earth in the cedars' somber gloom and heard the clumsy knell of clods upon the wood and answered No when Judith at the grave's mounded end said, 'He was a Catholic. Do any of you all know how Catholics——' and Theophilus McCaslin said, 'Catholic be damned; he was a soldier. And I can pray for any Confedrit soldier' and then cried in his old man's shrill harsh loud cacophonous voice: 'Yaaaay, Forrest! Yaaaay, John Sartoris! Yaaaaaay!' And something walked with Judith and Clytie back across that sunset field and answered in some curious serene suspension to the serene quiet voice which talked of plowing corn and cutting winter wood, and in the lamplit kitchen helped this time to cook the meal and helped to eat it too within the room beyond whose ceiling he no longer lay, and went to bed (yes, took a candle from that firm untrembling hand and

*thought 'She did not even weep' and then in a lamp-
gloomed mirror saw my own face and thought 'Nor did
you either') within that house where he had sojourned
for another brief (and this time final) space and left no
trace of him, not even tears. Yes. One day he was not.
Then he was. Then he was not. It was too short, too fast,
too quick; six hours of a summer afternoon saw it all
—a space too short to leave even the imprint of a body
on a mattress, and blood can come from anywhere—if
there was blood, since I never saw him. For all I was
allowed to know, we had no corpse; we even had no
murderer (we did not even speak of Henry that day, not
one of us; I did not say—the aunt, the spinster—'Did
he look well or ill?' I did not say one of the thousand
trivial things with which the indomitable woman-blood
ignores the man's world in which the blood kinsman
shows the courage or cowardice, the folly or lust or fear,
for which his fellows praise or crucify him) who came
and crashed a door and cried his crime and vanished,
who for the fact that he was still alive was just that
much more shadowy than the abstraction which we had
nailed into a box—a shot heard only by its echo, a
strange gaunt half-wild horse, bridled and with empty
saddle, the saddle bags containing a pistol, a worn clean
shirt, a lump of iron-like bread, captured by a man four
miles away and two days later while trying to force the
crib door in his stable. Yes, more than that: he was
absent, and he was; he returned, and he was not; three
women put something into the earth and covered it, and
he had never been.*

Now you will ask me why I stayed there. I could say,

I do not know, could give ten thousand paltry reasons, all untrue, and be believed:—that I stayed for food, who could have combed ditch-banks and weed-beds, made and worked a garden as well at my own home in town as here, not to speak of neighbors, friends whose alms I might have accepted, since necessity has a way of obliterating from our conduct various delicate scruples regarding honor and pride; that I stayed for shelter, who had a roof of my own in fee simple now indeed; or that I stayed for company, who at home could have had the company of neighbors who were at least of my own kind, who had known me all my life and even longer in the sense that they thought not only as I thought but as my forbears thought, while here I had for company one woman whom, for all she was blood kin to me, I did not understand and, if what my observation warranted me to believe was true, I did not wish to understand, and another who was so foreign to me and to all that I was that we might have been not only of different races (which we were), not only of different sexes (which we were not), but of different species, speaking no language which the other understood, the very simple words with which we were forced to adjust our days to one another being even less inferential of thought or intention than the sounds which a beast and a bird might make to each other. But I dont say any of these. I stayed there and waited for Thomas Sutpen to come home. Yes. You will say (or believe) that I waited even then to become engaged to him; if I said I did not, you would believe I lied. But I do say I did not. I waited for him exactly as Judith and Clytie waited for him: because now he was all we had, all that gave us any reason for continuing to exist, to eat food and sleep and wake and rise again: knowing that he would need us, knowing as we did (who knew him) that he would begin at once to salvage what was left of Sutpen's Hundred and restore it. Not that we would or did need him. (I had never for one instant thought of marriage, never for one instant imagined that he would look at me, see me, since he never had. You may believe me, because I shall make no bones to say so when the moment comes to tell you when I did think of it.) No. It did not even require the first day of the life we were to lead together to show us that we did not need him, had not the need for any man so long as Wash Jones lived or stayed there—I who had kept my father's house and he alive for almost four years, Judith who had done the same out here, and Clytie who could cut a cord of wood or run a furrow better (or at least quicker) than Jones himself.—And this the sad fact, one of the saddest: that weary tedium which the heart and spirit feel when they no longer need that to whose need they (the spirit and the heart) are necessary. No. We did not need him, not even vicariously, who could not even join him in his furious (that almost mad intention which he brought home with him, seemed to project, radiate ahead of him before he even dismounted) desire to restore the place to what it had been that he had sacrificed pity and gentleness and love and all the soft virtues for—if he had ever had them to sacrifice, felt their lack, desired them of others. Not even that. Neither Judith nor I wanted that. Perhaps it was because we did not believe it could be done, but I think it was more than that: that we now existed in an apathy which was almost peace, like that of the blind unsentient earth itself which dreams after no flower's stalk nor bud, envies not the airy musical solitude of the springing leaves it nourishes.

So we waited for him. We led the busy eventless lives of three nuns in a barren and poverty-stricken convent: the walls we had were safe, impervious enough, even if it did not matter to the walls whether we ate or not. And amicably, not as two white women and a negress, not as three negroes or three whites, not even as three women, but merely as three creatures who still possessed the need to eat but took no pleasure in it, the need to sleep but from no joy in weariness or regeneration, and in whom sex was some forgotten atrophy like the rudimentary gills we call the tonsils or the still-opposable thumbs for old climbing. We kept the house, what part of it we lived in, used; we kept the room which Thomas Sutpen would return to—not that one which he left, a husband, but the one to which he should return a sonless widower, barren of that posterity which he doubtless must have wanted who had gone to the trouble and expense of getting children and housing them among imported furniture beneath crystal chandeliers—just as we kept Henry's room, as Judith and Clytie kept it that is, as if he had not run up the stairs that summer afternoon and then run down again; we grew and tended and harvested with our own hands the food we ate, made and worked that garden just as we cooked and ate the food which came out of it: with no distinction among the three of us of age or color but just as to who *could build this fire or stir this pot or weed this bed or carry this apron full of corn to the mill for meal with least cost to the general good in time or expense of other duties. It was as though we were one being, interchangeable and indiscriminate, which kept that garden growing, spun thread and wove the cloth we wore, hunted and found and rendered the meagre ditch-side herbs to protect and guarantee what spartan compromise we dared or had the time to make with illness, harried and nagged that Jones into working the corn and cutting the wood which was to be our winter's warmth and sustenance;—the three of us, three women: I drafted by circumstance at too soon an age into a pinch-penny housewifery which might have existed just as well upon a lighthouse rock, which had not even taught me how to cultivate a bed of flowers, let alone a kitchen garden, which had taught me to look upon fuel and meat as something appearing by its own volition in a woodbox or on a pantry shelf; Judith created by circumstance (circumstance? a hundred years of careful nurturing, perhaps not by blood, not even Coldfield blood, but certainly by the tradition in which Thomas Sutpen's ruthless will had carved a niche) to pass through the soft insulated and unscathed cocoon stages: bud, served prolific queen, then potent and soft-handed matriarch of old age's serene and well-lived content—Judith handicapped by what in me was a few years' ignorance but which in her was ten generations of iron prohibition, who had not learned that first principle of penury which is to scrimp and save for the sake of scrimping and saving, who (and abetted by Clytie) would cook twice*

*what we could eat and three times what we could afford
and give it to anyone, any stranger in a land already
beginning to fill with straggling soldiers who stopped
and asked for it; and (but not least) Clytie. Clytie, not
inept, anything but inept: perverse inscrutable and paradox: free, yet incapable of freedom who had never once
called herself a slave, holding fidelity to none like the
indolent and solitary wolf or bear (yes, wild: half untamed black, half Sutpen blood: and if 'untamed' be
synonymous with 'wild', then 'Sutpen' is the silent unsleeping viciousness of the tamer's lash) whose false
seeming holds it docile to fear's hand but which is not,
which if this be fidelity, fidelity only to the prime fixed
principle of its own savageness;—Clytie who in the very
pigmentation of her flesh represented that debacle which
had brought Judith and me to what we were and which
had made of her (Clytie) that which she declined to be
just as she had declined to be that from which its purpose
had been to emancipate her, as though presiding aloof
upon the new, she deliberately remained to represent to
us the threatful portent of the old.*

*We were three strangers. I do not know what Clytie
thought, what life she led which the food we raised and
cooked in unison, the cloth we spun and wove together,
nourished and sheltered. But I expected that because she
and I were open, ay honorable, enemies. But I did not
even know what Judith thought and felt. We slept in
the same room, the three of us (this for more than to
conserve the firewood which we had to carry in ourselves. We did it for safety. It was winter soon and
already soldiers were beginning to come back—the*

*stragglers, not all of them tramps, ruffians, but men
who had risked and lost everything, suffered beyond
endurance and had returned now to a ruined land, not
the same men who had marched away but transformed
—and this the worst, the ultimate degradation to which
war brings the spirit, the soul—into the likeness of that
man who abuses from very despair and pity the beloved
wife or mistress who in his absence has been raped. We
were afraid. We fed them; we gave them what and all
we had and we would have assumed their wounds and
left them whole again if we could. But we were afraid
of them.), we waked and fulfilled the endless tedious
obligations which the sheer holding to life and breath
entailed; we would sit before the fire after supper, the
three of us in that state where the very bones and muscles
are too tired to rest, when the attenuated and invincible
spirit has changed and shaped even hopelessness into the
easy obliviousness of a worn garment, and talk, talk of
a hundred things—the weary recurrent triviata of our
daily lives, of a thousand things but not of one. We
talked of him, Thomas Sutpen, of the end of the War
(we could all see it now) and when he would return, of
what he would do: how begin the Herculean task which
we knew he would set himself, into which (oh yes, we
knew this too) he would undoubtedly sweep us with the
old ruthlessness whether we would or no; we talked of
Henry, quietly—that normal useless impotent woman-
worrying about the absent male—as to how he fared, if
he were cold or hungry or not, just as we talked of his
father, as if both they and we still lived in that time
which that shot, those running mad feet, had put a*

*period to and then obliterated, as though that afternoon
had never been. But not once did we mention Charles
Bon. There were two afternoons in the late fall when
Judith was absent, returning at supper time serene and
calm. I did not ask and I did not follow her, yet I knew
and I knew that Clytie knew that she had gone to clear
that grave of dead leaves and the sere brown refuse of
the cedars—that mound vanishing slowly back into the
earth, beneath which we had buried nothing. No, there
had been no shot. That sound was merely the sharp and
final clap-to of a door between us and all that was, all
that might have been—a retroactive severance of the
stream of event: a forever crystallised instant in imponderable time accomplished by three weak yet indomitable women which, preceding the accomplished fact which
we declined, refused, robbed the brother of the prey, reft
the murderer of a victim for his very bullet. That was
how we lived for seven months. And then one afternoon
in January Thomas Sutpen came home; someone looked
up where we were preparing the garden for another
year's food and saw him riding up the drive. And then
one evening I became engaged to marry him.*

*It took me just three months. (Do you mind how I
dont say he, but I?) Yes, I, just three months, who for
twenty years had looked on him (when I did—had to
—look) as an ogre, some beast out of a tale to frighten
children with; who had seen his own get upon my dead
sister's body already begin to destroy one another, yet
who must come to him like a whistled dog at that first
opportunity, that noon when he who had been seeing me
for twenty years should first raise his head and pause*

and look at me. Oh, I hold no brief for myself who could (and would; ay, doubtless have already) give you a thousand specious reasons good enough for women, ranging from woman's natural inconsistency to the desire (or even hope) for possible wealth, position, or even the fear of dying manless which (so they will doubtless tell you) old maids always have, or for revenge. No. I hold no brief for me. I could have gone home and I did not. Perhaps I should have gone home. But I did not. As Judith and Clytie did, I stood there before the rotting portico and watched him ride up on that gaunt and jaded horse on which he did not seem to sit but rather seemed to project himself ahead like a mirage, in some fierce dynamic rigidity of impatience which the gaunt horse, the saddle, the boots, the leaf-colored and threadbare coat with its tarnished and flapping braid containing the sentient though nerveless shell, could not keep up with, which seemed to precede him as he dismounted and out of which he said 'Well, daughter' and stooped and touched his beard to Judith's forehead, who had not, did not, move, who stood rigid and still and immobile of face, and within which they spoke four sentences, four sentences of simple direct words behind beneath above which I felt that same rapport of communal blood which I had sensed that day while Clytie held me from the stairs: 'Henry's not——?' 'No. He's not here.' —'Ah. And——?' 'Yes. Henry killed him.' and then burst into tears. Yes, burst, who had not wept yet, who had brought down the stairs that afternoon and worn ever since that cold calm face which had stopped me in midrunning at that closed door; yes, burst, as if that entire accumulation of seven months were erupting spontaneously from every pore in one incredible evacuation (she not moving, not moving a muscle) and then vanishing, disappearing as instantaneously as if the very fierce and arid aura which he had enclosed her in were drying the tears faster than they emerged: and still standing with his hands on her shoulders and looked at Clytie and said, 'Ah, Clytie' and then at me—the same face which I had last seen, only a little thinner, the same ruthless eyes, the hair grizzled a little now, and no recognition in the face at all until Judith said, 'It's Rosa. Aunt Rosa. She lives here now.'

That was all. He rode up the drive and into our lives again and left no ripple save those instantaneous and incredible tears. Because he himself was not there, not in the house where we spent our days, had not stopped there. The shell of him was there, using the room which we had kept for him and eating the food which we produced and prepared as if it could neither feel the softness of the bed nor make distinction between the viands either as to quality or taste. Yes. He wasn't there. Something ate with us; we talked to it and it answered questions; it sat with us before the fire at night and, rousing without any warning from some profound and bemused complete inertia, talked, not to us, the six ears, the three minds capable of listening, but to the air, the waiting grim decaying presence, spirit, of the house itself, talking that which sounded like the bombast of a madman who creates within his very coffin walls his fabulous immeasurable Camelots and Carcassonnes.

Not absent from the place, the arbitrary square of earth which he had named Sutpen's Hundred: not that at all. He was absent only from the room, and that because he had to be elsewhere, a part of him encompassing each ruined field and fallen fence and crumbling wall of cabin or cotton house or crib; himself diffused and in solution held by that electric furious immobile urgency and awareness of short time and the need for haste as if he had just drawn breath and looked about and realised that he was old (he was fifty-nine) and was concerned (not afraid: concerned) not that old age might have left him impotent to do what he intended to do, but that he might not have time to do it in before he would have to die. We were right about what he would intend to do: that he would not even pause for breath before undertaking to restore his house and plantation as near as possible to what it had been. We did not know how he would go about it, nor I believe did he. He could not have known, who came home with nothing, to nothing, to four years less than nothing. But it did not stop him, intimidate him. His was that cold alert fury of the gambler who knows that he may lose anyway but that with a second's flagging of the fierce constant will he is sure to: and who keeps suspense from ever quite crystallising by sheer fierce manipulation of the cards or dice until the ducts and glands of luck begin to flow again. He did not pause, did not take that day or two to let the bones and flesh of fifty-nine recuperate—the day or two in which he might have talked, not about us and what we had been doing, but about himself, the past four years (for all he ever told us, there might not have been any war at all, or it on another planet and no stake of his risked on it, no flesh and blood of his to suffer by it)—that natural period during which bitter though unmaimed defeat might have exhausted itself to something like peace, like quiet in the raging and incredulous recounting (which enables man to bear with living) of that feather's balance between victory and disaster which makes that defeat unbearable which, turning against him, yet declined to slay him who, still alive, yet cannot bear to live with it.

We hardly ever saw him. He would be gone from dawn until dark, he and Jones and another man or two that he had got from somewhere and paid with something, perhaps the same coin in which he had paid that foreign architect—cajolery, promise, threat, and at last force. That was the winter when we began to learn what carpet-bagger meant and people—women—locked doors and windows at night and began to frighten each other with tales of negro uprisings, when the ruined, the four years' fallow and neglected land lay more idle yet while men with pistols in their pockets gathered daily at secret meeting places in the towns. He did not make one of these; I remember how one night a deputation called, rode out through the mud of early March and put him to the point of definite yes or no, with them or against them, friend or enemy: and he refused, declined, offered them (with no change of gaunt ruthless face nor level voice) defiance if it was defiance they wanted, telling them that if every man in the South would do as he himself was doing, would see to the restoration of his own land, the general land and South would save

*itself: and ushered them from the room and from the
house and stood plain in the doorway holding the lamp
above his head while their spokesman delivered his ultimatum: 'This may be war, Sutpen', and answered, 'I
am used to it.' Oh yes, I watched him, watched his old
man's solitary fury fighting now not with the stubborn
yet slowly tractable earth as it had done before, but now
against the ponderable weight of the changed new time
itself as though he were trying to dam a river with his
bare hands and a shingle: and this for the same spurious
delusion of reward which had failed (failed? betrayed:
and would this time destroy) him once; I see the analogy
myself now: the accelerating circle's fatal curving
course of his ruthless pride, his lust for vain magnificence, though I did not then. And how could I? turned
twenty true enough yet still a child, still living in that
womb-like corridor where the world came not even as
living echo but as dead incomprehensible shadow, where
with the quiet and unalarmed amazement of a child I
watched the miragy antics of men and women—my
father, my sister, Thomas Sutpen, Judith, Henry,
Charles Bon—called honor, principle, marriage, love,
bereavement, death; the child who watching him was
not a child but one of that triumvirate mother-woman
which we three, Judith Clytie and I, made, which fed
and clothed and warmed the static shell and so gave vent
and scope to the fierce vain illusion and so said, 'At last
my life is worth something, even though it only shields
and guards the antic fury of an insane child.' And then
one afternoon (I was in the garden with a hoe, where
the path came up from the stable lot) I looked up and*

saw him looking at me. He had seen me for twenty years, but now he was looking at me; he stood there in the path looking at me, in the middle of the afternoon. That was it: that it should have been in the middle of the afternoon, when he should not have been anywhere near the house at all but miles away and invisible somewhere among his hundred square miles which they had not troubled to begin to take away from him yet, perhaps not even at this point or at that point but diffused (not attenuated to thinness but enlarged, magnified, encompassing as though in a prolonged and unbroken instant of tremendous effort embracing and holding intact that ten-mile square while he faced from the brink of disaster, invincible and unafraid, what he must have known would be the final defeat) but instead of that standing there in the path looking at me with something curious and strange in his face as if the barnlot, the path at the instant when he came in sight of me had been a swamp out of which he had emerged without having been forewarned that he was about to enter light, and then went on—the face, the same face: it was not love; I do not say that, not gentleness or pity: just a sudden over-burst of light, illumination, who had been told that his son had done murder and vanished and said 'Ah.—Well, Clytie.' He went on to the house. But it was not love: I do not claim that; I hold no brief for myself, I do not excuse it. I could have said that he had needed, used me; why should I rebel now, because he would use me more? but I did not say it; I could say this time, I do not know, and I would tell the truth. Because I do not know. He was gone; I did not even

*know that either since there is a metabolism of the spirit
as well as of the entrails, in which the stored accumula-
tions of long time burn, generate, create and break some
maidenhead of the ravening meat; ay, in a second's
time;—yes, lost all the shibboleth erupting of cannot,
will not, never will in one red instant's fierce oblitera-
tion. This was my instant, who could have fled then and
did not, who found that he had gone on and did not
remember when he had walked away, who found my
okra bed finished without remembering the completing
of it, who sat at the supper table that night with the
familiar dream-cloudy shell which we had grown used
to (he did not look at me again during the meal; I might
have said then, To what deluded sewer-gush of dreaming does the incorrigible flesh betray us: but I did not)
and then before the fire in Judith's bedroom sat as we
always did until he came in the door and looked at us
and said, 'Judith, you and Clytie——' and ceased, still
entering, then said, 'No, never mind. Rosa will not
mind if you both hear it too, since we are short for time
and busy with what we have of it' and came and
stopped and put his hand on my head and (I do not
know what he looked at while he spoke, save that by the
sound of his voice it was not at us nor at anything in
that room) said, 'You may think I made your sister
Ellen no very good husband. You probably do think so.
But even if you will not discount the fact that I am
older now, I believe I can promise that I shall do no
worse at least for you.'*

*That was my courtship. That minute's exchanged
look in a kitchen garden, that hand upon my head in*

*his daughter's bedroom; a ukase, a decree, a serene and
florid boast like a sentence (ay, and delivered in the same
attitude) not to be spoken and heard but to be read
carved in the bland stone which pediments a forgotten
and nameless effigy. I do not excuse it. I claim no brief,
no pity, who did not answer 'I will' not because I was
not asked, because there was no place, no niche, no
interval for reply. Because I could have made one. I
could have forced that niche myself if I had willed to—
a niche not shaped to fit mild 'Yes' but some blind
desperate female weapon's frenzied slash whose very
gaping wound had cried 'No! No!' and 'Help!' and
'Save me!' No, no brief, no pity, who did not even move,
who sat beneath that hard oblivious childhood ogre's
hand and heard him speak to Judith now, heard Judith's
feet, saw Judith's hand, not Judith—that palm in which
I read as from a printed chronicle the orphaning, the
hardship, the bereave of love; the four hard barren years
of scoriating loom, of axe and hoe and all the other tools
decreed for men to use: and upon it lying the ring which
he gave Ellen in the church almost thirty years ago. Yes,
analogy and paradox and madness too. I sat there and
felt not watched him slip the ring onto my finger in my
turn (he was sitting now also, in the chair which we
called Clytie's while she stood just beyond the firelight's
range beside the chimney) and listened to his voice as
Ellen must have listened in her own spirit's April thirty
years ago: he talking not about me or love or marriage,
not even about himself and to no sane mortal listening
nor out of any sanity, but to the very dark forces of fate
which he had evoked and dared, out of that wild brag-*

gart dream where an intact Sutpen's Hundred which no more had actual being now (and would never have again) than it had when Ellen first heard it, as though in the restoration of that ring to a living finger he had turned all time back twenty years and stopped it, froze it. Yes. I sat there and listened to his voice and told myself, 'Why, he is mad. He will decree this marriage for tonight and perform his own ceremony, himself both groom and minister; pronounce his own wild benediction on it with the very bedward candle in his hand: and I mad too, for I will acquiesce, succumb; abet him and plunge down.' No, I hold no brief, ask no pity. If I was saved that night (and I was saved; mine was to be some later, colder sacrifice when we—I—should be free of all excuse of the surprised importunate traitorous flesh) it was no fault, no doing of my own but rather because, once he had restored the ring, he ceased to look at me save as he had looked for the twenty years before that afternoon, as if he had reached for the moment some interval of sanity such as the mad know, just as the sane have intervals of madness to keep them aware that they are sane. It was more than that even. For three months now he had seen me daily though he had not looked at me since I merely made one of that triumvirate who received his gruff unspoken man's gratitude for the spartan ease we supplied, not to his comfort perhaps but at least to the mad dream he lived in. But for the next two months he did not even see me. Perhaps the reason was the obvious one: he was too busy; that having accomplished his engagement (granted that was what he wanted) he did not need to see me. Certainly he did not:

there was not even any date set for the wedding. It was almost as though that very afternoon did not exist, had never happened. I might not have even been there in the house. Worse: I could have gone, returned home, and he would not have missed me. I was (whatever it was he wanted of me—not my being, my presence: just my existence, whatever it was that Rosa Coldfield or any young female no blood kin to him represented in whatever it was he wanted—because I will do him this credit: he had never once thought about what he asked me to do until the moment he asked it because I know that he would not have waited two months or even two days to ask it)—my presence was to him only the absence of black morass and snarled vine and creeper to that man who had struggled through a swamp with nothing to guide or drive him—no hope, no light: only some incorrigibility of undefeat—and blundered at last and without warning onto dry solid ground and sun and air— if there could have been such thing as sun to him, if anyone or any thing could have competed with the white glare of his madness. Yes, mad, yet not so mad. Because there is a practicality to viciousness: the thief, the liar, the murderer even, has faster rules than virtue ever has; why not madness too? If he was mad, it was only his compelling dream which was insane and not his methods: it was no madman who bargained and cajoled hard manual labor out of men like Jones; it was no madman who kept clear of the sheets and hoods and night-galloping horses with which men who were once his acquaintances even if not his friends discharged the canker suppuration of defeat; it was no madman's plan or tactics which gained him at the lowest possible price the sole woman available to wive him, and by the one device which could have gained his point;—not madman, no: since surely there is something in madness, even the demoniac, which Satan flees, aghast at his own handiwork, and which God looks on in pity—some spark, some crumb to leaven and redeem that articulated flesh, that speech sight hearing taste and being which we call human man. But no matter. I will tell you what he did and let you be the judge. (Or try to tell you, because there are some things for which three words are three too many, and three thousand words that many words too less, and this is one of them. It can be told; I could take that many sentences, repeat the bold blank naked and outrageous words just as he spoke them, and bequeath you only that same aghast and outraged unbelief I knew when I comprehended what he meant; or take three thousand sentences and leave you only that Why? Why? and Why? that I have asked and listened to for almost fifty years.) But I will let you be the judge and let you tell me if I was not right.

You see, I was that sun, or thought I was who did believe there was that spark, that crumb in madness which is divine, though madness know no word itself for terror or for pity. There was an ogre of my childhood which before my birth removed my only sister to its grim ogre-bourne and produced two half phantom children whom I was not encouraged, and did not desire, to associate with as if my late-born solitude had taught me presentiment of that fateful intertwining, warned me of that fatal snarly climax before I knew the name

for murder—and I forgave it; there was a shape which
rode away beneath a flag and (demon or no) coura-
geously suffered—and I did more than just forgive: I
slew it, because the body, the blood, the memory which
that ogre had dwelt in returned five years later and held
out its hand and said 'Come' as you might say it to a
dog, and I came. Yes, the body, the face, with the right
name and memory, even the correct remembering of
what and whom (except myself: and was that not but
further proof?) it had left behind and returned to: but
not the ogre; villain true enough, but a mortal fallible
one less to invoke fear than pity: but no ogre; mad true
enough, but I told myself, Why should not madness be
its own victim also? or, Why may it be not even madness but solitary despair in titan conflict with the lonely
and foredoomed and indomitable iron spirit: but no
ogre, because it was dead, vanished, consumed somewhere in flame and sulphur-reek perhaps among the
lonely craggy peaks of my childhood's solitary remembering—or forgetting; I was that sun, who believed that
he (after that evening in Judith's room) was not oblivious of me but only unconscious and receptive like the
swamp-freed pilgrim feeling earth and tasting sun and
light again and aware of neither but only of darkness'
and morass's lack—who did believe there was that
magic in unkin blood which we call by the pallid name
of love that could be, might be sun for him (though I
the youngest, weakest) where Judith and Clytie both
would cast no shadow; yes, I the youngest there yet
potently without measured and measurable age since I
alone of them could say, 'O furious mad old man, I hold

*no substance that will fit your dream but I can give you
airy space and scope for your delirium.' And then one
afternoon—oh there was a fate in it: afternoon and
afternoon and afternoon: do you see? the death of hope
and love, the death of pride and principle, and then the
death of everything save the old outraged and aghast
unbelieving which has lasted for forty-three years—he
returned to the house and called me, shouting from the
back gallery until I came down; oh I told you he had
not thought of it until that moment, that prolonged
moment which contained the distance between the house
and wherever it was he had been standing when he
thought of it: and this too coincident: it was the very
day on which he knew definitely and at last exactly how
much of his hundred square miles he would be able to
save and keep and call his own on the day when he
would have to die, that no matter what happened to him
now, he would at least retain the shell of Sutpen's Hundred even though a better name for it would now be
Sutpen's One—called, shouted for me until I came
down. He had not even waited to tether his horse; he
stood with the reins over his arm (and no hand on my
head now) and spoke the bald outrageous words exactly
as if he were consulting with Jones or with some other
man about a bitch dog or a cow or mare.*

*They will have told you how I came back home. Oh
yes, I know: 'Rosie Coldfield, lose him, weep him;
caught a man but couldn't keep him'—Oh yes, I know
(and kind too; they would be kind): Rosa Coldfield,
warped bitter orphaned country stick called Rosa Coldfield, safely engaged at last and so off the town, the*

county; they will have told you: How I went out there to live for the rest of my life, seeing in my nephew's murdering an act of God enabling me ostensibly to obey my dying sister's request that I save at least one of the two children which she had doomed by conceiving them but actually to be in the house when he returned who, being a demon, would therefore be impervious to shot and shell and so would return; I waiting for him because I was young still (who had buried no hopes to bugles, beneath a flag) and ripe for marrying in this time and place where most of the young men were dead and all the living ones either old or already married or tired, too tired for love; he my best my only chance in this: an environment where at best and even lacking war my chances would have been slender enough since I was not only a Southern gentlewoman but the very modest character of whose background and circumstances must needs be their own affirmation since had I been the daughter of a wealthy planter I could have married almost anyone but being the daughter merely of a small store-keeper I could even afford to accept flowers from almost no one and so would have been doomed to marry at last some casual apprentice-clerk in my father's business;—Yes, they will have told you: who was young and had buried hopes only during that night which was four years long when beside a shuttered and unsleeping candle she embalmed the War and its heritage of suffering and injustice and sorrow on the backsides of the pages within an old account book, embalming blotting from the breathable air the poisonous secret effluvium of lusting and hating and killing;

—they will have told you: daughter of an embusqué who had to turn to a demon, a villain: and therefore she had been right in hating her father since if he had not died in that attic she would not have had to go out there to find food and protection and shelter and if she had not had to depend on his food and clothing (even if she did help to grow and weave it) to keep her alive and warm until simple justice demanded that she make what return for it he might require of her commensurate with honor she would not have become engaged to him and if she had not become engaged to him she would not have had to lie at night asking herself Why and Why and Why as she has done for forty-three years: as if she had been instinctively right even as a child in hating her father and so these forty-three years of impotent and unbearable outrage were the revenge of some sophisticated and ironic sterile nature on her for having hated that which gave her life.—Yes, Rosa Coldfield engaged at last who, lacking the fact that her sister had bequeathed her at least something of shelter and kin, might have become a charge upon the town: and now Rosie Coldfield, lose him, weep him; found a man but failed to keep him; Rosa Coldfield who would be right only right, being right, is not enough for women who had rather be wrong than just that who want the man who was wrong to admit it. And that's what she cant forgive him for: not for the insult, not even for having jilted her: but for being dead. Oh yes, I know, I know: How two months later they learned that she had packed up her belongings (that is, put on the shawl and hat again) and come back to town, to live alone in the house

*where her parents were dead and gone and where Judith
would come now and then and bring her some of what
food they had out at Sutpen's Hundred and which only
dire necessity, the brute inexplicable flesh's stubborn will
to live, brought her (Miss Coldfield) to accept. And it
dire indeed: because now the town—farmers passing,
negro servants going to work in white kitchens—would
see her before sunup gathering greens along garden
fences, pulling them through the fence since she had no
garden of her own, no seed to plant one with, no tools
to work it with herself even if she had known completely
how who had had only the freshman year at gardening
and doubtless would not have worked it if she had
known who had never surrendered; reaching through
the garden fence and gathering vegetables who would
have been welcome to enter the garden and get them and
they would have even done the gathering and sent them
to her since there were more people than Judge Benbow
who would leave baskets of provisions on her front porch
at night but she would not permit them who would not
even use a stick to reach through the fence and draw the
vegetables to where she could grasp them, the reach of her
unaided arm being the limit of brigandage which she
never passed, and it not to keep from being seen stealing
which sent her forth before the town was awake because
if she had had a nigger she would have sent him forth
in broad daylight to forage, where, she would not have
cared, exactly as the cavalry heroes whom she wrote
verse about would have sent their men.—Yes, Rosie
Coldfield, lose him, weep him; caught a beau but
couldn't keep him; (oh yes, they will tell you) found a*

*beau and was insulted, something heard and not for-
given, not so much for the saying of it but for having
thought it about her so that when she heard it she realised like thunderclap that it must have been in his mind
for a day, a week, even a month maybe, he looking at
her daily with that in his mind and she not even knowing it. But I forgave him. They will tell you different,
but I did. Why shouldn't I? I had nothing to forgive;
I had not lost him because I never owned him: a certain
segment of rotten mud walked into my life, spoke that
to me which I had never heard before and never shall
again, and then walked out; that was all. I never owned
him; certainly not in that sewer sense which you would
mean by that and maybe think (but you are wrong) I
mean. That did not matter. That was not even the nub
of the insult. I mean that he was not owned by anyone
or anything in this world, had never been, would never
be, not even by Ellen, not even by Jones' granddaughter.
Because he was not articulated in this world. He was
a walking shadow. He was the light-blinded bat-like
image of his own torment cast by the fierce demoniac
lantern up from beneath the earth's crust and hence in
retrograde, reverse; from abysmal and chaotic dark to
eternal and abysmal dark completing his descending (do
you mark the gradation?) ellipsis, clinging, trying to
cling with vain unsubstantial hands to what he hoped
would hold him, save him, arrest him—Ellen (do you
mark them?), myself, then last of all that fatherless
daughter of Wash Jones' only child who, so I heard once,
died in a Memphis brothel—to find severance (even if
not rest and peace) at last in the stroke of a rusty scythe.*

I was told, informed of that too, though not by Jones this time but by someone else kind enough to turn aside and tell me he was dead. 'Dead?' I cried. 'Dead? You? You lie; you're not dead; heaven cannot, and hell dare not, have you!' But Quentin was not listening, because there was also something which he too could not pass—that door, the running feet on the stairs beyond it almost a continuation of the faint shot, the two women, the negress and the white girl in her underthings (made of flour sacking when there had been flour, of window curtains when not) pausing, looking at the door, the yellowed creamy mass of old intricate satin and lace spread carefully on the bed and then caught swiftly up by the white girl and held before her as the door crashed in and the brother stood there, hatless, with his shaggy bayonet-trimmed hair, his gaunt worn unshaven face, his patched and faded gray tunic, the pistol still hanging against his flank: the two of them, brother and sister, curiously alike as if the difference in sex had merely sharpened the common blood to a terrific, an almost unbearable, similarity, speaking to one another in short brief staccato sentences like slaps, as if they stood breast to breast striking one another in turn, neither making any attempt to guard against the blows:

Now you cant marry him.

Why cant I marry him?

Because he's dead.

Dead?

Yes. I killed him.

He (Quentin) couldn't pass that. He was not even listening to her; he said, "Ma'am? What's that? What did you say?"

"There's something in that house."

"In that house? It's Clytie. Dont she——"

"No. Something living in it. Hidden in it. It has been out there for four years, living hidden in that house."

VI

There was snow on Shreve's overcoat sleeve, his ungloved blond square hand red and raw with cold, vanishing. Then on the table before Quentin, lying on the open text book beneath the lamp, the white oblong of envelope, the familiar blurred mechanical *Jefferson Jan 10 1910 Miss* and then, opened, the *My dear son* in his father's sloped fine hand out of that dead dusty summer where he had prepared for Harvard so that his father's hand could lie on a strange lamplit table in Cambridge; that dead summer twilight—the wistaria, the cigar-smell, the fireflies—attenuated up from Mississippi and into this strange room, across this strange iron New England snow:

> *My dear son,*
> *Miss Rosa Coldfield was buried yesterday. She remained in the coma for almost two weeks and two days ago she died without regaining consciousness and without pain they say and whatever they mean by that since it has always seemed to me that the only painless death must be that which takes the intelligence by violent surprise and from the rear so to speak since if death be anything at all beyond a*

brief and peculiar emotional state of the bereaved
it must be a brief and likewise peculiar state of the
subject as well and if aught can be more painful to
any intelligence above that of a child or an idiot
than a slow and gradual confronting with that
which over a long period of bewilderment and
dread it has been taught to regard as an irrevocable
and unplumbable finality, I do not know it. And
if there can be either access of comfort or cessation
of pain in the ultimate escape from a stubborn and
amazed outrage which over a period of forty-three
years has been companionship and bread and fire
and all, I do not know that either—

—bringing with it that very September evening itself (and he soon needing, required, to say "No,
neither aunt cousin nor uncle Rosa. Miss Rosa. Miss
Rosa Coldfield, an old lady that died young of outrage in 1866 one summer" and then Shreve, "You
mean she was no kin to you, no kin to you at all, that
there was actually one Southern Bayard or Guine-
vere who was no kin to you? then what did she die
for?" and that not Shreve's first time, nobody's first
time in Cambridge since September: *Tell about the*
South. What's it like there. What do they do there. Why
do they live there. Why do they live at all)—that very
September evening when Mr Compson stopped
talking at last, he (Quentin) walked out of his father's talking at last because it was now time to go,
not because he had heard it all because he had not
been listening since he had something which he still

was unable to pass: that door, that gaunt tragic dramatic self-hypnotised youthful face like the tragedian in a college play, an academic Hamlet waked from some trancement of the curtain's falling and blundering across the dusty stage from which the rest of the cast had departed last commencement, the sister facing him across the wedding dress which she was not to use, not even to finish, the two of them slashing at one another with twelve or fourteen words and most of these the same words repeated two or three times so that when you boiled it down they did it with eight or ten. And she (Miss Coldfield) had on the shawl, as he had known she would, and the bonnet (black once but faded now to that fierce muted metallic green of old peacock feathers) and the black reticule almost as large as a carpet bag containing all the keys which the house possessed: cupboard closet and door, some of which would not even turn in locks which, shot home, could be solved by any child with a hairpin or a wad of chewing gum, some of which no longer even fit the locks they had been made for like old married people who no longer have anything in common, to do or to talk about, save the same general weight of air to displace and breathe and general oblivious biding earth to bear their weight;—that evening, the twelve miles behind the fat mare in the moonless September dust, the trees along the road not rising soaring as trees should but squatting like huge fowl, their leaves ruffled and heavily separate like the feathers of panting fowls, heavy with sixty days of

dust, the roadside undergrowth coated with heat-
vulcanised dust and, seen through the dustcloud in
which the horse and buggy moved, appeared like
masses stranding delicate and rigid and immobly
upward at perpendicular's absolute in some old dead
volcanic water refined to the oxygenless first principle of liquid, the dustcloud in which the buggy
moved not blowing away because it had been raised
by no wind and was supported by no air but evoked,
materialised about them, instantaneous and eternal,
cubic foot for cubic foot of dust to cubic foot for
cubic foot of horse and buggy, peripatetic beneath
the branch-shredded vistas of flat black fiercely and
heavily starred sky, the dustcloud moving on, en-
closing them with not threat exactly but maybe
warning, bland, almost friendly, warning, as if to
say, *Come on if you like. But I will get there first;
accumulating ahead of you I will arrive first, lifting,
sloping gently upward under hooves and wheels so that
you will find no destination but will merely abrupt
gently onto a plateau and a panorama of harmless and
inscrutable night and there will be nothing for you to
do but return and so I would advise you not to go, to
turn back now and let what is, be;* he (Quentin) agreeing to this, sitting in the buggy beside the implacable doll-sized old woman clutching her cotton
umbrella, smelling the heat-distilled old woman-
flesh, the heat-distilled camphor in the old fold-
creases of the shawl, feeling exactly like an electric
bulb blood and skin since the buggy disturbed not
enough air to cool him with motion, created not

enough motion within him to make his skin sweat, thinking *Good Lord yes, let's dont find him or it, try to find him or it, risk disturbing him or it:* (then Shreve again, "Wait. Wait. You mean that this old gal, this Aunt Rosa——"

"Miss Rosa," Quentin said.

"All right all right.——that this old dame, this Aunt Rosa——"

"Miss Rosa, I tell you."

"All right all right all right.——that this old—— this Aunt R—— All right all right all right all right. ——that hadn't been out there, hadn't set foot in the house even in forty-three years, yet who not only said there was somebody hidden in it but found somebody that would believe her, would drive that twelve miles out there in a buggy at midnight to see if she was right or not?"

"Yes," Quentin said.

"That this old dame that grew up in a household like an overpopulated mausoleum, with no call or claim on her time but the hating of her father and aunt and her sister's husband in peace and comfort and waiting for the day when they would prove not only to themselves but to everybody else that she had been right: so one night the aunt slid down the rainpipe with a horse trader and she was right about the aunt so that fixed that: then her father nailed himself up in the attic to keep from being drafted into the Rebel army and starved to death so that fixed that except for the unavoidable possibility that when the moment came for him to admit to himself

that she had been right he may not have been able
to speak or may not have had anyone to tell it to: so
she was right about the father too since if he hadn't
made General Lee and Jeff Davis mad he wouldn't
have had to nail himself up and die and if he hadn't
died he wouldn't have left her an orphan and a
pauper and so situated, left susceptible to a situation
where she could receive this mortal affront: and
right about the brother-in-law because if he hadn't
been a demon his children wouldn't have needed
protection from him and she wouldn't have had to
go out there and be betrayed by the old meat and
find instead of a widowed Agamemnon to her Cassandra an ancient stiff-jointed Pyramus to her eager
though untried Thisbe who could approach her in
this unbidden April's compounded demonry and
suggest that they breed together for test and sample
and if it was a boy they would marry; would not
have had to be blown back to town on the initial
blast of that horror and outrage to eat of gall and
wormwood stolen through paling fences at dawn: so
this was not fixed at all and forever because she
couldn't even tell it because of who her successor
was, not because he found a successor by just turning around and no day's loss of time even but because of who the successor was, that she might
conceivably have ever suffered a situation where she
could or would have to decline any office which her
successor could have been deemed worthy, even by
a demon, to fill; this not fixed at all since when the
moment came for him to admit he had been wrong

she would have the same trouble with him she had
with her father, he would be dead too since she
doubtless foresaw the scythe if for no other reason
than that it would be the final outrage and affront
like the hammer and nails in her father's business—
that scythe, symbolic laurel of a caesar's triumph—
that rusty scythe loaned by the demon himself to
Jones more than two years ago to cut the weeds
away from the shanty doorway to smooth the path
for rutting—that rusty blade garlanded with each
successive day's gaudy ribbon or cheap bead for the
(how did she put it? slut wasn't all, was it?) to walk
in—that scythe beyond whose symbolic shape he,
even though dead, even when earth itself declined
any longer to bear his weight, jeered at her?"

"Yes," Quentin said.

"That this Faustus, this demon, this Beelzebub
fled hiding from some momentary flashy glare of his
Creditor's outraged face exasperated beyond all endurance, hiding, scuttling into respectability like a
jackal into a rockpile so she thought at first until she
realised that he was not hiding, did not want to hide,
was merely engaged in one final frenzy of evil and
harm-doing before the Creditor overtook him this
next time for good and all;—this Faustus who appeared suddenly one Sunday with two pistols and
twenty subsidiary demons and skuldugged a hundred miles of land out of a poor ignorant Indian and
built the biggest house on it you ever saw and went
away with six wagons and came back with the crystal tapestries and the Wedgwood chairs to furnish it

and nobody knew if he had robbed another steamboat or had just dug up a little more of the old loot,
who hid horns and tail beneath human raiment and
a beaver hat and chose (bought her, outswapped his
father-in-law, wasn't it?) a wife after three years to
scrutinise weigh and compare, not from one of the
local ducal houses but from the lesser baronage
whose principality was so far decayed that there
would be no risk of his wife bringing him for dowry
delusions of grandeur before he should be equipped
for it yet not so far decayed but that she might keep
them both from getting lost among the new knives
and forks and spoons that he had bought—a wife
who not only would consolidate the hiding but
could would and did breed him two children to fend
and shield both in themselves and in their progeny
the brittle bones and tired flesh of an old man against
the day when the Creditor would run him to earth
for the last time and he couldn't get away: and so
sure enough the daughter fell in love, the son the
agent for the providing of that living bulwark between him (the demon) and the Creditor's bailiff
hand until the son should marry and thus insure him
doubled and compounded—and then the demon
must turn square around and run not only the fiancé
out of the house and not only the son out of the
house but so corrupt seduce and mesmerise the son
that he (the son) should do the office of the outraged
father's pistol-hand when fornication threatened: so
that the demon should return from the war five
years later and find accomplished and complete the

situation he had been working for: son fled for good now with a noose behind him, daughter doomed to spinsterhood—and then almost before his foot was out of the stirrup he (the demon) set out and got himself engaged again in order to replace that progeny the hopes of which he had himself destroyed?"

"Yes," Quentin said.

"Came back home and found his chances of descendants gone where his children had attended to that, and his plantation ruined, fields fallow except for a fine stand of weeds, and taxes and levies and penalties sowed by United States marshals and such and all his niggers gone where the Yankees had attended to that, and you would have thought he would have been satisfied: yet before his foot was out of the stirrup he not only set out to try to restore his plantation to what it used to be, like maybe he was hoping to fool the Creditor by illusion and obfuscation by concealing behind the illusion that time and change had not elapsed and occurred the fact that he was now almost sixty years old until he could get himself a new batch of children to bulwark him, but chose for this purpose the last woman on earth he might have hoped to prevail on, this Aunt R——all right all right all right.—that hated him, that had always hated him, yet choosing her with a kind of outrageous bravado as if a kind of despairing conviction of his irresistibility or invulnerability were a part of the price he had got for whatever it was he had sold the Creditor since according to the old dame he never had had a soul;

proposed to her and was accepted—then three months later, with no date ever set for the wedding and marriage itself not mentioned one time since, and on the very day when he established definitely that he would be able to keep at least some of his land and how much, he approached her and suggested they breed like a couple of dogs together, inventing with fiendish cunning the thing which husbands and fiancés have been trying to invent for ten million years: the thing that without harming her or giving her grounds for civil or tribal action would not only blast the little dream-woman out of the dovecote but leave her irrevocably husbanded (and himself, husband or fiancé, already safely cuckolded before she can draw breath) with the abstract carcass of outrage and revenge; who said it and was free now, forever more now of threat or meddling from anyone since he had at last eliminated the last member of his late wife's family, free now: son fled to Texas or California or maybe even South America, daughter doomed to spinsterhood to live until he died, since after that it wouldn't matter, in that rotting house, caring for him and feeding him, raising chickens and peddling the eggs for the clothes she and Clytie couldn't make: so that he didn't even need to be a demon now but just mad impotent old man who had realised at last that his dream of restoring his Sutpen's Hundred was not only vain but that what he had left of it would never support him and his family and so running his little crossroads store with a stock of plowshares and hame strings

and calico and kerosene and cheap beads and ribbons and a clientele of freed niggers and (what is it?
the word? white what?—Yes, trash) with Jones for
clerk and who knows maybe what delusions of making money out of the store to rebuild the plantation;
who had escaped twice now, got himself into it and
been freed by the Creditor who set his children to
destroying one another before he had posterity, and
he decided that maybe he was wrong in being free
and so got into it again and then decided that he was
wrong in being unfree and so got out of it again—
and then turned right around and bought his way
back into it with beads and calico and striped candy
out of his own showcase and off his shelves?"

"Yes," Quentin said. *He sounds just like Father* he
thought, glancing (his face quiet, reposed, curiously
almost sullen) for a moment at Shreve leaning forward into the lamp, his naked torso pink-gleaming
and baby-smooth, cherubic, almost hairless, the
twin moons of his spectacles glinting against his
moonlike rubicund face, smelling (Quentin) the
cigar and the wistaria, seeing the fireflies blowing
and winking in the September dusk. *Just exactly like
Father if Father had known as much about it the night
before I went out there as he did the day after I came
back* thinking *Mad impotent old man who realised at
last that there must be some limit even to the capabilities
of a demon for doing harm, who must have seen his
situation as that of the show girl, the pony, who realises
that the principal tune she prances to comes not from
horn and fiddle and drum but from a clock and calen-*

dar, must have seen himself as the old wornout cannon which realises that it can deliver just one more fierce shot and crumble to dust in its own furious blast and recoil, who looked about upon the scene which was still within his scope and compass and saw son gone, vanished, more insuperable to him now than if the son were dead since now (if the son still lived) his name would be different and those to call him by it strangers and whatever dragon's outcropping of Sutpen blood the son might sow on the body of whatever strange woman would therefore carry on the tradition, accomplish the hereditary evil and harm under another name and upon and among people who will never have heard the right one; daughter doomed to spinsterhood who had chosen spinsterhood already before there was anyone named Charles Bon since the aunt who came to succor her in bereavement and sorrow found neither but instead that calm absolutely impenetrable face between a homespun dress and sunbonnet seen before a closed door and again in a cloudy swirl of chickens while Jones was building the coffin and which she wore during the next year while the aunt lived there and the three women wove their own garments and raised their own food and cut the wood they cooked it with (excusing what help they had from Jones who lived with his granddaughter in the abandoned fishing camp with its collapsing roof and rotting porch against which the rusty scythe which Sutpen was to lend him, make him borrow to cut away the weeds from the door—and at last forced him to use though not to cut weeds, at least not vegetable weeds—would lean for two years) and wore still after the aunt's indigna-

tion had swept her back to town to live on stolen garden
truck and out of anonymous baskets left on her front
steps at night, the three of them, the two daughters negro
and white and the aunt twelve miles away watching
from her distance as the two daughters watched from
theirs the old demon, the ancient varicose and despairing Faustus fling his final main now with the Creditor's
hand already on his shoulder, running his little country
store now for his bread and meat, haggling tediously
over nickels and dimes with rapacious and poverty-
stricken whites and negroes, who at one time could have
galloped for ten miles in any direction without crossing
his own boundary, using out of his meagre stock the
cheap ribbons and beads and the stale violently-colored
candy with which even an old man can seduce a fifteen-
year-old country girl, to ruin the granddaughter of his
partner, this Jones—this gangling malaria-ridden
white man whom he had given permission fourteen
years ago to squat in the abandoned fishing camp with
the year-old grandchild—Jones, partner porter and
clerk who at the demon's command removed with his
own hand (and maybe delivered too) from the showcase
the candy beads and ribbons, measured the very cloth
from which Judith (who had not been bereaved and did
not mourn) helped the granddaughter to fashion a dress
to walk past the lounging men in, the side-looking and
the tongues, until her increasing belly taught her embar-
rassment—or perhaps fear;—Jones who before '61 had
not even been allowed to approach the front of the house
and who during the next four years got no nearer than
the kitchen door and that only when he brought the

game and fish and vegetables on which the seducer-to-
be's wife and daughter (and Clytie too, the one remaining servant, negro, the one who would forbid him to
pass the kitchen door with what he brought) depended
on to keep life in them, but who now entered the house
itself on the (quite frequent now) afternoons when the
demon would suddenly curse the store empty of customers and lock the door and repair to the rear and in the
same tone in which he used to address his orderly or even
his house servants when he had them (and in which he
doubtless ordered Jones to fetch from the showcase the
ribbons and beads and candy) direct Jones to fetch the
jug, the two of them (and Jones even sitting now who
in the old days, the old dead Sunday afternoons of
monotonous peace which they spent beneath the scuppernong arbor in the back yard, the demon lying in the
hammock while Jones squatted against a post, rising
from time to time to pour for the demon from the
demijohn and the bucket of spring water which he had
fetched from the spring more than a mile away then
squatting again, chortling and chuckling and saying
'Sho, Mister Tawm' each time the demon paused)—the
two of them drinking turn and turn about from the jug
and the demon not lying down now nor even sitting but
reaching after the third or second drink that old man's
state of impotent and furious undefeat in which he
would rise, swaying and plunging and shouting for his
horse and pistols to ride single-handed into Washington
and shoot Lincoln (a year or so too late here) and Sherman both, shouting, 'Kill them! Shoot them down like
the dogs they are!' and Jones: 'Sho, Kernel; sho now' and

*catching him as he fell and commandeering the first
passing wagon to take him to the house and carry him
up the front steps and through the paintless formal door
beneath its fanlight imported pane by pane from
Europe which Judith held open for him to enter with no
change, no alteration in that calm frozen face which she
had worn for four years now, and on up the stairs and
into the bedroom and put him to bed like a baby and
then lie down himself on the floor beside the bed though
not to sleep since before dawn the man on the bed would
stir and groan and Jones would say, 'Hyer I am, Kernel. Hit's all right. They aint whupped us yit, air they?'
—this Jones who after the demon rode away with the
regiment when the granddaughter was only eight years
old would tell people that he 'was lookin after Major's
place and niggers' even before they had time to ask him
why he was not with the troops and perhaps in time
came to believe the lie himself, who was among the first
to greet the demon when he returned, to meet him at the
gate and say, 'Well, Kernel, they kilt us but they aint
whupped us yit, air they?' who even worked, labored,
sweat at the demon's behest during that first furious
period while the demon believed he could restore by sheer
indomitable willing the Sutpen's Hundred which he
remembered and had lost, labored with no hope of pay
or reward who must have seen long before the demon did
(or would admit it) that the task was hopeless—blind
Jones who apparently saw still in that furious lecherous
wreck the old fine figure of the man who once galloped
on the black thoroughbred about that domain two
boundaries of which the eye could not see from any point*

"Yes," Quentin said.

So that Sunday morning came and the demon up and away before dawn, Judith thinking she knew why since that morning the black stallion which he rode to Virginia and led back had a son born on his wife Penelope, only it was not that foal which the demon had got up early to look at and it was almost a week before they caught, found, the old negress, the midwife who was squatting beside the quilt pallet that dawn while Jones sat on the porch where the rusty scythe had leaned for two years, so that she could tell how she heard the horse and then the demon entered and stood over the pallet with the riding whip in his hand and looked down at the mother and the child and said, 'Well, Milly, too bad you're not a mare like Penelope. Then I could give you a decent stall in the stable' and turned and went out and the old negress squatted there and heard them, the voices, he and Jones: 'Stand back. Dont you touch me, Wash.' —'I'm going to tech you, Kernel' and she heard the whip too though not the scythe, no whistling air, no blow, nothing since always that which merely consummates punishment evokes a cry while that which evokes the last silence occurs in silence. And that night they finally found him and fetched him home in a wagon and carried him, quiet and bloody and with his teeth still showing in his parted beard (which was hardly grizzled although his hair was almost white now) in the light of the lanterns and the pine torches, up the steps where the tearless and stonefaced daughter held the door open for him too who used to like to drive fast to church and who rode fast there this time, only when it was all over he had never reached the church since the daughter (the woman of thirty now and looking older, not as the weak grow old, either enclosed in a static ballooning of already lifeless flesh or through a series of stages of gradual collapsing whose particles adhere not to some iron and still impervious framework but to one another as though in some communal and oblivious and mindless life of their own like a colony of maggots, but as the demon himself had grown old: with a kind of condensation, an anguished emergence of the primary indomitable ossification which the soft color and texture, the light electric aura of youth, had merely temporarily assuaged but never concealed—the spinster in homemade and shapeless clothing, with hands which could either transfer eggs or hold a plow straight in furrow) decided that he should be driven in to that same Methodist church in town where he had married her mother before returning to the grave in the cedar grove, who borrowed two half-wild young mules to pull the wagon: so he rode fast toward church as far as he went, in his homemade coffin, in his regimentals and sabre and embroidered gauntlets, until the young mules bolted and turned the wagon over and tumbled him, sabre plumes and all, into a ditch from which the daughter extricated him and fetched him back to the cedar grove and read the service herself. And no tears, no bereavement this time too, whether or not it was because she had no time to mourn since she ran the store herself now until she found a buyer for it, not keeping it open but carrying the keys to it in her apron pocket, hailed from the kitchen or the garden or even from the field since she and Clytie now did all the *plowing which was done, now that Jones was gone too, having followed the demon within twelve hours on that same Sunday (and maybe to the same place; maybe They would even have a scuppernong vine for them and no compulsions now of bread or ambition or fornication or vengeance and maybe they wouldn't even have to drink only they would miss this now and then without knowing what it was that they missed but not often; serene, pleasant, unmarked by time or change of weather, only just now and then something, a wind, a shadow, and the demon would stop talking and Jones would stop guffawing and they would look at one another, groping, grave, intent, and the demon would say, 'What was it, Wash? Something happened. What was it?' and Jones looking at the demon, groping too, sober too, saying, 'I dont know, Kernel. Whut?' each watching the other. Then the shadow would fade, the wind die away until at last Jones would say, serene, not even triumphant: 'They mought have kilt us, but they aint whupped us yit, air they?')—hailed by women and children with pails and baskets, whereupon she or Clytie would go to the store, unlock it, serve the customer, lock the store and return: until she sold the store at last and spent the money for a tombstone.* —("How was it?" Shreve said. "You told me; how was it? you and your father shooting quail, the gray day after it had rained all night and the ditch the horses couldn't cross so you and your father got down and gave the reins to—what was his name? the nigger on the mule? Luster.—Luster to lead them around the ditch" and he and his father crossed just as the rain began to come down again gray and solid and slow, making no sound, Quentin not aware yet of just where they were because he had been riding with his head lowered against the drizzle, until he looked up the slope before them where the wet yellow sedge died upward into the rain like melting gold and saw the grove, the clump of cedars on the crest of the hill dissolving into the rain as if the trees had been drawn in ink on a wet blotter—the cedars beyond which, beyond the ruined fields beyond which, would be the oak grove and the gray huge rotting deserted house half a mile away. Mr Compson had stopped to look back at Luster on the mule, the towsack he had been using for saddle now wrapped around his head, his knees drawn up under it, leading the horses on down the ditch to find a place to cross. "Better get on out of the rain," Mr Compson said. "He's not going to come within a hundred yards of those cedars anyway."

They went on up the slope. They could not see the two dogs at all, only the steady furrowing of the sedge where, invisible, the dogs quartered the slope until one of them flung up his head to look back. Mr Compson gestured with his hand toward the trees, he and Quentin following. It was dark among the cedars, the light more dark than gray even, the quiet rain, the faint pearly globules, materialising on the gun barrels and the five headstones like drops of not-quite-congealed meltings from cold candles on the marble: the two flat heavy vaulted slabs, the other three headstones leaning a little awry, with here and there a carved letter or even an entire word momentary and legible in the faint light which the raindrops brought particle by particle into the gloom and released; now the two dogs came in, drifted in like smoke, their hair close-plastered with damp, and curled down in one indistinguishable and apparently inextricable ball for warmth. Both the flat slabs were cracked across the middle by their own weight (and vanishing into the hole where the brick coping of one vault had fallen in was a smooth faint path worn by some small animal—possum probably—by generations of some small animal since there could have been nothing to eat in the grave for a long time) though the lettering was quite legible: *Ellen Coldfield Sutpen. Born October 9, 1817. Died January 23, 1863* and the other: *Thomas Sutpen, Colonel, 23rd Mississippi Infantry, C.S.A. Died August 12, 1869:* this last, the date, added later, crudely with a chisel, who even dead did not divulge where and when he had been born. Quentin looked at the stones quietly, thinking *Not beloved wife of. No. Ellen Coldfield Sutpen* "I wouldn't have thought they would have had any money to buy marble with in 1869," he said.

"He bought them himself," Mr Compson said. "He bought the two of them while the regiment was in Virginia, after Judith got word to him that her mother was dead. He ordered them from Italy, the best, the finest to be had—his wife's complete and his with the date left blank: and this while on active service with an army which had not only the highest

mortality rate of any before or since but which had
a custom of electing a new set of regimental officers
each year (and by which system he was at the moment entitled to call himself colonel, since he had
been voted in and Colonel Sartoris voted out only
last summer) so that for all he could know, before
his order could be filled or even received he might
be already under ground and his grave marked (if at
all) by a shattered musket thrust into the earth, or
lacking that he might be a second lieutenant or even
a private—provided of course that his men would
have the courage to demote him—yet he not only
ordered the stones and managed to pay for them,
but stranger still he managed to get them past a
seacoast so closely blockaded that the incoming run-
ners refused any cargo except ammunition——" It
seemed to Quentin that he could actually see them:
the ragged and starving troops without shoes, the
gaunt powder-blackened faces looking backward
over tattered shoulders, the glaring eyes in which
burned some indomitable desperation of undefeat
watching that dark interdict ocean across which a
grim lightless solitary ship fled with in its hold two
thousand precious pounds-space containing not bullets, not even something to eat, but that much bombastic and inert carven rock which for the next year
was to be a part of the regiment, to follow it into
Pennsylvania and be present at Gettysburg, moving
behind the regiment in a wagon driven by the
demon's body servant through swamp and plain and
mountain pass, the regiment moving no faster than

the wagon could, with starved gaunt men and gaunt spent horses knee deep in icy mud or snow, sweating and cursing it through bog and morass like a piece of artillery, speaking of the two stones as 'Colonel' and 'Mrs Colonel'; then through the Cumberland Gap and down through the Tennessee mountains, travelling at night to dodge Yankee patrols, and into Mississippi in the late fall of '64, where the daughter waited whose marriage he had interdict and who was to be a widow the next summer though apparently not bereaved, where his wife was dead and his son self-excommunicated and -banished, and put one of the stones over his wife's grave and set the other upright in the hall of the house, where Miss Coldfield possibly (maybe doubtless) looked at it every day as though it were his portrait, possibly (maybe doubtless here too) reading among the lettering more of maiden hope and virgin expectation than she ever told Quentin about, since she never mentioned the stone to him at all, and (the demon) drank the parched corn coffee and ate the hoe cake which Judith and Clytie prepared for him and kissed Judith on the forehead and said, 'Well, Clytie' and returned to the war, all in twenty-four hours; he could see it; he might even have been there. Then he thought *No. If I had been there I could not have seen it this plain*

"But that dont explain the other three," he said. "They must have cost something too."

"Who would have paid for them?" Mr Compson said. Quentin could feel him looking at him.

"Think." Quentin looked at the three identical headstones with their faint identical lettering, slanted a little in the soft loamy decay of accumulated cedar needles, these decipherable too when he looked close, the first one: *Charles Bon. Born in New Orleans, Louisiana. Died at Sutpen's Hundred, Mississippi, May 3, 1865. Aged 33 years and 5 months.* He could feel his father watching him.

"She did it," he said. "With that money she got when she sold the store."

"Yes," Mr Compson said. Quentin had to stoop and brush away some of the cedar needles to read the next one. As he did so one of the dogs rose and approached him, thrusting its head in to see what he was looking at like a human being would, as if from association with human beings it had acquired the quality of curiosity which is an attribute only of men and apes.

"Get away," he said, thrusting the dog back with one hand while with the other he brushed the cedar needles away, smoothing with his hand into legibility the faint lettering, the graved words: *Charles Etienne Saint-Valery Bon. 1859–1884* feeling his father watching him, remarking before he rose that the third stone bore that same date, 1884. "It couldn't have been the store this time," he said. "Because she sold the store in '70, and besides 1884 is the same date that's on hers" thinking how it would have been terrible for her sure enough if she had wanted to put *Beloved Husband of* on that first one.

"Ah," Mr Compson said. "That was the one your

grandfather attended to. Judith came into town one day and brought him the money, some of it, where she got it from he never knew, unless it was what she had left out of the price of the store which he sold for her; brought the money in with the inscription (except the date of death of course) all written out as you see it, during that three weeks while Clytie was in New Orleans finding the boy to fetch him back though your grandfather of course did not know this, money and inscription not for herself but for him."

"Oh," Quentin said.

"Yes. They lead beautiful lives—women. Lives not only divorced from, but irrevocably excommunicated from, all reality. That's why although their deaths, the instant of dissolution, are of no importance to them since they have a courage and fortitude in the face of pain and annihilation which would make the most spartan man resemble a puling boy, yet to them their funerals and graves, the little puny affirmations of spurious immortality set above their slumber, are of incalculable importance. You had an aunt once (you do not remember her because I never saw her myself but only heard the tale) who was faced with a serious operation which she became convinced she would not survive, at a time when her nearest female kin was a woman between whom and herself there had existed for years one of those bitter inexplicable (to the man mind) amicable enmities which occur between women of the same blood, whose sole worry about departing this world was to get rid of a certain brown dress which she owned and knew that the kinswoman knew she had never liked, which must be burned, not given away but burned in the back yard beneath the window where, by being held up to the window (and suffering excruciating pain) she could see it burned with her own eyes, because she was convinced that after she died the kinswoman, the logical one to take charge, would bury her in it."

"And did she die?" Quentin said.

"No. As soon as the dress was consumed she began to mend. She stood the operation and recovered and outlived the kinswoman by several years. Then one afternoon she died peacefully of no particular ailment and was buried in her wedding gown."

"Oh," Quentin said.

"Yes. But there was one afternoon in the summer of '70 when one of these graves (there were only three here then) was actually watered by tears. Your grandfather saw it; that was the year Judith sold the store and your grandfather attended to it for her and he had ridden out to see her about the matter and he witnessed it: the interlude, the ceremonial widowhood's bright dramatic pageantry. He didn't know at the time how the octoroon came to be here, how Judith could even have known about her to write her where Bon was dead. But there she was, with the eleven-year-old boy who looked more like eight. It must have resembled a garden scene by the Irish poet, Wilde: the late afternoon, the dark cedars

with the level sun in them, even the light exactly
right and the graves, the three pieces of marble
(your grandfather had advanced Judith the money
to buy the third stone with against the price of the
store) looking as though they had been cleaned and
polished and arranged by scene shifters who with
the passing of twilight would return and strike them
and carry them, hollow fragile and without weight,
back to the warehouse until they should be needed
again; the pageant, the scene, the act, entering upon
the stage—the magnolia-faced woman a little
plumper now, a woman created of by and for darkness whom the artist Beardsley might have dressed,
in a soft flowing gown designed not to infer bereavement or widowhood but to dress some interlude of slumbrous and fatal insatiation, of passionate
and inexorable hunger of the flesh, walking beneath
a lace parasol and followed by a bright gigantic
negress carrying a silk cushion and leading by the
hand the little boy whom Beardsley might not only
have dressed but drawn—a thin delicate child with
a smooth ivory sexless face who, after his mother
handed the negress the parasol and took the cushion
and knelt beside the grave and arranged her skirts
and wept, never released the negress' apron but
stood blinking quietly who, having been born and
lived all his life in a kind of silken prison lighted by
perpetual shaded candles, breathing for air the milk-
like and absolutely physical lambence which his
mother's days and hours emanated, had seen little
enough of sunlight before, let alone out-of-doors,

trees and grass and earth; and last of all, the other woman, Judith *(who, not bereaved, did not need to mourn* Quentin thought, thinking *Yes, I have had to listen too long)* who stood just inside the cedars, in the calico dress and the sunbonnet to match it, both faded and shapeless—the calm face, the hands which could plow or cut wood and cook or weave cloth folded before her, standing in the attitude of an indifferent guide in a museum, waiting, probably not even watching. Then the negress came and handed the octoroon a crystal bottle to smell and helped her to rise and took up the silk cushion and gave the octoroon the parasol and they returned to the house, the little boy still holding to the negress' apron, the negress supporting the woman with one arm and Judith following with that face like a mask or like marble, back to the house, across the tall scaling portico and into the house where Clytie was cooking the eggs and the cornbread on which she and Judith lived.

"She stayed a week. She passed the rest of that week in the one remaining room in the house whose bed had linen sheets, passed it in bed, in the new lace and silk and satin negligees subdued to the mauve and lilac of mourning—that room airless and shuttered, impregnated behind the sagging closed blinds with the heavy fainting odor of her flesh, her days, her hours, her garments, of eau-de-cologne from the cloth upon her temples, of the crystal phial which the negress alternated with the fan as she sat beside the bed between trips to the door to receive the trays

which Clytie carried up the stairs—Clytie, who did
that fetching and carrying as Judith made her, who
must have perceived whether Judith told her or not
that it was another negro whom she served, yet who
served the negress just as she would quit the kitchen
from time to time and search the rooms downstairs
until she found that little strange lonely boy sitting
quietly on a straight hard chair in the dim and shadowy library or parlor, with his four names and his
sixteenth-part black blood and his expensive esoteric
Fauntleroy clothing who regarded with an aghast
fatalistic terror the grim coffee-colored woman who
would come on bare feet to the door and look in at
him, who gave him not teacakes but the coarsest
cornbread spread with as coarse molasses (this sur-
reptitiously, not that the mother or the duenna
might object, but because the household did not
have food for eating between meals), gave it to him,
thrust it at him with restrained savageness, and who
found him one afternoon playing with a negro boy
about his own size in the road outside the gates and
cursed the negro child out of sight with level and
deadly violence and sent him, the other, back to the
house in a voice the very absence from which of
vituperation or rage made it seem just that much
more deadly and cold.

"Yes, Clytie, who stood impassive beside the
wagon on that last day, following the second ceremonial to the grave with the silk cushion and the
parasol and the smelling-bottle, when mother and
child and duenna departed for New Orleans. And

your grandfather never knew if it was Clytie who
watched, kept in touch by some means, waited for
the day, the moment, to come, the hour when the
little boy would be an orphan, and so went herself
to fetch him; or if it was Judith who did the waiting
and the watching and sent Clytie for him that winter, that December of 1871;—Clytie who had never
been further from Sutpen's Hundred than Jefferson
in her life, yet who made that journey alone to New
Orleans and returned with the child, the boy of
twelve now and looking ten, in one of the outgrown
Fauntleroy suits but with a new oversize overall
jumper coat which Clytie had bought for him (and
made him wear, whether against the cold or
whether not your grandfather could not say either)
over it and what else he owned tied up in a bandana
handkerchief—this child who could speak no English as the woman could speak no French who had
found him, hunted him down, in a French city and
brought him away, this child with a face not old but
without age, as if he had had no childhood, not in
the sense that Miss Rosa Coldfield says she had no
childhood, but as if he had not been human born but
instead created without agency of man or agony of
woman and orphaned by no human being (your
grandfather said you did not wonder what had become of the mother, you did not even care: death or
elopement or marriage: who would not grow from
one metamorphosis—dissolution or adultery—to
the next carrying along with her all the old accumulated rubbish-years which we call memory,

the recognisable *I*, but changing from phase to phase as the butterfly changes once the cocoon is cleared, carrying nothing of what was into what is, leaving nothing of what is behind but eliding complete and intact and unresisting into the next avatar as the overblown rose or magnolia elides from one rich June to the next, leaving no bones, no substance, no dust of whatever dead pristine soulless rich surrender anywhere between sun and earth) but produced complete and subject to no microbe in that cloyed and scented maze of shuttered silk as if he were the delicate and perverse spirit-symbol, immortal page of the ancient immortal Lilith, entering the actual world not at the age of one second but of twelve years, the delicate garments of his pagehood already half concealed beneath that harsh and shapeless denim cut to an iron pattern and sold by the millions—that burlesque uniform and regalia of the tragic burlesque of the sons of Ham;—a slight silent child who could not even speak English, picked suddenly up out of whatever debacle the only life he knew had disintegrated into, by a creature whom he had seen once and learned to dread and fear yet could not flee, held helpless and passive in a state which must have been some incredible compound of horror and trust, since although he could not even talk to her (they made, they must have made, that week's journey by steamboat among the cotton bales on the freight deck, eating and sleeping with negroes, where he could not even tell his companion when he was hungry or when he had to relieve

himself) and so could have only suspected, sur-
mised, where she was taking him, could have known
nothing certainly except that all he had ever been
familiar with was vanishing about him like smoke,
yet he made no resistance, returning quietly and
docilely to that decaying house which he had seen
one time, where the fierce brooding woman who
had come and got him lived with the calm white one
who was not even fierce, who was not anything
except calm, who to him did not even have a name
yet who was somehow so closely related to him as
to be the owner of the one spot on earth where he
had ever seen his mother weep;—returned, crossed
that strange threshold, that irrevocable demarcation,
not led, not dragged, but driven and herded by that
stern implacable presence, into that gaunt and barren household where his very silken remaining
clothes, his delicate shirt and stockings and shoes
which still remained to remind him of what he had
once been, vanished, fled from arms and body and
legs as if they had been woven of chimaeras or of
smoke.—Yes, sleeping in the trundle bed beside Judith's, beside that of the woman who looked upon
him and treated him with a cold unbending detached gentleness more discouraging than the fierce
ruthless constant guardianship of the negress who,
with a sort of invincible spurious humility slept on
a pallet on the floor, the child lying there between
them unasleep in some hiatus of passive and hopeless despair aware of this, aware of the woman on
the bed whose every look and action toward him,

whose every touch of the capable hands seemed at the moment of touching his body to lose all warmth and become imbued with cold implacable antipathy, and the woman on the pallet upon whom he had already come to look as might some delicate talonless and fangless wild beast crouched in its cage in some hopeless and desperate similitude of ferocity (and your grandfather said, 'Suffer little children to come unto Me': and what did He mean by that? how, if He meant that little children should need to *be* suffered to approach Him, what sort of earth had He created; that if they had to *suffer* in order to approach Him, what sort of heaven did He have?) look upon the human creature who feeds it, who fed him, thrust food which he himself could discern to be the choicest of what they had, food which he realised had been prepared for him by deliberate sacrifice, with that curious blend of savageness and pity, of yearning and hatred; who dressed him and washed him, thrust him into tubs of water too hot or too cold yet against which he dared make no outcry, and scrubbed him with harsh rags and soap, sometimes scrubbing at him with repressed fury as if she were trying to wash the smooth faint olive tinge from his skin as you might watch a child scrubbing at a wall long after the epithet, the chalked insult, has been obliterated;—lying there unsleeping in the dark between them, feeling them unasleep too, feeling them thinking about him, projecting about him and filling the thunderous solitude of his despair louder than speech could: *You are*

*not up here in this bed with me, where through no fault
nor willing of your own you should be, and you are not
down here on this pallet floor with me, where through
no fault nor willing of your own you must and will be,
not through any fault or willing of our own who would
not what we cannot just as we will and wait for what
must be.*

"And your grandfather did not know either just
which of them it was who told him that he was,
must be, a negro, who could neither have heard yet
nor recognised the term 'nigger', who even had no
word for it in the tongue he knew who had been
born and grown up in a padded silken vacuum cell
which might have been suspended on a cable a thousand fathoms in the sea, where pigmentation had
no more moral value than the silk walls and the
scent and the rose-colored candle shades, where the
very abstractions which he might have observed—
monogamy and fidelity and decorum and gentleness
and affection—were as purely rooted in the flesh's
offices as the digestive processes. Your grandfather
did not know if he was sent from the trundle bed at
last or if he quitted it by his own wish and will; if
when the time came when his loneliness and grief
became calloused, he retired himself from Judith's
bedroom or was sent from it, to sleep in the hall
(where Clytie had likewise moved her pallet)
though not on a pallet like her but on a cot, elevated
still and perhaps not by Judith's decree either but by
the negress' fierce inexorable spurious humility; and
then in the attic, the cot moved there, the few gar-

ments (the rags of the silk and broadcloth in which he had arrived, the harsh jeans and homespun which the two women bought and made for him, he accepting them with no thanks, no comment, accepting his garret room with no thanks, no comment, asking for and making no alteration in its spartan arrangements that they knew of until that second year when he was fourteen and one of them, Clytie or Judith, found hidden beneath his mattress the shard of broken mirror: and who to know what hours of amazed and tearless grief he might have spent before it, examining himself in the delicate and outgrown tatters in which he perhaps could not even remember himself, with quiet and incredulous incomprehension) hanging behind a curtain contrived of a piece of old carpet nailed across a corner. And Clytie sleeping in the hall below, barring the foot of the attic stairs, guarding his escape or exit as inexorably as a Spanish duenna, teaching him to chop wood and to work the garden and then to plow as his strength (his resiliency rather, since he would never be other than light in the bone and almost delicate) increased—the boy with his light bones and womanish hands struggling with what anonymous avatar of intractable Mule, whatever tragic and barren clown was his bound fellow and complement beneath his first father's curse, getting the hang of it gradually and the two of them, linked by the savage steel-and-wood male symbol, ripping from the prone rich female earth corn to feed them both while Clytie watched, never out of sight of

him, with that brooding fierce unflagging jealous
care, hurrying out whenever anyone white or black
stopped in the road as if to wait for the boy to
complete the furrow and pause long enough to be
spoken to, sending the boy on with a single quiet
word or even gesture a hundred times more fierce
than the level murmur of vituperation with which
she drove the passerby on. So he (your grandfather)
believed that it was neither of them. Not Clytie,
who guarded him as if he were a Spanish virgin,
who even before she could have even suspected that
he would ever come there to live, had interrupted
his first contact with a nigger and sent him back to
the house; not Judith, who could have refused at any
time to let him sleep in that white child's bed in her
room, who even if she could not have reconciled
herself to his sleeping on the floor could have forced
Clytie to take him into another bed with her, who
would have made a monk, a celibate, of him perhaps
yet not a eunuch, who may not have permitted him
to pass himself for a foreigner, yet who certainly
would not have driven him to consort with negroes.
Your grandfather didn't know, even though he did
know more than the town, the countryside, knew,
which was that there was a strange little boy living
out there who had apparently emerged from the
house for the first time at the age of about twelve
years, whose presence was not even unaccountable
to the town and county since they now believed
they knew why Henry had shot Bon and they wondered only where and how Clytie and Judith had

managed to keep him concealed all the time, believing now that it had been a widow who had buried Bon even though she had no paper to show for it, and only the incredulous (and shocked) speculation of your grandfather who, though he had that hundred dollars and the written directions in Judith's hand for this fourth tombstone in his safe at the time, had not yet associated the boy with the child he had seen two years ago when the octoroon came there to weep at the grave, to believe that the child might be Clytie's, got by its father on the body of his own daughter—a boy seen always near the house with Clytie always nearby, then a youth learning to plow and Clytie somewhere nearby too and it soon well known with what grim and unflagging alertness she discovered and interrupted any attempt to speak to him, and only your grandfather to couple at last the boy, the youth, with the child who had been there three or four years ago to visit that grave; —your grandfather to whose office Judith came that afternoon five years later and he could not remember when he had seen her in Jefferson before—the woman of forty now, in the same shapeless calico and faded sunbonnet, who would not even sit down, who despite the impenetrable mask which she used for face emanated a terrible urgency, who insisted that they walk on toward the courthouse while she talked, told him, toward the crowded room where the justice's court sat, the crowded room which they entered and your grandfather saw him, the boy (only a man now) handcuffed to an officer, his other

arm in a sling and his head bandaged since they had
taken him to the doctor first, your grandfather gradually learning what had happened or as much of it
as he could since the Court itself couldn't get very
much out of the witnesses, the ones who had fled
and sent for the sheriff, the ones (excepting that one
whom he had injured too badly to be present) with
whom he had fought—a negro ball held in a cabin
a few miles from Sutpen's Hundred and he there,
present and your grandfather never to know how
often he had done this before, whether he had gone
there to engage in the dancing or for the dice game
in progress in the kitchen where the trouble started,
trouble which he and not the negroes started according to the witnesses and for no reason, no accu-
sation of cheating, nothing; and he making no
denial, saying nothing, refusing to speak at all, sitting there sullen pale and silent: so that at this point
all truth, evidence vanished into a moiling clump of
negro backs and heads and black arms and hands
clutching sticks of stove wood and cooking imple-
ments and razors, the white man the focal point of
it and using a knife which he had produced from
somewhere, clumsily, with obvious lack of skill and
practice, yet with deadly earnestness and a strength
which his slight build denied, a strength composed
of sheer desperate will and imperviousness to the
punishment, the blows and slashes which he took in
return and did not even seem to feel;—no cause, no
reason for it; none to ever know exactly what happened, what curses and ejaculations which might

have indicated what it was that drove him and only your grandfather to fumble, grope, grasp the presence of that furious protest, that indictment of heaven's ordering, that gage flung into the face of what is with a furious and indomitable desperation which the demon himself might have shown, as if the child and then the youth had acquired it from the walls in which the demon had lived, the air which he had once walked in and breathed until that moment when his own fate which he had dared in his turn struck back at him; only your grandfather to sense that because the justice and the others present did not recognise him, did not recognise this slight man with his bandaged head and arm, his sullen impassive (and now bloodless) olive face, who refused to answer any questions, make any statement: so that the justice (Jim Hamblett it was) was already making his speech of indictment when your grandfather entered, utilising opportunity and audience to orate, his eyes already glazed with that cessation of vision of people who like to hear themselves talk in public: 'At this time, while our country is struggling to rise from beneath the iron heel of a tyrant oppressor, when the very future of the South as a place bearable for our women and children to live in depends on the labor of our own hands, when the tools which we have to use, to depend on, are the pride and integrity and forbearance of black men and the pride and integrity and forbearance of white; that you, I say, a white man, a white——' and your grandfather trying to reach him, stop him, trying to push through the crowd, saying, 'Jim. Jim. *Jim!*' and it already too late, as if Hamblett's own voice had waked him at last or as if someone had snapped his fingers under his nose and waked him, he looking at the prisoner now but saying 'white' again even while his voice died away as if the order to stop the voice had been shocked into short circuit, and every face in the room turned toward the prisoner as Hamblett cried, '*What are you? Who and where did you come from?*'

"Your grandfather got him out, quashed the indictment and paid the fine and brought him back to his office and talked to him while Judith waited in the anteroom. 'You are Charles Bon's son,' he said. 'I dont know,' the other answered, harsh and sullen. 'You dont remember?' your grandfather said. The other did not answer. Then your grandfather told him he must go away, disappear, giving him money to go on: 'Whatever you are, once you are among strangers, people who dont know you, you can be whatever you will. I will make it all right; I will talk to—to——What do you call her?' And he had gone too far now, but it was too late to stop; he sat there and looked at that still face which had no more expression than Judith's, nothing of hope nor pain: just sullen and inscrutable and looking down at the calloused womanish hands with their cracked nails which held the money while your grandfather thought how he could not say 'Miss Judith', since that would postulate the blood more than ever. Then he thought *I dont even know whether he wants*

to hide it or not. So he said Miss Sutpen. 'I will tell
Miss Sutpen, not where you are going of course,
because I wont know that myself. But just that you
are gone and that I knew you were going and that
you will be all right.'

"So he departed, and your grandfather rode out
to tell Judith, and Clytie came to the door and
looked full and steadily at his face and said nothing
and went to call Judith, and your grandfather
waited in that dim shrouded parlor and knew that
he would not have to tell either of them. He did not
have to. Judith came presently and stood and looked
at him and said, 'I suppose you wont tell me.'—'Not
wont, cant,' your grandfather said. 'But not now
because of any promise I made him. But he has
money; he will be——' and stopped, with that forlorn little boy invisible between them who had come
there eight years ago with the overall jumper over
what remained of his silk and broadcloth, who had
become the youth in the uniform—the tattered hat
and the overalls—of his ancient curse, who had become the young man with a young man's potence
yet was still that lonely child in his parchment-and-
denim hairshirt, and your grandfather speaking the
lame vain words, the specious and empty fallacies
which we call comfort, thinking *Better that he were
dead, better that he had never lived:* then thinking
what vain and empty recapitulation that would be
to her if he were to say it, who doubtless had already
said it, thought it, changing only the person and the
number. He returned to town. And now, next time,

he was not sent for; he learned it as the town learned it: by that country grapevine whose source is among negroes, and he, Charles Etienne Saint-Valery Bon, already returned (not home again; returned) before your grandfather learned how he had come back, appeared, with a coal black and ape-like woman and an authentic wedding license, brought back by the woman since he had been so severely beaten and mauled recently that he could not even hold himself on the spavined and saddleless mule on which he rode while his wife walked beside it to keep him from falling off; rode up to the house and apparently flung the wedding license in Judith's face with something of that invincible despair with which he had attacked the negroes in the dice game. And none ever to know what incredible tale lay behind that year's absence which he never referred to and which the woman who, even a year later and after their son was born, still existed in that aghast and automaton-like state in which she had arrived, did not, possibly could not, recount but which she seemed to exude gradually and by a process of terrific and incredulous excretion like the sweat of fear or anguish: how he had found her, dragged her out of whatever two dimensional backwater (the very name of which, town or village, she either had never known or the shock of her exodus from it had driven the name forever from her mind and memory) her mentality had been capable of coercing food and shelter from, and married her, held her very hand doubtless while she made the laborious cross on the register before she even knew his name or knew that he was not a white man (and this last none knew even now if she knew for certain, even after the son was born in one of the dilapidated slave cabins which he rebuilt after renting his parcel of land from Judith); how there followed something like a year composed of a succession of periods of utter immobility like a broken cinema film, which the white-colored man who had married her spent on his back recovering from the last mauling he had received, in frowsy stinking rooms in places—towns and cities —which likewise had no names to her, broken by other periods, intervals, of furious and incomprehensible and apparently reasonless moving, progression—a maelstrom of faces and bodies through which the man thrust, dragging her behind him, toward or from what, driven by what fury which would not let him rest, she did not know, each one to end, finish, as the one before it had so that it was almost a ritual—the man apparently hunting out situations in order to flaunt and fling the ape-like body of his charcoal companion in the faces of all and any who would retaliate: the negro stevedores and deckhands on steamboats or in city honky-tonks who thought he was a white man and believed it only the more strongly when he denied it; the white men who, when he said he was a negro, believed that he lied in order to save his skin, or worse: from sheer besotment of sexual perversion; in either case the result the same: the man with body and limbs almost as light and delicate as a girl's giving the first blow, usually unarmed and heedless of the numbers opposed to him, with that same fury and implacability and physical imperviousness to pain and punishment, neither cursing nor panting, but laughing.

"So he showed Judith the license and took his wife, already far gone with the child, to the ruined cabin which he had chosen to repair and installed her, kenneled her with a gesture perhaps, and returned to the house. And nobody to know what transpired that evening between him and Judith, in whatever carpetless room furnished with whatever chairs and such which they had not had to chop up and burn to cook food or for warmth or maybe to heat water for illness from time to time—the woman who had been widowed before she had been a bride, the son of the man who had bereaved her and a hereditary negro concubine, who had not resented his black blood so much as he had denied the white, and this with a curious and outrageous exaggeration in which was inherent its own irrevocability, almost exactly as the demon himself might have done it. (*Because there was love* Mr Compson said *There was that letter she brought and gave to your grandmother to keep* He (Quentin) could see it, as plainly as he saw the one open upon the open text book on the table before him, white in his father's dark hand against his linen leg in the September twilight where the cigar-smell, the wistaria-smell, the fireflies drifted, thinking *Yes. I have heard too much, I have been told too much; I have had to listen to too much, too long* thinking *Yes, almost exactly like Father: that letter, and who to know what moral restoration she might have contemplated in the privacy of that house, that room, that night, what hurdling of iron old traditions since she had seen almost everything else she had learned to call stable vanish like straws in a gale;* —*she sitting there beside the lamp in a straight chair, erect, in the same calico save that the sunbonnet would be missing now, the head bare now, the once coal-black hair streaked with gray now while he faced her, standing. He would not have sat; perhaps she would not even have asked him to, and the cold level voice would not be much louder than the sound of the lamp's flame: 'I was wrong. I admit it. I believed that there were things which still mattered just because they had mattered once. But I was wrong. Nothing matters but breath, breathing, to know and to be alive. And the child, the license, the paper. What about it? That paper is between you and one who is inescapably negro; it can be put aside, no one will anymore dare bring it up than any other prank of a young man in his wild youth. And as for the child, all right. Didn't my own father beget one? and he none the worse for it? We will even keep the woman and the child if you wish; they can stay here and Clytie will . . . ' watching him, staring at him yet not moving, immobile, erect, her hands folded motionless on her lap, hardly breathing as if he were some wild bird or beast which might take flight at the expansion and contraction of her nostrils or the movement of her breast: 'No: I. I will. I will raise it, see that it. . . . It does not need to have any name; you will neither have to see it*

*again nor to worry. We will have General Compson sell
some of the land; he will do it, and you can go. Into the
North, the cities, where it will not matter even if——
But they will not. They will not dare. I will tell them
that you are Henry's son and who could or would dare
to dispute——' and he standing there, looking at her or
not looking at her she cannot tell since his face would
be lowered—the still expressionless thin face, she watching him, not daring to move, her voice murmuring,
clear enough and full enough yet hardly reaching him:
'Charles': and he: 'No, Miss Sutpen': and she again, still
without moving, not stirring so much as a muscle, as
if she stood on the outside of the thicket into which she
had cajoled the animal which she knew was watching
her though she could not see it, not quite cringing, not
in any terror or even alarm but in that restive light
incorrigibility of the free which would leave not even a
print on the earth which lightly bore it and she not
daring to put out the hand with which she could have
actually touched it but instead just speaking to it, her
voice soft and swooning, filled with that seduction, that
celestial promise which is the female's weapon: 'Call me
Aunt Judith, Charles'*) Yes, who to know if he said
anything or nothing, turning, going out, she still
sitting there, not moving, not stirring, watching
him, still seeing him, penetrating walls and darkness
too to watch him walk back down the weedy lane
between the deserted collapsed cabins toward that
one where his wife waited, treading the thorny and
flint-paved path toward the Gethsemane which he
had decreed and created for himself, where he had

crucified himself and come down from his cross for a moment and now returned to it.

"Not your grandfather. He knew only what the town, the county, knew: that the strange little boy whom Clytie had used to watch and had taught to farm, who had sat, a grown man, in the justice's court that day with his head bandaged and one arm in a sling and the other in a handcuff, who had vanished and then returned with an authentic wife resembling something in a zoo, now farmed on shares a portion of the Sutpen plantation, farmed it pretty well, with solitary and steady husbandry within his physical limitations, the body and limbs which still looked too light for the task which he had set himself, who lived like a hermit in the cabin which he rebuilt and where his son was presently born, who consorted with neither white nor black (Clytie did not watch him now; she did not need to) and who was not seen in Jefferson but three times during the next four years and then to appear, be reported by the negroes who seemed to fear either him or Clytie or Judith, as being either blind or violently drunk in the negro store district on Depot Street, where your grandfather would come and take him away (or if he were too drunk, had become violent, the town officers) and keep him until his wife, the black gargoyle, could hitch the team back into the wagon and come, with nothing alive about her but her eyes and hands, and load him into it and take him home. So they did not even miss him from town at first; it was the County Medical Officer who told your grandfather that he had yellow fever and that Judith had had him moved into the big house and was nursing him and now Judith had the disease too, and your grandfather told him to notify Miss Coldfield and he (your grandfather) rode out there one day. He did not dismount; he sat his horse and called until Clytie looked down at him from one of the upper windows and told him 'they didn't need nothing'. Within the week your grandfather learned that Clytie had been right, or was right now anyway, though it was Judith who died first."

"Oh," Quentin said.—*Yes* he thought *Too much, too long* remembering how he had looked at the fifth grave and thought how whoever had buried Judith must have been afraid that the other dead would contract the disease from her, since her grave was at the opposite side of the enclosure, as far from the other four as the enclosure would permit, thinking *Father wont have to say 'think' this time* because he knew who had ordered and bought that headstone before he read the inscription on it, thinking about, imagining what careful printed directions Judith must have roused herself (from delirium possibly) to write down for Clytie when she knew that she was going to die; and how Clytie must have lived during the next twelve years while she raised the child which had been born in the old slave cabin and scrimped and saved the money to finish paying out the stone on which Judith had paid his grandfather the hundred dollars twenty-four years ago and which, when his grandfather tried to refuse it, she (Clytie) set the rusty can full of nickels and dimes and frayed paper money on the desk and walked out of the office without a word. He had to brush the clinging cedar needles from this one also to read it, watching these letters also emerge beneath his hand, wondering quietly how they could have clung there, not have been blistered to ashes at the instant of contact with the harsh and unforgiving threat: *Judith Coldfield Sutpen. Daughter of Ellen Coldfield. Born October 3, 1841. Suffered the Indignities and Travails of this World for 42 Years, 4 Months, 9 Days, and went to Rest at Last February 12, 1884. Pause, Mortal; Remember Vanity and Folly and Beware* thinking (Quentin) *Yes. I didn't need to ask who invented that, put that one up,* thinking, *Yes, to too much, too long. I didn't need to listen then but I had to hear it and now I am having to hear it all over again because he sounds just like Father: Beautiful lives—women do. In very breathing they draw meat and drink from some beautiful attenuation of unreality in which the shades and shapes of facts—of birth and bereavement, of suffering and bewilderment and despair—move with the substanceless decorum of lawn party charades, perfect in gesture and without significance or any ability to hurt. Miss Rosa ordered that one. She decreed that headstone of Judge Benbow. He had been the executor of her father's estate, appointed by no will since Mr Coldfield left neither will nor estate except the house and the rifled shell of the store. So he appointed himself, elected himself probably out of some conclave of neighbors and citizens who came together to discuss her affairs and what to do with her after they realised that nothing under the sun, certainly no man nor committee of men, would ever persuade her to go back to her niece and brother-in-law*

*—the same citizens and neighbors who left baskets of
food on her doorstep at night, the dishes (the plates
containing the food, the napkins which covered it) from
which she never washed but returned soiled to the empty
basket and set the basket back on the same step where she
had found it as if to carry completely out the illusion
that it had never existed or at least that she had never
touched, emptied, it, had not come out and taken the
basket up with that air which had nothing whatever of
furtiveness in it nor even defiance, who doubtless tasted
the food, criticised its quality or cooking, chewed and
swallowed it and felt it digest yet still clung to that
delusion, that calm incorrigible insistence that that
which all incontrovertible evidence tells her is so does
not exist, as women can;—that same self deluding
which declined to admit that the liquidation of the store
had left her something, that she had been left anything
but a complete pauper, who would not accept the actual
money from the sale of the store from Judge Benbow yet
would accept the money's value (and after a few years,
over-value) in a dozen ways: would use casual negro
boys who happened to pass the house, stopping them and
commanding them to rake her yard and they doubtless
as aware as the town was that there would be no mention of pay from her, that they would not even see her
again though they knew she was watching them from
behind the curtains of a window, but that Judge Benbow would pay them—would enter the stores and command objects from the shelves and showcases exactly as
she commanded that two hundred dollar headstone from
Judge Benbow, and walk out of the store with them—
who with the same aberrant cunning which would not*

wash the dishes and napkins from the baskets declined to have any discussion of her affairs with Benbow since she must have known that the sums which she had received from him must have years ago over-balanced (he, Benbow, had in his office a portfolio, a fat one, with Estate of Goodhue Coldfield. Private *written across it in indelible ink. After the Judge died his son Percy opened it. It was filled with racing forms and cancelled betting tickets on horses whose very bones were no man knew where now, which had won and lost races on the Memphis track forty years ago, and a ledger, a careful tabulation in the Judge's hand, each entry indicating the date and the horse's name and his wager and whether he won or lost; and another one showing how for forty years he had put each winning and an amount equal to each loss, to that mythical account) whatever the store had brought*

But you were not listening, because you knew it all already, had learned, absorbed it already without the medium of speech somehow from having been born and living beside it, with it, as children will and do: so that what your father was saying did not tell you anything so much as it struck, word by word, the resonant strings of remembering, who had been here before, seen these graves more than once in the rambling expeditions of boyhood whose aim was more than the mere hunting of game, just as you had seen the old house too, been familiar with how it would look before you even saw it, became large enough to go out there one day with four or five other boys of your size and age and dare one another to evoke the ghost, since it would have to be haunted, could not but be haunted although it had stood

*there empty and unthreatening for twenty-six years
and nobody to meet or report any ghost until the wagon
full of strangers moving from Arkansas tried to stop
and spend the night in it and something happened before
they could begin to unload the wagon even, what they
did not or could not or would not tell but which had
them back in the wagon and the mules going back down
the drive at a gallop, all in about ten minutes, not to
stop until they reached Jefferson—the rotting shell with
its sagging portico and scaling walls, its sagging blinds
and blank-shuttered windows, set in the middle of the
domain which had reverted to the state and had been
bought and sold and bought and sold again and again
and again. No, you were not listening; you didn't have
to: then the dogs stirred, rose; you looked up and sure
enough, just as your father had said he would, Luster
had halted the mule and the two horses in the rain about
fifty yards from the cedars, sitting there with his knees
drawn up under the towsack and enclosed by the cloudy
vapor of the steaming animals as though he were looking at you and your father out of some lugubrious and
painless purgatory. 'Come on in out of the rain, Luster,'
your father said. 'I wont let the old Colonel hurt you.'
—'Yawl come on and less go home,' Luster said. 'Aint
no more hunting today.'—'We'll get wet,' your father
said. 'I'll tell you what: we'll ride on over to that old
house. We can keep good and dry there.' But Luster
didn't budge, sitting there in the rain and inventing
reasons not to go to the house—that the roof would leak
or that you would all three catch cold with no fire or
that you would all get so wet before you reached it that
the best thing to do would be to go straight home: and*

your father laughing at Luster but you not laughing so much because even though you were not black like Luster was, you were not any older, and you and Luster had both been there that day when the five of you, the five boys all of an age, began daring one another to enter the house long before you reached it, coming up from the rear, into the old street of the slave quarters—a jungle of sumach and persimmon and briers and honeysuckle, and the rotting piles of what had once been log walls and stone chimneys and shingle roofs among the undergrowth except one, that one; you coming up to it; you didn't see the old woman at all at first because you were watching the boy, the Jim Bond, the hulking slack-mouthed saddle-colored boy a few years older and bigger than you were, in patched and faded yet quite clean shirt and overalls too small for him, working in the garden patch beside the cabin: so you didn't even know she was there until all of you started and whirled as one and found her watching you from a chair tilted back against the cabin wall—a little dried-up woman not much bigger than a monkey and who might have been any age up to ten thousand years, in faded voluminous skirts and an immaculate headrag, her bare coffee-colored feet wrapped around the chair rung like monkeys do, smoking a clay pipe and watching you with eyes like two shoe buttons buried in the myriad wrinkles of her coffee-colored face, who just looked at you and said without even removing the pipe and in a voice almost like a white woman's: 'What do you want?' and after a moment one of you said 'Nothing' and then you were all running without knowing which of you began to

*run first nor why since you were not scared, back across
the fallow and rain-gutted and brier-choked old fields
until you came to the old rotting snake fence and crossed
it, hurled yourselves over it, and then the earth, the
land, the sky and trees and woods, looked different
again, all right again*

"Yes," Quentin said.

"And that was the one Luster was talking about
now," Shreve said, "And your father watching you
again because you hadn't heard the name before,
hadn't even thought that he must have a name that
day when you saw him in the vegetable patch, and
you said, 'Who? Jim what?' and Luster said, 'Das
him. Bright-colored boy whut stay wid dat ole
woman' and your father still watching you and you
said, 'Spell it' and Luster said, 'Dat's a lawyer word.
Whut dey puts you under when de Law ketches
you. I des spells readin words.' And that was him,
the name Bond now and he wouldn't care about
that, who had inherited what he was from his
mother and only what he could never have been
from his father, and if your father had asked him if
he was Charles Bon's son he not only would not
have known either, he wouldn't have cared: and if
you had told him he was, it would have touched and
then vanished from what you (not he) would have
had to call his mind long before it could have set up
any reaction at all, either of pride or pleasure, anger
or grief?"

"Yes," Quentin said.

"And that he lived in that cabin behind the

haunted house for twenty-six years, he and the old woman who must be more than seventy now yet who had no white hair under that headrag, whose flesh had not sagged but looked instead like she had grown old up to a certain point just like normal people do, then had stopped, and instead of turning gray and soft she had begun to shrink so that the skin of her face and hands broke into a million tiny cross-hair wrinkles and her body just grew smaller and smaller like something being shrunk in a furnace, like the Bornese do their captured heads—who might well have been the ghost if one was ever needed, if anybody ever had so little else to do as to prowl around the house, which there was not; if there could have been anything in it to protect from prowlers, which there was not; if there had been anyone of them left to hide or need concealment in it, which there was not. And yet this old gal, this Aunt Rosa, told you that someone was hiding out there and you said it was Clytie or Jim Bond and she said No and you said it would have to be because the demon was dead and Judith was dead and Bon was dead and Henry gone so far he hadn't even left a grave: and she said No and so you went out there, drove the twelve miles at night in a buggy and you found Clytie and Jim Bond both in it and you said You see? and she (the Aunt Rosa) still said No and so you went on: and there was?"

"Yes."

"Wait then," Shreve said. "For God's sake wait.")

VII

There was no snow on Shreve's arm now, no sleeve on his arm at all now: only the smooth cupid-fleshed forearm and hand coming back into the lamp and taking a pipe from the empty coffee can where he kept them, filling it and lighting it. So it is zero outside, Quentin thought; soon he will raise the window and do deep-breathing in it, clench-fisted and naked to the waist, in the warm and rosy orifice above the iron quad. But he had not done so yet, and now the moment, the thought, was an hour past and the pipe lay smoked out and overturned and cold, with a light sprinkling of ashes about it, on the table before Shreve's crossed pink bright-haired arms while he watched Quentin from behind the two opaque and lamp-glared moons of his spectacles. "So he just wanted a grandson," he said. "That was all he was after. Jesus, the South is fine, isn't it. It's better than the theatre, isn't it. It's better than Ben Hur, isn't it. No wonder you have to come away now and then, isn't it."

Quentin did not answer. He sat quite still, facing the table, his hands lying on either side of the open text book on which the letter rested: the rectangle of paper folded across the middle and now open, three quarters open, whose bulk had raised half itself by the leverage of the old crease in weightless and paradoxical levitation, lying at such an angle that he could not possibly have read it, deciphered it, even without this added distortion. Yet he seemed to be looking at it, or as near as Shreve could tell, he was, his face lowered a little, brooding, almost sullen. "He told Grandfather about it," he said. "That time when the architect escaped, tried to, tried to escape into the river bottom and go back to New Orleans or wherever it was, and he—" ("The demon, hey?" Shreve said. Quentin did not answer him, did not pause, his voice level, curious, a little dreamy yet still with that overtone of sullen bemusement, of smoldering outrage: so that Shreve, still too, resembling in his spectacles and nothing else (from the waist down the table concealed him; anyone entering the room would have taken him to be stark naked) a baroque effigy created out of colored cake dough by someone with a faintly nightmarish affinity for the perverse, watched him with thoughtful and intent curiosity.)"—sent word in to Grandfather and some others and got his dogs and his wild niggers out and hunted the architect down and made him take earth in a cave under the river bank two days later. That was in the second summer, when they had finished all the brick and had the foundations laid and most of the big timbers cut and trimmed, and one day the architect couldn't stand it anymore or he was afraid he would starve or that the wild niggers (and maybe

Colonel Sutpen too) would run out of grub and eat him or maybe he got homesick or maybe he just had to go—" ("Maybe he had a girl," Shreve said. "Or maybe he just wanted a girl. You said the demon and the niggers didn't have but two." Quentin did not answer this either; again he might not have heard, talking in that curious repressed calm voice as though to the table before him or the book upon it or the letter upon the book or his hands lying on either side of the book.) "—and so he went. He seemed to vanish in broad daylight, right out from the middle of twenty-one people. Or maybe it was just Sutpen's back that was turned, and that the niggers saw him go and didn't think it needed mentioning; that being wild men they probably didn't know what Sutpen himself was up to and him naked in the mud with them all day. So I reckon they never did know what the architect was there for, supposed to do or had done or could do or was, so maybe they thought Sutpen had sent him, told him to go away and drown himself, go away and die, or maybe just go away. So he did, jumped up in broad daylight, in his embroidered vest and Fauntleroy tie and a hat like a Baptist congressman and probably carrying the hat in his hand, and ran into the swamp and the niggers watched him out of sight and then went back to work and Sutpen didn't see it, didn't even miss him until night, suppertime probably, and the niggers told him and he declared a holiday tomorrow because he would have to get out and borrow some dogs. Not that he would have needed dogs, with his niggers to trail, but maybe he thought that the guests, the others, would not be used to trailing with niggers and would expect dogs. And Grandfather (he was young then too) brought some champagne and some of the others brought whiskey and they began to gather out there a little after sundown, at his house that didn't even have walls yet, that wasn't anything yet but some lines of bricks sunk into the ground but that was all right because they didn't go to bed anyhow, Grandfather said, they just sat around the fire with the champagne and the whiskey and a quarter of the last venison he had killed, and about midnight the man with the dogs came. Then it was daylight and the dogs had a little trouble at first because some of the wild niggers had run out about a mile of the trail just for fun. But they got the trail straightened out at last, the dogs and the niggers in the bottom and most of the men riding along the edge of it where the going was good. But Grandfather and Colonel Sutpen went with the dogs and the niggers because Sutpen was afraid the niggers might catch the architect before he could reach them. He and Grandfather had to walk a good deal, sending one of the niggers to lead the horses on around the bad places until they could ride again. Grandfather said it was fine weather and the trail lay pretty good but he said it would have been fine if the architect had just waited until October or November. And so he told Grandfather something about it.

"His trouble was innocence. All of a sudden he discovered, not what he wanted to do but what he just had to do, had to do it whether he wanted to or not, because if he did not do it he knew that he could never live with himself for the rest of his life, never live with what all the men and women that had died to make him had left inside of him for him to pass on, with all the dead ones waiting and watching to see if he was going to do it right, fix things right so that he would be able to look in the face not only the old dead ones but all the living ones that would come after him when he would be one of the dead. And that at the very moment when he discovered what it was, he found out that this was the last thing in the world he was equipped to do because he not only had not known that he would have to do this, he did not even know that it existed to be wanted, to need to be done, until he was almost fourteen years old. Because he was born in West Virginia, in the mountains where—" ("Not in West Virginia," Shreve said. "—What?" Quentin said. "Not in West Virginia," Shreve said. "Because if he was twenty-five years old in Mississippi in 1833, he was born in 1808. And there wasn't any West Virginia in 1808 because—" "All right," Quentin said. "—West Virginia wasn't admitted—" "All right all right," Quentin said. "—into the United States until—" "All right all right all right," Quentin said.) "—where what few other people he knew lived in log cabins boiling with children like the one he was born in—men and grown boys who hunted or lay before the fire on the floor while the women and older girls stepped back and forth across them to reach the fire to cook, where the only colored people were Indians and you only looked down at them over your rifle sights, where he had never even heard of, never imagined, a place, a land divided neatly up and actually owned by men who did nothing but ride over it on fine horses or sit in fine clothes on the galleries of big houses while other people worked for them; he did not even imagine then that there was any such way to live or to want to live, or that there existed all the objects to be wanted which there were, or that the ones who owned the objects not only could look down on the ones that didn't, but could be supported in the down-looking not only by the others who owned objects too but by the very ones that were looked down on that didn't own objects and knew they never would. Because where he lived the land belonged to anybody and everybody and so the man who would go to the trouble and work to fence off a piece of it and say 'This is mine' was crazy; and as for objects, nobody had any more of them than you did because everybody had just what he was strong enough or energetic enough to take and keep, and only that crazy man would go to the trouble to take or even want more than he could eat or swap for powder and whiskey. So he didn't even know there was a country all divided and fixed and neat with a people living on it all divided and fixed and neat because of what color their skins happened to be and what they happened to own, and where a certain few men not only had the power of life and death and barter and sale over others, they had living human men to perform the endless repetitive personal offices such as pouring the very whiskey from the jug and putting the glass into his hand or pulling off his boots for him to go to bed that all men have had to do for themselves since time began and would have to do until they died and which no man ever has or ever will like to do but which no man that he knew had ever anymore thought of evading than he had thought of evading the effort of chewing and swallowing and breathing. When he was a child he didn't listen to the vague and cloudy tales of Tidewater splendor that penetrated even his mountains because then he could not understand what the people meant, and when he became a boy he didn't listen to them because there was nothing in sight to compare and gauge the tales by and so give the words life and meaning, and no chance that he ever would (certainly no belief or thought that someday he might), and because he was too busy doing the things that boys do; and when he got to be a youth and curiosity itself exhumed the tales which he did not know he had heard and speculated about them, he was interested and would have liked to see the places once, but without envy or regret, because he just thought that some people were spawned in one place and some in another, some spawned rich (lucky, he may have called it: or maybe he called lucky, rich) and some not, and that (so he told Grandfather) the men themselves had little to do with the choosing and less of the regret because (he told Grandfather this too) it had never once occurred to him that any man should take any such blind accident as that as authority or warrant to look down at others, any others. So he had hardly heard of such a world until he fell into it.

"That's how it was. They fell into it, the whole family, returned to the coast from which the first Sutpen had come (when the ship from the Old Bailey reached Jamestown probably), tumbled head over heels back to Tidewater by sheer altitude, elevation and gravity, as if whatever slight hold the family had had (he said something to Grandfather about his mother dying about that time and how his pap said she was a fine wearying woman and that he would miss her; and something about how it was the wife that had got his father even that far West) on the mountain had broken and now the whole passel of them from the father through the grown daughters down to one that couldn't even walk yet, sliding back down out of the mountains and skating in a kind of accelerating and sloven and inert coherence like a useless collection of flotsam on a flooded river moving by some perverse automotivation such as inanimate objects sometimes show, backward against the very current of the stream, across the Virginia plateau and into the slack lowlands about the mouth of the James River. He didn't know why they moved, or didn't remember the reason if he ever knew it—whether it was optimism, hope in his father's breast or nostalgia, since he didn't know just where his father had come from, whether the coun-

try to which they returned was it or not, or even if
his father knew, remembered, wanted to remember
and find it again;—whether somebody, some trav-
eler, had told him of some easy place or time, some
escape from the hardship of getting food and keeping warm in the mountain way, or if perhaps somebody his father knew once or who knew his father
once and remembered him, happened to think about
him, or someone kin to him who had tried to forget
him and couldn't quite do it, had sent for him and
he obeying, going not for the promised job but for
the ease, having faith perhaps in the blood kinship
to evade the labor if it was kinship, in his own inertia
and in whatever gods had watched over him this far
if it were not. But he—" ("The demon," Shreve
said) "—didn't know, or remember, whether he had
ever heard, been told, the reason or not. All he
remembered was that one morning the father rose
and told the older girls to pack what food they had,
and somebody wrapped up the baby and somebody
else threw water on the fire and they walked down
the mountain to where roads existed. They had a
lopsided two-wheeled cart and two spavined oxen
now. He told Grandfather he did not remember just
where nor when nor how his father had got it, and
he (he was ten then; the two older boys had left
home some time before and had not been heard of
since) driving the oxen since almost as soon as they
got the cart his father began the practice of accomplishing that part of the translation devoted to motion flat on his back in the cart, oblivious among the

quilts and lanterns and well buckets and bundles of clothing and children, snoring with alcohol. That was how he told it. He didn't remember if it was weeks or months or a year they traveled (except that one of the older girls who had left the cabin unmarried was still unmarried when they finally stopped, though she had become a mother before they lost the last blue mountain range), whether it was that winter and then spring and then summer overtook and passed them on the road or whether they overtook and passed in slow succession the seasons as they descended or whether it was the descent itself that did it and they not progressing parallel in time but descending perpendicularly through temperature and climate—a (you couldn't call it a period because as he remembered it or as he told Grandfather he did, it didn't have either a definite beginning or a definite ending. Maybe attenuation is better)—an attenuation from a kind of furious inertness and patient immobility while they sat in the cart outside the doors of doggeries and taverns and waited for the father to drink himself insensible, to a sort of dreamy and destinationless locomotion after they had got the old man out of whatever shed or outhouse or barn or ditch and loaded him into the cart again and during which they did not seem to progress at all but just to hang suspended while the earth itself altered, flattened and broadened out of the mountain cove where they had all been born, mounting, rising about them like a tide in which the strange harsh rough faces about the doggery doors into which the old man was just entering or was just being carried or thrown out (and this one time by a huge bull of a nigger, the first black man, slave, they had ever seen, who emerged with the old man over his shoulder like a sack of meal and his—the nigger's—mouth loud with laughing and full of teeth like tombstones) swam up and vanished and were replaced; the earth, the world, rising about them and flowing past as if the cart moved on a treadmill (and it now spring and now summer and they still moving on toward a place they had never seen and had no conception of, let alone wanted to go to; and from a place, a little lost spot on the side of a hill back to which probably not one of them— excepting possibly the usually insensible father who made one stage of the journey accompanied by the raspberry-colored elephants and snakes which he seems to have been hunting for—could have led the way) bringing into and then removing from their sober static country astonishment the strange faces and places, both faces and places—doggeries and taverns now become hamlets, hamlets now become villages, villages now towns and the country flattened out now with good roads and fields and niggers working in the fields while white men sat fine horses and watched them, and more fine horses and men in fine clothes, with a different look in the face from mountain men about the taverns where the old man was not even allowed to come in by the front door and from which his mountain drinking manners got him ejected before he would have time to get drunk good (so that now they began to make really pretty good time) and no laughter and jeers to the ejecting now, even if the laughter and jeers had been harsh and without much gentleness in them.

"That's the way he got it. He had learned the difference not only between white men and black ones, but he was learning that there was a difference between white men and white men not to be measured by lifting anvils or gouging eyes or how much whiskey you could drink then get up and walk out of the room. That is, he had begun to discern that without being aware of it yet. He still thought that that was just a matter of where you were spawned and how; lucky or not lucky; and that the lucky ones would be even slower and lother than the unlucky to take any advantage of it or credit for it, feel that it gave them anything more than the luck; that they would feel if anything more tender toward the unlucky than the unlucky would ever need to feel toward them. He was to find all that out later. He remembered when he did it, because that was the same second when he discovered the innocence. It was not the second, the moment, that he was long about: it was the getting to it: the moment when they must have realised, believed at last that they were no longer traveling, moving, going somewhere—not the being still at last and in a fashion settled, because they had done that before on the road; he remembered how one time the gradual difference in comfort between the presence and absence of shoes and warm clothing occurred in one place: a cowshed where the sister's baby was born and, as he told Grandfather, for all he could remember, locate in elapsed time, conceived too. Because they were stopped now at last. He didn't know where they were. For a time, during the first days or weeks or months, the woodsman's instinct which he had acquired from the environment where he grew up or maybe had been bequeathed him by the two brothers who had vanished, one of which had been as far West as the Mississippi River one time— bequeathed him along with the wornout buckskin garments and such which they left in the cabin when they departed the last time for good—and which he had sharpened by boy's practice at small game and such, kept him oriented so that he could have (so he said) found his way back to the mountain cabin in time. But that was past now, the moment when he last could have said exactly where he had been born now weeks and months (maybe a year, the year, since that was when he became confused about his age and was never able to straighten it out again, so that he told Grandfather that he did not know within a year on either side just how old he was) behind him. So he knew neither where he had come from nor where he was nor why. He was just there, surrounded by the faces, almost all the faces which he had ever known, always known (though the number of them, despite the efforts of the unmarried sister who pretty soon, so he told Grandfather, and still without any wedding had another baby, decreasing, thinning out, because of the climate, the warmth, the dampness) living in a cabin that was almost a replica of the mountain one except that it didn't sit up in the bright wind but sat instead beside a big flat river that sometimes showed no current at all and even sometimes ran backward, where his sisters and brothers seemed to take sick after supper and die before the next meal, where regiments of niggers with white men watching them planted and raised things that he had never heard of (the old man did something too, something besides drink now. At least, he would leave the cabin after breakfast and return sober to supper, and he fed them somehow) and the man who owned all the land and the niggers and apparently the white men who superintended the work, lived in the biggest house he had ever seen and spent most of the afternoon (he told how he would creep up among the tangled shrubbery of the lawn and lie hidden and watch the man) in a barrel stave hammock between two trees, with his shoes off and a nigger who wore every day better clothes than he or his father and sisters had ever owned and ever expected to, who did nothing else but fan him and bring him drinks; and he (he was eleven or twelve or thirteen now because this was where he realised that he had irrevocably lost count of his age) lying there all afternoon while the sisters would come from time to time to the door of the cabin two miles away and scream at him for wood or water, watching that man who not only had shoes in the summertime too, but didn't even have to wear them.

"But he still didn't envy the man he was watching. He coveted the shoes, and probably he would have liked for his father to have a broadcloth monkey to hand him the jug and to carry the wood and water into the cabin for his sisters to wash and cook with and keep the house warm so that he himself would not have to do it. Maybe he even realised, understood the pleasure it would have given his sisters for their neighbors (other whites like them, who lived in other cabins not quite as well built and not at all as well kept and preserved as the ones the nigger slaves lived in but still nimbused with freedom's bright aura, which the slave quarters were not for all their sound roofs and white wash) to see them being waited on. Because he had not only not lost the innocence yet, he had not yet discovered that he possessed it. He no more envied the man than he would have envied a mountain man who happened to own a fine rifle. He would have coveted the rifle, but he would himself have supported and confirmed the owner's pride and pleasure in its ownership because he could not have conceived of the owner taking such crass advantage of the luck which gave the rifle to him rather than to another as to say to other men: *Because I own this rifle, my arms and legs and blood and bones are superior to yours* except as the victorious outcome of a fight with rifles: and how in the world could a man fight another man with dressed-up niggers and the fact that he could lie in a hammock all afternoon with his shoes off? and what in the world would he be fighting for if he did?

He didn't even know he was innocent that day when his father sent him to the big house with the message. He didn't remember (or did not say) what the message was, apparently he still didn't know exactly just what his father did, what work (or maybe supposed to do) the old man had in relation to the plantation—a boy either thirteen or fourteen, he didn't know which, in garments his father had got from the plantation commissary and had worn out and which one of the sisters had patched and cut down to fit him and he no more conscious of his appearance in them or of the possibility that anyone else would be than he was of his skin, following the road and turning into the gate and following the drive up past where still more niggers with nothing to do all day but plant flowers and trim grass were working, and so to the house, the portico, the front door, thinking how at last he was going to see the inside of it, see what else a man was bound to own who could have a special nigger to hand him his liquor and pull off his shoes that he didn't even need to wear, never for one moment thinking but what the man would be as pleased to show him the balance of his things as the mountain man would have been to show the powder horn and bullet mold that went with the rifle. Because he was still innocent. He knew it without being aware that he did; he told Grandfather how, before the monkey nigger who came to the door had finished saying what he did, he seemed to kind of dissolve and a part of him turn and rush back through the two years they had lived

there like when you pass through a room fast and
look at all the objects in it and you turn and go back
through the room again and look at all the objects
from the other side and you find out you had never
seen them before, rushing back through those two
years and seeing a dozen things that had happened
and he hadn't even seen them before: a certain flat
level silent way his older sisters and the other white
women of their kind had of looking at niggers, not
with fear or dread but with a kind of speculative
antagonism not because of any known fact or reason
but inherited by both white and black, the sense,
effluvium of it passing between the white women in
the doors of the sagging cabins and the niggers in
the road and which was not quite explainable by the
fact that the niggers had better clothes, and which
the niggers did not return as antagonism or in any
sense of dare or taunt but through the very fact that
they were apparently oblivious of it, too oblivious of
it (you knew that you could hit them, he told
Grandfather, and they would not hit back or even
resist. But you did not want to, because they (the
niggers) were not it, not what you wanted to hit;
that when you hit them you would just be hitting
a child's toy balloon with a face painted on it, a face
slick and smooth and distended and about to burst
into laughing and so you did not dare strike it because it would merely burst and you would rather
let it walk on out of your sight than to have stood
there in the loud laughing)—of talk at night before
the fire when they had company or had themselves

gone visiting after supper to another cabin, the
voices of the women sober enough, even calm, yet
filled with a quality dark and sullen and only some
man, usually his father in drink, to break out into
harsh recapitulation of his own worth, the respect
which his own physical prowess commanded from
his fellows, and the boy of either thirteen or fourteen or maybe twelve knowing that the men and the
women were talking about the same thing though it
had never once been mentioned by name, like when
people talk about privation without mentioning the
siege, about sickness without ever naming the epi-
demic;—of one afternoon when he and his sister
were walking along the road and he heard the carriage coming up behind them and stepped off the
road and then realised that his sister was not going
to give way to it, that she still walked in the middle
of the road with a sort of sullen implacability in the
very angle of her head and he shouted at her: and
then it was all dust and rearing horses and glinting
harness buckles and wheel spokes; he saw two parasols in the carriage and the nigger coachman in a
plug hat shouting: 'Hoo dar, gal! Git outen de way
dar!' and then it was over, gone: the carriage and the
dust, the two faces beneath the parasols glaring
down at his sister: then he was throwing vain clods
of dirt after the dust as it spun on, knowing now,
while the monkey-dressed nigger butler kept the
door barred with his body while he spoke, that it had
not been the nigger coachman that he threw at at all,
that it was the actual dust raised by the proud deli-

cate wheels, and just that vain;—of one night late when his father came home, blundered into the cabin; he could smell the whiskey even while still dulled with broken sleep, hearing that same fierce exultation, vindication, in his father's voice: 'We whupped one of Pettibone's niggers tonight' and he roused at that, waked at that, asking which one of Pettibone's niggers and his father said he did not know, had never seen the nigger before: and he asked what the nigger had done and his father said, 'Hell fire, that goddamn son of a bitch Pettibone's nigger.'—how, without knowing it then since he had not yet discovered innocence, he must have meant the question the same way his father meant the answer: no actual nigger, living creature, living flesh to feel pain and writhe and cry out. He could even seem to see them: the torch-disturbed darkness among trees, the fierce hysterical faces of the white men, the balloon face of the nigger. Maybe the nigger's hands would be tied or held but that would be all right because they were not the hands with which the balloon face would struggle and writhe for freedom, not the balloon face: it was just poised among them, levitative and slick with paper-thin distension. Then someone would strike the balloon one single desperate and despairing blow and then he would seem to see them fleeing, running, with all about them, overtaking them and passing and going on and then returning to overwhelm them again, the roaring waves of mellow laughter meaningless and terrifying and loud. And now he stood there

before that white door with the monkey nigger barring it and looking down at him in his patched
made-over jeans clothes and no shoes and I dont
reckon he had even ever experimented with a comb
because that would be one of the things that his
sisters would keep hidden good—who had never
thought about his own hair or clothes or anybody
else's hair or clothes until he saw that monkey nigger, who through no doing of his own happened to
have had the felicity of being housebred in Richmond maybe, looking—" ("Or maybe even in
Charleston," Shreve breathed.) "—at them and he
never even remembered what the nigger said, how
it was the nigger told him, even before he had had
time to say what he came for, never to come to that
front door again but to go around to the back.

"He didn't even remember leaving. All of a sudden he found himself running and already some
distance from the house, and not toward home. He
was not crying, he said. He wasn't even mad. He
just had to think, so he was going to where he could
be quiet and think, and he knew where that place
was. He went into the woods. He says he did not
tell himself where to go: that his body, his feet, just
went there—a place where a game trail entered a
cane brake and an oak tree had fallen across it and
made a kind of cave where he kept an iron griddle
that he would cook small game on sometimes. He
said he crawled back into the cave and sat with his
back against the uptorn roots, and thought. Because
he couldn't get it straight yet. He couldn't even

realise yet that his trouble, his impediment, was innocence because he would not be able to realise that
until he got it straight. So he was seeking among
what little he had to call experience for something
to measure it by, and he couldn't find anything. He
had been told to go around to the back door even
before he could state his errand, who had sprung
from a people whose houses didn't have back doors
but only windows and anyone entering or leaving
by a window would be either hiding or escaping,
neither of which he was doing. In fact, he had actually come on business, in the good faith of business
which he had believed that all men accepted. Of
course he had not expected to be invited in to eat a
meal since time, the distance from one cooking pot
to the next, did not need to be measured in hours or
days; perhaps he had not expected to be asked into
the house at all. But he did expect to be listened to
because he had come, been sent, on some business
which, even though he didn't remember what it was
and maybe at the time (he said) he might not even
have comprehended, was certainly connected somehow with the plantation that supported and endured
that smooth white house and that smooth white
brass-decorated door and the very broadcloth and
linen and silk stockings the monkey nigger stood in
to tell him to go around to the back before he could
even state the business. It was like he might have
been sent with a lump of lead or even a few molded
bullets so that the man who owned the fine rifle
could shoot it, and the man came to the door and

told him to leave the bullets on a stump at the edge of the woods, not even letting him come close enough to look at the rifle.

"Because he was not mad. He insisted on that to Grandfather. He was just thinking, because he knew that something would have to be done about it; he would have to do something about it in order to live with himself for the rest of his life and he could not decide what it was because of that innocence which he had just discovered he had, which (the innocence, not the man, the tradition) he would have to compete with. He had nothing to compare and gauge it by but the rifle analogy, and it would not make sense by that. He was quite calm about it, he said, sitting there with his arms around his knees in his little den beside the game trail where more than once when the wind was right he had seen deer pass within ten feet of him, arguing with himself quietly and calmly while both debaters agreed that if there were only someone else, some older and smarter person to ask. But there was not, there was only himself, the two of them inside that one body which was maybe thirteen or maybe fourteen or maybe was already fifteen but would never know it for certain forever more, arguing quiet and calm: *But I can shoot him.* (Not the monkey nigger. It was not the nigger anymore than it had been the nigger that his father had helped to whip that night. The nigger was just another balloon face slick and distended with that mellow loud and terrible laughing so that he did not dare to burst it, looking down at him from within the half closed door during that instant in which, before he knew it, something in him had escaped and—he unable to close the eyes of it—was looking out from within the balloon face just as the man who did not even have to wear the shoes he owned, whom the laughter which the balloon held barricaded and protected from such as he, looked out from whatever invisible place he (the man) happened to be at the moment, at the boy outside the barred door in his patched garments and splayed bare feet, looking through and beyond the boy, he himself seeing his own father and sisters and brothers as the owner, the rich man (not the nigger) must have been seeing them all the time—as cattle, creatures heavy and without grace, brutely evacuated into a world without hope or purpose for them, who would in turn spawn with brutish and vicious prolixity, populate, double treble and compound, fill space and earth with a race whose future would be a succession of cut-down and patched and made-over garments bought on exorbitant credit because they were white people, from stores where niggers were given the garments free, with for sole heritage that expression on a balloon face bursting with laughter which had looked out at some unremembered and nameless progenitor who had knocked at a door when he was a little boy and had been told by a nigger to go around to the back.): *But I can shoot him:* and the other: *No. That wouldn't do no good:* and the first: *What shall we do then?* and the other: *I dont know:* and the first: *But I can shoot him.*

I could slip right up there through them bushes and lay there until he come out to lay in the hammock and shoot him: and the other: *No. That wouldn't do no good:* and the first: *Then what shall we do?* and the other: *I dont know.*

"Now he was hungry. It was before dinner when he went to the big house, and now there was no sun at all where he crouched though he could still see sun in the tops of the trees around him. But his stomach had already told him it was late and that it would be later still when he reached home. And then he said he began to think *Home. Home* and that he thought at first that he was trying to laugh and that he kept on telling himself it was laughing even after he knew better; home, as he came out of the woods and approached it, still hidden yet, and looked at it—the rough partly rotten log walls, the sagging roof whose missing shingles they did not replace but just set pans and buckets under the leaks, the leanto room which they used for kitchen and which was all right because in good weather it didn't even matter that it had no chimney since they did not attempt to use it at all when it rained, and his sister pumping rhythmic up and down above a washtub in the yard, her back toward him, shapeless in a calico dress and a pair of the old man's shoes unlaced and flapping about her bare ankles and broad in the beam as a cow, the very labor she was doing brutish and stupidly out of all proportion to its reward: the very primary essence of labor, toil, reduced to its crude absolute which only a beast

could and would endure; and now (he said) the
thought striking him for the first time as to what he
would tell his father when the old man asked him
if he had delivered the message, whether he would
lie or not, since if he did lie he would be found out
maybe at once, since probably the man had already
sent a nigger down to see why whatever it was his
father had failed to do and had sent the excuse for
was not done—granted that that was what his errand to the house had been, which (granted his old
man) it probably was. But it didn't happen at once
because his father was not at home yet. So it was
only the sister, as if she had been waiting not for the
wood but just for him to return, for the opportunity
to use her vocal cords, nagging at him to fetch the
wood and he not refusing, not objecting, just not
hearing her, paying any attention to her because he
was still thinking. Then the old man came and the
sister told on him and the old man made him fetch
the wood: and still nothing said about the errand
while they ate supper nor when he went and lay
down on the pallet where he slept and where he
went to bed by just lying down, only not to sleep
now, just lying there with his hands under his head
and still nothing said about it and he still not knowing if he was going to lie or not. Because he said how
the terrible part of it had not occurred to him yet,
he just lay there while the two of them argued inside
of him, speaking in orderly turn, both calm, even
leaning backward to be calm and reasonable and
unrancorous: *But I can kill him.—No. That wouldn't*

*do no good—Then what shall we do about it?—I dont
know:* and he just listening, not especially interested
he said, hearing the two of them without listening.
Because what he was thinking about now he hadn't
asked for. It was just there, natural in a boy, a child,
and he not paying any attention to it either because
it was what a boy would have thought, and he knew
that to do what he had to do in order to live with
himself he would have to think it out straight as a
man would, thinking *The nigger never give me a
chance to tell him what it was and so he* (not the nigger
now either) *wont know it and whatever it is wont get
done and he wont know it aint done until too late so
he will get paid back that much for what he set that
nigger to do and if it only was to tell him that the stable,
the house, was on fire and the nigger wouldn't even let
me tell him, warn him* and then he said that all of a
sudden it was not thinking, it was something shouting it almost loud enough for his sisters on the other
pallet and his father in the bed with the two youngest and filling the room with alcohol snoring, to
hear too: *He never even give me a chance to say it. Not
even to tell it, say it:* it too fast, too mixed up to be
thinking, it all kind of shouting at him at once,
boiling out and over him like the nigger laughing:
*He never gave me a chance to say it and Pap never asked
me if I told him or not and so he cant even know that
Pap sent him any message and so whether he got it or
not cant even matter, not even to Pap; I went up to that
door for that nigger to tell me never to come to that
front door again and I not only wasn't doing any good*

to him by telling it or any harm to him by not telling it, there aint any good or harm either in the living world that I can do to him. It was like that, he said, like an explosion—a bright glare that vanished and left nothing, no ashes nor refuse: just a limitless flat plain with the severe shape of his intact innocence rising from it like a monument; that innocence instructing him as calm as the others had ever spoken, using his own rifle analogy to do it with, and when it said *them* in place of *he* or *him,* it meant more than all the human puny mortals under the sun that might lie in hammocks all afternoon with their shoes off: 'If you were fixing to combat them that had the fine rifles, the first thing you would do would be to get yourself the nearest thing to a fine rifle you could borrow or steal or make, wouldn't it?' and he said Yes. 'But this aint a question of rifles. So to combat them you have got to have what they have that made them do what he did. You got to have land and niggers and a fine house to combat them with. You see?' and he said Yes again. He left that night. He waked before day and departed just like he went to bed: by rising from the pallet and tiptoeing out of the house. He never saw any of his family again.

"He went to the West Indies." Quentin had not moved, not even to raise his head from its attitude of brooding bemusement upon the open letter which lay on the open textbook, his hands lying on the table before him on either side of the book and the letter, one half of which slanted upward from the transverse crease without support, as if it had learned half the secret of levitation. "That was how he said it. He and Grandfather were sitting on a log now because the dogs had faulted. That is, they had treed—a tree from which he (the architect) could not have escaped yet which he had undoubtedly mounted because they found the sapling pole with his suspenders still knotted about one end of it that he had used to climb the tree though at first they could not understand why the suspenders and it was three hours before they comprehended that the architect had used architecture, physics, to elude them as a man always falls back upon what he knows best in a crisis—the murderer upon murder, the thief thieving, the liar lying. He (the architect) knew about the wild negroes even if he couldn't have known that Sutpen would get dogs; he had chosen that tree and hauled that pole up after him and calculated stress and distance and trajectory and had crossed a gap to the next nearest tree that a flying squirrel could not have crossed and traveled from there on from tree to tree for almost half a mile before he put foot on the ground again. It was three hours before one of the wild niggers (the dogs wouldn't leave the tree; they said he was in it) found where he had come down. So he and Grandfather sat on the log and talked, and one of the wild niggers went back to camp for grub and the rest of the whiskey and they blew the other men in with horns and they ate, and he told Grandfather some more of it while they waited.

"He went to the West Indies. That's how he said it: not how he managed to find where the West Indies were nor where ships departed from to go there, nor how he got to where the ships were and got in one nor how he liked the sea nor about the hardships of a sailor's life and it must have been hardship indeed for him, a boy of fourteen or fifteen who had never seen the ocean before, going to sea in 1823. He just said, 'So I went to the West Indies,' sitting there on the log with Grandfather while the dogs still bayed the tree where they believed the architect was because he would have to be there— saying it just like that day thirty years later when he sat in Grandfather's office (in his fine clothes now, even though they were a little soiled and worn with three years of war, with money to rattle in his pocket and his beard at its prime too: beard body and intellect at that peak which all the different parts that make a man reach, where he can say *I did all that I set out to do and I could stop here if I wanted to and no man to chide me with sloth, not even myself* —and maybe this the instant which Fate always picks out to blackjack you, only the peak feels so sound and stable that the beginning of the falling is hidden for a little while—with his head flung up a little in that attitude that nobody ever knew exactly who he had aped it from or if he did not perhaps learn it too from the same book out of which he taught himself the words, the bombastic phrases with which Grandfather said he even asked you for a match for his cigar or offered you the cigar—and

nothing of vanity, nothing comic in it either Grandfather said, because of that innocence which he had
never lost because after it finally told him what to
do that night he forgot about it and didn't know that
he still had it) and told Grandfather—told him,
mind; not excusing, asking for no pity; not explaining, asking for no exculpation: just told Grandfather
how he had put his first wife aside like eleventh and
twelfth century kings did: 'I found that she was not
and could never be, through no fault of her own,
adjunctive or incremental to the design which I had
in mind, so I provided for her and put her aside.'—
telling Grandfather in that same tone while they sat
on the log waiting for the niggers to come back with
the other guests and the whiskey: 'So I went to the
West Indies. I had had some schooling during a part
of one winter, enough to have learned something
about them, to realise that they would be most suitable to the expediency of my requirements.' He
didn't remember how he came to go to the school.
That is, why his father decided all of a sudden to
send him, what nebulous vision or shape might have
evolved out of the fog of alcohol and nigger-beating
and scheming to avoid work which his old man
called his mind—the image not of ambition nor
glory, not to see his son better himself for his own
sake, probably not even some blind instant of revolt
against that same house whose roof had leaked on
probably a hundred families like his which had come
and lived beneath it and vanished and left no trace,
nothing, not even rags and broken crockery, but

was probably mere vindictive envy toward one or two men, planters, whom he had to see every now and then. Anyway, he was sent to school for about three months one winter—an adolescent boy of thirteen or fourteen in a room full of children three or four years younger than he and three or four years further advanced, and he not only probably bigger than the teacher (the kind of teacher that would be teaching a one-room country school in a nest of Tidewater plantations) but a good deal more of a man, who probably brought into the school with him along with his sober watchful mountain reserve a good deal of latent insubordination that he would not be aware of any more than he would be aware at first that the teacher was afraid of him. It would not be intractability and maybe you couldn't call it pride either, but maybe just the self reliance of mountains and solitude, since some of his blood at least (his mother was a mountain woman, a Scottish woman who, so he told Grandfather, never did quite learn to speak English) had been bred in mountains, but which, whatever it was, was that which forbade him to condescend to memorise dry sums and such but which did permit him to listen when the teacher read aloud.—Sent to school, 'where,' he told Grandfather, 'I learned little save that most of the deeds, good and bad both, incurring opprobrium or plaudits or reward either, within the scope of man's abilities, had already been performed and were to be learned about only from books. So I listened when he would read to us. I realise now that on most of these occasions he resorted to reading aloud only when he saw that the moment had come when his entire school was on the point of rising and leaving the room. But whatever the reason, he read to us and I anyway listened, though I did not know that in that listening I was equipping myself better for what I should later design to do than if I had learned all the addition and subtraction in the book. That was how I learned of the West Indies. Not where they were, though if I had known at the time that that knowledge would someday serve me, I would have learned that too. What I learned was that there was a place called the West Indies to which poor men went in ships and became rich, it didn't matter how, so long as that man was clever and courageous: the latter of which I believed that I possessed, the former of which I believed that, if it were to be learned by energy and will in the school of endeavor and experience, I should learn. I remember how I remained one afternoon when school was out and waited for the teacher, waylaid him (he was a smallish man who always looked dusty, as if he had been born and lived all his life in attics and store rooms) and stepped out. I recall how he started back when he saw me and how I thought at the time that if I were to strike him there would be no resulting outcry but merely the sound of the blow and a puff of dust in the air as when you strike a rug hanging from a line. I asked him if it were true, if what he had read us about the men who got rich in the West Indies were true. "Why not?" he answered, starting back. "Didn't you hear me read it from the book?"—"How do I know that what you read was in the book?" I said. I was that green, that countrified, you see. I had not then learned to read my own name; although I had been attending the school for almost three months, I daresay I knew no more than I did when I entered the schoolroom for the first time. But I had to know, you see. Perhaps a man builds for his future in more ways than one, builds not only toward the body which will be his tomorrow or next year, but toward actions and the subsequent irrevocable courses of resultant action which his weak senses and intellect cannot foresee but which ten or twenty or thirty years from now he will take, will have to take in order to survive the act. Perhaps it was that instinct and not I who grasped one of his arms as he drew back (I did not actually doubt him. I think that even then, even at my age, I realised that he could not have invented it, that he lacked that something which is necessary in a man to enable him to fool even a child by lying. But you see, I had to be sure, had to take whatever method that came to my hand to make sure. And there was nothing else to hand except him) glaring at me and beginning to struggle, and I holding him and saying—I was quite calm, quite calm; I just had to know—saying, "Suppose I went there and found out that it was not so?" and he shrieking now, shouting "Help! Help!" so that I let him go. So when the time came when I realised that to accomplish my design I should need first of all and above all things money in considerable quantities and in the quite immediate future, I remembered what he had read to us and I went to the West Indies.'

"Then the other guests began to ride up, and after a while the niggers came back with the coffee pot and a deer haunch and the whiskey (and one bottle of champagne which they had overlooked, Grandfather said) and he stopped talking for a while. He didn't tell anymore of it until they had eaten and were sitting around smoking while the niggers and the dogs (they had to drag the dogs away from the tree, but especially away from the sapling pole with the architect's suspenders tied to it, as if it was not only that the pole was the last thing the architect had touched but it was the thing his exultation had touched when he saw another chance to elude them, and so it was not only the man but the exultation too which the dogs smelled that made them wild) made casts in all directions, getting further and further away until just before sundown one of the niggers whooped and he (he hadn't spoken for some time, Grandfather said, lying there on one elbow, in the fine boots and the only pants he had and the shirt he had put on when he came out of the mud and washed himself off after he realised that he would have to hunt the architect down himself if he wanted him back alive probably, not talking himself and maybe not even listening while the men talked about cotton and politics, just smoking the cigar Grandfather had given him and looking at the fire embers and maybe making that West Indian voyage again that he had made when he was fourteen and didn't even know where he was going or if he would ever get there or not, no more way of knowing whether the men who said the ship was going there were lying or not than he had of knowing whether or not the school teacher was telling the truth about what was in the book. And he never told whether the voyage was hard or not, how much he must have had to endure to make it. Which of course he did have to endure, but then he believed that all necessary was courage and shrewdness and the one he knew he had and the other he believed he could learn if it were to be taught, and it probably the hardship of the voyage which comforted him that the men who said the ship was going to the West Indies had not lied to him because at that time, Grandfather said, he probably could not have believed in anything that was easy.)——he said, 'There it is' and got up and they all went on and found where the architect had come back to the ground again, with a gain of almost three hours. So they had to go fast now and there wasn't much time to talk, or at least, Grandfather said, he did not appear to intend to resume. Then the sun went down and the other men had to start back to town; they all went except Grandfather, because he wanted to listen some more. So he sent word in by one of the others (he was not married then either) that he would not be home, and he and Sutpen went on until the light failed. Two of the niggers (they were thirteen miles from Sutpen's camp then) had already gone back to get blankets and more grub. Then it was dark and the niggers began to light pine knots and they went on for a little while yet, gaining what they could now since they knew that the architect would have had to den soon after dark to keep from traveling in a circle. That was how Grandfather remembered it: he and Sutpen leading their horses (he would look back now and then and see the horses' eyes shining in the torch light and the horses' heads tossing and the shadows slipping along their shoulders and flanks) and the dogs and the niggers (the niggers mostly still naked except for a pair of pants here and there) with the pine torches smoking and flaring above them and the red light on their round heads and arms and the mud they wore in the swamp to keep the mosquitoes off dried hard and shiny, glinting like glass or china and the shadows they cast taller than they were at one moment then gone the next and even the trees and brakes and thickets there one moment and gone the next though you knew all the time that they were still there because you could feel them with your breathing, as though, invisible, they pressed down and condensed the invisible air you breathed. And he said how Sutpen was talking about it again, telling him again before he realised that this was some more of it, and he said how he thought how there was something about a man's destiny (or about the man) that caused the destiny to shape itself to him like his clothes did, like the same coat that new might have fitted a thousand men, yet after one man has worn it for a while it fits

no one else and you can tell it anywhere you see
it even if all you see is a sleeve or a lapel: so that
his—" ("the demon's," Shreve said) "—destiny had
fitted itself to him, to his innocence, his pristine
aptitude for platform drama and childlike heroic
simplicity just as the fine broadcloth uniform which
you could have seen on ten thousand men during
those four years, which he wore when he came in
the office on that afternoon thirty years later had
fitted itself to the swaggering of all his gestures and
to the forensic verbiage in which he stated calmly,
with that frank innocence which we call 'of a child'
except that a human child is the only living creature
that is never either frank or innocent, the most simple and the most outrageous things. He was telling
some more of it, already into what he was telling yet
still without telling how he got to where he was nor
even how what he was now involved in (obviously
at least twenty years old now, crouching behind a
window in the dark and firing the muskets through
it which someone else loaded and handed to him)
came to occur, getting himself and Grandfather
both into that besieged Haitian room as simply as he
got himself to the West Indies by saying that he
decided to go to the West Indies and so he went
there; this anecdote no deliberate continuation of
the other one but merely called to his mind by the
picture of the niggers and torches in front of them;
he not telling how he got there, what had happened
during the six years between that day when he, a
boy of fourteen who knew no tongue but English

and not much of that, had decided to go to the West Indies and become rich, and this night when, overseer or foreman or something to a French sugar planter, he was barricade in the house with the planter's family (and now Grandfather said there was the first mention—a shadow that almost emerged for a moment and then faded again but not completely away—of the——" ("It's a girl," Shreve said. "Dont tell me. Just go on.") "——whom he was to tell Grandfather thirty years afterward he had found unsuitable to his purpose and so put aside, though providing for her) and a few frightened half-breed servants which he would have to turn from the window from time to time and kick and curse into helping the girl load the muskets which he and the planter fired through the windows, and I reckon Grandfather was saying 'Wait wait for God's sake wait' about like you are until he finally did stop and back up and start over again with at least some regard for cause and effect even if none for logical sequence and continuity. Or maybe it was the fact that they were sitting again now, having decided that they had gone far enough for that night, and the niggers had made camp and cooked supper and they (he and Grandfather) drank some of the whiskey and ate and then sat before the fire drinking some more of the whiskey and he telling it all over and still it was not absolutely clear—the how and the why he was there and what he was—since he was not talking about himself. He was telling a story. He was not bragging about something he had done; he was just telling a story about something a man named Thomas Sutpen had experienced, which would still have been the same story if the man had had no name at all, if it had been told about any man or no man over whiskey at night.

"That may have been what slowed him down. But it was not enough to clarify the story much. He still was not recounting to Grandfather the career of somebody named Thomas Sutpen. Grandfather said the only mention he ever made to those six or seven years which must have existed somewhere, must have actually occurred, was about the patois he had to learn in order to oversee the plantation, and the French he had to learn, maybe not to get engaged to be married, but which he would certainly need to be able to repudiate the wife after he had already got her—how, so he told Grandfather, he had believed that courage and shrewdness would be enough but found that he was wrong and how sorry he was that he had not taken the schooling along with the West Indian lore when he discovered that all people did not speak the same tongue and realised that he would not only need courage and skill, he would have to learn to speak a new language, else that design to which he had dedicated himself would die still-born. So he learned the language just like he learned to be a sailor I reckon, because Grandfather asked him why he didn't get himself a girl to live with and learn it the easy way and Grandfather said how he sat there with the firelight on his face and the beard and his eyes quiet and sort of bright, and said—and Grandfather said it was the only time he ever knew him to say anything quiet and simple: 'On this night I am speaking of (and until my first marriage, I might add) I was still a virgin. You will probably not believe that, and if I were to try to explain it you would disbelieve me more than ever. So I will only say that that too was a part of the design which I had in my mind' and Grandfather said, 'Why shouldn't I believe it?' and he looking at Grandfather still with that quiet bright expression about the eyes, saying, 'But do you? Surely you dont hold me in such small contempt as to believe that at twenty I could neither have suffered temptation nor offered it?' and Grandfather said, 'You're right. I shouldn't believe it. But I do.' So it was no tale about women, and certainly not about love: the woman, the girl, just that shadow which could load a musket but could not have been trusted to fire one out the window that night (or the seven or eight nights while they huddled in the dark and watched from the windows the barns or granaries or whatever it is you harvest sugar into, and the fields too, blazing and smoking: he said how you could smell it, you could smell nothing else, the rank sweet rich smell as if the hatred and the implacability, the thousand secret dark years which had created the hatred and implacability, had intensified the smell of the sugar: and Grandfather said how he remembered then that he had seen Sutpen each time decline sugar for his coffee and so he (Grandfather) knew why now but he asked anyway to be sure and Sutpen told him it

was true; that he had not been afraid until after the
fields and barns were all burned and they had even
forgot about the smell of the burning sugar, but that
he had never been able to bear sugar since)—the girl
just emerging for a second of the telling, in a single
word almost, so that Grandfather said it was like he
had just seen her too for a second by the flash of one
of the muskets—a bent face, a single cheek, a chin
for an instant beyond a curtain of fallen hair, a white
slender arm raised, a delicate hand clutching a ram-
rod, and that was all. No more detail and information about that than about how he got from the field,
his overseeing, into the besieged house when the
niggers rushed at him with their machetes, than
how he got from the rotting cabin in Virginia to the
fields he oversaw: and this, Grandfather said, more
incredible to him than the getting there from Virginia because that did infer time, a space the getting
across which did indicate something of leisureliness
since time is longer than any distance, while the
other, the getting from the fields into the barricaded
house, seemed to have occurred with a sort of violent abrogation which must have been almost as
short as his telling about it—a very condensation of
time which was the gauge of its own violence, and
he telling it in that pleasant faintly forensic anecdotal manner apparently just as he remembered it, was
impressed by it through detached and impersonal
interest and curiosity which even fear (that once
when he mentioned fear by that same inverse process of speaking of a time when he was not afraid,

before he became afraid, he put it) failed to leaven
very much. Because he was not afraid until after it
was all over, Grandfather said, because that was all
it was to him—a spectacle, something to be watched
because he might not have a chance to see such
again, since his innocence still functioned and he
not only did not know what fear was until afterward, he did not even know that at first he was not
terrified; did not even know that he had found the
place where money was to be had quick if you were
courageous and shrewd (he did not mean shrewdness, Grandfather said. What he meant was un-
scrupulousness only he didn't know that word
because it would not have been in the book from
which the school teacher read. Or maybe that was
what he meant by courage, Grandfather said) but
where high mortality was concomitant with the
money and the sheen on the dollars was not from
gold but from blood—a spot of earth which might
have been created and set aside by Heaven itself,
Grandfather said, as a theatre for violence and injustice and bloodshed and all the satanic lusts of human
greed and cruelty, for the last despairing fury of all
the pariah-interdict and all the doomed—a little island set in a smiling and fury-lurked and incredible
indigo sea, which was the halfway point between
what we call the jungle and what we call civiliza-
tion, halfway between the dark inscrutable continent from which the black blood, the black bones
and flesh and thinking and remembering and hopes
and desires, was ravished by violence, and the cold

known land to which it was doomed, the civilised
land and people which had expelled some of its own
blood and thinking and desires that had become too
crass to be faced and borne longer, and set it homeless and desperate on the lonely ocean—a little lost
island in a latitude which would require ten thousand years of equatorial heritage to bear its climate,
a soil manured with black blood from two hundred
years of oppression and exploitation until it sprang
with an incredible paradox of peaceful greenery and
crimson flowers and sugar cane sapling size and
three times the height of a man and a little bulkier
of course but valuable pound for pound almost with
silver ore, as if nature held a balance and kept a book
and offered a recompense for the torn limbs and
outraged hearts even if man did not, the planting of
nature and man too watered not only by the wasted
blood but breathed over by the winds in which the
doomed ships had fled in vain, out of which the last
tatter of sail had sunk into the blue sea, along which
the last vain despairing cry of woman or child had
blown away;—the planting of men too: the yet intact bones and brains in which the old unsleeping
blood that had vanished into the earth they trod still
cried out for vengeance. And he overseeing it, riding peacefully about on his horse while he learned
the language (that meagre and fragile thread,
Grandfather said, by which the little surface corners
and edges of men's secret and solitary lives may be
joined for an instant now and then before sinking
back into the darkness where the spirit cried for the

first time and was not heard and will cry for the last time and will not be heard then either), not knowing that what he rode upon was a volcano, hearing the air tremble and throb at night with the drums and the chanting and not knowing that it was the heart of the earth itself he heard, who believed (Grandfather said) that earth was kind and gentle and that darkness was merely something you saw, or could not see in; overseeing what he oversaw and not knowing that he was overseeing it, making his daily expeditions from an armed citadel until the day itself came. And he not telling that either, how that day happened, the steps leading up to it because Grandfather said he apparently did not know, comprehend, what he must have been seeing every day because of that innocence—a pig's bone with a little rotten flesh still clinging to it, a few chicken feathers, a stained dirty rag with a few pebbles tied up in it found on the old man's pillow one morning and none knew (least of all, the planter himself who had been asleep on the pillow) how it had come there because they learned at the same time that all the servants, the half breeds, were missing, and he did not know until the planter told him that the stains on the rag were neither dirt nor grease but blood, nor that what he took to be the planter's gallic rage was actually fear, terror, and he just curious and quite interested because he still looked upon the planter and the daughter both (he told Grandfather how until that first night of the siege he had not once thought that he did not know the girl's chris-

tian name, whether he had ever heard it or not. He
also told Grandfather, dropped this into the telling
as you might flick the joker out of a pack of fresh
cards without being able to remember later whether
you had removed the joker or not, that the old man's
wife had been a Spaniard, and so it was Grandfather
and not Sutpen who realised that until that first
night of the attack he had possibly not seen the girl
as much as a dozen times) as foreigners;—the body
of one of the half breeds found at last (he found it,
hunted for it for two days without even knowing
that what he was meeting was a blank wall of black
secret faces, a wall behind which almost anything
could be preparing to happen and, as he learned
later, almost anything was, and on the third day
found the body where he could not possibly have
missed it during the first hour of the first day if it
had been there) and he sitting on the log, Grandfather said, telling it, making the gestures to tell it
with, whom Grandfather himself had seen fight
naked chest to chest with one of his wild niggers by
the light of the camp fire while his house was building and who still fought with them by lantern light
in the stable after he had got at last that wife who
would be adjunctive to the forwarding of that design he had in mind, and no bones about the fighting
either, no handshaking and gratulations while he
washed the blood off and donned his shirt because
at the end of it the nigger would be flat on his back
with his chest heaving and another nigger throwing
water on him;—sitting there and telling Grand-

father how at last he found the half breed, or what used to be the half breed, and that he (Sutpen) had seen as much as most men and had done as much as most, including some things which he did not boast about: but that there were some things which a man who pretended to be civilised saw when he had to but which he did not talk about, so he would only say that he found the half breed at last and so began to comprehend that the situation might become serious; then the house, the barricade, the five of them —the planter, the daughter, two women servants and himself—shut up in it and the air filled with the smoke and smell of burning cane and the glare and smoke of it on the sky and the air throbbing and trembling with the drums and the chanting—the little lost island beneath its down-cupped bowl of alternating day and night like a vacuum into which no help could come, where not even winds from the outer world came but only the trades, the same weary winds blowing back and forth across it and burdened still with the weary voices of murdered women and children homeless and graveless about the isolating and solitary sea—while the two servants and the girl whose christian name he did not yet know loaded the muskets which he and the father fired at no enemy but at the Haitian night itself, lancing their little vain and puny flashes into the brooding and blood-weary and throbbing darkness: and it the very time of year, the season between hurricanes and any hope of rain: and how on the eighth night the water gave out and something had

to be done so he put the musket down and went out
and subdued them. That was how he told it: he went
out and subdued them, and when he returned he
and the girl became engaged to marry and Grandfather saying 'Wait wait' sure enough now, saying,
'But you didn't even know her; you told me that
when the siege began you didn't even know her
name' and he looked at Grandfather and said, 'Yes.
But you see, it took me some time to recover.' Not
how he did it. He didn't tell that either, that of no
moment to the story either; he just put the musket
down and had someone unbar the door and then bar
it behind him, and walked out into the darkness and
subdued them, maybe by yelling louder, maybe by
standing, bearing more than they believed any
bones and flesh could or should (should, yes: that
would be the terrible thing: to find flesh to stand
more than flesh should be asked to stand); maybe at
last they themselves turning in horror and fleeing
from the white arms and legs shaped like theirs and
from which blood could be made to spurt and flow
as it could from theirs and containing an indomitable spirit which should have come from the same
primary fire which theirs came from but which
could not have, could not possibly have (he showed
Grandfather the scars, one of which, Grandfather
said, came pretty near leaving him that virgin for the
rest of his life too) and then daylight came with no
drums in it for the first time in eight days, and they
emerged (probably the man and the daughter) and
walked across the burned land with the bright sun

shining down on it as if nothing had happened, walking now in what must have been an incredible desolate solitude and peaceful quiet, and found him and brought him to the house: and when he recovered he and the girl were engaged. Then he stopped."

"All right," Shreve said. "Go on."

"I said he stopped," Quentin said.

"I heard you. Stopped what? How got engaged and then stopped yet still had a wife to repudiate later? You said he didn't remember how he got to Haiti, and then he didn't remember how he got into the house with the niggers surrounding it. Now are you going to tell me he didn't even remember getting married? That he got engaged and then he decided he would stop, only one day he found out he hadn't stopped but on the contrary he was married? And all you called him was just a virgin?"

"He stopped talking, telling it," Quentin said. He had not moved, talking apparently (if to anything) to the letter lying on the open book on the table between his hands. Opposite him Shreve had filled the pipe and smoked it out again. It lay again overturned, a scattering of white ashes fanning out from the bowl, onto the table before his crossed naked arms with which he appeared at the same time both to support and hug himself, since although it was only eleven oclock the room was beginning to cool toward that point where about midnight there would be only enough heat in the radiators to keep the pipes from freezing, though (he would not per-

form his deep-breathing in the open window tonight at all) he had yet to go to the bedroom and
return first with his bathrobe on and next with his
overcoat on top of the bathrobe and Quentin's overcoat on his arm. "He just said that he was now
engaged to be married and then he stopped telling
it. He just stopped, Grandfather said, flat and final
like that, like that was all there was, all there could
be to it, all of it that made good listening from one
man to another over whiskey at night. Maybe it
was." His (Quentin's) face was lowered. He spoke
still in that curious, that almost sullen flat tone
which had caused Shreve to watch him from the
beginning with intent detached speculation and curiosity, to watch him still from behind his (Shreve's)
expression of cherubic and erudite amazement
which the spectacles intensified or perhaps actually
created. "He just got up and looked at the whiskey
bottle and said, 'No more tonight. We'll get to sleep;
we want to get an early start tomorrow. Maybe we
can catch him before he limbers up.'

"But they didn't. It was late afternoon before they
caught him—the architect I mean—and then only
because he had hurt his leg trying to architect himself across the river. But he made a mistake in the
calculation this time so the dogs and the niggers
bayed him and the niggers making the racket now
(Grandfather said how maybe the niggers believed
that by fleeing the architect had voluntarily surrendered his status as interdict meat, had voluntarily
offered the gambit by fleeing, which the niggers had

accepted by chasing him and won by catching him, and that now they would be allowed to cook and eat him, both victors and vanquished accepting this in the same spirit of sport and sportsmanship and no rancor or hard feelings on either side) as they hauled him out (all the men who had started the race yesterday had come back except three, and the ones that returned had brought others, so there were more of them now than when the race started, Grandfather said)—hauled him out of his cave under the river bank: a little man with one sleeve missing from his frock coat and his flowered vest ruined by water and mud where he had fallen in the river and one pants leg ripped down so they could see where he had tied up his leg with a piece of his shirt tail and the rag bloody and the leg swollen, and his hat was completely gone. They never did find it so Grandfather gave him a new hat the day he left when the house was finished. It was in Grandfather's office and Grandfather said the architect took the new hat and looked at it and burst into tears.—a little harried wild-faced man with a two-days' stubble of beard, who came out of the cave fighting like a wildcat, hurt leg and all, with the dogs barking and the niggers whooping and hollering with deadly and merry anticipation, like they were under the impression that since the race had lasted more than twenty-four hours the rules would be automatically abrogated and they would not have to wait to cook him until Sutpen waded in with a short stick and beat niggers and dogs all away, leaving the architect standing

there, not scared worth a damn either, just panting
a little and Grandfather said a little sick in the face
where the niggers had mishandled his leg in the heat
of the capture, and making them a speech in French,
a long one and so fast that Grandfather said probably another Frenchman could not have understood
all of it. But it sounded fine; Grandfather said even
he—all of them—could tell that the architect was
not apologising; it was fine, Grandfather said, and
he said how Sutpen turned toward him but he
(Grandfather) was already approaching the architect, holding out the bottle of whiskey already un-
corked. And Grandfather saw the eyes in the gaunt
face, the eyes desperate and hopeless but indomitable too, invincible too, not beaten yet by a damn
sight Grandfather said, and all that fifty-odd hours
of dark and swamp and sleeplessness and fatigue and
no grub and nowhere to go and no hope of getting
there: just a will to endure and a foreknowing of
defeat but not beat yet by a damn sight: and he took
the bottle in one of his little dirty coon-like hands
and raised the other hand and even fumbled about
his head for a second before he remembered that the
hat was gone, then flung the hand up in a gesture
that Grandfather said you simply could not de-
scribe, that seemed to gather all misfortune and defeat that the human race ever suffered into a little
pinch in his fingers like dust and fling it backward
over his head, and raised the bottle and bowed first
to Grandfather then to all the other men sitting their
horses in a circle and looking at him, and then he

took not only the first drink of neat whiskey he ever took in his life but the drink of it that he could no more have conceived himself taking than the Brahmin can believe that that situation can conceivably arise in which he will eat dog."

Quentin ceased. At once Shreve said, "All right. Dont bother to say he stopped now; just go on." But Quentin did not continue at once—the flat, curiously dead voice, the downcast face, the relaxed body not stirring except to breathe; the two of them not moving except to breathe, both young, both born within the same year: the one in Alberta, the other in Mississippi; born half a continent apart yet joined, connected after a fashion in a sort of geographical transubstantiation by that Continental Trough, that River which runs not only through the physical land of which it is the geologic umbilical, not only runs through the spiritual lives of the beings within its scope, but is very Environment itself which laughs at degrees of latitude and temperature, though some of these beings, like Shreve, have never seen it—the two of them who four months ago had never laid eyes on one another yet who since had slept in the same room and eaten side by side of the same food and used the same books from which to prepare to recite in the same freshman courses, facing one another across the lamplit table on which lay the fragile pandora's box of scrawled paper which had filled with violent and unratiocinative djinns and demons this snug monastic coign, this dreamy and heatless alcove of what we call the best of thought. "Just dont bother," Shreve said. "Just get on with it."

"That would take thirty years," Quentin said. "It was thirty years before he told Grandfather any more of it. Maybe he was too busy. All his time for spare talking taken up with furthering that design which he had in mind, and his only relaxation fighting his wild niggers in the stable where the men could hitch their horses and come up from the back and not be seen from the house because he was already married now, his house finished and he already arrested for stealing it and freed again so that was all settled, with a wife and two children—no, three—in it and his land cleared and planted with the seed Grandfather loaned him and him getting rich good and steady now——"

"Yes," Shreve said; "Mr Coldfield: what was that?"

"I dont know," Quentin said. "Nobody ever did know for certain. It was something about a bill of lading, some way he persuaded Mr Coldfield to use his credit: one of those things that when they work you were smart and when they dont you change your name and move to Texas: and Father said how Mr Coldfield must have sat back there in his little store and watched his wagonload of stock double maybe every ten years or at least not lose any ground and seen the chance to do that very same thing all the time, only his conscience (not his courage: Father said he had plenty of that) wouldn't let him. Then Sutpen came along and offered to do it, he and Mr Coldfield to divide the loot if it worked, and he (Sutpen) to take all the blame if it didn't. And Mr Coldfield let him. Father said it was because Mr Coldfield did not believe it would work, that they would get away with it, only he couldn't quit thinking about it, and so when they tried it and it failed he (Mr Coldfield) would be able to get it out of his mind then; and that when it did fail and they were caught, Mr Coldfield would insist on taking his share of the blame as penance and expiation for having sinned in his mind all those years. Because Mr Coldfield never did believe it would work, so when he saw that it was going to work, had worked, the least thing he could do was to refuse to take his share of the profits; that when he saw that it had worked it was his conscience he hated, not Sutpen; —his conscience and the land, the country which had created his conscience and then offered the opportunity to have made all that money to the conscience which it had created, which could do nothing but decline; hated that country so much that he was even glad when he saw it drifting closer and closer to a doomed and fatal war; that he would have joined the Yankee army, Father said, only he was not a soldier and knew that he would either be killed or die of hardship and so not be present on that day when the South would realise that it was now paying the price for having erected its economic edifice not on the rock of stern morality but on the shifting sands of opportunism and moral brigandage. So he chose the only gesture he could think of to impress his disapproval on those who should outlive the fighting and so participate in the remorse—"

"Sure," Shreve said. "That's fine. But Sutpen. The design. Get on, now."

"Yes," Quentin said. "The design.—Getting richer and richer. It must have looked fine and clear ahead for him now: house finished, and even bigger and whiter than the one he had gone to the door of that day and the nigger came in his monkey clothes and told him to go to the back, and he with his own brand of niggers even, which the man who lay in the hammock with his shoes off didn't have, to cull one from and train him to go to the door when his turn came for a little boy without any shoes on and with his pap's cutdown pants for clothes to come and knock on it. Only Father said that that wasn't it now, that when he came to Grandfather's office that day after the thirty years, and not trying to excuse now anymore than he had tried in the bottom that night when they ran the architect, but just to explain now, trying hard to explain now because now he was old and knew it, knew it was being old that he had to talk against: time shortening ahead of him that could and would do things to his chances and possibilities even if he had no more doubt of his bones and flesh than he did of his will and courage, telling Grandfather that the boy-symbol at the door wasn't it because the boy-symbol was just the figment of the amazed and desperate child; that now he would take that boy in where he would never again need to stand on the outside of a white door and knock at it: and not at all for mere shelter but so that that boy, that whatever nameless stranger, could shut that door himself forever behind him on all that he had ever known, and look ahead along the still undivulged light rays in which his descendants who might not even ever hear his (the boy's) name, waited to be born without even having to know that they had once been riven forever free from brutehood just as his own (Sutpen's) children were——"

"Dont say it's just me that sounds like your old man," Shreve said. "But go on. Sutpen's children. Go on."

"Yes," Quentin said. "The two children" thinking *Yes. Maybe we are both Father. Maybe nothing ever happens once and is finished. Maybe happen is never once but like ripples maybe on water after the pebble sinks, the ripples moving on, spreading, the pool attached by a narrow umbilical water-cord to the next pool which the first pool feeds, has fed, did feed, let this second pool contain a different temperature of water, a different molecularity of having seen, felt, remembered, reflect in a different tone the infinite unchanging sky, it doesn't matter: that pebble's watery echo whose fall it did not even see moves across its surface too at the original ripple-space, to the old ineradicable rhythm* thinking *Yes, we are both Father. Or maybe Father and I are both Shreve, maybe it took Father and me both to*

make Shreve or Shreve and me both to make Father or
maybe Thomas Sutpen to make all of us. "Yes, the two
children, the son and the daughter by sex and age
so glib to the design that he might have planned that
too, by character mental and physical so glib to it
that he might have culled them out of the celestial
herd of seraphs and cherubim like he chose his
twenty niggers out of whatever swapping there
must have been when he repudiated that first wife
and that child when he discovered that they would
not be adjunctive to the forwarding of the design.
And Grandfather said there was no conscience
about that, that Sutpen sat in the office that afternoon after thirty years and told him how his conscience had bothered him somewhat at first but that
he had argued calmly and logically with his conscience until it was settled, just as he must have
argued with his conscience about his and Mr Coldfield's bill of lading (only probably not as long here,
since time here would be pressing) until that was
settled;—how he granted that by certain lights there
was injustice in what he did but that he had obviated
that as much as lay in his power by being above-
board in the matter; that he could have simply deserted her, could have taken his hat and walked out,
but he did not: and that he had what Grandfather
would have to admit was a good and valid claim, if
not to the whole place which he alone had saved, as
well as the lives of all the white people on it, at least
to that portion of it which had been specifically
described and deeded to him in the marriage settle-

ment which he had entered in good faith, with no reservations as to his obscure origin and material equipment, while there had been not only reservation but actual misrepresentation on their part and misrepresentation of such a crass nature as to have not only voided and frustrated without his knowing it the central motivation of his entire design, but would have made an ironic delusion of all that he had suffered and endured in the past and all that he could ever accomplish in the future toward that design—which claim he had voluntarily relinquished, taking only the twenty niggers out of all he might have claimed and which many another man in his place would have insisted upon keeping and (in which contention) would have been supported by both legal and moral sanction even if not the delicate one of conscience: and Grandfather not saying 'Wait wait' now because it was that innocence again, that innocence which believed that the ingredients of morality were like the ingredients of pie or cake and once you had measured them and balanced them and mixed them and put them into the oven it was all finished and nothing but pie or cake could come out.—Yes, sitting there in Grandfather's office trying to explain with that patient amazed recapitulation, not to Grandfather and not to himself because Grandfather said that his very calmness was indication that he had long since given up any hope of ever understanding it, but trying to explain to circumstance, to fate itself, the logical steps by which he had arrived at a result absolutely and forever incredible, repeating the clear and simple synopsis of his history (which he and Grandfather both now knew) as if he were trying to explain it to an intractable and unpredictable child: 'You see, I had a design in my mind. Whether it was a good or a bad design is beside the point; the question is, Where did I make the mistake in it, what did I do or misdo in it, whom or what injure by it to the extent which this would indicate. I had a design. To accomplish it I should require money, a house, a plantation, slaves, a family—incidentally of course, a wife. I set out to acquire these, asking no favor of any man. I even risked my life at one time, as I told you, though as I also told you I did not undertake this risk purely and simply to gain a wife, though it did have that result. But that is beside the point also: suffice that I had the wife, accepted her in good faith, with no reservations about myself, and I expected as much from them. I did not even demand, mind, as one of my obscure origin might have been expected to do (or at least be condoned in the doing) out of ignorance of gentility in dealing with gentleborn people. I did not demand; I accepted them at their own valuation while insisting on my own part upon explaining fully about myself and my progenitors: yet they deliberately withheld from me the one fact which I have reason to know they were aware would have caused me to decline the entire matter, otherwise they would not have withheld it from me —a fact which I did not learn until after my son was born. And even then I did not act hastily. I could

have reminded them of these wasted years, these
years which would now leave me behind with my
schedule not only the amount of elapsed time which
their number represented, but that compensatory
amount of time represented by their number which
I should now have to spend to advance myself once
more to the point I had reached and lost. But I did
not. I merely explained how this new fact rendered
it impossible that this woman and child be incorpo-
rated in my design, and following which, as I told
you, I made no attempt to keep not only that which
I might consider myself to have earned at the risk
of my life but which had been given to me by signed
testimonials, but on the contrary I declined and resigned all right and claim to this in order that I
might repair whatever injustice I might be considered to have done by so providing for the two persons whom I might be considered to have deprived
of anything I might later possess: and this was
agreed to, mind; agreed to between the two parties.
And yet, and after more than thirty years, more than
thirty years after my conscience had finally assured
me that if I had done an injustice, I had done what
I could to rectify it——' and Grandfather not saying Wait now but saying, hollering maybe even:
'Conscience? Conscience? Good God, man, what
else did you expect? Didn't the very affinity and
instinct for misfortune of a man who had spent that
much time in a monastery even, let alone one who
had lived that many years as you lived them, tell you
better than that? didn't the dread and fear of females

which you must have drawn in with the primary mammalian milk teach you better? What kind of abysmal and purblind innocence could that have been which someone told you to call virginity? what conscience to trade with which would have warranted you in the belief that you could have bought immunity from her for no other coin but justice?'——"

It was at this point that Shreve went to the bedroom and put on the bathrobe. He did not say Wait, he just rose and left Quentin sitting before the table, the open book and the letter, and went out and returned in the robe and sat again and took up the cold pipe, though without filling it anew or lighting it as it was. "All right," he said. "So that Christmas Henry brought him home, into the house, and the demon looked up and saw the face he believed he had paid off and discharged twenty-eight years ago. Go on."

"Yes," Quentin said. "Father said he probably named him himself. Charles Bon. Charles Good. He didn't tell Grandfather that he did, but Grandfather believed he did, would have. That would have been a part of the cleaning up, just as he would have done his share toward cleaning up the exploded caps and musket cartridges after the siege if he hadn't been sick (or maybe engaged); he would have insisted on it maybe, the conscience again which could not allow her and the child any place in the design even though he could have closed his eyes and, if not fooled the rest of the world as they had fooled him, at least have frightened any man out of speaking the secret aloud—the same conscience which would not permit the child, since it was a boy, to bear either his name or that of its maternal grandfather, yet which would also forbid him to do the customary and provide a quick husband for the discarded woman and so give his son an authentic name. He chose the name himself, Grandfather believed, just as he named them all—the Charles Goods and the Clytemnestras and Henry and Judith and all of them—that entire fecundity of dragons' teeth as Father called it. And Father said——"

"Your father," Shreve said. "He seems to have got an awful lot of delayed information awful quick, after having waited forty-five years. If he knew all this, what was his reason for telling you that the trouble between Henry and Bon was the octoroon woman?"

"He didn't know it then. Grandfather didn't tell him all of it either, like Sutpen never told Grandfather quite all of it."

"Then who did tell him?"

"I did." Quentin did not move, did not look up while Shreve watched him. "The day after we—— after that night when we——"

"Oh," Shreve said. "After you and the old aunt. I see. Go on. And Father said——"

"——said how he must have stood there on the front gallery that afternoon and waited for Henry and the friend Henry had been writing home about all fall to come up the drive, and that maybe after

Henry wrote the name in the first letter Sutpen probably told himself it couldn't be, that there was a limit even to irony beyond which it became either just vicious but not fatal horseplay or harmless coincidence, since Father said that even Sutpen probably knew that nobody yet ever invented a name that somebody didn't own now or hadn't owned once: and they rode up at last and Henry said, 'Father, this is Charles' and he——" ("the demon," Shreve said) "——saw the face and knew that there are situations where coincidence is no more than the little child that rushes out onto a football field to take part in the game and the players run over and around the unscathed head and go on and shock together and in the fury of the struggle for the facts called gain or loss nobody even remembers the child nor saw who came and snatched it back from dissolution;—— that he stood there at his own door, just as he had imagined, planned, designed, and sure enough and after fifty years the forlorn nameless and homeless lost child came to knock at it and no monkey-dressed nigger anywhere under the sun to come to the door and order the child away; and Father said that even then, even though he knew that Bon and Judith had never laid eyes on one another, he must have felt and heard the design—house, position, posterity and all—come down like it had been built out of smoke, making no sound, creating no rush of displaced air and not even leaving any debris. And he not calling it retribution, no sins of the father come home to roost; not even calling it bad luck, but just a mistake: that mistake which he could not discover himself and which he came to Grandfather, not to excuse but just to review the facts for an impartial (and Grandfather said he believed, a legally trained) mind to examine and find and point out to him. Not moral retribution you see: just an old mistake in fact which a man of courage and shrewdness (the one of which he now knew he possessed, the other of which he believed that he had now learned, acquired) could still combat if he could only find out what the mistake had been. Because he did not give up. He never did give up; Grandfather said that his subsequent actions (the fact that for a time he did nothing and so perhaps helped to bring about the very situation which he dreaded) were not the result of any failing of courage or shrewdness or ruthlessness, but were the result of his conviction that it had all come from a mistake and until he discovered what that mistake had been he did not intend to risk making another one.

"So he invited Bon into the house, and for the two weeks of the vacation (only it didn't take that long; Father said that probably Mrs Sutpen had Judith and Bon already engaged from the moment she saw Bon's name in Henry's first letter) he watched Bon and Henry and Judith, or watched Bon and Judith rather because he would have already known about Henry and Bon from Henry's letters about him from the school; watched them for two weeks, and did nothing. Then Henry and Bon went back to school and now the nigger groom that fetched the

mail back and forth each week between Oxford and
Sutpen's Hundred brought letters to Judith now
that were not in Henry's hand (and that not necessary either, Father said, because Mrs Sutpen was
already covering the town and county both with
news of that engagement that Father said didn't
exist yet) and still he did nothing. He didn't do
anything at all until spring was almost over and
Henry wrote that he was bringing Bon home with
him to stay a day or two before Bon went home.
Then Sutpen went to New Orleans. Whether he
chose that time to go in order to get Bon and his
mother together and thrash the business out for
good and all or not, nobody knows, just as nobody
knows whether he ever saw the mother or not while
he was there, if she received him or refused to receive him; or if she did and he tried once more to
come to terms with her, buy her off maybe with
money now, since Father said that a man who could
believe that a scorned and outraged and angry
woman could be bought off with formal logic would
believe that she could be placated with money too,
and it didn't work; or if Bon was there and it was
Bon himself who refused the offer, though nobody
ever did know if Bon ever knew Sutpen was his
father or not, whether he was trying to revenge his
mother or not at first and only later fell in love, only
later succumbed to the current of retribution and
fatality which Miss Rosa said Sutpen had started and
had doomed all his blood to, black and white both.
But it didn't work evidently, and the next Christmas

came and Henry and Bon came to Sutpen's Hundred again and now Sutpen saw that there was no help for it, that Judith was in love with Bon and whether Bon wanted revenge or was just caught and sunk and doomed too, it was all the same. So it seems that he sent for Henry that Christmas eve just before supper time (Father said that maybe by now, after his New Orleans trip, he had learned at last enough about women to know it wouldn't do any good to go to Judith first) and told Henry. And he knew what Henry would say and Henry said it and he took the lie from his son and Henry knew by his father taking the lie that what his father had told him was true; and Father said that he (Sutpen) probably knew what Henry would do too and counted on Henry doing it because he still believed that it had been only a minor tactical mistake, and so he was like a skirmisher who is outnumbered yet cannot retreat who believes that if he is just patient enough and clever enough and calm enough and alert enough he can get the enemy scattered and pick them off one by one. And Henry did it. And he (Sutpen) probably knew what Henry would do next too, that Henry too would go to New Orleans to find out for himself. Then it was '61 and Sutpen knew what they would do now, not only what Henry would do but what he would force Bon to do; maybe (being a demon—though it would not require a demon to foresee war now) he even foresaw that Henry and Bon would join that student company at the University; he may have had some

way of watching, knowing the day their names appeared on the roster, some way of knowing where
the company was even before Grandfather became
colonel of the regiment the company was in until he
got hurt at Pittsburg Landing (where Bon was
wounded) and came home to get used to not having
any right arm and Sutpen came home in '64 with the
two tombstones and talked to Grandfather in the
office that day before both of them went back to the
war;—knew all the time where Henry and Bon
were, that they had been all the time in Grandfather's regiment where Grandfather could look
after them in a fashion even if Grandfather didn't
know that he was doing it—even if they needed
watching, because Sutpen must have known about
the probation too, what Henry was doing now:
holding all three of them—himself and Judith and
Bon—in that suspension while he wrestled with his
conscience to make it come to terms with what he
wanted to do just like his father had that time more
than thirty years ago, maybe even turned fatalist like
Bon now and giving the war a chance to settle the
whole business by killing him or Bon or both of
them (but with no help, no fudging, on his part
because it was him that carried Bon to the rear after
Pittsburg Landing) or maybe he knew that the
South would be whipped and then there wouldn't
be anything left that mattered that much, worth
getting that heated over, worth protesting against or
suffering for or dying for or even living for. That
was the day he came to the office, his——" ("the

demon's," Shreve said) "——one day of leave at home, came home with his tombstones and Judith was there and I reckon he looked at her and she looked at him and he said, 'You know where he is' and Judith didn't lie to him, and (he knew Henry) he said, 'But you have not heard from him yet' and Judith didn't lie about that either and she didn't cry either because both of them knew what would be in the letter when it came so he didn't have to ask, 'When he writes you that he is coming, you and Clytie will start making the wedding dress' even if Judith would have lied to him about that, which she would not have: so he put one of the stones on Ellen's grave and set the other one up in the hall and came in to see Grandfather, trying to explain it, seeing if Grandfather could discover that mistake which he believed was the sole cause of his problem, sitting there in his worn and shabby uniform, with his worn gauntlets and faded sash and (he would have had the plume by all means. He might have had to discard his sabre, but he would have had the plume) the plume in his hat broken and frayed and soiled, with his horse saddled and waiting in the street below and a thousand miles to ride to find his regiment, yet he sitting there on the one afternoon of his leave as though he had a thousand of them, as if there were no haste nor urgency anywhere under the sun and that when he departed he had no further to go than the twelve miles out to Sutpen's Hundred and a thousand days or maybe even years of monotony and rich peace, and he, even after he would become dead, still there, still watching the fine grandsons and great-grandsons springing as far as eye could reach; he still, even though dead in the earth, that same fine figure of a man that Wash Jones called him, but not now. Now fogbound by his own private embattlement of personal morality: that picayune splitting of abstract hairs while (Grandfather said) Rome vanished and Jericho crumbled, that *this would be right if* or *that would be wrong but* of slowing blood and stiffening bones and arteries that Father says men resort to in senility who while young and supple and strong reacted to a single simple Yes and a single simple No as instantaneous and complete and unthinking as the snapping on and off of electricity, sitting there and talking and now Grandfather not knowing what he was talking about because now Grandfather said he did not believe that Sutpen himself knew because even yet Sutpen had not quite told him all of it. And this that morality again, Grandfather said: that morality which would not permit him to malign or traduce the memory of his first wife, or at least the memory of the marriage even though he felt that he had been tricked by it, not even to an acquaintance in whose confidence and discretion he trusted enough to wish to justify himself, not even to his son by another marriage in order to preserve the status of his life's attainment and desire, except as a last resort. Not that he would hesitate then, Grandfather said: but not until then. He had been tricked by it himself, but he had extricated himself without asking or receiving help

from any man; let anyone else who might be so
imposed upon do the same.—Sitting there and mor-
alising on the fact that, no matter which course he
chose, the result would be that that design and plan
to which he had given fifty years of his life had just
as well never have existed at all by almost exactly
fifty years, and Grandfather not knowing what
choice he was talking about even, what second
choice he was faced with until the very last word he
spoke before he got up and put on his hat and shook
Grandfather's left hand and rode away; this second
choice, need to choose, as obscure to Grandfather as
the reason for the first, the repudiation, had been: so
that Grandfather did not even say 'I dont know
which you should choose' not because that was all
he could have said and so to say that would be less
than no answer at all, but that anything he might
have said would have been less than no answer at all
since Sutpen was not listening, did not expect an
answer, who had not come for pity and there was
no advice that he could have taken, and justification
he had already coerced from his conscience thirty
years ago. And he still knew that he had courage,
and though he may have come to doubt lately that
he had acquired that shrewdness which at one time
he believed he had, he still believed that it existed
somewhere in the world to be learned and that if it
could be learned he would yet learn it—and maybe
even this, Grandfather said: if shrewdness could not
extricate him this second time as it had before, he
could at least depend on the courage to find him will

and strength to make a third start toward that design
as it had found him to make the second with—who
came into the office not for pity and not for help
because Grandfather said he had never learned how
to ask anybody for help or anything else and so he
would not have known what to do with the help if
Grandfather could have given it to him, but came
just with that sober and quiet bemusement, hoping
maybe (if he hoped at all, if he were doing anything
but just thinking out loud at all) that the legal mind
might perceive and clarify that initial mistake which
he still insisted on, which he himself had not been
able to find: 'I was faced with condoning a fact
which had been foisted upon me without my
knowledge during the process of building toward
my design, which meant the absolute and irrevocable negation of the design; or in holding to my
original plan for the design in pursuit of which I had
incurred this negation. I chose, and I made to the
fullest what atonement lay in my power for whatever injury I might have done in choosing, paying
even more for the privilege of choosing as I chose
than I might have been expected to, or even (by law)
required. Yet I am now faced with a second necessity to choose, the curious factor of which is not, as
you pointed out and as first appeared to me, that the
necessity for a new choice should have arisen, but
that either choice which I might make, either course
which I might choose, leads to the same result: either I destroy my design with my own hand, which
will happen if I am forced to play my last trump

card, or do nothing, let matters take the course which I know they will take and see my design complete itself quite normally and naturally and successfully to the public eye, yet to my own in such fashion as to be a mockery and a betrayal of that little boy who approached that door fifty years ago and was turned away, for whose vindication the whole plan was conceived and carried forward to the moment of this choice, this second choice devolving out of that first one which in its turn was forced on me as the result of an agreement, an arrangement which I had entered in good faith, concealing nothing, while the other party or parties to it concealed from me the one very factor which would destroy the entire plan and design which I had been working toward, concealed it so well that it was not until after the child was born that I discovered that this factor existed'——"

"Your old man," Shreve said. "When your grandfather was telling this to him, he didn't know any more what your grandfather was talking about than your grandfather knew what the demon was talking about when the demon told it to him, did he? And when your old man told it to you, you wouldn't have known what anybody was talking about if you hadn't been out there and seen Clytie. Is that right?"

"Yes," Quentin said. "Grandfather was the only friend he had."

"The demon had?" Quentin didn't answer, didn't move. It was cold in the room now. The heat was

almost gone out of the radiators: the cold iron
fluting stern signal and admonition for sleeping, the
little death, the renewal. It had been some time now
since the chimes had rung eleven. "All right,"
Shreve said. He was hugging himself into the bathrobe now as he had formerly hugged himself inside
his pink naked almost hairless skin. "He chose. He
chose lechery. So do I. But go on." His remark was
not intended for flippancy nor even derogation. It
was born (if from any source) of that incorrigible
unsentimental sentimentality of the young which
takes the form of hard and often crass levity—to
which, by the way, Quentin paid no attention whatever, resuming as if he had never been interrupted,
his face still lowered, still brooding apparently on
the open letter upon the open book between his
hands.

"He left for Virginia that night. Grandfather said
how he went to the window and watched him ride
across the square on the gaunt black stallion, erect
in his faded gray, the hat with its broken plume
cocked a little yet not quite so much as the beaver
of the old days, as if (Grandfather said) even with
his martial rank and prerogatives he did not quite
swagger like he used to do, not because he was
chastened by misfortune or spent or even war-
wearied but as though even while riding he was still
bemused in that state in which he struggled to hold
clear and free above a maelstrom of unpredictable
and unreasoning human beings, not his head for
breath and not so much his fifty years of effort and

striving to establish a posterity, but his code of logic
and morality, his formula and recipe of fact and
deduction whose balanced sum and product declined, refused to swim or even float;—saw him approach the Holston House and saw old Mr
McCaslin and two other old men hobble out and
stop him, he sitting the stallion and talking to them
and his voice not raised, Grandfather said, yet the
very sober quality of his gestures and the set of his
shoulders forensic, oratorical. Then he went on. He
could still reach Sutpen's Hundred before dark, so
it was probably after supper that he headed the stallion toward the Atlantic Ocean, he and Judith facing one another again for maybe a full minute, he
not needing to say 'I will stop it if I can', she not
needing to say 'Stop it then—if you can' but just
goodbye, the kiss on the brow and no tears; a word
to Clytie and to Wash: master to slave, baron to
retainer: 'Well, Clytie, take care of Miss Judith.—
Wash, I'll send you a piece of Abe Lincoln's coat tail
from Washington' and I reckon Wash answering
like it used to be under the scuppernongs with the
demijohn and the well bucket: 'Sho, Kernel; kill
ever one of the varmints!' So he ate the hoecake and
drank the parched acorn coffee and rode away.
Then it was '65 and the army (Grandfather had
gone back to it too; he was a brigadier now though
I reckon this was for more reason than because he
just had one arm) had retreated across Georgia and
into Carolina and they all knew it wouldn't be very
much longer now. Then one day Lee sent Johnston

some reinforcements from one of his corps and
Grandfather found out that the Twenty-third Mississippi was one of the regiments. And he (Grandfather) didn't know what had happened: whether
Sutpen had found out in some way that Henry had
at last coerced his conscience into agreeing with him
as his (Henry's) father had done thirty years ago,
whether Judith perhaps had written her father that
she had heard from Bon at last and what she and
Bon intended to do, or if the four of them had just
reached as one person that point where something
had to be done, had to happen, he (Grandfather)
didn't know. He just learned one morning that
Sutpen had ridden up to Grandfather's old regiment's headquarters and asked and received permission to speak to Henry and did speak to him and
then rode away again before midnight."

"So he got his choice made, after all," Shreve said.
"He played that trump after all. And so he came
home and found——"

"Wait," Quentin said.

"——what he must have wanted to find or anyway what he was going to find——"

"Wait, I tell you!" Quentin said, though still he
did not move nor even raise his voice—that voice
with its tense suffused restrained quality: "I am telling" *Am I going to have to hear it all again* he
thought *I am going to have to hear it all over again
I am already hearing it all over again I am listening
to it all over again I shall have to never listen to anything else but this again forever so apparently not only*

*a man never outlives his father but not even his friends
and acquaintances do:*—(that at least regarding
which he should have needed no word nor warning
even if Judith would have sent him one, sent him
acknowledgement that she was beaten, who according to Mr Compson would no more have sent him
acknowledgement that he had beat her than she
waited (who Miss Coldfield said was not bereaved)
and met him on his return, not with the fury and
despair perhaps which he might have expected even
though knowing as little, having learned as little,
about women as Mr Compson said he had, yet certainly with something other than the icy calm with
which, according to Miss Coldfield, she met him—
the kiss again after almost two years, on the brow;
the voices, the speeches, quiet, contained, almost
impersonal: "And—?" "Yes. Henry killed him" followed by the brief tears which ceased on the instant
when they began, as if the moisture consisted of a
single sheet or layer thin as a cigarette paper and in
the shape of a human face; the "Ah, Clytie. Ah,
Rosa.—Well, Wash. I was unable to penetrate far
enough behind the Yankee lines to cut a piece from
that coat tail as I promised you"; the (from Jones)
guffaw, the chortle, the old imbecile stability of the
articulated mud which, Mr Compson said, outlasts
the victories and the defeats both: "Well, Kernel,
they kilt us but they aint whupped us yit, air they?":
and that was all. He had returned. He was home
again where his problem now was haste, passing
time, the need to hurry. *He was not concerned,* Mr

Compson said, *about the courage and the will, nor
even about the shrewdness now. He was not for one
moment concerned about his ability to start the third
time. All that he was concerned about was the possibility that he might not have time sufficient to do it in,
regain his lost ground in. He did not waste any of what
time he had either. The will and the shrewdness too he
did not waste, though he doubtless did not consider it
to have been either his will or his shrewdness which
supplied waiting to his hand the opportunity, and it
was probably less of shrewdness and more of courage
than even will which got him engaged to Miss Rosa
within a period of three months and almost before she
was aware of the fact—Miss Rosa, the chief disciple and
advocate of that cult of demon-harrying of which he
was the chief object (even though not victim), engaged
to him before she had got accustomed to having him in
the house;—yes, more of courage than even will, yet
something of shrewdness too: the shrewdness acquired in
excruciating driblets through the fifty years suddenly
capitulant and retroactive or suddenly sprouting and
flowering like a seed lain fallow in a vacuum or in a
single iron clod. Because he seemed to perceive without
stopping, in that passage through the house which was
an unbroken continuation of the long journey from
Virginia, the pause not to greet his family but merely
to pick up Jones and drag him on out to the brier-choked
fields and fallen fences and clap axe or mattock into his
hands, the one weak spot, the one spot vulnerable to
assault in Miss Rosa's embattled spinsterhood, and to
assault and carry this in one stride, with something of*

the ruthless tactical skill of his old master (the Twenty-third Mississippi was in Jackson's corps at one time). And then the shrewdness failed him again. It broke down, it vanished into that old impotent logic and morality which had betrayed him before: and what day might it have been, what furrow might he have stopped dead in, one foot advanced, the unsentient plow handles in his instantaneous unsentient hands, what fence panel held in midair as though it had no weight by muscles which could not feel it, when he realised that there was more in his problem than just lack of time, that the problem contained some super-distillation of this lack: that he was now past sixty and that possibly he could get but one more son, had at best but one more son in his loins, as the old cannon might know when it has just one more shot in its corporeality. So he suggested what he suggested to her, and she did what he should have known she would do and would have known probably if he had not bogged himself again in his morality which had all the parts but which refused to run, to move. Hence the proposal, the outrage and unbelief; the tide, the blast of indignation and anger upon which Miss Rosa vanished from Sutpen's Hundred, her air-ballooned skirts spread upon the flood, chip-light, her bonnet (possibly one of Ellen's which she had prowled out of the attic) clapped fast onto her head rigid and precarious with rage. And he standing there with the reins over his arm, with perhaps something like smiling inside his beard and about the eyes which was not smiling but the crinkled concentration of furious thinking: —the haste, the need for it; the urgency but not fear, not

*concern: just the fact that he had missed that time,
though luckily it was just a spotting shot with a light
charge, and the old gun, the old barrel and carriage none
the worse; only next time there might not be enough
powder for both a spotting shot and then a full-sized
load;—the fact that the thread of shrewdness and courage and will ran onto the same spool which the thread
of his remaining days ran onto and that spool almost
near enough for him to reach out his hand and touch it.
But this was no grave concern yet, since it (the old logic,
the old morality which had never yet failed to fail him)
was already falling into pattern, already showing him
conclusively that he had been right, just as he knew he
had been, and therefore what had happened was just a
delusion and did not actually exist)*

"No," Shreve said; "you wait. Let me play a
while now. Now, Wash. Him (the demon) standing
there with the horse, the saddled charger, the
sheathed sabre, the gray waiting to be laid peaceful
away among the moths and all lost save dishonor:
then the voice of the faithful grave-digger who
opened the play and would close it, coming out of
the wings like Shakespeare's very self: 'Well, Kernel, they mought have whupped us but they aint kilt
us yit, air they?'——" This was not flippancy either.
It too was just that protective coloring of levity
behind which the youthful shame of being moved
hid itself, out of which Quentin also spoke, the reason for Quentin's sullen bemusement, the (on both
their parts) flipness, the strained clowning: the two
of them, whether they knew it or not, in the cold

room (it was quite cold now) dedicated to that best of ratiocination which after all was a good deal like Sutpen's morality and Miss Coldfield's demonising —this room not only dedicated to it but set aside for it and suitably so since it would be here above any other place that it (the logic and the morality) could do the least amount of harm;—the two of them back to back as though at the last ditch, saying No to Quentin's Mississippi shade who in life had acted and reacted to the minimum of logic and morality, who dying had escaped it completely, who dead remained not only indifferent but impervious to it, somehow a thousand times more potent and alive. There was no harm intended by Shreve and no harm taken, since Quentin did not even stop. He did not even falter, taking Shreve up in stride without comma or colon or paragraph:

"——no reserve to risk a spotting shot with now so he started this one like you start a rabbit out of a brier patch, with a little chunk of dried mud thrown by hand. Maybe it was the first string of beads out of his and Wash's little store where he would get mad at his customers, the niggers and the trash and the haggling, and turn them out and lock the door and drink himself blind. And maybe Wash delivered the beads himself, Father said, that was down at the gate when he rode back from the war that day, that after he went away with the regiment would tell folks that he (Wash) was looking after Kernel's place and niggers until after a while maybe he even believed it. Father's mother said how when

the Sutpen niggers first heard about what he was
saying, they would stop him in the road that came
up out of the bottom where the old fishing camp was
that Sutpen let him and the granddaughter (she was
about eight then) live in. There would be too many
of them for him to whip them all, to even try to, risk
trying to: and they would ask him why he wasn't at
the war and he would say, 'Git outen my road,
niggers!' and then it would be the outright laughing, asking one another (except it was not one another but him): 'Who him, calling us niggers?' and
he would rush at them with a stick and them avoid-
ing him just enough, not mad at all, just laughing.
And he was still carrying fish and animals he killed
(or maybe stole) and vegetables up to the house
when that was about all Mrs Sutpen and Judith (and
Clytie too) had to live on, and Clytie would not let
him come into the kitchen with the basket even,
saying, 'Stop right there, white man. Stop right
where you is. You aint never crossed this door while
Colonel was here and you aint going to cross it
now.' Which was true, only Father said there was
a kind of pride in it: that he had never tried to enter
the house, even though he believed that if he had
tried, Sutpen would not have let them repulse him;
like (Father said) he might have said to himself *The
reason I wont try it aint that I refuse to give any black
nigger the chance to tell me I cant but because I aint
going to force Mister Tom to have to cuss a nigger or
take a cussing from his wife on my account* But they
would drink together under the scuppernong arbor

on the Sunday afternoons, and on the week days he would see Sutpen (the fine figure of the man as he called it) on the black stallion, galloping about the plantation, and Father said how for that moment Wash's heart would be quiet and proud both and that maybe it would seem to him that this world where niggers, that the Bible said had been created and cursed by God to be brute and vassal to all men of white skin, were better found and housed and even clothed than he and his granddaughter—that this world where he walked always in mocking and jeering echoes of nigger laughter, was just a dream and an illusion and that the actual world was the one where his own lonely apotheosis (Father said) galloped on the black thoroughbred, thinking maybe, Father said, how the Book said that all men were created in the image of God and so all men were the same in God's eyes anyway, looked the same to God at least, and so he would look at Sutpen and think *A fine proud man. If God Himself was to come down and ride the natural earth, that's what He would aim to look like.* Maybe he even delivered the first string of beads himself, and Father said maybe each of the ribbons afterward during the next three years while the girl matured fast like girls of that kind do; or anyway he would know and recognise each and every ribbon when he saw it on her even when she lied to him about where and how she got it, which she probably did not, since she would be bound to know that he had been seeing the ribbons in the showcase every day for three years and would have known them as well as he knew his own shoes. And not only he knew them, but all the other men, the customers and the loungers, the white and the black that would be sitting and squatting about the store's gallery to watch her pass, not quite defiant and not quite cringing and not quite flaunting the ribbons and the beads, but almost; not quite any of them but a little of all: bold sullen and fearful. But Father said how Wash's heart was probably still quiet even after he saw the dress and spoke about it, probably only a little grave now and watching her secret defiant frightened face while she told him (before he had asked, maybe too insistent, too quick to volunteer it) that Miss Judith had given it to her, helped her to make it: and Father said maybe he realised all of a sudden and without warning that when he passed the men on the gallery they would look after him too and that they already knew that which he had just thought they were probably thinking. But Father said his heart was still quiet, even now, and that he answered, if he answered at all, stopped the protestations and disclaimers at all: 'Sho, now. Ef Kernel and Miss Judith wanted to give hit to you, I hope you minded to thank them.'—Not alarmed, Father said: just thoughtful, just grave; and Father said how that afternoon Grandfather rode out to see Sutpen about something and there was nobody in the front of the store and he was about to go out and go up to the house when he heard the voices from the back and he walked on toward them and so he overheard them before he could begin to not listen

and before he could make them hear him calling
Sutpen's name. Grandfather couldn't see them yet,
he hadn't even got to where they could hear him
yet, but he said he knew exactly how they would be:
Sutpen having already told Wash to get the jug out
and then Wash spoke and Sutpen beginning to turn,
realising that Wash wasn't getting the jug before he
comprehended the import of what Wash was saying, then comprehending that and still half turned
and then all of a sudden kind of reared back and
flinging his head up, looking at Wash and Wash
standing there, not cringing either, in that attitude
dogged and quiet and not cringing, and Sutpen said,
'What about the dress?' and Grandfather said it was
Sutpen's voice that was short and sharp: not Wash's;
that Wash's voice was just flat and quiet, not abject:
just patient and slow: 'I have knowed you for going
on twenty years now. I aint never denied yit to do
what you told me to do. And I'm a man past sixty.
And she aint nothing but a fifteen-year-old gal.' and
Sutpen said, 'Meaning that I'd harm the girl? I, a
man as old as you are?' and Wash: 'If you was arra
other man, I'd say you was as old as me. And old or
no old, I wouldn't let her keep that dress nor nothing else that come from your hand. But you are
different.' and Sutpen: 'How different?' and Grandfather said how Wash did not answer and that he
called again now and neither of them heard him; and
then Sutpen said: 'So that's why you are afraid of
me?' and Wash said, 'I aint afraid. Because you are
brave. It aint that you were a brave man at one

second or minute or hour of your life and got a
paper to show hit from General Lee. But you are
brave, the same as you are alive and breathing.
That's where it's different. Hit dont need no ticket
from nobody to tell me that. And I know that whatever your hands tech, whether hit's a regiment of
men or a ignorant gal or just a hound dog, that you
will make hit right.' Then Grandfather heard
Sutpen move, sudden and sharp, and Grandfather
said he reckoned, thought just about what he imagined Wash was thinking. But all Sutpen said was,
'Get the jug.'—'Sho, Kernel,' Wash said.

"So that Sunday came, a year after that day and
three years after he had suggested to Miss Rosa that
they try it first and if it was a boy and lived, they
would be married. It was before daylight and he was
expecting his mare to foal to the black stallion, so
when he left the house before day that morning
Judith thought he was going to the stable, who
knew what and how much about her father and
Wash's granddaughter nobody knew, how much
she could not have helped but know from what
Clytie must have known (may have or may not have
told her, whether or no) since everybody else white
or black in the neighborhood knew who had ever
seen the girl pass in the ribbons and beads which
they all recognised, how much she may have refused
to discover during the fitting and sewing of that
dress (Father said Judith actually did this; this was
no lie that the girl told Wash: the two of them alone
all day long for about a week in the house: and what

they must have talked about, what Judith must have talked about while the girl stood around in what she possessed to call under clothes, with her sullen defiant secret watchful face, answering what, telling what that Judith may or may not have tried to shut her eyes to, nobody knew). So it was not until he failed to return at dinner time that she went or sent Clytie to the stable and found that the mare had foaled in the night but that her father was not there. And it was not until midafternoon that she found a halfgrown boy and paid him a nickel to go down to the old fish camp and ask Wash where Sutpen was, and the boy walked whistling around the corner of the rotting cabin and saw maybe the scythe first, maybe the body first lying in the weeds which Wash had not yet cut, and as he screamed he looked up and saw Wash in the window, watching him. Then about a week later they caught the nigger, the midwife, and she told how she didn't know that Wash was there at all that dawn when she heard the horse and then Sutpen's feet and he came in and stood over the pallet where the girl and the baby were and said, 'Penelope—("that was the mare")—foaled this morning. A damned fine colt. Going to be the spit and image of his daddy when I rode him North in '61. Do you remember?' and the old nigger said she said, 'Yes, Marster' and that he jerked the riding whip toward the pallet and said, 'Well? Damn your black hide: horse or mare?' and that she told him and that he stood there for a minute and he didn't move at all, with the riding whip against his leg and the

lattices of sunlight from the unchinked wall falling
upon him, across his white hair and his beard that
hadn't turned at all yet, and she said she saw his eyes
and then his teeth inside his beard and that she
would have run then only she couldn't, couldn't
seem to make her legs bear to get up and run: and
then he looked at the girl on the pallet again and
said, 'Well, Milly; too bad you're not a mare too.
Then I could give you a decent stall in the stable'
and turned and went out. Only she could not move
even yet, and she didn't even know that Wash was
outside there; she just heard Sutpen say, 'Stand
back, Wash. Dont you touch me': and then Wash,
his voice soft and hardly loud enough to reach her:
'I'm going to tech you, Kernel': and Sutpen again:
'Stand back, Wash!' sharp now, and then she heard
the whip on Wash's face but she didn't know if she
heard the scythe or not because now she found out
that she could move, get up, run out of the cabin and
into the weeds, running——"

"Wait," Shreve said; "wait. You mean that he
had got the son at last that he wanted, yet still
he——"

"——walked the three miles and back before midnight to fetch the old nigger, then sat on the sagging
gallery until daylight came and the granddaughter
stopped screaming inside the cabin and he even
heard the baby once, waiting for Sutpen. And Father said his heart was quiet then too, even though
he knew what they would be saying in every cabin
about the land by nightfall, just as he had known

what they were saying during the last four or five
months while his granddaughter's condition (which
he had never tried to conceal) could no longer be
mistaken: *Wash Jones has fixed old Sutpen at last. It
taken him twenty years to do it, but he has got a holt
of old Sutpen at last where Sutpen will either have to
tear meat or squeal* That's what Father said he was
thinking while he waited outside on the gallery
where the old nigger had sent him, ordered him out,
standing there maybe by the very post where the
scythe had leaned rusting for two years, while the
granddaughter's screams came steady as a clock now
but his own heart quiet, not at all concerned nor
alarmed; and Father said that maybe while he stood
befogged in his fumbling and groping (that morality
of his that was a good deal like Sutpen's, that told
him he was right in the face of all fact and usage and
everything else) which had always been somehow
mixed up and involved with galloping hooves even
during the old peace that nobody remembered, and
in which during the four years of the war which he
had not attended the galloping had been only the
more gallant and proud and thunderous;—Father
said that maybe he got his answer; that maybe there
broke free and plain in midgallop against the yellow
sky of dawn the fine proud image of the man on the
fine proud image of the stallion and that the fumbling and the groping broke clear and free too, not
in justification or explanation or extenuation or excuse, Father said, but as the apotheosis lonely, ex-
plicable, beyond all human fouling: *He is bigger than*

all them Yankees that killed us and ourn, that killed his wife and widowed his daughter and druv his son from home, that stole his niggers and ruined his land; bigger than this whole county that he fit for and in payment for which has brung him to keeping a little country store for his bread and meat; bigger than the scorn and denial which hit helt to his lips like the bitter cup in the Book. And how could I have lived nigh to him for twenty years without being touched and changed by him? Maybe I am not as big as he is and maybe I did not do any of the galloping. But at least I was drug along where he went. And me and him can still do hit and will ever so, if so be he will show me what he aims for me to do; and maybe still standing there and holding the stallion's reins after Sutpen had entered the cabin, still hearing the galloping, watching the proud galloping image merge and pass, galloping through avatars which marked the accumulation of years, time, to the fine climax where it galloped without weariness or progress, forever and forever immortal beneath the brandished sabre and the shot-torn flags rushing down a sky in color like thunder; stood there and heard Sutpen inside the house speak his single sentence of salutation inquiry and farewell to the granddaughter, and Father said that for a second Wash must not have felt the very earth under his feet while he watched Sutpen emerge from the house, the riding whip in his hand, thinking quietly, like in a dream: *I kaint have heard what I know I heard. I just know I kaint* thinking *That was what got him up. It was that colt. It aint me or mine either. It*

wasn't even his own that got him out of bed maybe
feeling no earth, no stability, even yet, maybe not
even hearing his own voice when Sutpen saw his
face (the face of the man who in twenty years he
had no more known to make any move save at
command than he had the stallion which he rode)
and stopped: 'You said if she was a mare you could
give her a decent stall in the stable', maybe not
even hearing Sutpen when he said, sudden and
sharp: 'Stand back. Dont you touch me' only he
must have heard that because he answered it: 'I'm
going to tech you, Kernel' and Sutpen said 'Stand
back, Wash' again before the old woman heard the
whip. Only there were two blows with the whip;
they found the two welts on Wash's face that
night. Maybe the two blows even knocked him
down; maybe it was while he was getting up that
he put his hand on the scythe——"

"Wait," Shreve said; "for Christ's sake wait. You
mean that he——"

"——sat there all that day in the little window
where he could watch the road; probably laid the
scythe down and went straight into the house where
maybe the granddaughter on the pallet asked querulously what it was and he answered, 'Whut? Whut
racket, honey?' and maybe he tried to persuade her
to eat too—the side meat he had probably brought
home from the store Saturday night or maybe the
candy, trying to tempt her with it maybe—the
nickel's worth of stale jellified glue out of a striped
sack, and maybe ate himself and then sat at the

window where he could look out above the body and the scythe in the weeds below, and watch the road. Because he was sitting there when the half grown boy came around the corner of the house whistling and saw him. And Father said he must have realised then that it would not be much after dark when it would happen; that he must have sat there and sensed, felt them gathering with the horses and dogs and guns—the curious and the vengeful—men of Sutpen's own kind, who used to eat at his table with him back when he (Wash) had yet to approach nearer the house than the scuppernong arbor—men who had led the way, shown the other and lesser ones how to fight in battles, who might also possess signed papers from the generals saying that they were among the first and foremost of the brave—who had galloped also in the old days arrogant and proud on the fine horses about the fine plantations—symbol also of admiration and hope, instruments too of despair and grief; these it was whom he was expected to run from and it seeming to him probably that he had no less to run from than he had to run to; that if he ran he would be fleeing merely one set of bragging and evil shadows for another, since they (men) were all of a kind throughout all of earth which he knew, and he old, too old to run far even if he were to run who could never escape them, no matter how much or how far he ran; a man past sixty could not expect to run that far, far enough to escape beyond the boundaries of earth where such men lived, set the order and the rule of living: and Father said that maybe for the first time in his life he began to comprehend how it had been possible for Yankees or any other army to have whipped them—the gallant, the proud, the brave; the acknowledged and chosen best among them all to bear the courage and honor and pride. It would probably be about sunset now and probably he could feel them quite near now; Father said it probably seemed to him that he could even hear them: all the voices, the murmuring of tomorrow and tomorrow and tomorrow beyond the immediate fury: *Old Wash Jones come a tumble at last. He thought he had Sutpen, but Sutpen fooled him. He thought he had him, but old Wash Jones got fooled* and then maybe even saying it aloud, shouting it Father said: 'But I never expected that, Kernel! You know I never!' until maybe the granddaughter stirred and spoke querulously again and he went and quieted her and returned to talk to himself again but careful now, quiet now since Sutpen was close enough to hear him easy, without shouting: 'You know I never. You know I never expected or asked or wanted nothing from arra living man but what I expected from you. And I never asked that. I didn't think hit would need: I just said to myself *I dont need to. What need has a fellow like Wash Jones to question or doubt the man that General Lee himself said in a hand-wrote ticket that he was brave?* Brave' (and maybe it would be loud again, forgetting again) 'Brave! Better if narra one of them had ever rid back in '65' thinking *Better if his kind and mine too had never drawn the breath of life on this earth. Better that all who remain of us be blasted from the face of it than that another Wash Jones should see his whole life shredded from him and shrivel away like a dried shuck thrown onto the fire*

Then they rode up. He must have been listening to them as they came down the road, the dogs and the horses, and seen the lanterns since it was dark now. And Major de Spain who was sheriff then got down and saw the body, though he said he did not see Wash nor know that he was there until Wash spoke his name quietly from the window almost in his face: 'That you, Major?' De Spain told him to come on out and he said how Wash's voice was quite quiet when he said he would be out in just a minute; it was too quiet, too calm; so much too quiet and calm that de Spain said he did not realise for a moment that it was too calm and quiet: 'In just a minute. Soon as I see about my granddaughter.' 'We'll see to her,' de Spain said. 'You come on out.' 'Sho, Major,' Wash said. 'In just a minute.' So they waited in front of the dark house, and the next day Father said there were a hundred that remembered about the butcher knife that he kept hidden and razor-sharp—the one thing in his sloven life that he was ever known to take pride in or care of—only by the time they remembered all this it was too late. So they didn't know what he was about. They just heard him moving inside the dark house, then they heard the granddaughter's voice, fretful and querulous: 'Who is it? Light the lamp, Grandpaw' then his voice: 'Hit wont need no light, honey. Hit wont take but a minute' then de Spain drew his pistol and said, 'You, Wash! Come out of there!' and still Wash didn't answer, murmuring still to the granddaughter: 'Where air you?' and the fretful voice answering, 'Right here. Where else would I be? What is——' then de Spain said, 'Jones!' and he was already fumbling at the broken steps when the granddaughter screamed; and now all the men there claimed that they heard the knife on both the neckbones, though de Spain didn't. He just said he knew that Wash had come out onto the gallery and that he sprang back before he found out that it was not toward him Wash was running but toward the end of the gallery, where the body lay, but that he did not think about the scythe: he just ran backward a few feet when he saw Wash stoop and rise again and now Wash was running toward him. Only he was running toward them all, de Spain said, running into the lanterns so that now they could see the scythe raised above his head; they could see his face, his eyes too, as he ran with the scythe above his head, straight into the lanterns and the gun barrels, making no sound, no outcry while de Spain ran backward before him, saying, 'Jones! Stop! Stop, or I'll kill you. Jones! Jones! JONES!' ''

"Wait," Shreve said. "You mean that he got the son he wanted, after all that trouble, and then turned right around and——"

"Yes. Sitting in Grandfather's office that afternoon, with his head kind of flung back a little, explaining to Grandfather like he might have been explaining arithmetic to Henry back in the fourth grade: 'You see, all I wanted was just a son. Which seems to me, when I look about at my contemporary scene, no exorbitant gift from nature or circumstance to demand——' "

"*Will you wait?*" Shreve said. "——that with the son he went to all that trouble to get lying right there behind him in the cabin, he would have to taunt the grandfather into killing first him and then the child too?"

"—What?" Quentin said. "It wasn't a son. It was a girl."

"Oh," Shreve said. "——Come on. Let's get out of this damn icebox and go to bed."

VIII

There would be no deep breathing tonight. The window would remain closed above the frozen and empty quad beyond which the windows in the opposite wall were, with two or three exceptions, already dark; soon the chimes would ring for midnight, the notes melodious and tranquil, faint and clear as glass in the fierce (it had quit snowing) still air. "So the old man sent the nigger for Henry," Shreve said. "And Henry came in and the old man said 'They cannot marry because he is your brother' and Henry said 'You lie' like that, that quick: no space, no interval, no nothing between like when you press the button and get light in the room. And the old man just sat there, didn't even move and strike him and so Henry didn't say 'You lie' again because he knew now it was so; he just said 'It's not true', not 'I dont believe it' but 'It's not true' because he could maybe see the old man's face again now and demon or no it was a kind of grief and pity, not for himself but for Henry, because Henry was just young while he (the old man) knew that he still had the courage and even all the shrewdness too——"

Shreve stood beside the table, facing Quentin

again though not seated now. In the overcoat buttoned awry over the bathrobe he looked huge and shapeless like a disheveled bear as he stared at Quentin (the Southerner, whose blood ran quick to cool, more supple to compensate for violent changes of temperature perhaps, perhaps merely nearer the surface) who sat hunched in his chair, his hands thrust into his pockets as if he were trying to hug himself warm between his arms, looking somehow fragile and even wan in the lamplight, the rosy glow which now had nothing of warmth, coziness, in it, while both their breathing vaporised faintly in the cold room where there was now not two of them but four, the two who breathed not individuals now yet something both more and less than twins, the heart and blood of youth (Shreve was nineteen, a few months younger than Quentin. He looked exactly nineteen; he was one of those people whose correct age you never know because they look exactly that and so you tell yourself that he or she cannot possibly be that because he or she looks too exactly that not to take advantage of the appearance: so you never believe implicitly that he or she is either that age which they claim or that which in sheer desperation they agree to or which someone else reports them to be) strong enough and willing enough for two, for two thousand, for all. Not two of them in a New England college sitting-room but one in a Mississippi library sixty years ago, with holly and mistletoe in vases on the mantel or thrust behind, crowning and garlanding with the season and time the pictures on the walls, and a sprig or so decorating the photograph, the group—mother and two children—on the desk behind which the father sat when the son entered; and they—Quentin and Shreve—thinking how after the father spoke and before what he said stopped being shock and began to make sense, the son would recall later how he had seen through the window beyond his father's head the sister and the lover in the garden, pacing slowly, the sister's head bent with listening, the lover's head leaned above it while they paced slowly on in that rhythm which not the eyes but the heart marks and calls the beat and measure for, to disappear slowly beyond some bush or shrub starred with white bloom—jasmine, spiraea, honeysuckle, perhaps myriad scentless unpickable Cherokee roses—names, blooms which Shreve possibly had never heard and never seen although the air had blown over him first which became tempered to nourish them—and it would not matter here that the time had been winter in that garden too and hence no bloom nor leaf even if there had been someone to walk there and be seen there since, judged by subsequent events, it had been night in the garden also. But that did not matter because it had been so long ago. It did not matter to them (Quentin and Shreve) anyway, who could without moving, as free now of flesh as the father who decreed and forbade, the son who denied and repudiated, the lover who acquiesced, the beloved who was not bereaved, and with no tedious transition from hearth and garden (granted the garden) to saddle, be already clattering over the frozen ruts of that December night and that Christmas dawn, that day of peace and cheer, of holly and goodwill and logs on the hearth; not two of them there and then either but four of them riding the two horses through the iron darkness and that not mattering either: what faces and what names they called themselves and were called by so long as the blood coursed—the blood, the immortal brief recent intransient blood which could hold honor above slothy unregret and love above fat and easy shame.

"And Bon didn't know it," Shreve said. "The old man didn't move and this time Henry didn't say 'You lie', he said 'It's not true' and the old man said, 'Ask him. Ask Charles then' and then Henry knew that that was what his father had meant all the time and that that was what he meant himself when he told his father he lied, because what the old man said wasn't just 'He is your brother' but 'He has known all the time that he is yours and your sister's brother'. But Bon didn't. Listen, dont you remember how your father said it, about how not one time did he—the old guy, the demon—ever seem to wonder either how the other wife managed to find him, track him down, had never once seemed to wonder what she might have been doing all that time, how she might have passed that time, the thirty years since that day when he paid his bill with her and got it receipted, so he thought, and saw with his own eyes that it was (so he thought) destroyed, torn up

and thrown to the wind; never once wondered
about this but only that she had done it, had tracked
him down, could have and would have wanted to?
So it wasn't her that told Bon. She wouldn't have,
maybe for the reason that she knew he—the demon
—would believe she had. Or maybe she didn't get
around to telling him. Maybe she just never thought
that there could be anyone as close to her as a lone
child out of her own body who would have to be
told how she had been scorned and suffered. Or
maybe she was already telling it before he was big
enough to know words and so by the time he was
big enough to understand what was being told him
she had told it so much and so hard that the words
didn't make sense to her anymore either because
they didn't have to make sense to her, and so she had
got to the point where when she thought she was
saying it she was quiet, and when she thought she
was quiet it was just the hate and the fury and the
unsleeping and the unforgetting. Or maybe she
didn't intend for him to know it then. Maybe she
was grooming him for that hour and moment which
she couldn't foresee but that she knew would arrive
some day because it would have to arrive or else she
would have to do like the Aunt Rosa and deny that
she had ever breathed—the moment when he would
stand side by side (not face to face) with his father
where fate or luck or justice or whatever she called
it could do the rest (and it did, better than she could
have invented or hoped or even dreamed, and your
father said how being a woman she probably wasn't

even surprised)—grooming him herself, bringing
him on by hand herself, washing and feeding and
putting him to bed and giving him the candy and
the toys and the other child's fun and diversion and
needs in measured doses like medicine with her own
hand: not because she had to, who could have hired
a dozen or bought a hundred to do it for her with
the money, the jack that he (the demon) had voluntarily surrendered, repudiated to balance his moral
ledger: but like the millionaire who could have a
hundred hostlers and handlers but who has just the
one horse, the one maiden, the one moment, the one
matching of heart and muscle and will with the one
instant: and himself (the millionaire) patient in the
overalls and the sweat and the stable muck, bringing
him along to the moment when she would say 'He
is your father. He cast you and me aside and denied
you his name. Now go' and then sit down and let
God finish it: pistol or knife or rack; destruction or
grief or anguish: God to call the shot or turn the
wheel. Jesus, you can almost see him: a little boy
already come to learn, to expect, before he could
remember having learned his own name or the name
of the town where he lived or how to say either of
them, that every so often he would be snatched up
from playing and held, gripped between the two
hands fierce with (what passed at least with him for
it) love, against the two fierce rigid knees, the face
that he remembered since before remembering
began as supervising all the animal joys of palate and
stomach and entrails, of warmth and pleasure and

security, swooping down at him in a kind of blazing immobility: he taking the interruption as a matter of course, as just another natural phenomenon of existence; the face filled with furious and almost unbearable unforgiving almost like fever (not bitterness and despair: just implacable will for revenge) as just another manifestation of mammalian love—and he not knowing what in hell it was all about, who would be too young to curry any connected fact out of the fury and hate and the tumbling speed; not comprehending or caring: just curious, creating for himself (without help since who to help him) his own notion of that Porto Rico or Haiti or wherever it was he understood vaguely that he had come from like orthodox children do of heaven or the cabbage patch or wherever it was that they came from, except that his was different in that you were not supposed (your mother didn't intend to, anyway) to ever go back there (and maybe when you got as old as she was you would be horrified too every time you found hidden in your thoughts anything that just smelled or tasted like it might be a wish to go back there); which you were not supposed to know when and why you left but only that you had escaped, that whatever power had created the place for you to hate it had likewise got you away from the place so you could hate it good and never forgive it in quiet and monotony (though not exactly in what you would call peace); that you were to thank God you didn't remember anything about it yet at the same time you were not to, maybe dared not to,

ever forget it—he not even knowing maybe that he
took it for granted that all kids didn't have fathers
too and that getting snatched every day or so from
whatever harmless pursuit in which you were not
bothering anybody or even thinking about them, by
someone because that someone was bigger than you,
stronger than you, and being held for a minute or
five minutes under a kind of busted water pipe of
incomprehensible fury and fierce yearning and vindictiveness and jealous rage was a part of childhood
which all mothers of children had received in turn
from their mothers and from their mothers in turn
from that Porto Rico or Haiti or wherever it was we
all came from but none of us ever lived in: so that
when he grew up and had children he would have
to pass it on too (and maybe deciding then and there
that it was too much trouble and bother and that he
would not have any children or at least hoped he
would not) and hence no man had a father, no one
personal Porto Rico or Haiti, but all mother faces
which ever bred swooping down at those almost
calculable moments out of some obscure ancient
general affronting and outraging which the actual
living articulate meat had not even suffered but
merely inherited; all boy flesh that walked and
breathed stemming from that one ambiguous eluded
dark fatherhead and so brothered perennial and
ubiquitous everywhere under the sun——"

They stared at one another—glared rather—their
quiet regular breathing vaporising faintly and steadily in the now tomblike air. There was something

curious in the way they looked at one another, curious and quiet and profoundly intent, not at all as two young men might look at each other but almost as a youth and a very young girl might out of virginity itself—a sort of hushed and naked searching, each look burdened with youth's immemorial obsession not with time's dragging weight which the old live with but with its fluidity: the bright heels of all the lost moments of fifteen and sixteen. "Then he got older and got out from under the apron despite her (him too maybe; maybe the both of them) and he didn't even care. He found out that she was up to something and he not only didn't care, he didn't even care that he didn't know what it was; got older and found out that she had been shaping and tempering him to be the instrument for whatever it was her hand was implacable for, maybe came to believe (or saw) that she had tricked him into receiving that shape and temper, and didn't care about that too because probably by that time he had learned that there were three things and no more: breathing, pleasure, darkness; and without money there could be no pleasure, and without pleasure it would not even be breathing but mere protoplasmic inhale and collapse of blind unorganism in a darkness where light never began. And he had the money because he knew that she knew that the money was the only thing she could coerce and smoothe him into the barrier with when Derby Day came so she didn't dare pinch him there and she knew he knew it: so that maybe he even blackmailed her, bought her off that way: 'You give me the jack as I want it and I wont ask why or what for yet.' Or maybe she was so busy grooming him that she never thought of the money now, who probably never had had much time to remember it or count it or wonder how much there was in the intervals of the hating and the being mad, and so all to check him up about the money would be the lawyer and he (Bon) probably learned that the first thing: that he could go to his mother and hold the lawyer's feet to the fire anytime, like the millionaire horse has only to come in one time with a little extra sweat on him, and tomorrow he will have a new jock. Sure, that's who it would be: the lawyer, that lawyer with his private mad female millionaire to farm, who probably wasn't interested enough in the money to see whether the checks had any other writing on them when she signed them—that lawyer who, with Bon's mother already plotting and planning him since before he could remember (and even if she didn't know it or whether she knew it or not or would have cared or not) for that day when he should be translated quick into so much rich and rotting dirt, had already been plowing and planting and harvesting him and the mother both as if he already was—that lawyer who maybe had the secret drawer in the secret safe and the secret paper in it, maybe a chart with colored pins stuck into it like generals have in campaigns, and all the notations in code: *Today he finished robbing a drunken Indian of a hundred miles of virgin land, val. 25,000. At 2:31 today*

*came up out of swamp with final plank for house. val
in conj. with land 40,000. 7:52 p.m. today married.
Bigamy threat val. minus nil. unless quick buyer. Not
probable. Doubtless conjoined with wife same day. Say
1 year* and then with maybe the date and the hour
too: *Son. Intrinsic val. possible though not probable
forced sale of house & land plus val. crop minus child's
one quarter. Emotional val. plus 100% times nil. plus
val. crop. Say 10 years, one or more children. Intrinsic
val. forced sale house & improved land plus liquid
assets minus children's share. Emotional val. 100%
times increase yearly for each child plus intrinsic val.
plus liquid assets plus working acquired credit* and
maybe here with the date too: *Daughter* and you
could maybe even have seen the question mark after
it and the other words even: *daughter? daughter?
daughter?* trailing off not because thinking trailed
off, but on the contrary thinking stopping right still
then, backing up a little and spreading like when
you lay a stick across a trickle of water, spreading
and rising slow all around him in whatever place it
was that he could lock the door to and sit quiet and
subtract the money that Bon was spending on his
whores and his champagne from what his mother
had, and figure up how much would be left of it
tomorrow and next month and next year or until
Sutpen would be good and ripe—thinking about the
good hard cash that Bon was throwing away on his
horses and clothes and the champagne and gambling
and women (he would have known about the octoroon and the left handed marriage long before the

mother did even if it had been any secret; maybe he
even had a spy in the bedroom like he seems to have
had in Sutpen's; maybe he even planted her, said to
himself like you do about a dog: *He is beginning to
ramble. He needs a block. Not a tether: just a light block
of some sort, so he cant get inside of anything that might
have a fence around it*) and only him to try to check
it, or as much as he dared, and not getting far because he knew too that all Bon had to do was to go
to his mother and the racehorse would have a gold
eating trough if he wanted it and, if the jock wasn't
careful, a new jockey too—counting up the money,
figuring what he would net at this normal rate over
the next few years, against what it looked like would
be left of it to net from by that time, and meanwhile
crucified between his two problems: whether maybe
what he ought to do was to wash his hands of the
Sutpen angle and clean up what was left and light
out for Texas: except whenever he thought about
doing that he would have to think about all the
money that Bon had already spent, and that if he had
only gone to Texas ten years ago or five years ago
or even last year: so that maybe at night while he
would be waiting for the window to begin to turn
gray he would be like the Aunt Rosa said she was
and he would have to deny that he breathed (or
maybe wished he didn't) except for that two hundred percent. times the intrinsic value every New
Year's;—the water backing up from the stick and
rising and spreading about him steady and quiet as
light and him sitting there in the actual white glare

of clairvoyance (or second sight or faith in human misfortune and folly or whatever you want to call it) that was showing him not only what might happen but what was actually going to happen and him declining to believe it was going to happen, not because it had come to him as a vision, but because it would have to have love and honor and courage and pride in it; and believing it might happen, not because it was logical and possible, but because it would be the most unfortunate thing for all concerned that could occur; and though you could no more have proved vice or virtue or courage or cowardice to him without showing him the moving people than you could have proved death to him without showing him a corpse, he did believe in misfortune because of that rigorous and arduous dusty eunuch's training which taught to leave man's good luck and joys to God, who would in return surrender all his miseries and follies and misfortunes to the lice and fleas of Coke and Littleton. And the old Sabine——"

They stared—glared—at one another, their voices (it was Shreve speaking, though save for the slight difference which the intervening degrees of latitude had inculcated in them (differences not in tone or pitch but of turns of phrase and usage of words), it might have been either of them and was in a sense both: both thinking as one, the voice which happened to be speaking the thought only the thinking become audible, vocal; the two of them creating between them, out of the rag-tag and bob-

ends of old tales and talking, people who perhaps
had never existed at all anywhere, who, shadows,
were shadows not of flesh and blood which had
lived and died but shadows in turn of what were (to
one of them at least, to Shreve) shades too) quiet as
the visible murmur of their vaporising breath. The
chimes now began to ring for midnight, melodious
slow and faint beyond the closed, the snow-sealed,
window. "——the old Sabine, who couldn't to save
her life have told you or the lawyer or Bon or anybody else probably what she wanted, expected,
hoped for because she was a woman and didn't need
to want or hope or expect anything, but just to want
and expect and hope (and besides, your father said
that when you have plenty of good strong hating
you dont need hope because the hating will be
enough to nourish you);—the old Sabine (not so old
yet, but she would have just let herself go in the
sense that you keep the engines clean and oiled and
the best of coal in the bunkers but you dont bother
to shine the brightwork or holystone the decks anymore; just let herself go on the outside. Not fat; she
would burn it up too fast for that, shrivel it away in
the gullet between swallowing and stomach; no
pleasure in the chewing; having to chew just another nuisance like no pleasure in the clothing; having the old wear out and having to choose the new
just another nuisance: and no pleasure in the fine
figure he—" neither of them said 'Bon' "—cut in the
fine pants that fit his leg and the fine coats that fit
his shoulders nor in the fact that he had more

watches and cuff buttons and finer linen and horses
and yellow-wheeled buggies (not to mention the
gals) than most others did, but all that too just an
unavoidable nuisance that he would have to get shut
of before he could do her any good just like he had
to get shut of the teething and the chicken pox and
the light boy's bones in order to be able to do her
any good)—the old Sabine getting the faked reports
from the lawyer like reports sent back to headquarters from a battle front, with maybe a special nigger
in the lawyer's anteroom to do nothing else but
carry them and that maybe once in two years or five
times in two days, depending on when she would
begin to itch for news and began to worry him—the
report, the communiqué about how we are not far
behind him in Texas or Missouri or maybe California (California would be fine, that far away; conve-
nient, proof inherent in the sheer distance, the
necessity to accept and believe) and we are going to
catch up with him any day now and so do not
worry. So she wouldn't, she wouldn't worry at all:
she would just have out the carriage and go to the
lawyer, busting in in the black dress that looked like
a section of limp stove pipe and maybe not even a
hat but just a shawl over her head, so that the only
things missing would be the mop and the pail—
busting in and saying 'He's dead. I know he is dead
and how can he, how can he be', not meaning what
the Aunt Rosa meant: *where did they find or invent
a bullet that could kill him* but *How can he be allowed
to die without having to admit that he was wrong and*

suffer and regret it and so in the next two seconds
they would almost catch him (he—the lawyer—
would show her the actual letter, the writing in the
English she couldn't read, that had just come in, that
he had just sent for the nigger to carry to her when
she came in, and the lawyer done practised putting
the necessary date on the letter until he could do it
now while his back would be toward her, in the two
seconds it would take him to get the letter out of the
file)—catch him, get so close to him as to have ample
satisfaction that he was alive; so close indeed that he
would be able to get her out of the office before she
had sat down and into the carriage again and on the
way home again where, among the Florentine mirrors and Paris drapes and tufted camisoles, she
would still look like the one that had come in to
scrub the floors, in the black dress that the cook
wouldn't have looked at even when it was new five
or six years ago, holding, clutching the letter she
couldn't read (maybe the only word in it she could
even recognise would be the word 'Sutpen') in one
hand and brushing back a rope of lank iron-colored
hair with the other and not looking at the letter like
she was reading it even if she could have, but swooping at it, blazing down at it as if she knew she would
have only a second to read it in, only a second for
it to remain intact in after her eyes would touch
it, before it took fire and so would not be perused
but consumed, leaving her sitting there with a
black crumbling blank carbon ash in her hand.
And him—" (Neither of them said 'Bon') "—there

watching her, who had got old enough to have learned that what he thought was childhood wasn't childhood, that other children had been made by fathers and mothers where he had been created new when he began to remember, new again when he came to the point where his carcass quit being a baby and became a boy, new again when he quit being a boy and became a man, between a woman whom he had thought was feeding and washing and putting him to bed and finding him in the extra ticklings for his palate and his pleasure because he was himself, until he got big enough to find out that it wasn't him at all she was washing and feeding the candy and the fun to but it was a man that hadn't even arrived yet, whom even she had never seen yet, who would be something else beside that boy when he did arrive like the dynamite which destroys the house and the family and maybe even the whole community aint the old peaceful paper that maybe would rather be blowing aimless and light along the wind or the old merry sawdust or the old quiet chemicals that had rather be still and dark in the quiet earth like they had been before the meddling guy with ten-power spectacles came and dug them up and strained warped and kneaded them;— created between this woman and a hired lawyer (the woman who since before he could remember he now realised had been planning and grooming him for some moment that would come and pass and following which he saw that to her he would be little more than so much rich rotting dirt; the lawyer

who since before he could remember he now realised had been plowing and planting and watering
and manuring and harvesting him as if he already
was):—him watching her, lounging there against
the mantel maybe in the fine clothes, in the harem
incense odor of what you might call easy sanctity,
watching her looking at the letter, not even thinking *I am looking upon my mother naked* since if the
hating was nakedness, she had worn it long
enough now for it to do the office of clothing like
they say that modesty can do, does——

"So he went away. He went away to school at the
age of twenty-eight. And he wouldn't know nor
care about that either: which of them—mother or
lawyer—it was who decided he should go to school
nor why, because he had known all the time that his
mother was up to something and that the lawyer
was up to something, and he didn't care enough
about what either of them was to try to find out,
who knew that the lawyer knew that his mother was
up to something but that his mother didn't know
that the lawyer was up to something, and that it
would be all right with the lawyer if his mother got
whatever it was she wanted, provided he (the lawyer) got what he wanted one second before or at
least at the same time. He went away to school; he
said 'All right' and told the octoroon goodbye and
went to school, who not in all the twenty-eight
years had ever been told by anyone, 'Do as these
others do; have this task done at nine a.m. tomorrow
or Friday or Monday'; maybe it was even the oc-

toroon whom they (or the lawyer) used—the light block (not tether) which the lawyer had put on him to keep him from getting inside of something which might be found to have a fence around it later. Maybe the mother found out about the octoroon and the child and the ceremony and discovered more than the lawyer had (or would believe, who considered Bon only dull, not a fool) and sent for him and he came and lounged against the mantel again and maybe knowing what was up, what had happened before she told him, lounging there with an expression on his face you might call smiling except it was not that but just something you couldn't see through or past, and she watching him with maybe the lank iron-colored strand of hair down again and not even bothering to brush it back now because she was not looking at any letter now but her eyes blazing at him, her voice trying to blaze at him out of the urgency of alarm and fear, but she managing to keep it down since she could not talk about betrayal because she had not told him yet, and now, at this moment, she would not dare risk it;— he looking at her from behind the smiling that wasn't smiling but was just something you were not supposed to see beyond, saying, admitting it: 'Why not? All young men do it. The ceremony too. I didn't set out to get the child, but now that I have. . . . It's not a bad child, either' and she watching him, glaring at him and not being able to say what she would because she had put off too long now saying what she could: 'But you. This is different' and he

(she would not need to say it. He would know
because he already knew why she had sent for him,
even if he did not know and did not care what she
had been up to since before he could remember,
since before he could take a woman whether in love
or not): 'Why not? Men seem to have to marry some
day, sooner or later. And this is one whom I know,
who makes me no trouble. And with the ceremony,
that bother, already done. And as for a little matter
like a spot of negro blood——' not needing to talk
much, say much either, not needing to say *I seem to
have been born into this world with so few fathers that
I have too many brothers to outrage and shame while
alive and hence too many descendants to bequeath my
little portion of hurt and harm to, dead;* not that, just
'a little spot of negro blood——' and then to watch
the face, the desperate urgency and fear, then to
depart, kissing her maybe, her hand maybe which
would lie in his and even touch his lips like a dead
hand because of the desperate casting for this straw
or that; maybe as he went out he said *she will go to
him* (the lawyer); *if I were to wait five minutes I could
see her in the shawl. So probably by tonight I will be
able to know—if I cared to know.* Maybe by night he
did, maybe before that if they managed to find him,
get word to him, because she went to the lawyer.
And it was right in the lawyer's alley. Maybe before
she even got started telling it good that gentle white
glow began like when you turn up a wick; maybe
he could even almost see his hand writing on into
the space where the *daughter? daughter? daughter?*

never had quite showed. Because maybe that had been the lawyer's trouble and worry and concern all the time; that ever since she had made him promise he would never tell Bon who his father was, he had been waiting and wondering how to do it, since maybe he knew that if he were to tell Bon, Bon might believe it or he might not, but certainly he would go and tell his mother that the lawyer had told him and then he (the lawyer) would be sunk, not for any harm done because there would be no harm, since this could not alter the situation, but for having crossed his paranoiac client. Maybe while he would sit in his office adding and subtracting the money and adding what they would get out of Sutpen (he was never worried about what Bon would do when he found out; he had probably a long time ago paid Bon that compliment of thinking that even if he was too dull or too indolent to suspect or find out about his father himself, he wasn't fool enough not to be able to take advantage of it once somebody showed him the proper move; maybe if the thought had ever occurred to him that because of love or honor or anything else under heaven or jurisprudence either, Bon would not, would refuse to, he (the lawyer) would even have furnished proof that he no longer breathed)—maybe all the time it was this that racked him: how to get Bon where he would either have to find it out himself, or where somebody—the father or the mother—would have to tell him. So maybe she wasn't out of the office good—or at least as soon as he had had time to open

the safe and look in the secret drawer and make sure
that it was the University of Mississippi that Henry
attended—before his hand was writing steady and
even into the space where the *daughter? daughter?
daughter?* never had showed—and with the date
here too: *1859. Two children. Say 1860, 20 years. Increase 200% times intrinsic val. yearly plus liquid assets
plus credit earned. Approx'te val. 1860, 100,000. Query:
bigamy threat, Yes or No. Possible No. Incest threat:
Credible Yes* and the hand going back before it put
down the period, lining out the *Credible,* writing in
Certain, underlining it.

"And he didn't care about that too; he just said,
'All right.' Because maybe he knew now that his
mother didn't know and never would know what
she wanted, and so he couldn't beat her (maybe he
had learned from the octoroon that you cant beat
women anyhow and that if you are wise or dislike
trouble and uproar you dont even try to), and he
knew that all the lawyer wanted was just the money;
and so if he just didn't make the mistake of believing
that he could beat all of it, if he just remembered to
be quiet and be alert he could beat some of it.— So
he said, 'All right' and let his mother pack the fine
clothes and the fine linen into the bags and trunks,
and maybe he lounged into the lawyer's office and
watched from behind that something which could
have been called smiling while the lawyer made the
elbow motion about getting his horses onto the
steamboat and maybe buying him an extra special
body servant and arranging about the money and

all; watching from behind the smiling while the
lawyer did the heavy father even, talking about the
scholarship, the culture, the Latin and the Greek
that would equip and polish him for the position
which he would hold in life and how a man to be
sure could get that anywhere, in his own library
even, who had the will; but how there was something, some quality to culture which only the monastic, the cloistral monotony of a—say obscure and
small (though high class, high class) college;—and
he——" (neither of them said 'Bon'. Never at any
time did there seem to be any confusion between
them as to whom Shreve meant by 'he') "——listening courteous and quiet behind that expression
which you were not supposed to see past, asking at
last, interrupting maybe, courteous and affable—
nothing of irony, nothing of sarcasm—'What did
you say this college was?': and now a good deal of
elbow motion here while the lawyer would shuffle
through the papers to find the one from which he
could read that name which he had been memorising ever since he first talked to the mother: 'The
University of Mississippi, at'—— Where did you
say?"

"Oxford," Quentin said. "It's about forty miles
from——"

"——'Oxford.' And then the papers could be still
again because he would be talking: about a small
college only ten years old, about how there
wouldn't be anything to distract him from his stud-
ies there (where, in a sense, wisdom herself would

be a virgin or at least not very second hand) and
how he would have a chance to observe another and
a provincial section of the country in which his high
destiny (granted the outcome of this war which was
without doubt imminent, the successful conclusion
of which we all hoped for, had no doubt of) as the
man he would be and the economic power he would
represent when his mother passed on, was rooted;
and he listening behind that expression, saying,
'Then you dont recommend the law as a vocation?'
and now for just a moment the lawyer would stop,
but not long; maybe not long enough or perceptible
enough for you to call it pause: and he would be
looking at Bon too: 'It hadn't occurred to me that
the law might appeal to you' and Bon: 'Neither did
practising with a rapier appeal to me while I was
doing it. But I can recall at least one occasion in my
life when I was glad I had' and then the lawyer,
smooth and easy: 'Then by all means let it be the
law. Your mother will ag—be pleased.' 'All right,'
he said, not 'goodbye'; he didn't care; maybe not
even goodbye to the octoroon, to those tears and
lamentations and maybe even the clinging, the soft
despairing magnolia-colored arms about his knees,
and (say) three and a half feet above that boneless
steel gyves that expression which was not smiling
but just something not to be seen through. Because
you cant beat them: you just flee (and thank God
you can flee, can escape from that massy five-foot-
thick maggot-cheesy solidarity which overlays the
earth, in which men and women in couples are

ranked and racked like ninepins; thanks to whatever Gods for that masculine hipless tapering peg which fits light and glib to move where the cartridge-chambered hips of women hold them fast);—not goodbye: all right: and one night he walked up the gangplank between the torches and probably only the lawyer there to see him off and this not for godspeed but to make sure that he actually took the boat. And the new extra nigger opening the bags in the stateroom, spreading the fine clothes, and the ladies already gathered in the saloon for supper and the men in the bar, preparing for it but not he; he alone, at the rail, with a cigar maybe, watching the city drift and wink and glitter and sink away and then all motion cease, the boat suspended immobile and without progress from the stars themselves by the two ropes of spark-filled smoke streaming upward from the stacks. And who knows what thinking, what sober weighing and discarding, who had known for years that his mother was up to something even though he did not (probably believed he never would) know what; that the lawyer was up to something and though he knew that was just money, yet he knew that within his (the lawyer's) known masculine limitations he (the lawyer) could be almost as dangerous as the unknown quantity which was his mother; and now this—school, college—and he twenty-eight years old. And not only that, but this particular college, which he had never heard of, which ten years ago did not even exist; and knowing too that it was the lawyer who had chosen

it for him—what sober, what intent, what almost
frowning *Why? Why? Why this college, this particular
one above all others?*—maybe leaning there in that
solitude between panting smoke and engines and
almost touching the answer, aware of the jigsaw
puzzle picture integers of it waiting, almost lurking,
just beyond his reach, inextricable, jumbled, and
unrecognisable yet on the point of falling into pattern which would reveal to him at once, like a flash
of light, the meaning of his whole life, past—the
Haiti, the childhood, the lawyer, the woman who
was his mother. And maybe the letter itself right
there under his feet, somewhere in the darkness
beneath the deck on which he stood—the letter addressed not to Thomas Sutpen at Sutpen's Hundred
but to Henry Sutpen, Esquire, in Residence at the
University of Mississippi, near Oxford, Mississippi:
and one day Henry showed it to him and there was
no gentle spreading glow but a flash, a glare (who
not only had no visible father but had found himself
to be, even in infancy, enclosed by an unsleeping
cabal bent apparently on teaching him that he had
never had, that his mother had emerged from a sojourn in limbo, from that state of blessed amnesia in
which the weak senses can take refuge from the
godless dark forces and powers which weak human
flesh cannot stand, to wake pregnant, shrieking and
screaming and thrashing, not against the ruthless
agony of labor but in protest against the outrage of
her swelling loins; that he had been fathered on her
not through that natural process but had been blot-

ted onto and out of her body by the old infernal immortal male principle of all unbridled terror and darkness) in which he stood looking at the innocent face of the youth almost ten years his junior, while one part of him said *My brow my skull my jaw my hands* and the other said *Wait. Wait. You cant know yet. You cannot know yet whether what you see is what you are looking at or what you are believing. Wait. Wait.*—The letter which he——" it was not Bon he meant now, yet again Quentin seemed to comprehend without difficulty or effort whom he meant "——wrote maybe as soon as he finished that last entry in the record, into the *daughter? daughter? daughter?* while he thought *By all means he must not know now, must not be told before he can get there and he and the daughter*—not remembering anything about young love from his own youth and would not have believed it if he had, yet willing to use that too as he would have used courage and pride, think-ing not of any hushed wild importunate blood and light hands hungry for touching, but of the fact that this Oxford and this Sutpen's Hundred were only a day's ride apart and Henry already established in the University and so maybe for once in his life the lawyer even believed in God: *My Dear Mr Sutpen: The undersigned name will not be known to you, nor are the writer's position and circumstances, for all their reflected worth and (I hope) value, so unobscure as to warrant the hope that he will ever see you in person or you he—worth reflected from and value rendered to two persons of birth and position, one of whom, a lady and*

*widowed mother, resides in that seclusion befitting her
condition in the city from which this letter is inscribed,
the other of whom, a young gentleman her son, will
either be as you read this, or will shortly thereafter be
a petitioner before the same Bar of knowledge and wisdom as yourself. It is in his behalf that I write. No: I
will not say behalf; certainly I shall not let his lady
mother nor the young gentleman himself suspect that I
used that term, even to one, Sir, scion of the principal
family of that county as it is your fortunate lot to be.
Indeed, it were better for me if I had not written at all.
But I do; I have; it is irrevocable now; if you discern
aught in this letter which smacks of humility, take it as
coming not from the mother and certainly not from the
son, but from the pen of one whose humble position as
legal adviser and man of business to the above described
lady and young gentleman, whose loyalty and gratitude toward one whose generosity has found him (I do
not confess this; I proclaim it) in bread and meat and
fire and shelter over a period long enough to have taught
him gratitude and loyalty even if he had not known
them, has led him into an action whose means fall
behind its intention for the reason that he is only what
he is and professes himself to be, not what he would. So
take this, Sir, neither as the unwarranted insolence
which an unsolicited communication from myself to
you would be, not as a plea for sufferance on behalf of
an unknown, but as an introduction (clumsy though it
be) to one young gentleman whose position needs neither
detailing nor recapitulation in the place where this letter is read, of another young gentleman whose position*

requires neither detailing nor recapitulation in the place where it was written. —Not goodbye; all right, who had had so many fathers as to have neither love nor pride to receive or inflict, neither honor nor shame to share or bequeath; to whom one place was the same as another, like to a cat—cosmopolitan New Orleans or bucolic Mississippi: his own inherited and heritable Florentine lamps and gilded toilet seats and tufted mirrors, or a little jerkwater college not ten years old; champagne in the octoroon's boudoir or whiskey on a harsh new table in a monk's cell and a country youth, a bucolic heir apparent who had probably never spent a dozen nights outside of his paternal house (unless perhaps to lie fully dressed beside a fire in the woods listening to dogs running) until he came to school, whom he watched aping his clothing carriage speech and all and (the youth) completely unaware that he was doing it, who (the youth) over the bottle one night said, blurted—no, not blurted: it would be fumbling, groping: and he (the cosmopolite ten years the youth's senior almost, lounging in one of the silk robes the like of which the youth had never seen before and believed that only women wore) watching the youth blush fiery red yet still face him, still look him straight in the eye while he fumbled, groped, blurted with abrupt complete irrelevance: 'If I had a brother, I wouldn't want him to be a younger brother' and he: 'Ah?' and the youth: 'No. I would want him to be older than me' and he: 'No son of a landed father wants an older brother' and the youth: 'Yes. I do', looking straight at the other, the esoteric, the sybarite, standing (the youth) now, erect, thin (because he was young), his face scarlet but his head high and his eyes steady: 'Yes. And I would want him to be just like you' and he: 'Is that so? The whiskey's your side. Drink or pass.'

"And now," Shreve said, "we're going to talk about love." But he didn't need to say that either, any more than he had needed to specify which he he meant by he, since neither of them had been thinking about anything else; all that had gone before just so much that had to be overpassed and none else present to overpass it but them, as someone always has to rake the leaves up before you can have the bonfire. That was why it did not matter to either of them which one did the talking, since it was not the talking alone which did it, performed and accomplished the overpassing, but some happy marriage of speaking and hearing wherein each before the demand, the requirement, forgave condoned and forgot the faulting of the other—faultings both in the creating of this shade whom they discussed (rather, existed in) and in the hearing and sifting and discarding the false and conserving what seemed true, or fit the preconceived—in order to overpass to love, where there might be paradox and inconsistency but nothing fault nor false. "And now, love. He must have known all about her before he ever saw her—what she looked like, her private hours in that provincial women's world that even men of the family were not supposed to know a great deal about; he must have learned it without even having to ask a single question. Jesus, it must have kind of boiled out all over him. There must have been nights and nights while Henry was learning from him how to lounge about a bedroom in a gown and slippers such as women wore, in a faint though unmistakable effluvium of scent such as women used, smoking a cigar almost as a woman might smoke it, yet withal such an air of indolent and lethal assurance that only the most reckless man would have gratuitously drawn the comparison (and with no attempt to teach, train, play the mentor on his part—and then maybe yes; maybe who could know what times he looked at Henry's face and thought, not *there but for the intervening leaven of that blood which we do not have in common is my skull, my brow, sockets, shape and angle of jaw and chin and some of my thinking behind it, and which he could see in my face in his turn if he but knew to look as I know* but *there, just behind a little, obscured a little by that alien blood whose admixing was necessary in order that he exist is the face of the man who shaped us both out of that blind chancy darkness which we call the future; there—there—at any moment, second, I shall penetrate by something of will and intensity and dreadful need, and strip that alien leavening from it and look not on my brother's face whom I did not know I possessed and hence never missed, but my father's, out of the shadow of whose absence my spirit's posthumeity has never escaped;*—at what moment thinking, watching the eagerness which was without abjectness, the humility

which surrendered no pride—the entire proffering
of the spirit of which the unconscious aping of
clothes and speech and mannerisms was but the
shell—thinking *what cannot I do with this willing*
flesh and bone if I wish; this flesh and bone and spirit
which stemmed from the same source that mine did, but
which sprang in quiet peace and contentment and ran
in steady even though monotonous sunlight, where that
which he bequeathed me sprang in hatred and outrage
and unforgiving and ran in shadow—what could I not
mold of this malleable and eager clay which that father
himself could not—to what shape of what good there
might, must, be in that blood and none handy to take
and mold that portion of it in me until too late: or
what moments when he might have told himself
that it was nonsense, it could not be true; that such
coincidences only happened in books, thinking—
the weariness, the fatalism, the incorrigible cat for
solitude—*That young clodhopper bastard. How shall I*
get rid of him: and then the voice, the other voice:
You dont mean that: and he: *No. But I do mean the*
clodhopper bastard) and the days, the afternoons,
while they rode together (and Henry aping him
here too, who was the better horseman, who maybe
had nothing of what Bon would have called style
but who had done more of it, to whom a horse was
as natural as walking, who would ride anything
anywhere and at anything) while he must have
watched himself being swamped and submerged in
the bright unreal flood of Henry's speech, translated
(the three of them: himself and Henry and the sister

whom he had never seen and perhaps did not even
have any curiosity to see) into a world like a fairy
tale in which nothing else save them existed, riding
beside Henry, listening, needing to ask no questions, to prompt to further speech in any manner
that youth who did not even suspect that he and the
man beside him might be brothers, who each time
his breath crossed his vocal cords was saying *From
now on mine and my sister's house will be your house
and mine and my sister's lives your life,* wondering
(Bon)—or maybe not wondering at all—how if con-
ditions were reversed and Henry was the stranger
and he (Bon) the scion and still knew what he suspected, if he would say the same; then (Bon) agreeing at last, saying at last, 'All right. I'll come home
with you for Christmas', not to see the third inhabi-
tant of Henry's fairy tale, not to see the sister because he had not once thought of her: he had merely
listened about her: but thinking *So at last I shall see
him, whom it seems I was bred up never to expect to see,
whom I had even learned to live without,* thinking
maybe how he would walk into the house and see
the man who made him and then he would know;
there would be that flash, that instant of indisputable
recognition between them and he would know for
sure and forever—thinking maybe *That's all I want.
He need not even acknowledge me; I will let him understand just as quickly that he need not do that, that I do
not expect that, will not be hurt by that, just as he will
let me know that quickly that I am his son,* thinking
maybe, maybe again with that expression you might

call smiling but which was not, which was just
something that even just a clodhopper bastard was
not intended to see beyond: *I am my mother's son, at
least: I do not seem to know what I want either.* Because he knew exactly what he wanted; it was just
the saying of it—the physical touch even though in
secret, hidden—the living touch of that flesh
warmed before he was born by the same blood
which it had bequeathed him to warm his own flesh
with, to be bequeathed by him in turn to run hot and
loud in veins and limbs after that first flesh and then
his own were dead. So the Christmas came and he
and Henry rode the forty miles to Sutpen's Hundred, with Henry still talking, still keeping distended and light and iridescent with steady
breathing that fairy balloon-vacuum in which the
three of them existed, lived, moved even maybe, in
attitudes without flesh—himself and the friend and
the sister whom the friend had never seen and
(though Henry did not know it) had not even
thought about yet but only listened about from behind the more urgent thinking, and Henry probably
not even noticing that the nearer they came to home
the less Bon talked, had to say on any subject, and
maybe even (and certainly Henry would not know
this) listening less. And went into the house: and
maybe somebody looking at him would have seen
on his face an expression a good deal like the one—
that proffering with humility yet with pride too, of
complete surrender—which he had used to see on
Henry's face, and maybe he telling himself *I not only*

dont know what it is I want but apparently I am a good deal younger than I thought also: and saw face to face the man who might be his father, and nothing happened—no shock, no hot communicated flesh that speech would have been too slow even to impede—nothing. And he spent ten days there, not only the esoteric, the sybarite, the steel blade in the silken tesselated sheath which Henry had begun to ape at the University, but the object of art, the mold and mirror of form and fashion which Mrs Sutpen (so your father said) accepted him as and insisted (didn't your father say?) that he be (and would have purchased him as and paid for him with Judith even, if there had been no other bidder among the four of them—or didn't your father say?) and which he did remain to her until he disappeared, taking Henry with him, and she never saw him again and war and trouble and grief and bad food filled her days until maybe she didn't even remember after a while that she had ever forgot him. (And the girl, the sister, the virgin—Jesus, who to know what she saw that afternoon when they rode up the drive, what prayer, what maiden meditative dream ridden up out of whatever fabulous land, not in harsh stove iron but the silken and tragic Launcelot nearing thirty, ten years older than she was and wearied, sated with what experiences and pleasures, which Henry's letters must have created for her.) And the day came to depart and no sign yet; he and Henry rode away and still no sign, no more sign at parting than when he had seen it first, in that face where he might (he would believe) have seen for himself the truth and so would have needed no sign, if it hadn't been for the beard; no sign in the eyes which could see his face because there was no beard to hide it, could have seen the truth if it were there: yet no flicker in them: and so he knew it was in his face because he knew that the other had seen it there just exactly as Henry was to know the next Christmas eve in the library that his father was not lying by the fact that the father said nothing, did nothing. Maybe he even thought, wondered if perhaps that was not why the beard, if maybe the other had not hidden behind that beard against this very day, and if so, why? why? thinking *But why? Why?* since he wanted so little, could have understood if the other had wanted the signal to be in secret, would have been quick and glad to let it be in secret even if he could not have understood why, thinking in the middle of this *My God, I am young, young, and I didn't even know it; they didn't even tell me, that I was young,* feeling that same despair and shame like when you have to watch your father fail in physical courage, thinking *It should have been me that failed; me, I, not he who stemmed from that blood which we both bear before it could have become corrupt and tainted by whatever it was in Mother's that he could not brook.*—Wait," Shreve cried, though Quentin had not spoken: it had been merely some quality, some gathering of Quentin's still laxed and hunched figure which presaged speech, because Shreve said Wait. Wait. before Quentin could have begun to speak. "Because he hadn't even looked at her. Oh, he had seen her all right, he had had plenty of opportunity for that; he could not have helped but that because Mrs Sutpen would have seen to it—ten days of that kind of planned and arranged and executed privacies like the campaigns of dead generals in the text books, in libraries and parlors and drives in the buggy in the afternoons—all planned three months ago when Mrs Sutpen read Henry's first letter with Bon's name in it, until maybe even Judith too began to feel like the other one to a pair of goldfish: and him even talking to her too, or what talking he could have found to do to a country girl who probably never saw a man young or old before who sooner or later didn't smell like manure; talking to her about like he would talk to the old dame on the gold chairs in the parlor, except that in the one case he would have to make all the conversation and in the other he would not even be able to make his own escape but would have to wait for Henry to come and get him. And maybe he had even thought about her by that time; maybe at the times when he would be telling himself *it cant be so; he could not look at me like this every day and make no sign if it were so* he would even tell himself *She would be easy* like when you have left the champagne on the supper table and are walking toward the whiskey on the sideboard and you happen to pass a cup of lemon sherbet on a tray and you look at the sherbet and tell yourself, That would be easy too only who wants it.——Does that suit you?"

"But it's not love," Quentin said.

"Because why not? Because listen. What was it the old dame, the Aunt Rosa, told you about how there are some things that just have to be whether they are or not, have to be a damn sight more than some other things that maybe are and it dont matter a damn whether they are or not? That was it. He just didn't have time yet. Jesus, he must have known it would be. Like that lawyer thought, he wasn't a fool; the trouble was, he wasn't the kind of not-fool the lawyer thought he would be. He must have known it was going to happen. It would be like you passed that sherbet and maybe you knew you would even reach the sideboard and the whiskey, yet you knew that tomorrow morning you would want that sherbet, then you reached the whiskey and you knew you wanted that sherbet now; maybe you didn't even go to the sideboard, maybe you even looked back at that champagne on the supper table among the dirty haviland and the crumpled damask, and all of a sudden you knew you didn't want to go back there even. It would be no question of choosing, having to choose between the champagne or whiskey and the sherbet, but all of a sudden (it would be spring then, in that country where he had never spent a spring before and you said North Mississippi is a little harder country than Louisiana, with dogwood and violets and the early scentless flowers but the earth and the nights still a little cold and the hard tight sticky buds like young girls' nipples on alder and Judas trees and beech and maple and even something young in the cedars like he never saw before) you find that you dont want anything but that sherbet and that you haven't been wanting anything else but that and you have been wanting that pretty hard for some time—besides knowing that that sherbet is there for you to take. Not just for anybody to take but for you' to take, knowing just from looking at that cup that it would be like a flower that, if any other hand reached for it, it would have thorns on it but not for your hand; and him not used to that since all the other cups that had been willing and easy for him to take up hadn't contained sherbet but champagne or at least kitchen wine. And more than that. There was the knowing what he suspected might be so, or not knowing if it was so or not. And who to say if it wasn't maybe the possibility of incest, because who (without a sister: I dont know about the others) has been in love and not discovered the vain evanescence of the fleshly encounter; who has not had to realise that when the brief all is done you must retreat from both love and pleasure, gather up your own rubbish and refuse—the hats and pants and shoes which you drag through the world—and retreat since the gods condone and practise these and the dreamy immeasurable coupling which floats oblivious above the trammelling and harried instant, the: *was-not: is: was:* is a perquisite only of balloony and weightless elephants and whales: but maybe if there were sin too maybe you would not be permitted to escape, uncouple, return.—Aint that right?" He ceased; he could have been interrupted easily now. Quentin

could have spoken now, but Quentin did not. He
just sat as before, his hands in his trousers pockets,
his shoulders hugged inward and hunched, his face
lowered and he looking somehow curiously smaller
than he actually was because of his actual height and
spareness—that quality of delicacy about the bones,
articulation, which even at twenty still had something about it, some last echo about it, of adoles-
cence—that is, as compared with the cherubic
burliness of the other who faced him, who looked
younger, whose very superiority in bulk and displacement made him look even younger, as a plump
boy of twelve who outweighs the other by twenty
or thirty pounds still looks younger than the boy of
fourteen who had that plumpness once and lost it,
sold it (whether with his consent or not) for that
state of virginity which is neither boy's nor girl's.

"I dont know," Quentin said.

"All right," Shreve said. "Maybe I dont either.
Only, Jesus, some day you are bound to fall in love.
They just wouldn't beat you that way. It would be
like if God had got Jesus born and saw that He had
the carpenter tools and then never gave Him anything to build with them. Dont you believe that?"

"I dont know," Quentin said. He did not move.
Shreve looked at him. Even while they were not
talking their breaths in the tomblike air vaporised
gently and quietly. The chimes for midnight would
have rung some time ago now.

"You mean, it dont matter to you?" Quentin did
not answer. "That's right. Dont say it. Because I

would know you are lying.—All right then. Listen.
Because he never had to worry about the love because that would take care of itself. Maybe he knew
there was a fate, a doom on him, like what the old
Aunt Rosa told you about some things that just have
to be whether they are or not, just to balance the
books, write *Paid* on the old sheet so that whoever
keeps them can take it out of the ledger and burn it,
get rid of it. Maybe he knew then that whatever the
old man had done, whether he meant well or ill by
it, it wasn't going to be the old man who would have
to pay the check; and now that the old man was
bankrupt with the incompetence of age, who should
do the paying if not his sons, his get, because wasn't
it done that way in the old days? the old Abraham
full of years and weak and incapable now of further
harm, caught at last and the captains and the collec-
tors saying, 'Old man, we dont want you' and Abraham would say, 'Praise the Lord, I have raised about
me sons to bear the burden of mine iniquities and
persecutions; yea, perhaps even to restore my flocks
and herds from the hand of the ravisher: that I might
rest mine eyes upon my goods and chattels, upon
the generations of them and of my descendants increased an hundred fold as my soul goeth out from
me.' He knew all the time that the love would take
care of itself. Maybe that was why he didn't have to
think about her during those three months between
that September and that Christmas while Henry
talked about her to him, saying every time he
breathed: *Hers and my lives are to exist within and*

upon yours; did not need to waste any time over the love after it happened, backfired on him, why he never bothered to write her any letters (except that last one) which she would want to save, why he never actually proposed to her and gave her a ring for Mrs Sutpen to show around. Because the fate was on her too: the same old Abraham who was so old and weak now nobody would want him in the flesh on any debt; maybe he didn't even have to wait for that Christmas to see her to know this; maybe that's what it was that came out of the three months of Henry's talking that he heard without listening to: *I am not hearing about a young girl, a virgin; I am hearing about a narrow delicate fenced virgin field already furrowed and bedded so that all I shall need to do is drop the seeds in, caress it smooth again,* saw her that Christmas and knew it for certain and then forgot it, went back to school and did not even remember that he had forgotten it, because he did not have time then; maybe it was just one day in that spring you told about when he stopped and said, right quiet: *All right. I want to go to bed with who might be my sister. All right* and then forgot that too. Because he didn't have time. That is, he didn't have anything else but time, because he had to wait. But not for her. That was all fixed. It was the other. Maybe he thought it would be in the mail bag each time the nigger rode over from Sutpen's Hundred and Henry believing it was the letter from her that he was waiting for when what he was thinking was *Maybe he will write it then. He would just have to* write *'I am your father. Burn this'* and I would do it. *Or if not that, a sheet a scrap of paper with the one word 'Charles' in his hand, and I would know what he meant and he would not even have to ask me to burn it. Or a lock of his hair or a paring from his finger nail and I would know them because I believe now that I have known what his hair and his finger nails would look like all my life, could choose that lock and that paring out of a thousand.* And it did not come, and his letter went to her every two weeks and hers came back to him, and maybe he thought *If one of mine to her should come back to me unopened then. That would be a sign.* And that didn't happen: and then Henry began to talk about his stopping at Sutpen's Hundred for a day or so on his way home and he said all right to it, said *It will be Henry who will get the letter, the letter saying it is inconvenient for me to come at that time; so apparently he does not intend to acknowledge me as his son, but at least I shall have forced him to admit that I am.* And that one did not come either and the date was set and the family at Sutpen's Hundred notified of it and that letter did not come either and he thought *It will be then; I wronged him; maybe this is what he has been waiting for* and maybe his heart sprang then, maybe he said *Yes. Yes. I will renounce her; I will renounce love and all; that will be cheap, cheap, even though he say to me 'never look upon my face again; take my love and my acknowledgement in secret, and go' I will do that; I will not even demand to know of him what it was my mother did that justified his action toward her and me.* So the day came and

he and Henry rode the forty miles again, into the
gates and up the drive to the house. He knew what
would be there—the woman whom he had seen
once and seen through, the girl whom he had seen
through without even having to see once, the man
whom he had seen daily, watched out of his fearful
intensity of need and had never penetrated;—the
mother who had taken Henry aside before they had
been six hours in the house on that Christmas visit
and informed him of the engagement almost before
the fiancé had had time to associate the daughter's
name with the daughter's face: so that probably before they even reached school again, and without his
being aware that he had done so, Henry had already
told Bon what was in his mother's mind (who had
already told Bon what was in his); so that maybe
before they even started on Bon's second visit—(It
would be June now and what would it be in North
Mississippi? what was it you said? the magnolias in
bloom and the mockingbirds, and in fifty years
more, after they had gone and fought it and lost it
and come back home, the Decoration Day and the
veterans in the neat brushed hand-ironed gray and
the spurious bronze medals that never meant anything to begin with, and the chosen young girls in
white dresses bound at the waist with crimson
sashes and the band would play Dixie and all the old
doddering men would yell that you would not have
thought would have had wind enough to get there,
walk down town to sit on the rostrum even)—it
would be June now, with the magnolias and mock-

ingbirds in the moonlight and the curtains blowing in the June air of commencement and the music, fiddles and triangles, inside among the swirling and dipping hoops: and Henry would be a little tight, that should have been saying 'I demand to know your intentions toward my sister' but wasn't saying it, instead maybe blushing again even in the moonlight, but standing straight and blushing because when you are proud enough to be humble you dont have to cringe (who every time he breathed over his vocal cords he was saying *We belong to you; do as you will with us),* saying 'I used to think that I would hate the man that I would have to look at every day and whose every move and action and speech would say to me, I have seen and touched parts of your sister's body that you will never see and touch: and now I know that I shall hate him and that's why I want that man to be you', knowing that Bon would know what he meant, was trying to say, tell him, thinking, telling himself (Henry): *Not just because he is older than I am and has known more than I shall ever know and has remembered more of it; but because of my own free will, and whether I knew it at the time or not does not matter, I gave my life and Judith's both to him——"*

"That's still not love," Quentin said.

"All right," Shreve said. "Just listen.—— Rode the forty miles and into the gates and up to the house. And this time Sutpen wasn't even there. And Ellen didn't even know where he had gone, believing blandly and volubly that he had gone to Mem-

phis or maybe even to Saint Louis on business, and
Henry and Judith not even caring that much, and
only he, Bon, to know where Sutpen had gone,
saying to himself *Of course; he wasn't sure; he had to
go there to make sure,* telling himself that loud now,
loud and fast too so he would not, could not, hear
the thinking, the *But if he suspected, why not have told
me? I would have done that, gone to him first, who have
the blood after it was tainted and corrupt by whatever
it was in Mother;* loud and fast now, telling himself
*That's what it is; maybe he has gone on ahead to wait
for me; he left no message for me here because the others
are not to suspect yet and he knows that I will know
at once where he is when I find him gone,* thinking of
the two of them, the sombre vengeful woman who
was his mother and the grim rocklike man who had
looked at him every day for ten days with absolutely
no alteration of expression at all, facing one another
in grim armistice after almost thirty years in that
rich baroque drawing room in that house which he
called home since apparently everybody seemed to
have to have a home, the man who he was now sure
was his father not humble now either (and he, Bon,
proud of that), not saying even now *I was wrong* but
I admit that it is so— Jesus, think of his heart then,
during those two days, with the old gal throwing
Judith at him every minute now because she had
been spreading the news of the engagement confi-
dentially through the county ever since Christmas
—didn't your father say how she had even taken
Judith to Memphis in the spring to buy the trous-

seau?—and Judith neither having to accede to the throwing nor to resist it but just being, just existing and breathing like Henry did who maybe one morning during that spring waked up and lay right still in the bed and took stock, added the figures and drew the balance and told himself, *All right. I am trying to make myself into what I think he wants me to be; he can do anything he wants to with me; he has only to tell me what to do and I will do it; even though what he asked me to do looked to me like dishonor, I would still do it,* only Judith, being a female and so wiser than that, would not even consider dishonor: she would just say, *All right. I will do anything he might ask me to do and that is why he will never ask me to do anything that I consider dishonorable:* so that (maybe he even kissed her that time, the first time she had ever been kissed maybe and she too innocent to be coy or modest or even to know that she had been temporised with, maybe afterward just looking at him with a kind of peaceful and blank surprise at the fact that your sweetheart apparently kissed you the first time like your brother would—provided of course that your brother ever thought of, could be brought to, kissing you on the mouth) —so that when the two days were up and he was gone again and Ellen shrieking at her, 'What? No engagement, no troth, no ring?' she would be too astonished even to lie about it because that would be the first time it would have occurred to her that there had been no proposal.—Think of his heart then, while he rode to the River, and then on the steamboat itself where he walked up and down the deck, feeling through the deck the engines driving him nearer and nearer day and night to the moment which he must have realised now he had been waiting for ever since he had got big enough to comprehend. Of course every now and then he would have to say it pretty fast and loud, *That's all it is. He just wants to make sure first* to drown out the old *But why do it this way? Why not back there? He knows that I shall never make any claim upon any part of what he now possesses, gained at the price of what sacrifice and endurance and scorn (so they told me; not he: they) only he knows; knows that so well that it would never have occurred to him just as he knows it would never occur to me that this might be his reason, who is not only generous but ruthless, who must have surrendered everything he and Mother owned to her and to me as the price of repudiating her,* not because the doing it this way hurt him, flouted him and kept him in suspense that much unnecessary longer, because he didn't matter; whether he was irked or even crucified didn't matter: it was the fact that he had to be kept constantly reminded that he would not have done it this way himself, yet he had stemmed from the blood after whatever it was his mother had been or done had tainted and corrupted it.—Nearer and nearer, until suspense and puzzlement and haste and all seemed blended into one sublimation of passive surrender in which he thought only *All right. All right. Even this way. Even if he wants to do it this way. I will promise never to see her again. Never to see him again*. Then he reached home. And he never learned if Sutpen had been there or not. He never knew. He believed it, but he never knew—his mother the same sombre unchanged fierce paranoiac whom he had left in September, from whom he could learn nothing by indirection and whom he dared not ask outright—the very fact that he saw through the skillful questions of the lawyer (as to how he had liked the school and the people of that country and how perhaps—or had he not perhaps? —he had made friends up there among the country families) only that much more proof to him at that time that Sutpen had not been there, or at least the lawyer was not aware that he had, since now that he believed he had fathomed the lawyer's design in sending him to that particular school to begin with, he saw nothing in the questions to indicate that the lawyer had learned anything new since. (Or what he could have learned in that interview with the lawyer, because it would be a short one; it would be next to the shortest one ever to transpire between them, the shortest one of all next to the last one of course, the one which would occur in the next summer, when Henry would be with him.) Because the lawyer would not dare risk asking him outright, just as he (Bon) did not dare to ask his mother outright. Because, though the lawyer believed him to be rather a fool than dull or dense, yet even he (the lawyer) never for one moment believed that even Bon was going to be the kind of a fool he was going to be. So he told the lawyer nothing and the lawyer told him nothing, and the summer passed and September came and still the lawyer (his mother too) had not once asked him if he wanted to return to the school. So that at last he had to say it himself, that he intended to return; and maybe he knew that he had lost that move since there was nothing whatever in the lawyer's face save an agent's acquiescence. So he returned to school, where Henry was waiting (oh yes; waiting) for him, who did not even say 'You didn't answer my letters. You didn't even write to Judith' who had already said *What my sister and I have and are belongs to you* but maybe he did write to Judith now, by the first nigger post which rode to Sutpen's Hundred, about how it had been an uneventful summer and hence nothing to write about, with maybe *Charles Bon* plain and inelidible on the outside of the envelope and he thinking *He will have to see that. Maybe he will send it back* thinking *Maybe if it comes back nothing will stop me then and so maybe at last I will know what I am going to do.* But it didn't come back. And the others didn't come back. And the fall passed and Christmas came and they rode again to Sutpen's Hundred and this time he was not there again, he was in the field, he had gone to town, he was hunting—something; Sutpen not there when they rode up and Bon knew he had not expected him to be there, saying *Now. Now. Now. It will come now. It will come this time, and I am young, young, because I still dont know what I am going to do.* So maybe what he was doing that twilight (because he knew that Sutpen had returned, was now in the house; it would be like a wind, something, dark and chill, breathing upon him and he stopping, grave, quiet, alert, thinking *What? What is it?* Then he would know; he could feel the other entering the house, and he would let his held breath go quiet and easy, a profound exhalation, his heart quiet too) in the garden while he walked with Judith and talked to her, gallant and elegant and automatic (and Judith thinking about that like she thought about that first kiss back in the summer: *So that's it. That's what love is,* bludgeoned once more by disappointment but still unbowed);— maybe what he was doing there now was waiting, telling himself *Maybe even yet he will send for me. At least say it to me* even though he knew better: *He is in the library now, he has sent the nigger for Henry, now Henry is entering the room:* so that maybe he stopped and faced her, with something in his face that was smiling now, and took her by the elbows and turned her, easy and gentle, until she faced the house, and said 'Go. I wish to be alone to think about love' and she went just as she took the kiss that day, with maybe the feel of the flat of his hand light and momentary upon her behind. And he stood there facing the house until Henry came out, and they looked at one another for a while with no word said and then turned and walked together through the garden, across the lot and into the stable, where maybe there was a nigger there and maybe they saddled the two horses themselves and waited until the house nigger came with the two repacked saddlebags. And maybe he didn't even say then, 'But he sent no word to me?' "

Shreve ceased. That is, for all the two of them, Shreve and Quentin, knew he had stopped, since for all the two of them knew he had never begun, since it did not matter (and possibly neither of them conscious of the distinction) which one had been doing the talking. So that now it was not two but four of them riding the two horses through the dark over the frozen December ruts of that Christmas eve: four of them and then just two—Charles-Shreve and Quentin-Henry, the two of them both believing that Henry was thinking *He* (meaning his father) *has destroyed us all,* not for one moment thinking *He* (meaning Bon) *must have known or at least suspected this all the time; that's why he has acted as he has, why he did not answer my letters last summer nor write to Judith, why he has never asked her to marry him;* believing that that must have occurred to Henry, certainly during that moment after Henry emerged from the house and he and Bon looked at one another for a while without a word then walked down to the stable and saddled the horses, but that Henry had just taken that in stride because he did not yet believe it even though he knew that it was true, because he must have now understood with complete despair the secret of his whole attitude toward Bon from that first instinctive moment when he had seen him a year and a quarter ago; he knew, yet he did not, had to refuse to, believe. So it was four of them who rode the two horses through that night

and then across the bright frosty North Mississippi
Christmas day, in something very like pariah-hood
passing the plantation houses with sprigs of holly
thrust beneath the knockers on the doors and mistletoe hanging from the chandeliers and bowls of eggnog and toddy on tables in the halls and the blue
unwinded wood smoke standing above the plastered
chimneys of the slave quarters, to the River and the
steamboat. There would be Christmas on the boat
too: the same holly and mistletoe, the same eggnog
and toddy; perhaps, doubtless, a Christmas supper
and a ball, but not for them: the two of them in the
dark and the cold standing at the guard rail above
the dark water and still not talking since there was
nothing to say, the two of them (the four of them)
held in that probation, that suspension, by Henry
who knew but still did not believe, who was going
deliberately to look upon and prove to himself that
which, so Shreve and Quentin believed, would be
like death for him to learn. So it was four of them
still who got off the boat in New Orleans, which
Henry had never seen before (whose entire cosmopolitan experience, apart from his sojourn at the
school, consisted probably of one or two trips to
Memphis with his father to buy live stock or slaves)
and had no time to look at now—Henry who knew
yet did not believe, and Bon whom Mr Compson
had called a fatalist but who, according to Shreve
and Quentin, did not resist Henry's dictum and
design for the reason that he neither knew nor cared
what Henry intended to do because he had long

since realised that he did not know yet what he
himself was going to do;—four of them who sat in
that drawing room of baroque and fusty magnificence which Shreve had invented and which was
probably true enough, while the Haiti-born daughter of the French sugar planter and the woman who
Sutpen's first father-in-law had told him was a Spaniard (the slight dowdy woman with untidy gray-
streaked raven hair coarse as a horse's tail, with
parchment-colored skin and implacable pouched
black eyes which alone showed no age because they
showed no forgetting, whom Shreve and Quentin
had likewise invented and which was likewise probably true enough) told them nothing because she did
not need to because she had already told it, who did
not say, 'My son is in love with your sister?' but 'So
she has fallen in love with him' and then sat laughing harshly and steadily at Henry who could not
have lied to her even if he would have, who did not
even have to answer at all either Yes or No.—Four
of them there, in that room in New Orleans in 1860,
just as in a sense there were four of them here in this
tomblike room in Massachusetts in 1910. And Bon
may have, probably did, take Henry to call on the
octoroon mistress and the child, as Mr Compson
said, though neither Shreve nor Quentin believed
that the visit affected Henry as Mr Compson seemed
to think. In fact, Quentin did not even tell Shreve
what his father had said about the visit. Perhaps
Quentin himself had not been listening when Mr
Compson related (recreated?) it that evening at

home; perhaps at that moment on the gallery in the hot September twilight Quentin took that in stride without even hearing it just as Shreve would have, since both he and Shreve believed—and were probably right in this too—that the octoroon and the child would have been to Henry only something else about Bon to be, not envied but aped if that had been possible, if there had been time and peace to ape it in—peace not between men of the same race and nation but peace between two young embattled spirits and the incontrovertible fact which embattled them, since neither Henry and Bon, anymore than Quentin and Shreve, were the first young men to believe (or at least apparently act on the assumption) that wars were sometimes created for the sole aim of settling youth's private difficulties and discontents.

"So the old dame asked Henry that one question and then sat there laughing at him, so he knew then, they both knew then. And so now it would be short, this time with the lawyer, the shortest one of all. Because the lawyer would have been watching him; maybe there had even been a letter during that second fall while the lawyer was waiting and still nothing seemed to be happening up there (and maybe the lawyer was the reason why Bon never answered Henry's and Judith's letters during that summer: because he never got them)—a letter, two or maybe three pages of your humble and obedient e and t and c that boiled down to eighteen words *I know you are a fool, but just what kind of a fool are you going to be?*

and Bon was at least enough of a not-fool to do the boiling down.—Yes, watching him, not concerned yet, just considerably annoyed, giving Bon plenty of time to come to him, giving him all of a week maybe (after he—the lawyer—would have contrived to get hold of Henry and find out a good deal of what Henry was thinking without Henry ever knowing it) before he would contrive Bon too, and maybe so good at the contriving that even Bon would not know at once what was coming. It would be a short one. It would be no secret between them now; it would just be unsaid: the lawyer behind the desk (and maybe in the secret drawer the ledger where he had just finished adding in the last past year's interest compounded between the intrinsic and the love and pride at two hundred percent.)—the lawyer fretted, annoyed, but not at all concerned since he not only knew he had the screws, but he still did not really believe that Bon was that kind of a fool, though he was about to alter his opinion somewhat about the dullness, or at least the backwardness;— the lawyer watching him and saying, smooth and oily, since it would be no secret now, who would know now that Bon knew all he would ever know or would need to know to make the coup: 'Do you know that you are a very fortunate young man? With most of us, even when we are lucky enough to get our revenge, we must pay for it, sometimes in actual dollars. While you are not only in a position to get your revenge, clear your mother's name, but the balm with which you will assuage her injury

will have a collateral value which can be translated
into the things which a young man needs, which are
his due and which, whether we like it or not, may
be had only in exchange for hard dollars——' and
Bon not saying *What do you mean?* and not moving
yet; that is, the lawyer would not be aware that he
was beginning to move, continuing (the lawyer)
smooth and easy: 'And more than this, than the
revenge, as lagniappe to the revenge as it were, this
nosegay of an afternoon, this scentless prairie flower
which will not be missed and which might as well
bloom in your lapel as in another's; this—How do
you young men put it?—a nice little piece——' and
then he would see Bon, maybe the eyes, maybe he
would just hear the feet moving. And then, pistol
(derringer, horse pistol, revolver, whatever it was)
and all, he would be crouched back against the wall
behind the overturned chair, snarling, 'Stand back!
Stop!' then screaming 'Help! Help! He——!' then
just screaming, because he would hear and feel his
own wrenching bones before he could free his
fingers of the pistol, and his neck bone too as Bon
would strike him with the palm on one cheek and
then with the back of the hand on the other; maybe
he could even hear Bon too saying, 'Stop it. Hush.
I'm not going to hurt you' or maybe it was the
lawyer in him that said the Hush which he obeyed,
who got him back into the righted chair again, half
lying upon the desk; the lawyer in him that warned
him not to say *You will pay for this* but instead to
half lie there, nursing his wrenched hand in his

handkerchief while Bon stood looking down at him, holding the pistol by the barrel against his leg, saying, 'If you feel that you require satisfaction, of course you know——' and the lawyer, sitting back now, dabbing the handkerchief at his cheek now: 'I was wrong. I misunderstood your feeling about the matter. I ask your pardon' and Bon: 'Granted. As you wish. I will accept either an apology or a bullet, as you prefer' and the lawyer (there would be a faint fading red in his cheek, but that would be all: nothing in the voice or in the eyes): 'I see you are going to collect full measure for my unfortunate misconception—even ridicule. Even if I felt that right was on my side (which I do not) I would still have to decline your offer. I would not be your equal with pistols' and Bon: 'Nor with knives or rapiers too?' and the lawyer, smooth and easy: 'Nor knives or rapiers too.' So that now the lawyer wouldn't even need to say *You will pay for this* because Bon would be saying that for him, who would stand there with the lax pistol, thinking *But only with knives or pistols or rapiers. So I cant beat him. I could shoot him. I would shoot him with no more compunction than I would a snake or a man who cuckolded me. But he would still beat me.* thinking *Yes. He did beat me* while he—he —("Listen," Shreve said, cried. "It would be while he would be lying in a bedroom of that private house in Corinth after Pittsburg Landing while his shoulder got well two years later and the letter from the octoroon (maybe even the one that contained the photograph of her and the child) finally overtak-

ing him, wailing for money and telling him that the
lawyer had departed for Texas or Mexico or somewhere at last and that she (the octoroon) could not
find his mother either and so without doubt the
lawyer had murdered her before he stole the money,
since it would be just like both of them to flee or get
themselves killed without providing for her at all.")
—Yes, they knew now. And Jesus, think of him,
Bon, who had wanted to know, who had had the
most reason to want to know, who as far as he knew
had never had any father but had been created somehow between that woman who wouldn't let him
play with other children, and that lawyer who even
told the woman whether or not each time she
bought a piece of meat or a loaf of bread—two people neither of whom had taken pleasure or found
passion in getting him or suffered pain and travail
in borning him—who perhaps if one of the two had
only told him the truth, none of what happened
would ever have come to pass; while there was
Henry who had father and security and contentment and all, yet was told the truth by both of them
while he (Bon) was told by neither. And think of
Henry, who had said at first it was a lie and then
when he knew it was not a lie had still said 'I dont
believe it', who had found even in that 'I dont believe it' enough of strength to repudiate home and
blood in order to champion his defiance, and in
which championing he proved his contention to be
the false one and was more than ever interdict
against returning home; Jesus, think of the load he

had to carry, born of two Methodists (or of one long invincible line of Methodists) and raised in provincial North Mississippi, faced with incest, incest of all things that might have been reserved for him, that all his heredity and training had to rebel against on principle, and in a situation where he knew that neither incest nor training was going to help him solve it. So that maybe when they left and walked the streets that night and at last Bon said, 'Well? Now what?' Henry said, 'Wait. Wait. Let me get used to it.' And maybe it was two days or three days, and Henry said, 'You shall not. Shall not' and then it was Bon that said, 'Wait. I am your older brother: do you say *shall not* to me?' And maybe it was a week, maybe Bon took Henry to see the octoroon and Henry looked at her and said, 'Aint that enough for you?' and Bon said, 'Do you want it to be enough?' and Henry said, 'Wait. Wait. I must have time to get used to it. You will have to give me time.' Jesus, think how Henry must have talked during that winter and then that spring with Lincoln elected and the Alabama convention and the South began to draw out of the Union, and then there were two presidents in the United States and the telegraph brought the news about Charleston and Lincoln called out his army and it was done, irrevocable now, and Henry and Bon already decided to go without having to consult one another, who would have gone anyway even if they had never seen one another but certainly now, because after all you dont waste a war;—think how they must have talked, how Henry would say, 'But must you marry her? Do you have to do it?' and Bon would say, 'He should have told me. He should have told me, myself, himself. I was fair and honorable with him. I waited. You know now why I waited. I gave him every chance to tell me himself. But he didn't do it. If he had, I would have agreed and promised never to see her or you or him again. But he didn't tell me. I thought at first it was because he didn't know. Then I knew that he did know, and still I waited. But he didn't tell me. He just told you, sent me a message like you send a command by a nigger servant to a beggar or a tramp to clear out. Dont you see that?' and Henry would say, 'But Judith. Our sister. Think of her' and Bon: 'All right. Think of her. Then what?' because they both knew what Judith would do when she found it out because they both knew that women will show pride and honor about almost anything except love, and Henry said, 'Yes. I see. I understand. But you will have to give me time to get used to it. You are my older brother; you can do that little for me.' Think of the two of them: Bon who didn't know what he was going to do and had to say, pretend, he did; and Henry who knew what he was going to do and had to say he didn't. Then it was Christmas again, then 1861, and they hadn't heard from Judith because Judith didn't know for sure where they were because Henry wouldn't let Bon write to her yet; then they heard about the company, the University Grays, organising up at Oxford and maybe they had been waiting for that. So they took the steamboat North again, and more gayety and excitement on the boat now than Christmas even, like it always is when a war starts, before the scene gets cluttered up with bad food and wounded soldiers and widows and orphans, and them taking no part in it now either but standing at the rail again above the churning water, and maybe it would be two or three days, then Henry said suddenly, cried suddenly: 'But kings have done it! Even dukes! There was that Lorraine duke named John something that married his sister. The Pope excommunicated him but it didn't hurt! It didn't hurt! They were still husband and wife. They were still alive. They still loved!' then again, loud, fast: 'But you will have to wait! You will have to give me time! Maybe the war will settle it and we wont need to!' And maybe this was one place where your old man was right: and they rode into Oxford without touching Sutpen's Hundred and signed the company roster and then hid somewhere to wait, and Henry let Bon write Judith one letter; they would send it by hand, by a nigger that would steal into the quarters by night and give it to Judith's maid, and Judith sent the picture in the metal case and they rode on ahead to wait until the company got through making flags and riding about the state telling girls farewell and started for the front.

"Jesus, think of them. Because Bon would know what Henry was doing, just as he had always known what Henry was thinking since that first day when they had looked at one another. Maybe he would

know all the better what Henry was doing because
he did not know what he himself was going to do,
that he would not know until all of a sudden some
day it would burst clear and he would know then
that he had known all the time what it would be, so
he didn't have to bother about himself and so all he
had to do was just to watch Henry trying to reconcile what he (Henry) knew he was going to do with
all the voices of his heredity and training which said
No. No. You cannot. You must not. You shall not.
Maybe they would even be under fire now, with the
shells rushing and rumbling past overhead and
bursting and them lying there waiting to charge and
Henry would cry again, 'But that Lorraine duke did
it! There must have been lots in the world who have
done it that people dont know about, that maybe
they suffered for it and died for it and are in hell
now for it. But they did it and it dont matter now;
even the ones we do know about are just names now
and it dont matter now' and Bon watching him and
listening to him and thinking *It's because I dont know
myself what I am going to do and so he is aware that
I am undecided without knowing that he is aware.
Perhaps if I told him now that I am going to do it, he
would know his own mind and tell me, You shall not.*
And maybe your old man was right this time and
they did think maybe the war would settle it and
they would not have to themselves, or at least maybe
Henry hoped it would because maybe your old man
was right here too and Bon didn't care; that since
both of the two people who could have given him

a father had declined to do it, nothing mattered to him now, revenge or love or all, since he knew now that revenge could not compensate him nor love assuage. Maybe it wasn't even Henry who wouldn't let him write to Judith but Bon himself who did not write her because he didn't care about anything, not even that he didn't know yet what he was going to do. Then it was the next year and Bon was an officer now and they were moving toward Shiloh without knowing that either, talking again as they moved along in column, the officer dropping back alongside the file in which the private marched and Henry crying again, holding his desperate and urgent voice down to undertone: 'Dont you know yet what you are going to do?' while Bon would look at him for a moment with that expression which could have been smiling: 'Suppose I told you I did not intend to go back to her?' and Henry would walk there beside him, with his pack and his eight feet of musket, and he would begin to pant, panting and panting while Bon watched him: 'I am out in front of you a lot now; going into battle, charging, I will be out in front of you——' and Henry panting, 'Stop! Stop!' and Bon watching him with that faint thin expression about the mouth and eyes: '——and who would ever know? You would not even have to know for certain yourself, because who could say but what a Yankee ball might have struck me at the exact second you pulled your trigger, or even before——' and Henry panting and looking, glaring at the sky, with his teeth showing and the

sweat on his face and the knuckles of the hand on
his musket butt white, saying, panting, 'Stop! Stop!
Stop! Stop!' Then it was Shiloh, the second day and
the lost battle and the brigade falling back from
Pittsburg Landing——And listen," Shreve cried;
"wait, now; wait!" (glaring at Quentin, panting
himself, as if he had had to supply his shade not only
with a cue but with breath to obey it in): "Because
your old man was wrong here, too! He said it was
Bon who was wounded, but it wasn't. Because who
told him? Who told Sutpen, or your grandfather
either, which of them it was who was hit? Sutpen
didn't know because he wasn't there, and your
grandfather wasn't there either because that was
where he was hit too, where he lost his arm. So who
told them? Not Henry, because his father never saw
Henry but that one time and maybe they never had
time to talk about wounds and besides to talk about
wounds in the Confederate army in 1865 would be
like coal miners talking about soot; and not Bon,
because Sutpen never saw him at all because he was
dead;—it was not Bon, it was Henry; Bon that
found Henry at last and stooped to pick him up and
Henry fought back, struggled, saying, 'Let be! Let
me die! I wont have to know it then' and Bon said,
'So you do want me to go back to her' and Henry
lay there struggling and panting, with the sweat on
his face and his teeth bloody inside his chewed lip,
and Bon said, 'Say you do want me to go back to
her. Maybe then I wont do it. Say it' and Henry lay
there struggling, with the fresh red staining through

his shirt and his teeth showing and the sweat on his face until Bon held his arms and lifted him onto his back——"

First, two of them, then four; now two again. The room was indeed tomblike: a quality stale and static and moribund beyond any mere vivid and living cold. Yet they remained in it, though not thirty feet away was bed and warmth. Quentin had not even put on his overcoat, which lay on the floor where it had fallen from the arm of the chair where Shreve had put it down. They did not retreat from the cold. They both bore it as though in deliberate flagellant exaltation of physical misery transmogrified into the spirits' travail of the two young men during that time fifty years ago, or forty-eight rather, then forty-seven and then forty-six, since it was '64 and then '65 and the starved and ragged remnant of an army having retreated across Alabama and Georgia and into Carolina, swept onward not by a victorious army behind it but rather by a mounting tide of the names of lost battles from either side—Chickamauga and Franklin, Vicksburg and Corinth and Atlanta—battles lost not alone because of superior numbers and failing ammunition and stores, but because of generals who should not have been generals, who were generals not through training in contemporary methods or aptitude for learning them, but by the divine right to say 'Go there' conferred upon them by an absolute caste system; or because the generals of it never lived long enough to learn how to fight massed cautious accretionary battles, since

they were already as obsolete as Richard or Roland
or du Guesclin, who wore plumes and cloaks lined
with scarlet at twenty-eight and thirty and thirty-
two and captured warships with cavalry charges but
no grain nor meat nor bullets, who would whip
three separate armies in as many days and then tear
down their own fences to cook meat robbed from
their own smokehouses, who on one night and with
a handful of men would gallantly set fire to and
destroy a million dollar garrison of enemy supplies
and on the next night be discovered by a neighbor
in bed with his wife and be shot to death;—two,
four, now two again, according to Quentin and
Shreve, the two the four the two still talking—the
one who did not yet know what he was going to do,
the other who knew what he would have to do yet
could not reconcile himself—Henry citing himself
authority for incest, talking about his Duke John of
Lorraine as if he hoped possibly to evoke that condemned and excommunicated shade to tell him in
person that it was all right, as people both before and
since have tried to evoke God or devil to justify
them in what their glands insisted upon;—the two
the four the two facing one another in the tomblike
room: Shreve, the Canadian, the child of blizzards
and of cold in a bathrobe with an overcoat above it,
the collar turned up about his ears; Quentin, the
Southerner, the morose and delicate offspring of
rain and steamy heat in the thin suitable clothing
which he had brought from Mississippi, his overcoat
(as thin and vain for what it was as the suit) lying

on the floor where he had not even bothered to raise
it:

(——*the winter of '64 now, the army retreated across
Alabama, into Georgia; now Carolina was just at their
backs and Bon, the officer, thinking 'We will either be
caught and annihilated or Old Joe will extricate us and
we will make contact with Lee in front of Richmond
and then we will at least have the privilege of surrender': and then one day all of a sudden he thought of it,
remembered, how that Jefferson regiment of which his
father was now colonel was in Longstreet's corps, and
maybe from that moment the whole purpose of the retreat seemed to him to be that of bringing him within
reach of his father, to give his father one more chance.
So that it must have seemed to him now that he knew
at last why he had not been able to decide what he
wanted to do. Maybe he thought for just a second, 'My
God, I am still young; even after these four years I am
still young' but just for a second, because maybe in the
same breath he said, 'All right. Then I am young. But
I still believe, even though what I believe probably is
that war, suffering, these four years of keeping his men
alive and able in order to swap them blood and flesh for
the largest amount of ground at its bargain price, will
have changed him (which I know that it does not do)
to where he will say to me not: Forgive me: but: You
are my oldest son. Protect your sister; never see either of
us again:' Then it was '65 and what was left of the
Army of the West with nothing remaining now but the
ability to walk backward slow and stubborn and to
endure musketry and shelling; maybe they didn't even*

miss the shoes and overcoats and food any more now and that was why he could write about the captured stove polish like he did in the letter to Judith when he finally knew what he was going to do at last and told Henry and Henry said 'Thank God. Thank God', not for the incest of course but because at last they were going to do something, at last he could be something even though that something was the irrevocable repudiation of the old heredity and training and the acceptance of eternal damnation. Maybe he could even quit talking about his Lorraine duke then, because he could say now, 'It isn't yours nor his nor the Pope's hell that we are all going to: it's my mother's and her mother's and father's and their mother's and father's hell, and it isn't you who are going there, but we, the three—no: four of us. And so at least we will all be together where we belong, since even if only he went there we would still have to be there too since the three of us are just illusions that he begot, and your illusions are a part of you like your bones and flesh and memory. And we will all be together in torment and so we will not need to remember love and fornication, and maybe in torment you cannot even remember why you are there. And if we cannot remember all this, it cant be much torment'. Then they were in Carolina, that January and February of '65 and what was left of them had been walking backward for almost a year now and the distance between them and Richmond was less far than the distance they had come; the distance between them and the end a good deal less far. But to Bon it was not the space between them and defeat but the space between him and the other regiment, *between him and the hour, the moment: 'He will not even have to ask me; I will just touch flesh with him and I will say it myself: You will not need to worry; she shall never see me again'. Then March in Carolina and still the walking backward slow and stubborn and listening to the Northward now because there was nothing to hear from any other direction because in all the other directions it was finished now, and all they expected to hear from the North was defeat. Then one day (he was an officer; he would have known, heard, that Lee had detached some troops and sent them down to reinforce them; perhaps he even knew the names and numbers of the regiments before they arrived) he saw Sutpen. Maybe that first time Sutpen actually did not see him, maybe that first time he could tell himself, 'That was why; he didn't see me', so that he had to put himself in Sutpen's way, make his chance and situation. Then for the second time he looked at the expressionless and rock-like face, at the pale boring eyes in which there was no flicker, nothing, the face in which he saw his own features, in which he saw recognition, and that was all. That was all, there was nothing further now; perhaps he just breathed once quietly, with on his own face that expression which might at a glance have been called smiling while he thought, 'I could force him. I could go to him and force him', knowing that he would not because it was all finished now, that was all of it now and at last. And maybe it was that same night or maybe a night a week later while they were stopped (because even Sherman would have to stop sometimes at night) with the fires burning for warmth at least because at*

*least warmth is cheap and doesn't remain consumed,
that Bon said, 'Henry' and said, 'It wont be much
longer now and then there wont be anything left; we
wont even have anything to do left, not even the privilege of walking backward slowly for a reason, for the
sake of honor and what's left of pride. Not God; evidently we have done without Him for four years, only
He just didn't think to notify us; and not only not shoes
and clothing but not even any need for them, and not
only no land nor any way to make food, but no need
for the food since we have learned to live without that
too; and so if you dont have God and you dont need food
and clothes and shelter, there isn't anything for honor
and pride to climb on and hold to and flourish. And if
you haven't got honor and pride, then nothing matters.
Only there is something in you that doesn't care about
honor and pride yet that lives, that even walks backward for a whole year just to live; that probably even
when this is over and there is not even defeat left, will
still decline to sit still in the sun and die, but will be
out in the woods, moving and seeking where just will
and endurance could not move it, grubbing for roots
and such—the old mindless sentient undreaming meat
that doesn't even know any difference between despair
and victory, Henry'. And then Henry would begin to
say 'Thank God. Thank God' panting and saying
'Thank God', saying, 'Dont try to explain it. Just do
it' and Bon: 'You authorise me? As her brother you give
me permission?' and Henry: 'Brother? Brother? You are
the oldest: why do you ask me?' and Bon: 'No. He has
never acknowledged me. He just warned me. You are*

the brother and the son. Do I have your permission, Henry?' and Henry: 'Write. Write. Write'. So Bon wrote the letter, after the four years, and Henry read it and sent it off. But they didn't quit then and follow the letter. They still walked backward, slow and stubborn, listening toward the North for the end of it because it takes an awful lot of character to quit anything when you are losing, and they had been walking backward slow for a year now so all they had left was not the will but just the ability, the grooved habit to endure. Then one night they had stopped again since Sherman had stopped again, and an orderly came along the bivouac line and found Henry at last and said, 'Sutpen, the colonel wants you in his tent.')

"And so you and the old dame, the Aunt Rosa, went out there that night and the old nigger Clytie tried to stop you, stop her; she held your arm and said, 'Dont let her go up there, young marster' but you couldn't stop her either because she was strong with forty-three years of hate like forty-three years of raw meat and all Clytie had was just forty-five or fifty years of despair and waiting; and you, you didn't even want to be there at all to begin with. And you couldn't stop her either and then you saw that Clytie's trouble wasn't anger nor even distrust; it was terror, fear. And she didn't tell you in so many words because she was still keeping that secret for the sake of the man who had been her father too as well as for the sake of the family which no longer existed, whose here-to-fore inviolate and rotten mausoleum she still guarded;—didn't tell you in so

many words anymore than she told you in so many
words how she had been in the room that day when
they brought Bon's body in and Judith took from
his pocket the metal case she had given him with her
picture in it; she didn't tell you, it just came out of
the terror and the fear after she turned you loose and
caught the Aunt Rosa's arm and the Aunt Rosa
turned and struck her hand away and went on to the
stairs and Clytie ran at her again and this time the
Aunt Rosa stopped and turned on the second step
and knocked Clytie down with her fist like a man
would and turned and went on up the stairs: and
Clytie lay there on the floor, more than eighty years
old and not much more than five feet tall and looking like a little bundle of clean rags so that you went
and took her arm and helped her up and her arm felt
like a stick, as light and dry and brittle as a stick: and
she looked at you and you saw it was not rage but
terror, and not nigger terror because it was not
about herself but was about whatever it was that was
up stairs, that she had kept hidden up there for
almost four years; and she didn't tell you in the
actual words because even in the terror she kept the
secret; nevertheless she told you, or at least all of a
sudden you knew——"

He ceased again. It was just as well, since he had
no listener. Perhaps he was aware of it. Then suddenly he had no talker either, though possibly he
was not aware of this. Because now neither of them
was there. They were both in Carolina and the time
was forty-six years ago, and it was not even four

now but compounded still further, since now both of them were Henry Sutpen and both of them were Bon, compounded each of both yet either neither, smelling the very smoke which had blown and faded away forty-six years ago from the *bivouac fires burning in a pine grove, the gaunt and ragged men sitting or lying about them, talking not about the war yet all curiously enough (or perhaps not curiously at all) facing the South where further on in the darkness the pickets stood—the pickets who, watching to the South, could see the flicker and gleam of the Federal bivouac fires myriad and faint and encircling half the horizon and counting ten fires for each Confederate one, and between whom and which (Rebel picket and Yankee fire) the Yankee outposts watched the darkness also, the two picket lines so close that each could hear the challenge of the other's officers passing from post to post and dying away: and when gone, the voice, invisible, cautious, not loud yet carrying:*

—Hey, Reb.

—Yah.

—Where you fellers going?

—Richmond.

—So are we. Why not wait for us?

—We air.

The men about the fires would not hear this exchange, though they would presently hear the orderly plainly enough as he passes from fire to fire, asking for Sutpen and being directed on and so reaches the fire at last, the smoldering log, with his monotonous speech: 'Sutpen? I'm looking for Sutpen' until Henry sits up and says,

'Here.' He is gaunt and ragged and unshaven; because of the last four years and because he had not quite got his height when the four years began, he is not as tall by two inches as he gave promise of being, and not as heavy by thirty pounds as he probably will be a few years after he has outlived the four years, if he do outlive them.

—Here, he says.—What is it?

—The colonel wants you.

The orderly does not return with him. Instead, he walks alone through the darkness along a rutted road, a road rutted and cut and churned where the guns have passed over it that afternoon, and reaches the tent at last, one of the few tents, the canvas wall gleaming faintly from a candle within, the silhouette of a sentry before it, who challenges him.

—Sutpen, Henry says.—The colonel sent for me.

The sentry gestures him into the tent. He stoops through the entrance, the canvas falls behind him as someone, the only occupant of the tent, rises from a camp chair behind the table on which the candle sits, his shadow swooping high and huge up the canvas wall. He (Henry) comes to salute facing a gray sleeve with colonel's braid on it, one bearded cheek, a jutting nose, a shaggy droop of iron-riddled hair—a face which Henry does not recognise, not because he has not seen it in four years and does not expect to see it here and now, but rather because he is not looking at it. He just salutes the braided cuff and stands so until the other says,

—Henry.

Even now Henry does not start. He just stands so, the

*two of them stand so, looking at one another. It is the
older man who moves first, though they meet in the
center of the tent, where they embrace and kiss before
Henry is aware that he has moved, was going to move,
moved by what of close blood which in the reflex instant
arrogates and reconciles even though it does not yet
(perhaps never will) forgive, who stands now while his
father holds his face between both hands, looking at it.*

—Henry, Sutpen says.—My son.

*Then they sit, one on either side of the table, in the chairs
reserved for officers, the table (an open map lies on it)
and the candle between them.*

*—You were hit at Shiloh, Colonel Willow tells me,
Sutpen says.*

—Yes, sir, Henry says.

*He is about to say Charles carried me back but he does
not, because already he knows what is coming. He does
not even think Surely Judith didn't write him about
that letter or It was Clytie who sent him word somehow
that Charles has written her. He thinks neither of these.
To him it is logical and natural that their father should
know of his and Bon's decision: that rapport of blood
which should bring Bon to decide to write, himself to
agree to it and their father to know of it at the same
identical instant, after a period of four years, out of all
time. Now it does come, almost exactly as he has known
that it will:*

—I have seen Charles Bon, Henry.

*Henry says nothing. It is coming now. He says nothing,
he merely stares at his father—the two of them in leaf-
faded gray, a single candle, a crude tent walling them*

*away from a darkness where alert pickets face one an-
other and where weary men sleep without shelter, waiting for dawn and the firing, the weary backward
walking to commence again: yet in a second tent candle
gray and all are gone and it is the holly-decked Christmas library at Sutpen's Hundred four years ago and the
table not a camp table suitable for the spreading of maps
but the heavy carved rosewood one at home with the
group photograph of his mother and sister and himself
sitting upon it, his father behind the table and behind
his father the window above the garden where Judith
and Bon strolled in that slow rhythm where the heart
matches the footsteps and the eyes need only look at one
another.*

*—You are going to let him marry Judith, Henry.
Still Henry does not answer. It has all been said before,
and now he has had four years of bitter struggle following which, whether it be victory or defeat which he has
gained, at least he has gained it and has peace now, even
if the peace be mostly despair.*

*—He cannot marry her, Henry.
Now Henry speaks.*

*—You said that before. I told you then. And now,
and now it wont be much longer now and then we wont
have anything left: honor nor pride nor God since God
quit us four years ago only He never thought it necessary to tell us; no shoes nor clothes and no need for them;
not only no land to make food out of but no need for
the food and when you dont have God and honor and
pride, nothing matters except that there is the old mindless meat that dont even care if it was defeat or victory,*

that wont even die, that will be out in the woods and fields, grubbing up roots and weeds.—Yes. I have decided. Brother or not, I have decided. I will. I will.

—*He must not marry her, Henry.*

—*Yes. I said Yes at first, but I was not decided then. I didn't let him. But now I have had four years to decide in. I will. I am going to.*

—*He must not marry her, Henry. His mother's father told me that her mother had been a Spanish woman. I believed him; it was not until after he was born that I found out that his mother was part negro.*

Nor did Henry ever say that he did not remember leaving the tent. He remembers all of it. He remembers stooping through the entrance again and passing the sentry again; he remembers walking back down the cut and rutted road, stumbling in the dark among the ruts on either side of which the fires have now died to embers, so that he can barely distinguish the men sleeping on the earth about them. It must be better than eleven oclock, he thinks. And another eight miles tomorrow. If it were only not for those damned guns. Why doesn't Old Joe give the guns to Sherman. Then we could make twenty miles a day. We could join Lee then. At least Lee stops and fights some of the time. He remembers it. He remembers how he did not return to his fire but stopped presently in a lonely place and leaned against a pine, leaning quietly and easily, with his head back so he could look up at the shabby shaggy branches like something in wrought iron spreading motionless against the chill vivid stars of early spring, thinking I hope he remembers to thank Colonel Willow for letting us use* *his tent, thinking not what he would do but what he would have to do. Because he knew what he would do; it now depended on what Bon would do, would force him to do, since he knew that he would do it. So I must go to him, he thought, thinking, Now it is better than two oclock and it will be dawn soon.*

Then it was dawn, or almost, and it was cold: a chill which struck through the worn patched thin clothing, through the something of weariness and undernourishment; the passive ability, not the volitional will, to endure; there was light somewhere, enough of it for him to distinguish Bon's sleeping face from among the others where he lay wrapped in his blankets, beneath his spread cloak; enough light for him to wake Bon by and for Bon to distinguish his face (or perhaps something communicated by Henry's hand) because Bon does not speak, demand to know who it is: he merely rises and puts the cloak about his shoulders and approaches the smoldering fire and is kicking it into a blaze when Henry speaks:

—*Wait.*

Bon pauses and looks at Henry; now he can see Henry's face. He says,

—*You will be cold. You are cold now. You haven't been asleep, have you? Here.*

He swings the cloak from his shoulders and holds it out.

—*No, Henry says.*

—*Yes. Take it. I'll get my blanket.*

Bon puts the cloak about Henry and goes and takes up

his tumbled blanket and swings it about his shoulders, and they move aside and sit on a log. Now it is dawn. The east is gray; it will be primrose soon and then red with firing and once more the weary backward marching will begin, retreating from annihilation, falling back upon defeat, though not quite yet. There will be a little time yet for them to sit side by side upon the log in the making light of dawn, the one in the cloak, the other in the blanket; their voices are not much louder than the silent dawn itself:

—So it's the miscegenation, not the incest, which you cant bear.

Henry doesn't answer.

—And he sent me no word? He did not ask you to send me to him? No word to me, no word at all? That was all he had to do, now, today; four years ago or at any time during the four years. That was all. He would not have needed to ask it, require it, of me. I would have offered it. I would have said, I will never see her again before he could have asked it of me. He did not have to do this, Henry. He didn't need to tell you I am a nigger to stop me. He could have stopped me without that, Henry.

—No! *Henry cries.*—No! No! I will—I'll——

He springs up; his face is working; Bon can see his teeth within the soft beard which covers his sunken cheeks, and the whites of Henry's eyes as though the eyeballs struggled in their sockets as the panting breath struggled in his lungs—the panting which ceased, the breath held, the eyes too looking down at him where he sat on

*the log, the voice now not much louder than an expelled
breath:*

—*You said, could have stopped you. What do you
mean by that?*

*Now it is Bon who does not answer, who sits on the log
looking at the face stooped above him. Henry says, still
in that voice no louder than breathing:*

—*But now? You mean you——*

—*Yes. What else can I do now? I gave him the choice.
I have been giving him the choice for four years.*

—*Think of her. Not of me: of her.*

—*I have. For four years. Of you and her. Now I am
thinking of myself.*

—*No, Henry says.—No. No.*

—*I cannot?*

—*You shall not.*

—*Who will stop me, Henry?*

—*No, Henry says.—No. No. No.*

*Now it is Bon who watches Henry; he can see the whites
of Henry's eyes again as he sits looking at Henry with
that expression which might be called smiling. His hand
vanishes beneath the blanket and reappears, holding his
pistol by the barrel, the butt extended toward Henry.*

—*Then do it now, he says.*

*Henry looks at the pistol; now he is not only panting,
he is trembling; when he speaks now his voice is not even
the exhalation, it is the suffused and suffocating in-
breath itself:*

—*You are my brother.*

—*No I'm not. I'm the nigger that's going to sleep
with your sister. Unless you stop me, Henry.*

Suddenly Henry grasps the pistol, jerks it free of Bon's hand and stands so, the pistol in his hand, panting and panting; again Bon can see the whites of his inrolled eyes while he sits on the log and watches Henry with that faint expression about the eyes and mouth which might be smiling.

—Do it now, Henry, he says.

Henry whirls; in the same motion he hurls the pistol from him and stoops again, gripping Bon by both shoulders, panting.

—You shall not! he says.—You shall not! Do you hear me?

Bon does not move beneath the gripping hands; he sits motionless, with his faint fixed grimace; his voice is gentler than that first breath in which the pine branches begin to move a little:

—You will have to stop me, Henry. "And he never slipped away," Shreve said. "He could have, but he never even tried. Jesus, maybe he even went to Henry and said, 'I'm going, Henry' and maybe they left together and rode side by side dodging Yankee patrols all the way back to Mississippi and right up to that gate; side by side and it only then that one of them ever rode ahead or dropped behind and that when Henry spurred ahead and turned his horse to face Bon and took out the pistol; and Judith and Clytie heard the shot, and maybe Wash Jones was hanging around somewhere in the back yard and so he was there to help Clytie and Judith carry him into the house and lay him on the bed, and Wash went to town to tell the Aunt Rosa and the Aunt

Rosa comes boiling out that afternoon and finds Judith standing without a tear before the closed door, holding the metal case she had given him with her picture in it but that didn't have her picture in it now but that of the octoroon and the kid. And your old man wouldn't know about that too: why the black son of a bitch should have taken her picture out and put the octoroon's picture in, so he invented a reason for it. But I know. And you know too. Dont you? Dont you, huh?" He glared at Quentin, leaning forward over the table now, looking huge and shapeless as a bear in his swaddling of garments. "Dont you know? It was because he said to himself, 'If Henry dont mean what he said, it will be all right; I can take it out and destroy it. But if he does mean what he said, it will be the only way I will have to say to her, *I was no good; do not grieve for me.*' Aint that right? Aint it? By God, aint it?"

"Yes," Quentin said.

"Come on," Shreve said. "Let's get out of this refrigerator and go to bed."

IX

At first, in bed in the dark, it seemed colder than ever, as if there had been some puny quality of faint heat in the single light bulb before Shreve turned it off and that now the iron and impregnable dark had become one with the iron and icelike bedclothing lying upon the flesh slacked and thin-clad for sleeping. Then the darkness seemed to breathe, to flow back; the window which Shreve had opened became visible against the faintly unearthly glow of the outer snow as, forced by the weight of the darkness, the blood surged and ran warmer, warmer. "University of Mississippi," Shreve's voice said in the darkness to Quentin's right. "Bayard attenuated forty miles (it was forty miles, wasn't it?); out of the wilderness proud honor semesterial regurgitant."

"Yes," Quentin said. "They were in the tenth graduating class since it was founded."

"I didn't know there were ten in Mississippi that went to school at one time," Shreve said. Quentin didn't answer. He lay watching the rectangle of window, feeling the warming blood driving through his veins, his arms and legs. And now, although he was warm and though while he had sat in the cold room he merely shook faintly and steadily, now he began to jerk all over, violently and uncontrollably until he could even hear the bed, until even Shreve felt it and turned, raising himself (by the sound) onto his elbow to look at Quentin, though Quentin himself felt perfectly all right. He felt fine even, lying there and waiting in peaceful curiosity for the next violent unharbingered jerk to come. "Jesus, are you that cold?" Shreve said. "Do you want me to spread the overcoats on you?"

"No," Quentin said. "I'm not cold. I'm all right. I feel fine."

"Then what are you doing that for?"

"I dont know. I cant help it. I feel fine."

"All right. But let me know if you want the coats. Jesus, if I was going to have to spend nine months in this climate, I would sure hate to have come from the South. Maybe I wouldn't come from the South anyway, even if I could stay there. Wait. Listen. I'm not trying to be funny, smart. I just want to understand it if I can and I dont know how to say it better. Because it's something my people haven't got. Or if we have got it, it all happened long ago across the water and so now there aint anything to look at every day to remind us of it. We dont live among defeated grandfathers and freed slaves (or have I got it backward and was it your folks that are free and the niggers that lost?) and bullets in the dining room table and such, to be always reminding us to never forget. What is it? something you live and breathe in like air? a kind of vacuum filled with wraithlike and indomitable anger and pride and glory at and in happenings that occurred and ceased fifty years ago?

a kind of entailed birthright father and son and father and son of never forgiving General Sherman,
so that forever more as long as your children's children produce children you wont be anything but a
descendant of a long line of colonels killed in Pick-
ett's charge at Manassas?"

"Gettysburg," Quentin said. "You cant understand it. You would have to be born there."

"Would I then?" Quentin did not answer. "Do
you understand it?"

"I dont know," Quentin said. "Yes, of course I
understand it." They breathed in the darkness.
After a moment Quentin said: "I dont know."

"Yes. You dont know. You dont even know
about the old dame, the Aunt Rosa."

"Miss Rosa," Quentin said.

"All right. You dont even know about her. Except that she refused at the last to be a ghost. That
after almost fifty years she couldn't reconcile herself
to letting him lie dead in peace. That even after fifty
years she not only could get up and go out there to
finish up what she found she hadn't quite completed, but she could find someone to go with her and
bust into that locked house because instinct or something told her it was not finished yet. Do you?"

"No," Quentin said peacefully. He could taste the
dust. Even now, with the chill pure weight of the
snow-breathed New England air on his face, he
could taste and feel the dust of that breathless
(rather, furnace-breathed) Mississippi September
night. He could even smell the old woman in the
buggy beside him, smell the fusty camphor-reeking

shawl and even the airless black cotton umbrella in which (he would not discover until they had reached the house) she had concealed a hatchet and a flashlight. He could smell the horse; he could hear the dry plaint of the light wheels in the weightless permeant dust and he seemed to feel the dust itself move sluggish and dry across his sweating flesh just as he seemed to hear the single profound suspiration of the parched earth's agony rising toward the imponderable and aloof stars. Now she spoke, for the first time since they had left Jefferson, since she had climbed into the buggy with a kind of clumsy and fumbling and trembling eagerness (which he thought derived from terror, alarm, until he found that he was quite wrong) before he could help her, to sit on the extreme edge of the seat, small, in the fusty shawl and clutching the umbrella, leaning forward as if by leaning forward she would arrive the sooner, arrive immediately after the horse and before he, Quentin, would, before the prescience of her desire and need could warn its consummation. "Now," she said. "We are on the Domain. On his land, his and Ellen's and Ellen's descendants. They have taken it away from them since, I understand. But it still belongs to him, to Ellen and her descendants." But Quentin was already aware of that. Before she spoke he had said to himself, 'Now. Now' and (as during the long hot afternoon in the dim hot little house) it seemed to him that if he stopped the buggy and listened, he might even hear the galloping hooves; might even see at any moment now the black stallion and the rider rush across the road before them and gallop on—the rider who at one time owned, lock stock and barrel, everything he could see from a given point, with every stick and blade and hoof and heel on it to remind him (if he ever forgot it) that he was the biggest thing in their sight and in his own too; who went to war to protect it and lost the war and returned home to find that he had lost more than the war even, though not absolutely all; who said *At least I have life left* but did not have life but only old age and breathing and horror and scorn and fear and indignation: and all remaining to look at him with unchanged regard was the girl who had been a child when he saw her last, who doubtless used to watch him from window or door as he passed unaware of her as she would have looked at God probably, since everything else within her view belonged to him too. Maybe he would even stop at the cabin and ask for water and she would take the bucket and walk the mile and back to the spring to fetch it fresh and cool for him, no more thinking of saying "The bucket is empty" to him than she would have said it to God;—this the not-all, since at least there was breathing left.

Now Quentin began to breathe hard again, who had been peaceful for a time in the warm bed, breathing hard the heady pure snowborn darkness. She (Miss Coldfield) did not let him enter the gate. She said "Stop" suddenly; he felt her hand flutter on his arm and he thought, 'Why, she is afraid'. He could hear her panting now, her voice almost a wail of diffident yet iron determination: "I dont know what to do. I dont know what to do." ('I do,' he thought. 'Go back to town and go to bed.') But he did not say it. He looked at the two huge rotting gate posts in the starlight, between which no gates swung now, wondering from what direction Bon and Henry had ridden up that day, wondering what had cast the shadow which Bon was not to pass alive; if some living tree which still lived and bore leaves and shed or if some tree gone, vanished, burned for warmth and food years ago now or perhaps just gone; or if it had been one of the two posts themselves, thinking, wishing that Henry were there now to stop Miss Coldfield and turn them back, telling himself that if Henry were there now, there would be no shot to be heard by anyone. "She's going to try to stop me," Miss Coldfield whimpered. "I know she is. Maybe this far from town, out here alone at midnight, she will even let that negro man——And you didn't even bring a pistol. Did you?"

"Nome," Quentin said. "What is it she's got hidden there? What could it be? And what difference does it make? Let's go back to town, Miss Rosa."

She didn't answer this at all. She just said, "That's what I have got to find out", sitting forward on the seat, trembling now and peering up the tree-arched drive toward where the rotting shell of the house would be. "And now I will have to find it out," she whimpered, in a kind of amazed self-pity. She moved suddenly. "Come," she whispered, beginning to get out of the buggy.

"Wait," Quentin said. "Let's drive up to the house. It's a half a mile."

"No, no," she whispered, a tense fierce hissing of words filled with that same curious terrified yet implacable determination, as though it were not she who had to go and find out but she only the helpless agent of someone or something else who must know. "Hitch the horse here. Hurry." She got out, scrambled awkwardly down, before he could help her, clutching the umbrella. It seemed to him that he could still hear her whimpering panting where she waited close beside one of the posts while he led the mare from the road and tied one rein about a sapling in the weed-choked ditch. He could not see her at all, so close she stood against the post: she just stepped out and fell in beside him when he passed and turned into the gate, still breathing in those whimpering pants as they walked on up the rutted tree-arched drive. The darkness was intense; she stumbled; he caught her. She took his arm, clutching it in a dead rigid hard grip as if her fingers, her hand, were a small mass of wire. "I will have to take your arm," she whispered, whimpered. "And you haven't even got a pistol—Wait," she said. She stopped. He turned; he could not see her but he could hear her hurried breathing and then a rustling of cloth. Then she was prodding something at him. "Here," she whispered. "Take it." It was a hatchet; not sight but touch told him—a hatchet with a heavy worn handle and a heavy gapped rust-dulled blade.

"What?" he said.

"Take it!" she whispered, hissed. "You didn't bring a pistol. It's something."

"Here," he said; "wait."

"Come," she whispered. "You will have to let me take your arm, I am trembling so bad." They went on again, she clinging to one of his arms, the hatchet in his other hand. "We will probably need it to get into the house, anyway," she said, stumbling along beside him, almost dragging him. "I just know she is somewhere watching us," she whimpered. "I can feel her. But if we can just get to the house, get into the house——" The drive seemed interminable. He knew the place. He had walked from the gate to the house as a child, a boy, when distances seem really long (so that to the man grown the long crowded mile of his boyhood becomes less than the throw of a stone) yet now it seemed to him that the house would never come in sight: so that presently he found himself repeating her words: 'If we can just get to the house, get inside the house', telling himself, recovering himself in that same breath: 'I am not afraid. I just dont want to be here. I just dont want to know about whatever it is she keeps hidden in it'. But they reached it at last. It loomed, bulked, square and enormous, with jagged half-toppled chimneys, its roofline sagging a little; for an instant as they moved, hurried, toward it Quentin saw completely through it a ragged segment of sky with three hot stars in it as if the house were of one dimension, painted on a canvas curtain in which there was a tear; now, almost beneath it, the dead furnace-breath of air in which they moved seemed

to reek in slow and protracted violence with a smell
of desolation and decay as if the wood of which it
was built were flesh. She was trotting beside him
now, her hand trembling on his arm yet gripping it
still with that lifeless and rigid strength; not talking,
not saying words, yet producing a steady whimpering, almost a moaning, sound. Apparently she could
not see at all now, so that he had to guide her toward
where he knew the steps would be and then restrain
her, whispering, hissing, aping without knowing it
her own tense fainting haste: "Wait. This way. Be
careful, now. They're rotten." He almost lifted, carried, her up the steps, supporting her from behind
by both elbows as you lift a child; he could feel
something fierce and implacable and dynamic driving down the thin rigid arms and into his palms and
up his own arms; lying in the Massachusetts bed he
remembered how he thought, knew, said suddenly
to himself, 'Why, she's not afraid at all. It's something. But she's not afraid', feeling her flee out of his
hands, hearing her feet cross the gallery, overtaking
her where she now stood beside the invisible front
door, panting. "Now what?" he whispered.

"Break it," she whispered. "It will be locked,
nailed. You have the hatchet. Break it."

"But——" he began.

"Break it!" she hissed. "It belonged to Ellen. I am
her sister, her only living heir. Break it. Hurry." He
pushed against the door. It did not move. She
panted beside him. "Hurry," she said. "Break it."

"Listen, Miss Rosa," he said. "Listen."

"Give me the hatchet."

"Wait," he said. "Do you really want to go inside?"

"I'm going inside," she whimpered. "Give me the hatchet."

"Wait," he said. He moved along the gallery, guiding himself by the wall, moving carefully since he did not know just where the floor planks might be rotten or even missing, until he came to a window. The shutters were closed and apparently locked, yet they gave almost at once to the blade of the hatchet, making not very much sound—a flimsy and sloven barricading done either by an old feeble person—woman—or by a shiftless man; he had already inserted the hatchet blade beneath the sash before he discovered that there was no glass in it, that all he had to do now was to step through the vacant frame. Then he stood there for a moment, telling himself to go on in, telling himself that he was not afraid, he just didn't want to know what might be inside. "Well?" Miss Coldfield whispered from the door. "Have you opened it?"

"Yes," he said. He did not whisper, though he did not speak overloud; the dark room which he faced repeated his voice with hollow profundity, as an unfurnished room will. "You wait there. I'll see if I can open the door."—'So now I shall have to go in,' he thought, climbing over the sill. He knew that the room was empty; the echo of his voice had told him that, yet he moved as slowly and carefully here as he had along the gallery, feeling along the wall with his hand, following the wall when it turned, and found the door and passed through it. He would be in the hall now; he almost believed that he could hear Miss Coldfield breathing just beyond the wall beside him. It was pitch dark; he could not see, he knew that he could not see, yet he found that his eyelids and muscles were aching with strain while merging and dissolving red spots wheeled and vanished across the retinae. He went on; he felt the door under his hand at last and now he could hear Miss Coldfield's whimpering breathing beyond it as he fumbled for the lock. Then behind him the sound of the scraped match was like an explosion, a pistol; even before the puny following light appeared all his organs lifted sickeningly; he could not even move for a moment even though something of sanity roared silently inside his skull: 'It's all right! If it were danger, he would not have struck the match!' Then he could move, and turned to see the tiny gnomelike creature in headrag and voluminous skirts, the worn coffee-colored face staring at him, the match held in one coffee-colored and doll-like hand above her head. Then he was not watching her but watching the match as it burned down toward her fingers; he watched quietly as she moved at last and lit a second match from the first and turned; he saw then the square-ended saw chunk beside the wall and the lamp sitting upon it as she lifted the chimney and held the match to the wick. He remembered it, lying here in the Massachusetts bed and breathing fast now, now that peace and quiet had fled again. He remembered how she did not say one word to him, not Who are you? or What do you want here? but merely came with a bunch of enormous old fashioned iron keys, as if she had known all the time that this hour must come and that it could not be resisted, and opened the door and stepped back a little as Miss Coldfield entered. And how she (Clytie) and Miss Coldfield said no word to one another, as if Clytie had looked once at the other woman and knew that that would do no good; that it was to him, Quentin, that she turned, putting her hand on his arm and saying, "Dont let her go up there, young marster." And how maybe she looked at him and knew that would do no good either, because she turned and overtook Miss Coldfield and caught her arm and said, "Dont you go up there, Rosie" and Miss Coldfield struck the hand away and went on toward the stairs (and now he saw that she had a flashlight; he remembered how he thought, 'It must have been in the umbrella too along with the axe') and Clytie said, "Rosie" and ran after the other again, whereupon Miss Coldfield turned on the step and struck Clytie to the floor with a full-armed blow like a man would have, and turned and went on up the stairs. She (Clytie) lay on the bare floor of the scaling and empty hall like a small shapeless bundle of quiet clean rags. When he reached her he saw that she was quite conscious, her eyes wide open and calm; he stood above her, thinking, 'Yes. She is the one who owns the terror'. When he raised her it was like picking up a handful of sticks concealed in a rag bundle, so light she was. She could not stand; he had to hold her up, aware of some feeble movement or intention in her limbs until he realised that she was trying to sit on the bottom step. He lowered her to it. "Who are you?" she said.

"I'm Quentin Compson," he answered.

"Yes. I remember your grandpaw. You go up there and make her come down. Make her go away from here. Whatever he done, me and Judith and him have paid it out. You go and get her. Take her away from here." So he mounted the stairs, the worn bare treads, the cracked and scaling wall on one side, the balustrade with its intermittent missing spindles on the other. He remembered how he looked back and she was still sitting as he had left her, and that now (and he had not heard him enter) there stood in the hall below a hulking young light-colored negro man in clean faded overalls and shirt, his arms dangling, no surprise, no nothing in the saddle-colored and slack-mouthed idiot face. He remembered how he thought, 'The scion, the heir, the apparent (though not obvious)' and how he heard Miss Coldfield's feet and saw the light of the torch approaching along the upper hall and how she came and passed him, how she stumbled a little and caught herself and looked full at him as if she had never seen him before—the eyes wide and unseeing like a sleepwalker's, the face which had always been tallow-hued now possessing some still profounder, some almost unbearable, quality of bloodlessness— and he thought, 'What? What is it now? It's not shock. And it never has been fear. Can it be triumph?' and how she passed him and went on. He heard Clytie say to the man, "Take her to the gate, the buggy" and he stood there thinking, 'I should go with her' and then, 'But I must see too now. I will have to. Maybe I shall be sorry tomorrow, but I must see'. So when he came back down the stairs (and he remembered how he thought, 'Maybe my face looks like hers did, but it's not triumph') there was only Clytie in the hall, sitting still on the bottom step, sitting still in the attitude in which he had left her. She did not even look at him when he passed her. Nor did he overtake Miss Coldfield and the negro. It was too dark to go fast, though he could presently hear them ahead of him. She was not using the flashlight now; he remembered how he thought, 'Surely she cant be afraid to show a light now'. But she was not using it and he wondered if she were holding to the negro's arm now; he wondered that until he heard the negro's voice, flat, without emphasis or interest: "Wawkin better over here" and no answer from her, though he was close enough now to hear (or believe he did) her whimpering panting breath. Then he heard the other sound and he knew that she had stumbled and fallen; he could almost see the hulking slack-faced negro stopped in his tracks, looking toward the sound of the fall, waiting, without interest or curiosity, as he (Quentin) hurried forward, hurried toward the voices:

"You, nigger! What's your name?"

"Calls me Jim Bond."

"Help me up! You aint any Sutpen! You dont have to leave me lying in the dirt!"

When he stopped the buggy at her gate she did not offer to get out alone this time. She sat there until he got down and came around to her side; she still sat there, clutching the umbrella in one hand and the hatchet in the other, until he spoke her name. Then she stirred; he helped, lifted her down; she was almost as light as Clytie had been; when she moved it was like a mechanical doll, so that he supported and led her through the gate and up the short walk and into the doll-sized house and turned on the light for her and looked at the fixed sleep-walking face, the wide dark eyes as she stood there, still clutching the umbrella and the hatchet, the shawl and the black dress both stained with dirt where she had fallen, the black bonnet jerked forward and awry by the shock of the fall. "Are you all right now?" he said.

"Yes," she said. "Yes. I'm all right. Goodnight." —'Not thank you,' he thought: 'Just goodnight', outside the house now, breathing deep and fast now as he returned to the buggy, finding that he was about to begin to run, thinking quietly, 'Jesus. Jesus. Jesus', breathing fast and hard of the dark dead furnace-breath of air, of night where the fierce aloof stars hung. His own home was dark; he was still using the whip when he turned into the lane and then into the stable lot. He sprang out and took the mare from the buggy, stripping the harness from her and tumbling it into the harness room without stopping to hang it up, sweating, breathing fast and hard; when he turned at last toward the house he did begin to run. He could not help it. He was twenty years old; he was not afraid, because what he had seen out there could not harm him, yet he ran; even inside the dark familiar house, his shoes in his hand, he still ran, up the stairs and into his room and began to undress, fast, sweating, breathing fast. 'I ought to bathe,' he thought: then he was lying on the bed, naked, swabbing his body steadily with the discarded shirt, sweating still, panting: so that when, his eye-muscles aching and straining into the darkness and the almost dried shirt still clutched in his hand, he said 'I have been asleep' it was all the same, there was no difference: waking or sleeping he walked down that upper hall between the scaling walls and beneath the cracked ceiling, toward the faint light which fell outward from the last door and paused there, saying 'No. No' and then 'Only I must. I have to' and went in, entered the bare stale room whose shutters were closed too, where a second lamp burned dimly on a crude table; waking or sleeping it was the same: the bed, the yellow sheets and pillow, the wasted yellow face with closed, almost transparent eyelids on the pillow, the wasted hands crossed on the breast as if he were already a corpse; waking or sleeping it was the same and would be the same forever as long as he lived:

And you are——?
Henry Sutpen.
And you have been here——?
Four years.
And you came home——?
To die. Yes.
To die?
Yes. To die.
And you have been here——?

Four years.

And you are——?

Henry Sutpen.

It was quite cold in the room now; the chimes would ring for one any time now; the chill had a compounded, a gathered quality, as though preparing for the dead moment before dawn. "And she waited three months before she went back to get him," Shreve said. "Why did she do that?" Quentin didn't answer. He lay still and rigid on his back with the cold New England night on his face and the blood running warm in his rigid body and limbs, breathing hard but slow, his eyes wide open upon the window, thinking 'Nevermore of peace. Nevermore of peace. Nevermore. Nevermore. Nevermore'. "Do you suppose it was because she knew what was going to happen when she told it, took any steps, that it would be over then, finished, and that hating is like drink or drugs and she had used it so long that she did not dare risk cutting off the supply, destroying the source, the very poppy's root and seed?" Still Quentin didn't answer. "But at last she did reconcile herself to it, for his sake, to save him, to bring him into town where the doctors could save him, and so she told it then, got the ambulance and the men and went out there. And old Clytie maybe watching for just that out of the upstairs window for three months now: and maybe even your old man was right this time and when she saw the ambulance turn into the gate she believed it was that same black wagon for which she probably had had that nigger boy watching for three months

now, coming to carry Henry into town for the
white folks to hang him for shooting Charles Bon.
And I guess it had been him who had kept that
closet under the stairs full of tinder and trash all that
time too, like she told him to, maybe he not getting
it then either but keeping it full just like she told
him, the kerosene and all, for three months now,
until the hour when he could begin to howl—"
Now the chimes began, ringing for one oclock.
Shreve ceased, as if he were waiting for them to
cease or perhaps were even listening to them. Quentin lay still too, as if he were listening too, though
he was not; he just heard them without listening as
he heard Shreve without listening or answering,
until they ceased, died away into the icy air delicate
and faint and musical as struck glass. And he, Quentin, could see that too, though he had not been there
—the ambulance with Miss Coldfield between the
driver and the second man, perhaps a deputy sheriff,
in the shawl surely and perhaps even with the umbrella too, though probably no hatchet nor flashlight
in it now, entering the gate and picking its way
gingerly up the rutted and frozen (and now partially
thawed) drive; and it may have been the howling or
it may have been the deputy or the driver or it may
have been she who cried first: "It's on fire!" though
she would not have cried that; she would have said,
"Faster. Faster." leaning forward on this seat too—
the small furious grim implacable woman not much
larger than a child. But the ambulance could not go
fast in that drive; doubtless Clytie knew, counted

upon, that; it would be a good three minutes before
it could reach the house, the monstrous tinder-dry
rotten shell seeping smoke through the warped
cracks in the weather-boarding as if it were made of
gauze wire and filled with roaring and beyond
which somewhere something lurked which bellowed, something human since the bellowing was in
human speech, even though the reason for it would
not have seemed to be. And the deputy and the
driver would spring out and Miss Coldfield would
stumble out and follow them, running too, onto the
gallery too, where the creature which bellowed followed them, wraith-like and insubstantial, looking
at them out of the smoke, whereupon the deputy
even turned and ran at him, whereupon he retreated, fled, though the howling did not diminish
nor even seem to get any further away. They ran
onto the gallery too, into the seeping smoke, Miss
Coldfield screaming harshly, "The window! The
window!" to the second man at the door. But the
door was not locked; it swung inward; the blast of
heat struck them. The entire staircase was on fire.
Yet they had to hold her; Quentin could see it: the
light thin furious creature making no sound at all
now, struggling with silent and bitter fury, clawing
and scratching and biting at the two men who held
her, who dragged her back and down the steps as the
draft created by the open door seemed to explode
like powder among the flames as the whole lower
hall vanished. He, Quentin, could see it, could see
the deputy holding her while the driver backed the

ambulance to safety and returned, the three faces all a little wild now since they must have believed her; —the three of them staring, glaring at the doomed house: and then for a moment maybe Clytie appeared in that window from which she must have been watching the gates constantly day and night for three months—the tragic gnome's face beneath the clean headrag, against a red background of fire, seen for a moment between two swirls of smoke, looking down at them, perhaps not even now with triumph and no more of despair than it had ever worn, possibly even serene above the melting clapboards before the smoke swirled across it again.— and he, Jim Bond, the scion, the last of his race, seeing it too now and howling with human reason now since now even he could have known what he was howling about. But they couldn't catch him. They could hear him; he didn't seem to ever get any further away but they couldn't get any nearer and maybe in time they could not even locate the direction of the howling anymore. They—the driver and the deputy—held Miss Coldfield as she struggled: he (Quentin) could see her, them; he had not been there but he could see her, struggling and fighting like a doll in a nightmare, making no sound, foaming a little at the mouth, her face even in the sunlight lit by one last wild crimson reflection as the house collapsed and roared away, and there was only the sound of the idiot negro left.

"And so it was the Aunt Rosa that came back to town inside the ambulance," Shreve said. Quentin did not answer; he did not even say, *Miss Rosa*. He just lay there staring at the window without even blinking, breathing the chill heady pure snow-gleamed darkness. "And she went to bed because it was all finished now, there was nothing left now, nothing out there now but that idiot boy to lurk around those ashes and those four gutted chimneys and howl until someone came and drove him away. They couldn't catch him and nobody ever seemed to make him go very far away, he just stopped howling for a little while. Then after a while they would begin to hear him again. And so she died." Quentin did not answer, staring at the window; then he could not tell if it was the actual window or the window's pale rectangle upon his eyelids, though after a moment it began to emerge. It began to take shape in its same curious, light, gravity-defying attitude—the once-folded sheet out of the wistaria Mississippi summer, the cigar smell, the random blowing of the fireflies. "The South," Shreve said. "The South. Jesus. No wonder you folks all outlive yourselves by years and years and years." It was becoming quite distinct; he would be able to decipher the words soon, in a moment; even almost now, now, now.

"I am older at twenty than a lot of people who have died," Quentin said.

"And more people have died than have been twenty-one," Shreve said. Now he (Quentin) could read it, could finish it—the sloped whimsical ironic hand out of Mississippi attenuated, into the iron snow:

—or perhaps there is. Surely it can harm no one to believe that perhaps she has escaped not at all the privilege of being outraged and amazed and of not forgiving but on the contrary has herself gained that place or bourne where the objects of the outrage and of the commiseration also are no longer ghosts but are actual people to be actual recipients of the hatred and the pity. It will do no harm to hope—You see I have written hope, not think. So let it be hope.—that the one cannot escape the censure which no doubt he deserves, that the other no longer lack the commiseration which let us hope (while we are hoping) that they have longed for, if only for the reason that they are about to receive it whether they will or no. The weather was beautiful though cold and they had to use picks to break the earth for the grave yet in one of the deeper clods I saw a redworm doubtless alive when the clod was thrown up though by afternoon it was frozen again.

"So it took Charles Bon and his mother to get rid of old Tom, and Charles Bon and the octoroon to get rid of Judith, and Charles Bon and Clytie to get rid of Henry; and Charles Bon's mother and Charles Bon's grandmother got rid of Charles Bon. So it takes two niggers to get rid of one Sutpen, dont it?" Quentin did not answer; evidently Shreve did not want an answer now; he continued almost without a pause: "Which is all right, it's fine; it clears the whole ledger, you can tear all the pages out and burn them, except for one thing. And do you know what that is?" Perhaps he hoped for an answer this time, or perhaps he merely paused for emphasis, since he got no answer. "You've got one nigger left. One nigger Sutpen left. Of course you cant catch him and you dont even always see him and you never will be able to use him. But you've got him there still. You still hear him at night sometimes. Dont you?"

"Yes," Quentin said.

"And so do you know what I think?" Now he did expect an answer, and now he got one:

"No," Quentin said.

"Do you want to know what I think?"

"No," Quentin said.

"Then I'll tell you. I think that in time the Jim Bonds are going to conquer the western hemisphere. Of course it wont quite be in our time and of course as they spread toward the poles they will bleach out again like the rabbits and the birds do, so they wont show up so sharp against the snow. But it will still be Jim Bond; and so in a few thousand years, I who regard you will also have sprung from the loins of African kings. Now I want you to tell me just one thing more. Why do you hate the South?"

"I dont hate it," Quentin said, quickly, at once, immediately; "I dont hate it," he said. *I dont hate it* he thought, panting in the cold air, the iron New England dark: *I dont. I dont! I dont hate it! I dont hate it!*

CHRONOLOGY

1807   Thomas Sutpen born in West Virginia mountains. Poor whites of Scottish-English stock. Large family.

1817   Sutpen family moved down into Tidewater Virginia, Sutpen ten years old. Ellen Coldfield born in Tennessee.

1820   Sutpen ran away from home. Fourteen years old.

1827   Sutpen married first wife in Haiti.

1828   Goodhue Coldfield moved to Yoknapatawpha County (Jefferson) Mississippi: mother, sister, wife, and daughter Ellen.

1831   Charles Bon born, Haiti. Sutpen learns his wife has negro blood, repudiates her and child.

1833   Sutpen appears in Yoknapatawpha County, Mississippi, takes up land, builds his house.

1834   Clytemnestra (Clytie) born to slave woman.

1838   Sutpen married Ellen Coldfield.

1839   Henry Sutpen born, Sutpen's Hundred.

1841   Judith Sutpen born.

1845   Rosa Coldfield born.

The chronology and genealogy have been corrected in several instances to agree with the dates and facts of the novel.

1850 Wash Jones moves into abandoned fishing camp on Sutpen's plantation, with his daughter.

1853 Milly Jones born to Wash Jones' daughter.

1859 Henry Sutpen and Charles Bon meet at University of Mississippi. Judith and Charles meet that Xmas. Charles Etienne St. Valery Bon born, New Orleans.

1860 Xmas, Sutpen forbids marriage between Judith and Bon. Henry repudiates his birthright, departs with Bon.

1861 Sutpen, Henry, and Bon depart for war.

1863 Ellen Coldfield dies.

1864 Goodhue Coldfield dies.

1865 Henry kills Bon at gates. Rosa Coldfield moves out to Sutpen's Hundred.

1866 Sutpen becomes engaged to Rosa Coldfield, insults her. She returns to Jefferson.

1867 Sutpen takes up with Milly Jones.

1869 Milly's child is born. Wash Jones kills Sutpen.

1870 Charles E. St. V. Bon appears at Sutpen's Hundred.

1871 Clytie fetches Charles E. St. V. Bon to Sutpen's Hundred to live.

1881 Charles E. St. V. Bon returns with negro wife.

1882 Jim Bond born.

1884 Judith and Charles E. St. V. Bon die of yellow fever.

1909

September Rosa Coldfield and Quentin find Henry Sutpen hidden in the house.

December Rosa Coldfield goes out to fetch Henry to town, Clytie sets fire to the house.

GENEALOGY

THOMAS SUTPEN. Born in West Virginia mountains, 1807. One of several children of poor whites, Scotch-English stock. Established plantation of Sutpen's Hundred in Yoknapatawpha County, Mississippi, 1833. Married (1) Eulalia Bon, Haiti, 1827. (2) Ellen Coldfield, Jefferson, Mississippi, 1838. Major, later Colonel, —th Mississippi Infantry, C.S.A. Died, Sutpen's Hundred, 1869.

EULALIA BON. Born in Haiti. Only child of Haitian sugar planter of French descent. Married Thomas Sutpen, 1827, divorced from him, 1831. Died in New Orleans, date unknown.

CHARLES BON. Son of Thomas and Eulalia Bon Sutpen. Only child. Attended University of Mississippi, where he met Henry Sutpen and became engaged to Judith. Private, later lieutenant, —th Company, (University Grays) —th Mississippi Infantry, C.S.A. Died, Sutpen's Hundred, 1865.

GOODHUE COLDFIELD. Born in Tennessee. Moved to Jefferson, Miss., 1828, established small mercantile business. Died, Jefferson, 1864.

ELLEN COLDFIELD. Daughter of Goodhue Coldfield. Born in Tennessee, 1817. Married Thomas Sutpen, Jefferson, Miss., 1838. Died, Sutpen's Hundred, 1863.

ROSA COLDFIELD. Daughter of Goodhue Coldfield. Born, Jefferson, 1845. Died, Jefferson, 1910.

HENRY SUTPEN. Born, Sutpen's Hundred, 1839, son of Thomas and Ellen Coldfield Sutpen. Attended University of Mississippi. Private, —th Company, (University Grays) —th Mississippi Infantry, C.S.A. Died, Sutpen's Hundred, 1909.

JUDITH SUTPEN. Daughter of Thomas and Ellen Coldfield Sutpen. Born, Sutpen's Hundred, 1841. Became engaged to Charles Bon, 1860. Died, Sutpen's Hundred, 1884.

CLYTEMNESTRA SUTPEN. Daughter of Thomas Sutpen and a negro slave. Born, Sutpen's Hundred, 1834. Died, Sutpen's Hundred, 1909.

WASH JONES. Date and location of birth unknown. Squatter, residing in an abandoned fishing camp belonging to Thomas Sutpen, hanger-on of Sutpen, handy man about Sutpen's place while Sutpen was away between '61–'65. Died, Sutpen's Hundred, 1869.

MELICENT JONES. Daughter of Wash Jones. Date of birth unknown. Rumored to have died in a Memphis brothel.

MILLY JONES. Daughter of Melicent Jones. Born 1853. Died, Sutpen's Hundred, 1869.

UNNAMED INFANT. Daughter of Thomas Sutpen and Milly Jones. Born, died, Sutpen's Hundred, same day, 1869.

CHARLES ETIENNE DE SAINT VALERY BON. Only child of Charles Bon and an octoroon mistress whose name

is not recorded. Born, New Orleans, 1859. Married a
full-blood negress, name unknown, 1879. Died,
Sutpen's Hundred, 1884.

JIM BOND (BON). Son of Charles Etienne de Saint Valery Bon. Born, Sutpen's Hundred, 1882. Disappeared
from Sutpen's Hundred, 1910. Whereabouts unknown.

QUENTIN COMPSON. Grandson of Thomas Sutpen's
first Yoknapatawpha County friend. Born, Jefferson,
1891. Attended Harvard, 1909–1910. Died, Cambridge,
Mass., 1910.

SHREVLIN MCCANNON. Born, Edmonton, Alberta,
Canada, 1890. Attended Harvard, 1909–1914. Captain,
Royal Army Medical Corps, Canadian Expeditionary
Forces, France, 1914–1918. Now a practising surgeon,
Edmonton, Alta.

EDITOR'S NOTE

The text of *Absalom, Absalom!* reproduced here is that of the original typescript which Faulkner prepared for publication. This typescript, at the Alderman Library of the University of Virginia, is a clear text, and complete except for the chronology and genealogy. We have attempted in this volume to reproduce that text faithfully, even to the point of preserving certain of Faulkner's inconsistencies and eccentricities. Nevertheless, some corrections and regularizations have been deemed necessary. When possible, textual problems in the typescript have been solved by reference to Faulkner's holograph manuscript, at the Humanities Research Center of the University of Texas, and to the corrected galleys of the first edition, information about which has been generously supplied by Professor Carvel Collins.

There is not enough space here to provide a complete textual apparatus for this novel. The table appended is merely to record, for the interested reader, a highly selective sampling of some of the more significant variations between the present text and that of the ribbon typescript setting copy. Page and line numbers in the left column are keyed to this volume. The reading to the left of the bracket is that of the typescript (except for variants in the chronology and genealogy, which are those of the first edition); the reading to the right of the bracket is that of the present text. Parentheses following any entry indicate the source of the correction: ms = holograph manuscript; gal = galleys.

4.2–3	childrens'] children's
6.4	*With out*] *Without* (ms)
6.13	Because] "Because (ms)
6.14	So] "So (ms)
8.26	marshalls'] marshals'
10.9	land of] land or
20.18	wedding] wedding,
22.22	protection.'] protection.' "
22.26	childrens'] children's
24.15	Oh] "Oh (ms)
29.6	Papa.'] Papa,' (ms)
30.5	So] "So (gal)
31.3	falling] fell (gal)
31.8	anothers'] another's
31.8	their] their skins (ms)
35.7	Square] square
36.7	unforseen] unforeseen
57.21	Or] or (ms)
68.19	into,] into
76.24	clothes] clothes,
88.17	Why. . . . . .] Why . . .
89.30	wordly] worldly (ms)
90.27	them] them,
91.31	horse-and] horse- and (ms)
103.29	which] with which (ms)
104.3	not so much] not

104.18	dying] dyeing
105.23	abrogating] arrogating
116.22	believe] believe, (gal)
127.26	Ellen] Judith
129.14	past summer of] last summer of (ms)
130.27	Eve] eve (ms)
131.27	scene] scenes (ms)
133.30	wordly] worldly (ms)
143.26	he] He
143.27	either,] either. (ms)
144.8	himself] Himself
146.3–4	no one,] anyone, (ms)
156.11	alteration of] alteration or
158.17	perish . . . .] perish . . .
163.15	*IS*] IS
165.10	"—and] "——and
185.27	'Where] "Where (gal)
185.28	from?'] from?" (gal)
185.28	'I] "I (gal)
185.29	know.'] know." ' (gal)
212.28	*him*] *her*
218.11	*forty-five*] *forty-three*
219.26	That] that (ms)
220.7	dust cloud] dustcloud
221.8	Rosa——] Rosa——"
223.1	ths] the
227.30	*principle*] *principal*
227.30	*prances*] *prances to* (ms)
234.20	*they?)*] *they?')*
234.31	*ditch")*] *ditch"*
255.10	*from?*] *from?'*
260.25	*will. . . . .*] *will . . .*
260.30	*it. . . . .*] *it. . . .*

262.6   justice'] justice's
267.20   *streaming*] *steaming* (ms)
275.19   said.—"What] said. "—What (ms)
286.12   than] or
313.14   keep] kept
315.18   there:] there)
332.28   "—said] "——said
336.29   forsee] foresee
344.13   ocean] Ocean
346.8   whom] who
355.10   reckoned] reckoned,
356.23   —"(that] —("that
356.23   mare)"—] mare")—
379.5   too,] too)
384.28   have. . . . . . .] have. . . .
411.22   whom] who (ms)
417.10   Eve] eve
419.6   whom] who
424.7   all.)] all.")
433.29   *army*] *Army*
438.31   were] was
441.6   *abrogates*] *arrogates*
460.11   'Dont] "Dont (gal)
460.12   marster.'] marster." (gal)
461.21   Mrs] Miss (ms)
465.15   Nevermore Nevermore. Nevermore.]
         Nevermore. Nevermore. Nevermore.
         (ms)
473.5–6 [Ellen born 1818]] [Ellen b. 1817]
473.13   [Bon b. 1829]] [Bon b. 1831]
474.7   Velery] Valery
474.13   1862] 1863
474.29   smallpox] yellow fever

474.30   1910] 1909
475.17   Greys] Grays
475.23   1818] 1817
475.24   1862] 1863
476.4   Greys] Grays
476.5   1910] 1909
476.12   1910] 1909
476.26   VELERY] VALERY
476.31   Velery] Valery

ABOUT THE AUTHOR

William Faulkner, one of the greatest writers of the twentieth century, was born in New Albany, Mississippi, on September 25, 1897. He published his first book, *The Marble Faun*, a collection of poems, in 1924, but it is as a literary chronicler of life in the Deep South—particularly in the fictional Yoknapatawpha County, the setting for several of his novels—that he is most highly regarded. In such novels as *Sanctuary* (1931), *The Hamlet* (1940), *The Town* (1957), *The Mansion* (1959), he explored the full range of post–Civil War Southern life, focusing both on the personal histories of his characters (especially members of the Snopes family) and on the moral uncertainties of an increasingly dissolute society. His other novels include *The Sound and the Fury* (1929), *As I Lay Dying* (1930), *Light in August* (1932), *Absalom, Absalom!* (1936), *The Unvanquished* (1938), *Intruder in the Dust* (1948), *Requiem for a Nun* (1951), *A Fable* (1954), and *The Reivers* (1962). For the latter two books, he was awarded the Pulitzer Prize. He also wrote several volumes of short stories as well as collections of poems and essays.

In combining the use of symbolism with a stream-of-consciousness technique, he created a new approach to the writing of fiction. In 1949 he was awarded the Nobel Prize for Literature.

William Faulkner died in Byhalia, Mississippi, on July 6, 1962.

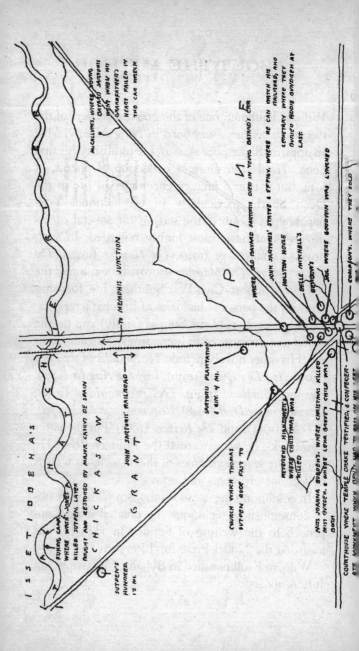

BYRON FOST SAW SNVA
GROVE,
MISS ROSA COLDFIELDS

BYRON SNOPES ROBBED,
OLD SAREY SARTORIS BANK,
WHICH FLEM SNOPES LATER
BECAME PRESIDENT OF

TO MOTTSTOWN,
WHERE JASON COMPSON
LOST HIS MONEY TRAIL
AND WHERE ANSE BUNDREN
AND HIS SONS HAD TO GO
IN ORDER TO REACH JEFFERSON

SWRATT'S

ARMSTID'S

TULL'S

VARNER'S STORE, WHERE
FLEM SNOPES GOT HIS
START

F R E N C H M A N' S   B E N D

BUNDREN'S

BRIDGE WHICH WASHED
AWAY SO ANSE BUNDREN
AND HIS SONS COULD NOT
CROSS IT WITH ADDIE'S
BODY

OLD FRENCHMAN PLACE,
WHICH FLEM SNOPES UNLOADED
ON HENRY ARMSTID AND JURATT, AND WHERE
POPEYE KILLED TOMMY

JEFFERSON,
YOKNAPATAWPHA CO.,
MISSISSIPPI

AREA. 2400 SQ. MI.
POPULATION, WHITES, 6298
NEGROES 9313

WILLIAM FAULKNER,
SOLE OWNER & PROPRIETOR.

P I N E   H I L L S

Y O K N A